WINTER'S CHARMS

CELIA LAKE

WELCOME TO WINTER!

This collection contains three novellas that take place during the winter holidays.

All three can be enjoyed without having read any previous books in my world, but the second and third novellas do have some spoilers for the events of the books where the main characters met.

Casting Nasturtiums takes place in 1919. When Seth returns from the War and finds his best friend, Golshan, wasting way in a care home. Together with Seth's wife Dilly, they need to figure out what their lives should look like now.

This polyamorous MMF romance was referred to briefly in *Eclipse* (Seth is Thesan's closest brother.)

In **Country Manners**, Kate and Giles make the most of an obligatory holiday visit to his family after their engagement. Fortunately for their good humour, they stumble across a small mystery and a bit of unexpected magic.

Kate and Giles met and fell in love in *Wards of the Roses*. That book mostly takes place in the summer of 1920. *Country Manners* takes place a year and a half later, in December 1921.

Chasing Legends explores some of the many mysteries of Schola. A small group of staff and associates are gathered over the winter holidays in 1926 for a feast, when there is a loud knock on the door of the Great Hall. Thesan, Isembard, Pross, and Ibis must combine their skills and talents to confront their fears and solve a centuries-old problem.

Thesan and Isembard fell in love during *Eclipse* (during the 1924-1925 school year), while Pross and Ibis met in the spring of 1926 during *Magician's Hoard*.

Casting Nasturtiums

CHAPTER I

JUNE 1919

"Now, remember, don't excite him. Rest is so very important, after all." Golshan had heard it all before, the long list of disapproved behaviour.

Golshan kept his eyes closed, tucking one hand under the blanket in his lap, so they wouldn't see his finger twitching, tapping. He tuned the words out again, as he usually did. He wanted to move, and he couldn't let it show. At least he was out on the terrace today, and the sun was shining. It was not a good day - he had not had a good day for a year - but it was not as awful a day as it might be.

He wondered who it was who was visiting. Not his family, certainly. Someone would come in two months. He knew the pattern now, could trace it out through the infinity of his life. Not anyone from the Ministry. They'd clearly washed their hands of him since the visit from a Healer three months ago. Nothing they could do, so sorry. Here was his pension, here was a medal. Here were the broken shards of the blade of his life.

It meant endless days looking out a window, or parked in a clunky Bath chair on a terrace. It would be one thing if they left him alone in his head. That was chaos, but it was a chaos he was used to. Far too often, there was someone reading aloud, or he was parked with others by a radio. None of that kept his mind occupied for more than a few seconds. It was always chasing off like a terrier after something in the garden.

He could feel the magic swirling around in his head again, wanting to poke out and do something, anything. He didn't have control of it, not properly. The nurses around him didn't understand any of it, and it wasn't as if he could explain the magic to them. The shreds and wisps that escaped were enough to make the ward gossip about ghosts, or about fairies, or any of the other things seen out of the corner of your eye, or ducking around a corner.

Golshan didn't want to scare anyone. Just like he'd never wanted to be difficult. That didn't change the fact he apparently was. All he wanted was something to hold on to. Something that made a day different from every other day. Perhaps with the summer to sit on the terrace and stare at the grass beyond, he might lure a fox or a rabbit or a bird to come closer. That was what his life had come down to, a few flickers of amusement poking through the fog.

If he didn't do something, he'd go completely out of his mind. And whatever else happened, some small part of him remembered how bad an idea that would be. He'd heard the whispers, what happened to patients who made too much trouble. Or at least too much obvious trouble. If he were lucky, he'd be sedated and sent off somewhere even more boring, where the staff did the bare minimum.

Whoever it was with the nurse just murmured. It was too soft for Golshan to make out who it was. A man, he thought. Something about it nagged at his mind.

"Corporal Soltani? You have a visitor. You let us know

just as soon as you get tired, or if you need any help at all. I'll be over at the table by the door, keeping an eye out." She gestured, and Golshan nodded, without bothering to open his eyes. A moment later, he heard her leather shoes clicking as she walked back across the stone. He tracked it automatically, as he always did, when he had any focus at all. They didn't like it when he was surprised. He didn't care for it either. It was the sort of trouble that would make things even worse.

There was a cough, just to the right of his chair, the sound of someone sitting.

"Golshan?"

It was a voice he hadn't expected to hear ever again, that clear baritone cracking in the middle. His eyes flew open, fixing on the man beside him. He looked remarkably good. Blond hair in an approved Army cut, far too short still. A suit that didn't fit well, too loose across the shoulders. Certainly not the shirt-sleeves and braces that suited him best, when he was bent over a bit of carving or carpentry.

Golshan blinked again, sure this must be some mirage or illusion or dream. Not a nightmare, never a nightmare. But this is what he'd seen in his dreams, every few nights, since he'd been shot. Or at least, since he'd come round in the field hospital, since he remembered.

"Seth." It came out in a rush, all hiss and breath. "You're not real."

Seth looked absolutely resolute. "I'm here. I'm sorry." He cut off at that.

"What do you mean?" Golshan twisted, peering at Seth now. "What do you have to be sorry for?" He held out a hand, carefully, glad that Seth had settled on his right. It was a little easier to angle that way.

Seth took hold of his hand. That was just the same. It

wasn't just the warmth of his touch that convinced him Seth was real and right here. It was the strength of Seth's grip and the places the calluses had settled from the hours he spent with a whittling knife.

"I'm sorry I wasn't here sooner." Seth swallowed, watching him, searchingly. "I don't even know what to say." He stopped, then tried again. "What happened to you? After, I mean."

Golshan took a breath. Part of his mind was circling, like it would in a duel, going out to fight, knife ready and his magic called to his hands. It pleased him, darkly, that that part of his mind was still there. He had thought it had been sliced away, drowned in mud and blood and drained out of him.

He kept tight control over his words, despite how they wanted to bubble out. "I was shot. I woke up in hospital. Non-magical. They sent me to another one, somewhere here in England. And now here." He gestured with his left hand, since Seth was still holding his right. "I've been here six months or so." They seemed endless, but he'd kept track, with the newspaper, once the days stopped dancing around in his head. "The day of Roosevelt's funeral, the papers kept going on about it."

Seth frowned, and Golshan knew that frown so well, when Seth was thinking, all the quiet in his head. Golshan could tell what he was working around to, and he squeezed. He'd never said it straight out to anyone else. The nurses and orderlies and doctors already knew. The other patients didn't care, except to complain about their own needs or, more likely, carry on with that so-British stiff upper lip. "I can't walk. The bullet hit my spine. A bit of feeling in my legs, but no strength, I can't move them." He didn't explain, didn't want to explain, all the other indignities.

It wasn't just the daily care to keep from soiling himself. It was the pneumonia he'd had in March and the way coughing was different. The things he didn't remember, when he was first in hospital. He'd been swimming up from unconsciousness to hear the tight, tense way people talked about him as if he were bound to die. And, of course, the fact he could do none of the things he'd been good at before. No climbing, no running, no tumbling. No duelling or fighting.

That last might be a relief, honestly. No one was going to ask him to use his knife for all the wrong reasons. Not any more.

When Seth spoke again, his voice was even softer. "You saved my life."

"Of course." As if he could have done anything else. He hadn't had to think about it, he'd just known, from the crack of the gun, what was about to happen. Golshan had always had a touch of premonition, and he remembered being grateful he'd been there, able to do something, anything. He didn't remember all of it, but he remembered flinging himself against Seth, putting himself in the way. He remembered twisting, how the bullet had slammed into his back, the searing pain. Then there had been nothing but the mud, and the memory of Seth's face, pale, wide-eyed, and terrified.

Seth just sat, squeezing his hand. Golshan let the silence wash over him. Seth had always been the one thing that made the bees in his head settle down and stop buzzing around. He hadn't thought he'd get that ever again. He hadn't dared let himself hope. No one else had come to see him, after all. Seth had always been different, but Golshan hadn't been sure, especially when the months had gone on and on, and he hadn't had any word at all.

As if Seth had read his mind, he spoke. "I wrote. I

never heard back. Some of the letters came back from the censors. The others just disappeared."

"Mmm." Golshan felt he should probably care more. He didn't want to right now. Golshan wanted to sit in the sun, and let Seth hold his hand, and soak up this moment. He was sure it would be forever until it happened again.

"I wrote to your family." Seth spoke again. "Wait, let me back up."

Golshan opened one eye, peering at him, then shrugged. "G'on?"

"I got demobbed last week. You know, not a priority by anyone's standards. The miners went first, the ironworkers. And agricultural work."

"People forget the world runs on wood. Who else kept our trenches from collapsing? Or makes houses?"

"Well, I admit. The sort of thing I make's not essential. But I guess our Ministry finally pushed things through. I got sent back to England a month ago. And then at least I could write, so Dilly knew to expect me home. And Mum and Dad and everyone."

Golshan peered at him, suddenly worried. "Are they all right?" Please, let them be all right. He hadn't dared to think about them.

"Dad had a bit of a time, but he's doing fine now. Mum's grand, and as soon as I said I was looking for you, she started baking. Can I leave a tin with you?"

The thought of someone baking for him - of Mistress Wain baking for him - almost made him cry. He screwed his eyes shut, nodding. "Does she know?"

"I didn't know. Dilly was sure you weren't dead. She checked the lists, every day, for both of us, but they wouldn't tell her anything when she wrote. I wasn't sure until yesterday where you were. And then I had to wait for visiting hours today. Do they really only let visitors come once a week? For two hours?"

Golshan shrugged. "Haven't exactly had a lot wanting to see me. Any of us."

Seth frowned again. "Your family?" Of course, if anything had happened to Seth, his entire family - even Lia, who was difficult - would have been showing up. They'd arrive en masse, inarguably there to see their son and brother. He'd saved Seth's life because he loved Seth. But Golshan knew, as he fell, that he'd also done it because he couldn't bear to be the reason Seth's mum was crying. She'd always been kind to him, far more than he'd ever deserved. He'd broken a lot of her things, over the summers, and more than just crockery.

Golshan shook his head. "My sister, every three months." She came dutifully and briefly, a public show of care that did neither of them any good. He'd wondered, more than once, if he'd been shunted here so everyone could ignore him, including his family.

"Surely you could go somewhere else?"

It was not, honestly, something Golshan had really considered, once it became clear his family had even less idea what to do with him than they had before. When he'd been a grown man, independent, a confirmed bachelor, they had managed. He appeared for the holiday meals and went away again. They didn't ask what he was up to and he didn't tell them about his lovers. "Who'd have me?"

Seth raised an eyebrow. "You don't object if I inquire?"

"It won't do any good." Golshan shrugged. He knew better than to argue when Seth got that note in his voice. He had only occasionally tried, and never won.

"We'll see about that." Seth shrugged, then returned to the question. "I got home a week ago. Dilly's grand, it was..." His voice went quiet again, with that particular note of awe and love and delight he got when he talked about her.

Golshan had known he could never come between them. Not once he'd seen how Dilly had shown up once she was done with school. He'd known he loved Seth since he was fifteen. He'd come back to school to start his third year.

They'd had a week apart at the end of the summer, full of family birthdays Golshan was expected to be at. It had been a week of feeling he was doing everything wrong. He'd come back to school glad to be somewhere on his own, with fewer expectations. At least their teachers didn't fuss about how he sat while he did his assignments, or that he needed breaks. So long as he got things done, and Seth helped make sure he did.

Third year, they'd had their own rooms. They'd ended up in Seth's, after he'd unpacked photographs and the little family shrine sculptures he'd carved so carefully out of wood. Eventually, they were sprawled on Seth's bed, just talking through the past week. All the bees had flown out of his head, and he'd tried, once, to kiss Seth.

It had been a mistake. Seth had looked startled, like the world had shifted, like the wood had twisted and gone to splinters in his hand. Golshan had pulled back, and stammered an apology and rammed any hint of that desire back down inside him. A moment later, Seth had taken his hand, squeezed it, and gone back to the easy talking that made everything good, without comment.

Golshan had taken all that wanting and shoved it into other things. Into learning all the martial magics he could, and a fair few of the protective ones. Into Materia, picking up tidbits about what material worked best for which task. When he'd discovered sex, when he'd had time and relative freedom to indulge, it had got a lot easier. It meant he had treasured the times curled up and talking with Seth, without expecting anything else.

Once Dilly showed up, Seth wanted Dilly. Dilly wanted Seth. They loved each other. Anyone who saw them knew that. And besides, theirs was an approved sort of relationship. Not like any of Golshan's. "Good." It was good. He was happy for them. "It'd been…"

"My leave, in 1917. Two years, near enough." He shrugged. "She didn't use a charm this time. Who knows, maybe we can start a family."

That hurt some, the idea they'd be doing more without him. That he'd be here, and they'd be there. Maybe Seth would visit regularly, but that was all. And yet, Seth was alive, and that would never be wrong.

There was a long silence, and when Golshan opened his eyes and peered at Seth, Seth was looking right back at him. "What?"

Seth spoke carefully now. "You can't stay here."

"Where else would have me? My family don't want me, they made that very clear. Besides, they say…"

"Do you want to be here?" Seth's voice was fierce now. "If you do, I'll stop."

"No." Goodness, no. But the idea he could be anywhere else was baffling. "They'll tell you, though, I need care, I need nurses, I had pneumonia in March."

"Has anyone from the Temple of Healing seen you?"

Golshan shrugged, leaning his head against the headrest. "They said they couldn't do anything." He didn't remember all of it, it had been a bad day to have a body. Too many people needed too many other things. The non-magical side was set up better for long-term care. Something like that. And there'd been no one to say otherwise, no one who cared about Golshan. He was a tick mark in a row of numbers, one more thing to be handled. Not a person.

"They owe you." Seth's voice was as sharp now as Golshan had ever heard. About him. In a way no one else ever was about him. "They owe you for taking you and using you, and then not caring what happened to you. I owe you. For saving my life."

Golshan's hand twisted. There was a split second where he might have stopped himself, but instead he caught Seth's wrist, as he was gesturing. "Don't say that. You don't owe me anything."

There was complete silence and stillness from both of them. Golshan was barely breathing, he was sure Seth was the same. The two of them were caught in the moment of a dance when everything stopped but the beat of his heart and knowing where the knife edge was.

Seth nodded, just once. "As you wish." Then he went on, as if rearranging the entire bureaucracy of the Army was a simple problem. "Do you want to come live with us?"

Golshan blinked. "You and Dilly?"

"Mmhmm." Seth was looking him up and down. "We've got a ground floor bedroom. My old one. There's a bath across the hall. We're not that far from the portal and the village." He must have been sorting it out in his head, as they talked, what they could do, so sure Dilly would just go along with it.

"You're mad." Golshan couldn't even begin to get his head around it. He knew he wasn't reacting right, but he couldn't figure out how to tell Seth not to get his hopes up.

"I'll ask. See what's possible." Golshan knew that tone. It meant that anything up to the impossible was on the table. "For now, what would be helpful? Books? Newspapers? Jumper? Mum would knit you something."

"It's June!" Golshan could at least argue against the jumper. For now. She'd probably start one tomorrow, so it would be done by autumn. "Tell me you'll come back."

A year ago, he could never have said it. Now, it was the only thing he wanted.

"Always. Every day they'll let me. Until we figure out something better." Golshan could almost believe it when Seth said it. He just nodded, wanting to trust it. At least he knew Seth would try. And he certainly couldn't argue Seth out of it. Then Seth was speaking again. "Anyone else you want me to tell? Your little black book?"

The list of Golshan's lovers had been long as his arm. He was sure a fair few of them were dead now. Golshan knew about a couple for certain. He'd seen notices from his vast and wide-ranging social circles about others, though not all of them.

He'd done a little of everything before the War. Before he signed up, he'd been running a vaudeville theatre for a year or so, quite successfully. He had no musical skill whatsoever, but he'd been good at managing the crises as they came up. And he'd always got on particularly well with the knife-throwers and mesmerists and contortionist acts. The touring companies had liked him because he didn't try to get the girls in private. "I'll think about it."

Seth nodded. "All right." He glanced up. "That nurse is coming over again. I promise I'll be back next week, or as soon as they let me. And I'll write. Here's the tin from Mum. There's a letter or two in there." All of a sudden, there was a biscuit tin, entirely out of season. It had a winter scene printed on it and it sat on his lap, taunting him.

There was one more squeeze of his hand, then a sudden impulse, like Golshan's all those years ago, where

Seth half-stood, then bent to kiss his forehead. "I'll be back."

Before Golshan could say anything, he heard Seth walking briskly, meeting the nurse maybe five feet away, enough behind Golshan he didn't need to guard his expressions. Seth would know he could hear. His hearing had always been excellent.

"What do I need to do to get him home?"

The nurse sounded startled. "That won't be possible." Then she recovered a bit, and her voice was firm. "He needs skilled care around the clock. He'll need it for the rest of his life. Poor dear." It was the sort of tone you might use about a somewhat dim dog.

"Still. What do I need to do to have him released to somewhere better suited?" Seth's voice was pleasant, but clear.

"We couldn't possibly. Besides, it's his family that could do that. And you're certainly not...." Her voice trailed off. Seth was blond and pale skinned and looked so much like he had been born from English soil, he might have grown there. Golshan was Persian, and further, with the sort of dark skin that wanted mustard yellows and bright reds, umbers and oranges. All the shades that marked him as being foreign. The convalescent blues, the required uniform, did him no favours at all, and made him look even more faded than he felt.

Seth's voice got soft. It was the kind of softness that a sensible person would worry about. "Golshan is family. I'll be having a chat with a few people. And be back next week. Take good care of him." He hesitated, and now Golshan could hear the need in Seth's voice. "Please. Take good care of him."

Something in the tone softened the nurse. "Let me walk you out, sir. Did you serve together, then? There are some pamphlets that explain things, so you understand his needs."

"In the trenches, in France. I was demobbed last week. But we've known each other since we were in school." Golshan heard the steps fade away, and now he finally let himself sink back in the chair.

CHAPTER 2
THIRTEEN DAYS LATER

Seth was lying on his back in the orchard, staring up into the trees. He could hear the bees buzzing back to the hives at the far corner, and the rustle of birds, an occasional chirp. He had the odd sense of wanting to take on both his role - being the steady, quiet one - and Golshan's. This conversation would be much better if Golshan were hanging upside down from the tree branch above him. Or circling him, distracted every few moments by a flower, or a leaf, or a dog.

They should get a dog of their own. Not yet. Not until they knew what was coming. He tucked the thought aside, as he'd done with so many others in the past month. Things to be done after they knew how to bring Golshan home. After they knew when they could. After they knew what he'd need. After Seth and Dilly made sure that happened.

He had his eyes closed again when he felt the shadow fall over him. He opened one eye, then the other, then held up his hand. "Dilly."

Seth would never get tired of that. He'd dreamed of

her almost every night in the War. The reality, of course, hadn't quite matched up. Not now he was home. But in almost every way, it was so much better than his memory. She didn't say a word about his twitches and starts, or the nightmares. She'd sleepily curl her hand over his hip, give him space, and nestle back against him when he'd settled.

"Heya, love." Dilly had been cooking. She had a smudge of flour on her nose, and one on her ear. He tugged her down, gently, by the hand, and she laughed, settling beside him as she spread her skirts out. "You've been out here a while. Supper in half an hour, the bread's just cooling."

It wouldn't be fancy, but that was the point. They were coming into harvest season now, where the gardens would start giving them plenty. Dilly and his mum had put up jar after jar last year, despite everything. And there were the chickens, and the sheep, and their share of the dairy from the family cows over at Lia and her husband's cottage, a half-mile away. Tonight would be cheese and chutney sandwiches, a simple salad, some of the berries and cream. It tasted like heaven, so different from the tinned mud from the trenches, and the boiled swill from behind the lines.

"Is everything sorted for tomorrow?" Dilly shifted, settling down to rest her head on his chest. He automatically stretched one arm along her side, the other stroking her hair where it was coming loose from the bun at the back of her neck. He remembered how this part went. He'd never forgotten it, even in the worst moments.

"I hope so." Seth let out a long breath. "I feel like I'm missing something. That it's going to come and bite me."

She was quiet for a good minute. When he didn't say anything, she made the slight clucking sound with her tongue, the one she only made when he was being a tad dense. "Love?"

"Yes?" He swallowed. "Tell me, please." It came out much more plaintive than he'd wanted or expected, but he felt overwhelmed.

That made her laugh. "What you're missing, love, is that if this were anyone else, you'd be talking it through with Golshan. Trusting he'd spot what you weren't seeing. His eye for that."

Seth grimaced, but then smiled hopefully at her. "Can you pretend?"

"Tell me then. One more time, all of it together."

Seth let his eyes close, his fingers still stroking along Dilly's hair. "I found him." That was what mattered most. "You'd told me he wasn't on the lists, but." He swallowed hard, tasting a bit of bile in his mouth. "The government didn't care. His family didn't care. They wouldn't even answer me."

"But you found him."

"Meredith helped." His cousin, the healer. Senior enough now - and owed enough favours - she'd been able to cut through the red tape. She hadn't been able to explain why Golshan was still in a non-magical convalescent home in London, but she'd introduced Seth to someone who knew who to ask.

He'd spent three days sitting on a series of hard wooden benches in grand buildings, where it seemed the world wheeled on, untroubled by war. They were full of men in pressed suits that had never seen mud, who walked briskly, barely paying attention to their surroundings. Seth suspected he'd never get that peace of mind back. Finally, one of them had sent him to a particular window, in the depths of the War Office, with a note.

The clerk had looked over his glasses, then taken the slip of paper Seth away, leaving him alone for nearly twenty minutes. He'd copied it, of course, into his notebook, like Thesan had told him. He felt like that piece of paper was his only hope of finding Golshan again.

When the clerk came back, he was carrying a large bound portfolio, and he flipped through it, copying information out onto a pre-printed form. Some small part of him wondered how many people like him had stood here, hoping.

"Meredith told me who to ask. He sent me to someone else, and then someone else. A dozen offices." He swallowed. "The last clerk was kind, at least."

"Kind?"

"When he'd filled out the form, he looked up. I don't know what I looked like. Drawn. A bit wild. He asked how I knew Golshan."

"What did you say?"

Seth shrugged. How did anyone explain a friendship like that, the person he'd carved his life around? Dilly had a sense of it, but she'd given them their space, while Seth was still at Schola. Seth's whole world outside of classes had been Golshan. Shepherding him through doing his assignments, making sure his impulsive ideas didn't get them into too much trouble but just enough trouble to be going on with.

But also the parts no one else saw, the times curled up in one of their rooms, Golshan talking about anything and everything. Seth had come to rely on the shapes that made in his head. Carvings, certainly, the little figures of people and animals he made for love and memory.

But also bigger things, how a box might slide best at the touch of fingers, what shape made a pleasing footboard for a bed, or the most comfortable chair. All the times they talked about materia, how this wood or that stone or this plant held magic and charms and enchantments, what that might do in the right hands.

He had something dancing at the edges of his mind, what his hands might do with a wheeled chair, with Golshan's ideas about which woods to use. Seth knew someone in the Trellech crafting guild who was a talented wheelwright, he'd been doing interesting things with bicycles.

Seth couldn't do anything with that yet. It was another thing for later. Along with repaving the paths out to the orchard, maybe some sort of platform that could be raised or lowered with ropes. Golshan loved being up in the trees, not just under them, he always had.

Dilly nudged him, just shifting her elbow. "Keep talking, you."

"I said we'd been in the trenches together. That he'd saved my life." He shrugged. It was a bare skeleton of an answer, but he had discovered it was the one no one ever questioned. "Then the hospital, the care home, wasn't open for visitors until the next day."

"You were entirely beside yourself. I do remember that."

He settled his hand along the curve of her head. "And you gave me something to drink and didn't fuss at me. Have I mentioned how glad I am to have you back?"

"We missed each other. Out of our proper place. Orbits, as your sister would say. Oh, she said she'd come by next week for a good visit. After things are settled. She brought round some more of that beer you like while you were out."

"Ta." He set that aside. It was one thing he did not have to worry about now. "And then I got to see him."

"For your very self." Dilly hesitated. "How is he?" It was the first time she'd asked for any kind of detail.

"Himself. Only." Seth shook his head. "It's wrong, seeing him that still. They had him in a Bath chair, not even something he could move on his own. You know what they're like, big basketwork things. Someone else has to push you. And the nurse, she told me not to excite him. He must have been dying, day by day. All the way inside his head, like he was when he had to go back to his family. And wearing convalescent blues."

"What's so wrong about them?" Trust her to find that one thing, the one that made him honestly furious about the indignity.

"No pockets." He'd been in them, briefly, after a ricochet injury to his arm that healed up fine in the end. All right, with a bit of help from a nurse with a touch of magic in her hands. He had her name and family address somewhere. He'd have to write and see if she'd made it through and offer to make something for her as a thank you. "Because a man in blues doesn't need money, or to hold anything, or any independence. It's awful." Nowhere for his whittling knife or a bit of wood, either.

Her mouth opened, making a small 'O' shape. "That's not the Golshan I know. And his family wouldn't talk to you?"

"They've never much liked me. We're below their station, a lot, by their standards. A cat might look at a king, but we're no cats. And they've never..." He shrugged. "If he'd done what he was supposed to, marry and have children, a proper woman from their own people, they might not have minded. But he didn't. Wouldn't. They think that if he hadn't spent so much time with me, he'd have made something of himself. Met the right people, got in with the Fox House families, the Gold Book clans."

Dilly snorted. "While you're the reason he didn't fail out of Schola his first year. When he turned up with no idea what to expect." She shook her head. "And then he was juggling half a dozen things after you left school. More duelling training, Materia, and the music hall. And his family never knew the half of it."

"Never." He smiled at the memory. "And you were setting your cap for me."

She turned her head to grin at him before settling back. "Any sensible woman would. Mmm. Kind and caring and good with your hands." She shrugged. "I loved you for how you were with him, honestly."

Seth had not actually heard her put it this way before. "You - " He stalled, then gathered up his courage. "You haven't said."

Dilly took a long breath. "I suppose I haven't put it in words. I knew. You knew. It was enough, before."

That did not answer his question. After a moment, she went on. "I kept watching you. My first year, I remember sitting there, in the House common room, or the library, seeing how you were with him. How you'd get him to do fifteen minutes of reading, and then something else, and then reading, and then something. How you'd let him tell you about things while you took notes, and then you'd hand the notes over, and he'd do better on the tests. And so would everyone who'd been listening. You were patient, but it wasn't the coddling kind of patient. It was giving him space to grow into, but be himself. Young as you were. As we all were."

"And you liked that, then?"

Dilly shrugged. "I thought, first, that you'd make a brilliant father. Not like my brother-in-law, who was a muchness at the time. You were kind. You saw things no one else noticed. You cared about them. And as I got a bit older, I got to thinking how that'd make a good lover. How could I not want a bit of that for me?"

"You've not had near enough." Seth's voice caught, because it hit home for him, now, how much she'd lost.

How much more he was blithely about to take away from her. "You could, you could say no."

"Say no to what, love?" He knew that note in her voice, the one that was setting her line in the dirt, to be crossed at his peril. He'd never heard it aimed at him before, just others.

"To Golshan coming here. It'll change everything."

She shrugged. "So I can't wander downstairs half-naked in the morning. That's not much to give up. Mind, I bet he'd not care one way or the other after he got over the first time. He's lusty, Seth-my-love. Not lewd."

Seth was entirely sure this was not how this sort of conversation was supposed to go. "Still. I just barrelled ahead, assuming. You should have stopped me sooner."

Dilly shifted then, to peer at his face. "Do I look like an idiot? Good grief, Seth, did you forget that much? You have loved that man since you and he showed up at school, at thirteen. You've been his friend, you've had his back as much as he's had yours. You finish each other's sentences, you always know where he is. You always will. I married you knowing that and I'll die knowing it, and be glad every time I think of it. Even before the part where he saved your life, I knew that."

It had the burr of her home in it, the broad vowels of Yorkshire, that she'd mostly muted since she came to school. And even now, she wasn't scolding. She was just laying it out, in blunt true words.

He couldn't argue. He knew he wouldn't win this if he tried, even if he did his very best. And he didn't want to. She was right about that. He'd be telling lies if he tried, the kinds of lies that would shatter both his crafting and his life. He let out a long breath. "You're sure."

"You bring him home. Here. We've space, thanks to your parents. I did my share volunteering in the hospitals during the War, I'm not afraid of that bit of work. And we've more hands to help, if we need it. Besides, you said that the place he's going to has some ideas."

Seth nodded. "Meredith again. There's a convalescent home for our people, with magic. Mostly for people whose magic got twisted in the War. They have some ideas for helping him, and honestly, I'm wondering if his magic's not tangled up now too. They're pretty sure they can get him more independent. Help him use magic to do things, maybe. They don't know if any of it will work. But they're willing to try, at least. And they're on the books as a proper care home, with nursing staff, so the transfer went through."

"Why wasn't he there already?" Dilly had an excellent point.

"No one who cared to ask, near as I can tell. Just assumed they were full up, which they were at the time, not whether they'd have space in a few months. Someone from the Ministry just wanted to tick the box on the form, didn't care what it meant to Golshan. For the rest of his life. He'd get adequate care. Stay alive. They didn't bother about actually living." Seth let out a shuddering breath. "That's a … Meredith's looking into it. Who else is stuck somewhere like that. It'll take a while. The Ministry doesn't like admitting that sort of thing. And the Temple of Healing's still overwhelmed with people who'd die without their care."

"They should be ashamed." Dilly shook her head. "And Golshan's going where, then?" The change of subject was welcome, she must be able to feel the roiling anger Seth felt.

"Bit north of Trellech. There's a portal. I can visit three times a week. For hours, if he wants."

"I'd say we, but I'm still hopeful."

That made him lift his head. "Really, not just wanting?" She'd been at the right time of her cycle to catch, but it was still too soon to be sure.

"A tad inconvenient, but we'll manage. And I could take the train down, sometime." She shrugged. "If not this month, maybe next. Now you're home, and for longer than a fortnight's leave."

He let out a long sigh. "Have I mentioned how much I love you?"

"Not since this morning. Mind, you were out all day. After supper, you can take me up to bed and show me again."

He laughed. "I suppose that's one way to distract my nerves."

Dilly paused for just an instant. "You still think something's going to go wrong. Why?"

"I don't know. I can't trust my instincts anymore. You're right they've all got out of tune, not having him around. Rough, unsanded. Splinters catching on things."

"You never have approved of lazy workmanship." Her voice was teasing, the muted alto he loved. "And you think another shoe's going to drop. On your head."

"That place, it's so rigid. What if we didn't do a form right? Or his family stirs themselves to object."

"Then you will figure out what needs fixing, and do it again. I know you. If need be, you will figure out how to spirit him away in the middle of the night. You won't leave him there. Remember, now he knows you've found him. That must mean a lot."

Seth swallowed. "We didn't even get to talk long. A few minutes. The same this week. I don't..." He gestured with his free hand. "I don't know what we are now."

"Love, you barely know who you are anymore. You've been to hell and back the long way round. Remember? We talked about this during your leave. These past weeks."

"Now you're being patient with me." He didn't mind. It was soothing to have someone who understood without making him explain. Two someones.

"I am. I learned from the best, and don't you forget it. Right. Go wash your hands, and I'll make up our sandwiches. After, you should do some carving. And then we'll go up to bed. That is the way sensible people have an evening like this. In the morning, you will put on a suit that makes you look like you know what you're doing. And you'll meet the nurse from the place Golshan's going, and you'll make sure he's settled."

"And then I'll come home." He had to try that on, hear it as well as think it.

"And then you'll come home. And, eventually, so will he."

CHAPTER 3
A WEEK LATER

Golshan sat, staring at the knife on the table in front of him.

It was his knife. It had not been his knife for over a year. He had not, honestly, thought he would ever see it again. And now, he could not bring himself to touch it.

Frankly, he wasn't sure what to do with himself at all. Friday, he had been swept away, and brought to this new place. It was certainly an improvement. There were fewer patients here, only about eighteen.

Rather than a long ward, he had his own room at the end of one of the ground floor wings, and the silence was deafening. He'd been so long crammed in with other people, in the trenches and then in the wards. He'd forgotten what it was like to have space for his magic to move. Whatever magic he might still have.

The place was not at all institutional. Everyone ate together, apparently, unless they preferred to be alone. Not just the patients, but the staff, with plenty of laughter and chatter about everything from a recent outing to the local wildlife to a book someone was reading. No one had pressed him to join in, or told him to buck up. They'd just smiled, included him when he showed an interest, and let him listen. No one censored the papers or the books.

The first morning, after the orderly helped with all the necessary tasks, he'd been dressed in better clothes, more comfortable. They were even, to his surprise, a deep red. Not the brighter shades he might have chosen, but much more what he liked than anything he'd worn for years. Not a uniform, certainly. They'd brought him a different kind of wheelchair, one he could theoretically push himself. They hadn't asked him to try, hadn't told him to do anything, actually.

He let his hand drift to the rim, rolling an inch back and forth, testing it out again while no one was focused on him. Otherwise, the first few days, he'd been offered a range of books and puzzles. They'd asked if he wanted to join in for any of the radio shows, or if he would prefer to sit on the terrace and be left alone.

Apparently, their practice was to give people several days to settle in, because this morning, Tuesday, had been different. After breakfast, he'd been wheeled down into the other wing of the house, to a large room at the end. It turned out to be an office, not of some greying administrator, but of Nurse Gospatrick, who was briskly in control of the entire place. She was older than he was, but he thought not yet forty, and she had the glowing health of someone who flourished in the country.

Nurse Gospatrick had been clear that she was not sure yet exactly what they would be able to do for him. But she had a plan to find that out. That it would involve physical exercises, magical ones, perhaps other forms. That they would sort out what he could do now, and what might be possible in a while. That perhaps he might spend a week at the Temple of Healing in Trellech, for further examination and time with the healing baths.

She had been certain he could have much more independence than he currently had. Nurse Gospatrick seemed convinced he would be able to get himself in and out of the chair, manage without an orderly, with an outside chance of even standing briefly. The fact he could feel his legs was, apparently, extremely promising.

He thought, frankly, that near all of that was fantasy, but he did not argue with her. She had a pragmatism to her, like Mistress Wain and her daughters, like Seth's Dilly, that he'd never been able to cross. His mother's sharp comments, he'd learned to ignore those, when he wasn't doing what she wanted. But he'd had a much harder time shaking off the people who wanted good things for him and somehow believed he should have them.

Besides, he didn't have the strength to argue. He barely remembered how to have a conversation, after all those months of being a lump.

Nurse Gospatrick had done something else, too. She had explained to him, to the best of her ability, bringing out illustrations and diagrams, what his injury actually meant. He had wondered, for a moment, if the delay before this meeting had been partly so she could study up. It had that hint of earnestness, especially after she admitted they'd never had a resident - she said resident, not patient - with quite his background.

Knowing what had happened, that the swelling around the bullet's path had done much of the damage, that that was the reason he could feel his legs, that helped, somehow. Much of the time in the previous places, they'd either been startled he had any feeling at all, or were stunned he'd lived past the first week.

Nurse Gospatrick had been blunt about that, too. In

her ongoing view, there was apparently no reason he shouldn't have a good long life, full of things he enjoyed. At least once he learned how to take care of himself, and they sorted out what would be a help. He was quite sure she hadn't meant to imply any kind of love life, but of course, it was not the sort of thing one could ask a nurse. Especially if one preferred men.

He was, however, going to be kept busy. And exhausted, Nurse Gospatrick had been clear about that. There would be hours devoted every day to learning how to manage things for himself, how to move, how to sit, how to breathe better. How to use tools and likely his magic to make things easier. Part of him wanted to resent that, all the effort he could see coming. But if he'd learned to duel, if he'd learned the music hall, presumably he could learn this too. Even if this time, he didn't have Seth to steady him through it.

He hadn't quite asked how long she expected him to be a resident, but in the end, she'd answered that for him. If he put the work in, if he kept up with his previous form, learning things, five or six months. They'd sort out what he needed as they went along.

Then he'd been wheeled off to lunch, and immediately after, out to the terrace on a beautiful day. Five minutes later, Seth had appeared, all smiles and delight. He hadn't said much, not to start. Seth had never been much given to words when other things would do just as well. He'd sat down next to Golshan and started carving. A new piece, not one he'd already started on. Golshan had sat there, watching him carve for a good forty minutes, before he said anything. Finally, he'd asked about Dilly, about Seth's mum and dad.

That led to going through each of the family, bit by bit, catching up on what was going on. Lia had another new baby, Orcus had come through the War well enough and gone back into the depths of a Ministry office. Thesan was loving being the Astronomy professor at Schola, especially now she had got through her second year of teaching. Though she'd had a hard time with her predecessor's death that past fall. Allie and Cel, the two younger sisters, were still in their apprenticeships, and doing well. Archie, the youngest, was just out of school and figuring out what to do with himself. Seth had several amusing stories about the process so far.

The sun moved, the shadows shifted. No one came to make Seth go away. Golshan had never been on the best terms with time, always too early or too late for any meeting, but this began to unsettle him. The past year had been made up of other people's rigid schedules he must yield to. Finally, he'd asked about it, and Seth had shrugged.

As it wound around to tea time, Seth finished what he'd been working on, and held it out on his palm. It was a wooden stick, about four inches long, thicker on one end, with a little rondel. Just the right size to roll in his hands or along one arm, maybe even down one thigh. Made to pick up and fiddle with.

It wasn't the first time Seth had made him something of the kind, but it had been ages since he'd had one in his hands. He'd stopped in the trenches. It was too easy for the movement to startle someone else. He'd instead taught himself endless card tricks. Someone always had a deck handy.

He looked up, and Seth had smiled, then brought out a wooden box, about a foot and a half long. Seth had put it down in front of him, without a comment. Once again, he'd stood, bent to kiss Golshan on the forehead, and then gone away, saying only that he'd be back for the afternoon on Thursday.

The box had held four things. The tallest was a carved wooden polecat the size of his flat hand. It was one of Golshan's favourite animals, for the clever lethality and curiosity. The wood was sanded smooth and polished to a fine sheen that felt like silk under his fingers. There were hours of work there. Days. There was a frame with photos of Seth and Dilly on one side and the whole of Seth's immediate family on the other. A small writing kit sat at the bottom, also Seth's making, with a pen and plenty of paper and ink.

And then there had been the knife. It had been wrapped in a silk handkerchief, but he'd known what it was. The leather sheath he'd brought to the War was now cleaned and smelling of linseed oil and beeswax. The hilt was still the same creamy ivory he remembered, with the four stones around the rim. The knife had been spotless, no hint of rust, the blade as sharp as it should be. He might have been born in Persia, but he was of Albion now, for better and for worse. There was one stone for each of the elements his lessons had drilled into him. One stone to anchor each flavour of magic.

He had not touched it, handling it with the silk between his skin and the cool ivory, desperately needing that insulation. While he was trying to decide if he should, there was a shadow behind him, and then a man came around, where Golshan could see him without twisting. "May I join you?"

Yes. No. He had no idea what he wanted. The man was older, later thirties, perhaps, and he looked every bit like officers looked, for all he was wearing a quite ordinary country suit. To be honest, he looked like Golshan's parents wanted him to look. He was a man secure in his place in the world. If he'd been darker of skin and hair, he might have been one of Golshan's brothers, fit to rule.

He had the straight spine of someone who had taken to the Army like a roc to the air. His golden hair had not begun to go silver. The man had the kind of face that had graced every heroic magazine of the War, exhorting the troops onward to bravery and their own slaughter. Not someone Golshan had seen about the place before.

In the end, Golshan shrugged and gestured at the other chairs. The man took the one facing him, not the one Seth had been in, which meant he was far enough away not to touch any of Golshan's things by accident. "Tea? It's about an hour to supper." He didn't introduce himself, but he wasn't wearing any kind of uniform or insignia. Another patient, then, perhaps.

Golshan shook his head. "Not for me." His voice came out creaky.

The man nodded. "You've been here since Friday, I gather. How are you settling in?"

How was he supposed to answer that? It was better than where he'd been. There was more to look at and listen to. He didn't have to hide his magic, not that he'd done any. No one seemed inclined to demand his cheerfulness. The staff had been prompt, competent, and careful to avoid hurting him. All of those were, he knew, good things, but he was not at all sure it was safe to say any of them. In the end, he shrugged. "It's quiet." Never mind that he wasn't sure what he thought about the quiet.

"And you have what you need to be comfortable? I'm sure they've offered books and entertainment, but if there's anything you prefer, someone will find it."

Golshan nodded. "Nice to have a change from the edited newspaper and the same handful of magazines." That seemed fair enough to share.

The man leaned back, then grinned suddenly, as if he'd not been able to keep the mask up for much longer.

"And you have no idea what to make of all this, do you? We're not like anywhere else."

Golshan raised an eyebrow, shifting a little in the chair. The basket chair had been far more limiting. He was still getting used to the idea he could change the set of his shoulders. "What are you like, then?"

"Think of it like a garden. Different plants need different things. The roses, they like a bit of bone meal and blood meal. The dainty flowers need something else, the ferns want shade, and so on."

Golshan's chin came up at the mention of the roses. He'd always been ridiculously fond of them, the riotous shades of colour, the way they had beauty and thorns. And besides, his name meant 'rose garden', it was only proper he take an interest. He'd also found the idea of beauty growing from blood and bone somehow reassuring. It gave him a hint of hope. "And are you a gardener?"

"Oh, no. Or only in the most amateur way." Something about the question amused him. His eyes crinkled up now, but the man was laughing with him, definitely not laughing at. Of course, he didn't answer the question properly. After a moment, the man went on, "What did you do, before?"

"I ran a music hall. Young for it, but I had a knack. I got hired on when they needed someone in a pinch, and turned out to be good at it. Plenty going on, never the same day twice. Plenty of people need a bit of a word or an ear, to keep the smiles rolling in." He'd done plenty of other things, too, keeping up his knifework and the magic that went with it. But that wasn't a thing he talked about, certainly not to a stranger.

"Ah, you're someone who likes that sort of thing. I do a bit of that, now, sorting out things between the Army, our

Ministry, their Ministry. Though there's rather less entertainment in the mix."

Golshan snorted. "Certainly less knife throwing and acrobatics."

He regretted the comment about the knife, immediately, but the other man's gaze never moved to the blade on the table. Instead, he nodded. "And you've had a chat with Nurse Gospatrick, about what she thinks we might do for you." Before Golshan could say anything, the man lifted his hand. "Now you're trying to figure out how to say, without being too rude, that you think she's dreaming. That you'll never have most of that."

Golshan's lips quirked. He wasn't sure what he felt, but it was certainly different. Intriguing. Like his mind was engaging again, properly, for the first time in a year, wanting to analyse all the pieces of what was going on. All his instincts, dormant though they had been, shouted that this man was guiding the conversation deliberately. The question, though, was where, and to what end. He shrugged, spreading his hands. "Different from what they've been telling me for a year."

The man leaned forward, resting his forearms on the table now. "I thought the same thing. I was with the King's Bays - a few of us magical chaps, attached to the regiment, for messages and special assignments. Quite early on - spring of 15 - I found myself in a room at the Temple of Healing, not at all sure what was going on. Before this place was a glint in anyone's eye." He said the last very fondly. There was a note to it that wasn't just about the place itself.

Golshan nodded, interested now, a bit despite himself. "And?"

"And Nurse Gospatrick swept in one day, took a look at me, and set about doing something that worked, rather than what she was told should be done. And then she did it for more people, and more. We've had, oh, a hundred and fifty people come through, now. Almost all of them doing things they were sure they'd never have again. Work. Family. Magic coming to their call, instead of running wild or being blocked. Whatever their pleasures were."

Golshan turned his head away, feigning interest in a slight movement along the line of the woods, across the garden. "Not much of that for me. I'm not going to walk again. Even the nurse didn't suggest that. No space back-stage for a chair."

The man coughed, but went on when Golshan didn't look back. "And an awful lot of stairs in the world. I spent enough time in a chair to know that, though I had different problems. But a music hall's not the only place with people who need a kind hand and a bit of sense. You might be grand at what I do now, finding people help. We've only just met, but you don't seem the sort to just sit around and collect your pension."

Golshan glanced back at him, then let his eyes fall again to the knife on the table.

"What we can promise you is that we'll get you as much of the world as we can. El - Nurse Gospatrick is quite sure you can learn to manage your own care. Get yourself in and out of a chair once we've found the right one for you. Your friend..." He hesitated for an instant, then gestured at the things on the table, all of them. "A very good friend."

Golshan looked up, suddenly, sharply, but there was no assumption there, no hint of innuendo. "Seth." As always, he heard how he said the name, the weight behind it he'd never been able to hide fully. "Been friends since our first week at Schola. And his wife." He fumbled for the photographs. "That's her. That's his mum and dad and all his brothers and sisters."

The other man nodded. "He's been clear we need to do right by you. And we will." He hesitated, then gestured at the frame. "His family, not the one you come from?"

"They were always kind to me. His Mum, especially. I spent a lot of the hols with them." Golshan teetered, trying to decide whether to say something more.

"And your own, mmm. Let me guess, they have no idea what to make of your injury, and perhaps would prefer to ignore it entirely?" There was a note there that made Golshan look up, some sense that this wasn't what the man knew most intimately, but it wasn't just words. The other man nodded. "I worried, for a good while, my parents thought the same. I was lucky. It was a misunderstanding. They'd been trying to find me and help. But there's nothing that makes up for someone not being there, when you hoped they would be."

Golshan looked away. "I was a changeling child for them. Grew up here, my brothers and sister didn't." He shrugged, but let his fingers brush the frame one more time.

"And the knife, that's a thing that matters." The man didn't press, something in his voice making it clear he wasn't asking anything. "It will be safe in your room, I promise."

Golshan swallowed, then the need to know burst out of him. "How can you be so sure?" He gestured at the knife, then at the house behind him. "About any of it?"

The man leaned forward, offering his hand. "My word on it. I'm Gospatrick. Roland Gospatrick. Elen - Nurse Gospatrick - is my wife."

CHAPTER 4
TWO WEEKS BEFORE CHRISTMAS

Seth waited as Golshan turned the wheelchair, looking around. He was glad he'd put all the time into getting the road regraded. Dad had been a grand help, talking everyone who used the portal into chipping in for the charmwork to smooth the road out properly. He'd pointed out it would make it better for anyone who had a cart or a pram or a wheelbarrow.

Today, it meant it had been easy enough for Golshan to push himself along smoothly, even on the incline up to the house. The new ramp to the front door looked grand, and Seth held the door open. They'd already brought Golshan's trunk of personal effects down. Seth had done that first thing this morning, while Golshan was making his goodbyes to everyone at the home.

Seth looked around. The house was not so different from what Golshan had known when it was Seth's parents living here, back in their school days. The colours were a bit different, deep greens, but mixed now with the deep golds and a few bits of glowing orange and red. They'd pulled out all the colours that always reminded him of Golshan.

"Are those because of me?" Golshan gestured at the pillows on the sofa.

Seth laughed. "Yes, but we've had them for years, you remember? They were on the window seat for a while. Come see the garden, not that it's much of a garden at the moment?"

Golshan gave him a searching look, but pushed himself along, aiming for the kitchen door. They'd rearranged the kitchen, to make an easier path past the table, to the door, and now it was smooth and easy. Golshan went straight through, pausing to open the door, leaning forward to nudge the latch with a bit of magic.

It was December, so the garden truly wasn't much. The rose bushes were stark and trimmed back for the year. It made the new paving stand out more, though, the broad stone paths snaking through the garden, to a central circular terrace perhaps eight feet across. One path curved away through the garden into a wooden pathway that led out to the orchard.

Golshan twisted around as Seth came over. "For me?"

"I've some ideas for the orchard, too. We'll try them out when the spring comes."

That got Seth an incredibly dubious look. "You know this isn't real."

"I set the path with my own two hands. My blisters are plenty real." Seth was amused, more than anything else. Well, amused, and desperately hoping this would work out. "The workshop's there." They could just see the corner from here, at the end of the other path through the roses.

Golshan hesitated. "Can we?"

"See your room first, then we can go out there." Seth was, honestly, much more nervous about Golshan's room.

The workshop was grand, it always was, all his tools set out, space for Golshan's wheelchair, if Golshan wanted to keep him company. A sofa, if Golshan preferred that.

"Your old room, you said." Abruptly, Golshan wheeled around without saying anything else, and went back into the house after fumbling a bit with the door. He completely ignored Dilly, who had come down into the kitchen.

Seth held up a hand, silently asking her to wait. She blew him a kiss, and turned to busy herself with something in the corner, getting things ready for supper. Seth trailed along as Golshan pushed the first door on the right open. He came up behind the chair, with Golshan stopped a few inches inside.

He thought it looked grand. A desk, broad enough to fit the chair comfortably beneath it. It was set under the window, so Golshan could look out at the garden as much as he liked. The bed, to the right, plenty of space on both sides. This room had once held Seth and both his brothers. It was spacious for just one, even with a larger bed and needing space for the chair. And the colours, he hoped the colours were right.

The walls were freshly whitewashed, but the bedspread had the ruby reds and glowing orange, colours of the flame and vitality. The linens were a deep green, and the curtains. Dilly had somehow found a printed fabric for the curtains that brought it all together, leaves overlapping with hints of red and orange berries.

The floors were stone, had been since the house was made, but Seth had seen to it that they'd take warming charms. No rugs, Nurse Gospatrick had suggested that might foul the chair. He'd built two sets of shelves and drawers, set with plenty of room to move around. Golshan's trunk against the left wall, ready to be unpacked. There was more than enough room on the walls to hang photographs or whatever other decoration Golshan might want.

Then Golshan wheeled in further before turning in a circle to face Seth. Seth, with the part of his mind that always looked at how well something functioned, still wasn't happy with how the current chair turned. Much better than before, but not good enough. Not yet. "You're serious." Golshan's tone was still disbelieving, as if he still didn't know what to do with this.

Seth spread his hands. "This is your home. We can change anything, if you like. The bed adjusts. New trick, and that's going to make me a nice bit of coin when I make more frames."

Golshan wheeled over to the bed and peered at it. "How? And am I your test case, then?"

Seth laughed. "You always are. There are words to lift or lower it. We can set them whenever you like. Pick something you're not likely to use otherwise. And one for warming. They said you might like that, some nights."

Golshan snorted. "Scarcely going to have someone else warming it with me."

The bitterness was there, though it was a passing comment. Seth just nodded. He didn't argue. Not right now. Oh, Golshan would have let him. He'd done it before, in their long afternoon conversations in the gardens at the Gospatrick place.

Golshan nodded, then suddenly, he was scooting past Seth. "Workshop." Seth shook his head and followed. Dilly had settled in the great room, and she leaned forward as Golshan went by without looking at her.

He hesitated in the doorway. "You all right, my love?" Her voice was quiet, checking in with him.

Seth shrugged. "He needs to sort things out. Bet there will be carving."

"We'd all worry if you weren't carving." Dilly nodded. "Ring if you want me to come out." That was a new trick too, a bell that he could ring from the workshop to let her know to come out. Or for him to come in.

By the time Seth snagged two bottles of beer from the kitchen, and got down to the workroom, Golshan was inside, the door ajar. Seth made his way in, to find that Golshan had already levered himself from the chair onto the sofa, the way they used to sit. He'd nudged the chair mostly out of the way, but where he could grab it later.

Seth had been given a couple of mornings of rather intensive training on that point. It was all about how important it was not to move someone's chair without permission, not even to be helpful. That it wasn't helpful. That he should treat it like moving the person.

In the back of his head, Seth had felt that wasn't entirely helpful in their case, because in the usual way of things. Golshan would have been curled up, head in Seth's lap as Seth worked, or leaning against him, or hanging upside down on the sofa, for a change of perspective. They had always been inclined to touch, as long as they'd known each other.

"Comfy? Beer." Seth handed it over. "Want me to get something to work on?"

"It's your workshop." Golshan said it as if that were the obvious thing. Then his voice went quiet. "Please."

Seth handed over the beer, set his own down on the other small table, and went to his workbench. He came back with a box he was working on carving, delicate little lines and his leather roll with his fine tools. He settled in, sitting cross-legged, Golshan on his right side, his off-hand.

They sat like that, like they had for years, on and off. Gradually, slowly, he felt Golshan shift to lean against his shoulder, as if he had to test it, like he couldn't rely on it.

Seth just kept carving. This was something that could go any number of directions. If the gouge went somewhere he hadn't planned, he would make art out of that.

He'd been doing that a lot since he came home. Following the pattern that unfolded, rather than forcing himself into the narrow lines he'd been taught. He thought - Dilly thought, too - it made for better work. Work he felt better about, certainly.

He'd been working for perhaps twenty minutes when Golshan spoke again. "It can't last."

Seth shrugged. "If you want something different, we'll sort that."

"I meant you. Dilly." Golshan gestured with his free hand, Seth caught the movement out of the corner of his eye. "You'll need the space. I won't. What am I supposed to do?"

"Right now, you're supposed to unpack, and settle in, and enjoy the holidays."

Golshan snorted, but it was much more his usual sort of snort. "Not my customs, luv."

"If you live in this house, there will be Christmas. Sorry, it's a rule. Lots of food. Mum must have knitted you a jumper, everyone home."

"All the more reason you need my room." Golshan gestured again, but Seth thought that was some serious progress. 'His' room, yes.

"Mum and Dad are putting Thesan up for a night or two. The others are staying at Lia's." Seth hesitated, but this was as good an opening as he was going to get. "We're hosting the feast part of it. You don't need to go to the larger family things. Dilly's not going, because that's the portal, and you can keep each other company."

They'd told Golshan that she was expecting - she was only barely showing, yet, especially in the looser dresses she generally preferred at home. But it hit differently now, apparently. "You'll need room for the baby."

"We have a perfectly good nursery upstairs. Or we will in another month or two."

"Upstairs." Golshan shook his head.

Seth turned his head. "Thinking about some options for that. I don't know what will work, not without you here to help. But we're hosting the feast because Lia refused to let me put a ramp at her place. Or move anything around. She may or may not get over her snit by Christmas, but we gave her plenty of time."

There was a long silence. Seth was not at all sure how to read it, what it meant, but he knew he shouldn't rush it. Rushing this kind of thing didn't work. Golshan could be lightning quick about so many things, but others, he wanted to circle, evaluate.

"What do you mean?" When Golshan spoke again, he sounded cautious.

Seth shifted. "Get more comfortable if you like, yeah?" After a moment, Golshan wriggled down, to rest his head on Seth's leg, like he used to do. Then he pushed up on one elbow, tugging at his trousers and legs to manually get them into a better position before settling down again. Seth let him rearrange without comment.

They'd told him, at the Gospatrick place, that Golshan had had a month of doing things for himself, without an orderly helping, to make sure he'd feel able to manage. Not because Seth wasn't willing to help - he was. But because that was independence. It meant he could go out if he wanted. It meant Seth and Dilly could go out. That Golshan would be able to have a bath when he wanted, or cook, or whatever he needed.

It was a sensible plan, but it had meant Seth had been

waiting impatiently. Impatience wasn't like him, that was Golshan, normally.

"I don't want you to lose your family." Golshan's voice was clear now and crisp. "You didn't say." It wasn't - quite - an accusation, but it was the sort of tone that strongly indicated Golshan's disapproval.

"I won't." Seth was entirely confident in this. "Not my family. Lia's being difficult. Casting nasturtiums."

Golshan peered up at him, and Seth went on. "You remember. It should be aspersions, really. Mum's always said casting nasturtiums."

"Your mother has always preferred the garden to anywhere else." Golshan sounded content at that, at least.

"She's looking forward to having you round to the new place. And she promises the roses here will be grand. And the rest of it." They were not too far down the road, in a much smaller place now, easier to take care of. "Nasturtiums. Lia likes the idea of supporting the troops, but she's all over our poor wounded veterans only at a sizable distance."

"You?" Golshan's voice had that edge to it now.

"She hasn't asked." Not about the wound in his arm, for all it had healed well. Not about any of the rest of it. "I wish her well, but I won't bend for her. Not anymore."

Golshan hesitated, then shifted his hand to rest on Seth's knee. The little quiet intimacies they'd lost for so long, he kept feeling them out. "You were angry, at that, at the old place."

"I was. I still am. You deserve better. All of us deserve better. Everyone there did. But you more than most." Seth had ideas about that, eventually. Now he had space in his head for anything other than getting Golshan home, safe, here.

"The rest of the family?"

"I can't promise they won't be daft about something. Make assumptions. But Mum is throwing her whole weight behind including you. She has knit you a stocking of your very own, I've seen it."

"Knit? I thought they were sewn." Golshan sounded baffled. "The ones in stories."

"Mum will give you chapter and verse on knitting being the way to create something that moulds to the leg. In this case, though, it is the fact it stretches that is key."

Golshan snorted. "Oranges in the toe, isn't that a thing?"

"I know they're not your customs. But an orange is an orange, and there were years that'd have been the best thing ever, aren't there?"

"Oh, yes." Golshan let out a long sigh. "No. Wait. This. This is the best thing we didn't have."

"Missed you too." Seth rested his carving on his other knee, letting his hand rest on Golshan's shoulder. It felt right, the weight against his leg, the shift of Golshan's shoulder. "So, yes. Lia's being rather awful. Everyone else is fine, or will sort it out. Well, no bets about Dad's sisters, but that's no different than usual."

Golshan shook his head. "I don't want." He stopped, as if he weren't sure he wanted to commit himself to this, then charged ahead. "I don't want you to lose things because of me. Ever."

"I'm not." Seth tried to put all his certainty into it. "It may take a little to sort out how things are now."

"And you're sure Dilly doesn't mind?"

"Look, let me get her to come down. Another new thing. See this, here?" He tapped the panel mounted on the wall by the sofa. Three even taps. "Tap this three times, and it'll ring a bell in the kitchen and our room upstairs. There's one in your room, too, rings all three places. Just in case you need something. Three times so you don't have to worry about hitting it accidentally."

"You seem to have thought of everything." Golshan sounded resigned more than anything.

"I'm trying to. I'm sure I've missed things. I'm quite sure I'll mess up sometime. But I also know you'll tell me, and we'll figure it out." Golshan shook his head, but went quiet, just leaning.

When the door opened a couple of minutes later, he pushed up on one arm, as Dilly said, "Stay. Does me good to see that again." She moved to settle down on one of the broad flat stools. "Hey, Golshan." Golshan made a small embarrassed sound, and she went on. "Seth's being a lot, isn't he?" It was conspiratorial, amused, and so very much like a mare setting the tone of the herd.

It was also impossible to argue with, because Seth was. Golshan sighed. "Yes." It was a long-suffering sort of sigh, but amused, all at the same time.

"Well, if you don't know how to make him stop, I certainly don't. I suspect we're better off giving him his head for a bit. Besides, we've both done our part."

"Both?" Now Golshan shifted, to peer at her, more clearly, his elbow on Seth's thigh.

"Who do you think got the linens? Or made your curtains? Or sorted out soap for the bath you should like? And I've some cooking you can help with, if you want, the next few days. Mince pies. Stew. You always are a help with the onions and carrots and turnips. Or not. Your choice."

Golshan shook his head. "It's a lot of choices."

Dilly shrugged. "You don't need to make any right now. We found things we're fairly sure you like. If you don't like them anymore, when you figure that out, say so, and we'll do something else. Or you can do something else. We're not..."

She hesitated, and Seth's eyes went wide, glad Golshan couldn't see this from how he was leaning. It was Dilly showing her own nerves, letting Golshan see that, deliberately. "Being a mum is plenty enough for me to do for someone. I'm not going to do that for you. You're a grown man, you've your own ideas of how things should be. But I'm fair sure we can work it out."

Golshan was quiet for a long time. "You'll tell me if I'm too much? Take up too much ...." His hand twisted in the air. "Everything?"

Dilly snorted. "Got a long way to go, Golshan. A very very long way."

CHAPTER 5
THAT EVENING

After supper, Seth and Dilly settled into what was clearly their evening routine. Seth did more carving. It was the small whittling, this time, with the charm to draw all the sawdust and shavings to a cloth in his lap. Dilly chatted while working on a bit of sewing, then she read aloud for a bit. Golshan settled in, just listening to them, until it got to be about half eight.

"It's been a long day. Let me go wash up, see how things go." Golshan thought this a civil way to let them have their space back, their time together.

Seth had looked up, opening his mouth, then closing it, before saying, carefully, "Can I come say good night when you're settled?"

Some people did not take a hint. On the other hand, he did not want to turn Seth down when Seth had that sort of look in his eyes. And frankly, Golshan didn't really want to turn him down at all. "Please. I'll be...." He shrugged. "A bit."

"Ring your bell when you're ready then."

He'd have to remember to do that. His shoulders were aching a bit more than he wanted. And it had been a long day. Sorting out a new bath, a different bathing room, that took more energy than he really had, but he also wanted to know how it worked. Seth had made a little platform in the tub itself that would rise and sink. The same trick as the bed, he realised. It made it far easier to transfer to the bath, soak, then get back to the chair.

Easier was still not easy, though. There was a lot of levering himself, trusting that the chair would not move or his hand slip on a bit of water. Putting his feet where he wanted them, one by one, still took real thought. By the time he was in the bath, he was more tired. But the water was properly hot and someone had left a vial of bath oil full of the scent of spices, one he rather liked. Nutmeg and cinnamon and a hint of cardamom.

Eventually, he got out of the bath, into night things, and finally into his new bed. He was smug that he'd not needed any help. It had all gone remarkably smoothly. He'd been well-prepared to be on his own, he realised, and it was deeply reassuring to know that he could, in fact, manage for himself. The bed was comfortably broad, with plenty of leverage for him to brace a hand and change how he was sitting or lying. And the covers felt just the right temperature, enough to keep his feet properly warm but not so heavy as to feel binding.

Finally, when he didn't have anything else he thought he needed to do, he hesitated, then tapped the wooden panel at the head of the bed three times. A minute later - just about enough time for Seth to pack things up and walk down the hall - there was a knock on the door.

"Come in." It felt odd to tell Seth to come in. It had been so long since it had been remotely relevant. Since there had been a door between them.

Seth pushed the door open. Somewhere in the process, he'd changed into pyjamas and a dressing gown, and that was definitely something Golshan hadn't seen for too many years. He patted the bed. "Plenty of space."

There was a flicker across Seth's face, something Golshan couldn't read, but then he settled down. Golshan had propped himself up with pillows. After a moment Seth leaned back against the head of the bed, on top of the covers, shifting another pillow under his shoulders.

This bed was certainly fully stocked, overflowing with soft puffy mounds of them, unlike the meagre flat things of that care home. Plenty to share. He wondered, for a moment, how much Seth had planned the sharing. It was one of those flickering thoughts that popped into his head, ran around, and then disappeared, leaving him unsure whether to put any weight on it.

"Anything need fixing right away? The bathroom or here?" Seth was speaking quietly now, the way he did when he could, just loud enough for Golshan to hear.

"It all worked fine." There were a few small things he might want to see if they could adjust. Maybe different handles on the sink, that he could reach more easily. A little shelf to put the bath things on that was closer. But those were tiny in the grand scheme, and he knew it. "You put a lot of thought into everything."

Seth blinked, then said, as if he were baffled. "Of course."

Golshan had never heard quite that tone from him before. There was something fragile there, now, something he hadn't seen before, except perhaps for that flash of anger, the first day he'd turned up, like an avenging angel. He wasn't sure how to ask, or what to do with the fact Seth wasn't, in fact, carving anything.

He had no idea what to ask next, and so of course the

thing that popped into his head was the thing he'd been afraid to ask about. "My knife." His voice cracked, and he winced, but forged on. "How did you get it back?"

Seth's face changed into a broad smile, suddenly more relaxed, though there was still something complicated. "Remember Jack Alton? Ambulance man, he was a conscientious objector?"

Golshan loved that Seth never used the derogatory 'conchie' for them. Not after he'd seen Golshan's face when someone did. Golshan had made friends with them, just like he'd made friends all down the trenches. He figured that anyone who went out with the stretchers was every bit as brave as the men who fought. "Yes?"

"He was on duty when they brought you in. And he knew you, and he knew the knife meant things. Not what, but he argued it was like the Gurkha regiments, that you'd want it back." He hesitated. "That I'd keep it as safe as I could until I could get it home."

Golshan thought about that, about how Seth could have sent it home, somehow. And how he hadn't. "And you kept it."

Seth closed his eyes, as if this were deeply difficult. "It was all I had of you. That, a few things in the dugout, photos." He turned his head away, off to the corner of the room, as he went on. "I wrote to your family. If they'd asked for it, I don't know what I'd have done. But they didn't. So I kept it. And hoped..." His voice cracked again. "I didn't know what to do without you."

Somehow, they had gone from something complicated to an abyss, diving down into a place Golshan had no idea how to navigate. Seth was fond, but Seth did not say such things. He showed them, with the work of his hands, a touch, an arm. Golshan had never expected that naked a statement. Again, his mind decided for him, before his wits could catch up. "You too?"

It made Seth snort, a release of something he'd been holding in for a long time. Seth slowly shifted to settle his hand, the left, on Golshan's hip. A moment later, Golshan threaded his fingers through. This was a reason for Seth not to be carving. A good reason. They sat there, neither of them saying anything, for a good minute, until Seth spoke again. "In the trenches - even behind the lines - it was so hard not to touch you. To have you there, and know I couldn't."

Golshan hesitated. He had always liked it, leaned into it, needed it. The way Seth settled him and made all the bees in his head stop buzzing around. He'd joked, more than once, that it was like Seth put out a steady stream of smoke, smoothing them into lazy slumber. He hadn't known Seth needed it too. They'd never talked about that. "Me too." He had kept catching himself, only his training, the way he'd honed his will to pretend to be the way other people were, keeping him from all those casual touches. "And then I was gone."

"Then you were gone. And I thought - I thought about a lot of things. That you might die. So many people did. And I didn't know, not until I found you, how many." He stopped, and swallowed. "Something like eight in ten people, paralysed like you were, die in the first week or two. Many of the rest in the next year."

Golshan said, a tad startled, "No one put a number on it for me." It made him shiver, and Seth leaned a little more against him, or Golshan leaned into him. He couldn't even tell anymore. Maybe that was why no one from the Ministry cared where he ended up. They didn't expect him to be there long.

"I just had that last sight of you. When they got you on the stretcher. You looked...." Seth broke off.

"Nightmares?" Golshan tried to say it lightly, but it was not a word made for that.

Seth nodded. "What happened. A hundred other ways you could have died. Sometimes other things in the trenches. But mostly you." He gestured, vaguely, with his free hand, at the box across the room, where the knife was. "The knife. I know it's complicated. You didn't tell me what they made you do when they pulled you out for other duties. I suppose you still can't."

Golshan did not want to have this conversation either, but on the other hand, talking to anyone about it would probably feel better. Nurse Elen had tried a few times, but she hadn't served the same way. Even Roland hadn't had the same thing. He could talk about the trenches, but not about the other work. Golshan had danced around it with one of the other residents. In the end they had both been too shy of each other to talk about any of the meat of the worst of it.

"You know a bit about what it is to me. More than most people."

Seth shifted a little, dropping Golshan's hand long enough to settle more on his right side, then settle an arm against him, fingers threading through Golshan's again. Golshan hesitated, then shifted enough to lean into that, sliding lower on the pillows. It let him look up, let him think a bit.

Seth waited for him to be comfortable, then nodded. "Your people, your family, where you come from. The knife is the first tool of magic, a casting blade. I've seen you use it, of course, but not in years." Then that fierceness was back. "I've seen what using it made you into."

Golshan shivered, unable to stop himself. He thought

about what he could say. He'd made certain promises when they'd discovered his skills. But curiously enough, no one had ever asked him to swear on the Silence, or on his magic, not to tell anyone. Maybe they'd always known this moment might come, sometime after the War, when it wouldn't matter. His word mattered, of course, but it gave him a little room, more than he'd realised.

"A knife is a useful thing in a fight. They'd send me out with one or two other people. Never the same ones twice, never much chance to talk to them. And we'd have a task or three. Getting something out of a house. Causing a distraction while other people did other things. A few times..." He hesitated, wanting to pull away now, and not being able to, not really.

"Yes?" Seth's voice had gone smooth and quiet. Not flat, but more like he was making space now with his words, like he'd made this space they were in with his hands.

"Killing people. Close enough I saw their faces." Golshan didn't know how to say it better than that, there was nothing good about it. He'd done it, and he'd done it well, because he had pride in his skills. And because when it came down to it, a quick, competent death was the kindest.

Seth didn't move at all, other than squeezing Golshan's hand. When he spoke again, it was, at first, about a completely different subject. "You remember us both talking about why we ended up in Horse House? Way back?"

"Second year." They'd found a patch of grass out on a cliff overlooking the ocean. Golshan had begged some rolls and jam from the kitchen, on one of the last gorgeous days of autumn. Just before they'd had to buckle down and get serious about turning assignments in. Or at least he had. Seth had always been on top of that.

"And we got to talking about horses. About how it's a herd, but it's also - they have hooves, and teeth, and they can run, and how they use that, when they fight instead."

"I'd been reading something about a herd that attacked. I forget where. Some dog. And about how you have these horses, and people think they're placid and useful, and it's much more complicated than that."

Seth nodded. "I keep thinking about your knife. That it's about who's in charge of the horse, and how they treat it. All the different things." He waves a hand. "Everyone thinks Horse House is simple. And to be fair, it's the only one of the seven whose animal is domesticated. Granted, a Chicken House or Cow House or Goat House would be a little silly."

"Goats are only barely domesticated." Golshan was now deeply distracted by considering what the House magics of a hypothetical Goat House might be. He suspected that might be more of the sticking point, as the average Schola student did not need more encouragement to be stubborn. Or to be committed to eating everything in sight.

Seth bumped Golshan with his shoulder, amiably, then hesitated, as if he wasn't sure that was a good thing to have done.

"I liked that." He was finding that telling people was much better. Otherwise, they made very odd assumptions about what hurt or didn't, or why. Even Seth. Seth settled in, shifting their joined hands a bit more onto Golshan's hip. That, however, he wasn't sure what to do with at all. He didn't want Seth to move. He didn't want him to feel self-conscious, but he had no idea what it meant.

"Horses." Seth sounded distracted now. "At any rate.

Horses defend themselves, they can be fierce. Dangerous. And maybe that's you." He hesitated. "Maybe that's me, too, only I'm not very good at it."

Golshan sucked in a breath. He'd hoped, somehow, in an endless dream of hoping things that would not ever come to pass, that the War would not have touched Seth so heavily. And yet, who could live in the trenches for years, and not have a well of anger in them. What sensible and kind man wouldn't be filled with fury about all the short-sighted, dangerous, warped choices so many people above them in the hierarchy had made. "You were angry because of what they made me become."

"How they made you use your knife. I knew you couldn't refuse. Not without a court martial."

Golshan shook his head. "They made that clear, the first time. And...." He shrugged, a small shrug. "I was competent. I was quick. I made it as painless as I could. Better me than a lot of other people, probably." Then, because he had to know, "Does it change how you see me?"

Seth didn't answer with words at first. Instead, he curled his arm around a little more, and then, after a fleeting hesitation, he leaned to kiss Golshan's cheek. "No."

There was complete silence again, both of them unsure what to do next. Or at least Golshan was unsure. It felt like the ground was changing under his feet, too fast for him to make sense of. Certainly not tonight. He swallowed, then he said, "Earlier, you asked if there was anything."

Immediately, Seth nodded. "Anything we can do."

"For the solstice could we, could we keep a few of my customs? Help me..." He gestured vaguely with his chin. "The Army tried to shatter my knife. What it means. I want to claim it back."

Seth didn't hesitate. "Of course. What, um. Which

customs are these?" Golshan had to admit, some of them could be a bit odd. If he were still here when the baby was born, there would be quite a few curious ones, with knives and skewers and ash and cotton. All sorts of protection magics so old no one was entirely sure which pieces did what in a magical sense. He'd insist on that. Whatever else.

In this case, the customs were rather simpler. "Red foods. Pomegranate, if we can get one. But beets would do, or did your mum put up jam? She must have put up jam." He gestured at the blanket over his legs. "Red for vitality, for dawn, for the glow of life, some people put it." It came out of him like a babbling stream, now, like he couldn't stop, but Seth wouldn't mind. Seth never minded that. "And we sit around and read poetry. I..." He grimaced. "I might ask you to find a bookshop?"

Seth laughed. "Bookshop, I can do. If you tell me what to look for. Or we can see how awful it is to go to South-wark together."

"Aren't there cobblestones?" Golshan remembered that, and he had quickly learned how awful those were in a chair.

"I can investigate. Advance intelligence. And how many of the shops have steps in. Which, all right, probably a lot. Which makes no sense when you think about it, people moving boxes of books in and out all the time." Then he shook his head. "Right. Red foods. Poetry. Anything else?"

Golshan shook his head. "Spring, um. Nowruz, there are quite a few things. Foods. Customs."

"That's spring equinox, right? We've some time to sort that out." Then Seth hesitated, and said, "I should let you rest. Which is, um. I should get some rest. We were up early, getting your trunk here."

Golshan squeezed his hand once. "Shoo. There's a

tomorrow." And that was the thing. There was. They didn't have to cram everything into today. It was going to take him a long time to get used to that.

Seth leaned to kiss his cheek, bafflingly, one more time, and then eased himself off the bed, padding back to the door, waving, then closing it behind him.

CHAPTER 6
CHRISTMAS DAY

Christmas Eve, the larger gathering of the extended family, had gone well. Seth had gone by himself, to Aunt Constance's home, and spent most of his time with the knot of cousins around his age, along with Thesan, Allie, and Cel. He'd made his proper bows to the older generation, of course, and collected a basket of things to bring back for Dilly, everyone sending along good wishes for the pregnancy.

They'd forgone presents this morning in the household. It was too soon yet to know what Golshan was pining for and wouldn't think to ask for, and he'd not had time to consider shopping. Seth's gift to Dilly, in private, had been the promise of a new set of wooden spoons and a beautifully smoothed wooden bowl, ready for cooking. Her last good spoon had split back in November. He'd been so busy sorting things out for Golshan and keeping up stock for the shops that sold his various carved goods he'd not had time to replace it yet. Her gift to him had been a half dozen new shirts, and a promise of new trousers and shoes. Fresh clothes for a new life.

The stockings had been grand, too, a mix of the orange, little sweets and caramels, carefully made in the kitchen and done up in twists of tinted waxed paper. And, of course, there'd been the mix of small useful items. Another stick for Golshan to fiddle with. Some pencils. A pencil case Dilly had sewn out of delightfully bright fabric, with an embroidered bird across it.

Golshan had treated the whole thing like an endless cauldron of pleasure, each new item getting the same delight as the first. Finally, his hand was all the way down in the toe, pulling out the orange like it was a magical golden ball. He'd tossed it lightly from hand to hand, then done a series of tricks, like he was still remembering them. Golshan had rolled the orange along his arm, then from his head down a shoulder, smoothly into his hand. He'd been so gleeful, when it worked, it had them all laughing and grinning, in a pile on the floor. They'd sprawled with their various treasures scattered in an arc around them.

It felt right. Good. Amazingly good. The morning had a glow to it, beyond the fact it was his first Christmas home in years. That they were alive, and here now, and maybe all the awfulness was behind them.

By noon, they were overrun. It wasn't just his brothers and sisters, or their parents - though eight more people in the house was a good start on it. But of course there were Lia and Cephus's children, all five of them, including the babe in arms. At one point in the afternoon, Dilly, his mum, Cel, and Allie were all in the kitchen. Seth found himself leaning against a wall in the great room, watching Golshan.

It wasn't just the usual. He'd found himself always aware of where Golshan was, through the late morning and early afternoon, as everyone began arriving. He kept thinking about what Dilly had said, back in June, that he'd always known. Thesan had come over, watching him, and leaned to whisper in his ear. "You're calculating new orbits." She'd sounded approving.

She was right, of course, she often was. It had changed. When they were at school, they'd been two stars, dancing around each other, gravity shifting everything around them both. Then Golshan had, perhaps, turned into a comet, swooping in and out of Seth's life on a more or less regular basis. They were not the sort to have a regular weekly lunch or night at the pub.

Sometimes he'd come home from his apprenticeship to find Golshan on the sofa, reading a book with one hand, and tossing something up and down in his other. Usually not a knife, but sometimes Seth had just stood there, hoping nothing would go wrong. It never did. Sometimes Golshan would turn up five times in as many days. Sometimes it would be three weeks between.

If Seth actually got worried, he'd write a note, and get one back, a few run-on paragraphs of all the things that were in Golshan's head at that particular moment. They'd be scratched out between the music hall, the duelling salle, and whichever of the Materia specialists he happened to be chatting up at the time. Often in more than one sense, Golshan had said, repeatedly, that Materia men were excellent with their hands, in all the best ways.

Now, though, they were having to sort out how to be stars, again. Perhaps he'd lean into that metaphor. They'd been distant, rocky balls of ice, hurtling through the dark of space, on their own, barely caught by gravity. At least for the past year. And now they were coming to find a place where they were at the centre. Some different configuration, some different way of being. Settling into a solar system, one that included Dilly.

He wanted this to work. Needed it to work. There was

something so right about it now, about coming down in the morning, to find Golshan at the kitchen table, sipping some tea. Or he'd come down early himself and go to the workshop. Sometime later in the morning, he'd hear the door open, revealing Golshan with a flask of tea and a few scones, scooting himself neatly into place.

Watching this time was different, too. He'd seen Golshan with little ones before, now and again, usually after some children's show at the music hall or some event meant to bring in an audience. He had a knack for meeting them where they were, bright and honest and open. Right now, he was half-buried in them. As a man going to be a father soon enough, Seth liked what he saw a great deal.

The oldest of Seth's nieces was now ten, a somewhat serious girl who kept her brothers and sister out of too much trouble. Golshan teased her, and did little illusion tricks, spinning stories out, until she laughed. The next oldest wanted to know everything. He asked why about the decorations, the fireplace, the mulled wine he wasn't allowed to drink yet, why Golshan smelled of different spices.

Golshan answered each and everyone, delighted, explaining the curry he'd made yesterday. All the while, he had the five-year-old peering up at him, standing on tiptoe to tell him things. He somehow had the toddler on his knee, braced sturdily. It was a proper picture.

At least it was until Lia came back from feeding the baby and immediately called her children over to her. There were tight little comments, the kind meant to be overheard, about how they shouldn't bother that man. How it wasn't kind.

That man. As if Golshan hadn't been here for a week every school hols, a month in the summer, since Seth went to school. Granted, Lia had been enough older she was out of school after their first year. She'd been tucked into a modest sort of apprenticeship with a cousin in being a proper wife and mother, tending the home. She'd always wanted a bit of direction, but Seth thought, not for the first time, that she might have been happier if she'd apprenticed or done something else first. Something that didn't define her solely by her family.

Golshan looked deflated, then. Seth went over, settling a hand on his shoulder, bending down to murmur. "Is she the only awful one?"

It got him one of those half-smiles, where Golshan was trying to remember how this worked, and not quite managing to be fine about anything. "Archie's a bit much. He keeps going on about the bohort league." He was now settled down drinking a beer, and not being troublesome.

"Food will be ready in a few, and that'll be a distraction for everyone. I don't think it'll come to an outright argument about whether Mum's mincemeat pies or Dilly's are better. Honestly, they're both grand. Why choose? But we can have comparative testing and praising." That made Golshan snort and relax.

The feasting itself went well enough. Everyone gathered around a long table they set up in the great room. They'd moved the chairs and sofa out of the way, and left space at the end for Golshan's chair. The truce lasted until they were sitting around, picking bits of meat off the goose.

Lia said, "So when are you moving on, then, Golshan?" Her voice was clipped.

Seth's chin came up immediately, but before he could say anything, Dilly cut in. Dilly, who had quietly made sure all the day's festivities went off brilliantly, from the stockings on the hearth this morning to the cooking. Seth had done his bit, of course, cleaning and getting everything ready. He and Golshan had diced up infinite vegetables for the side dishes, but Dilly was queen in this house.

"I beg your pardon?" Dilly had that edge, the one Seth had only heard a couple of times. "Golshan's staying just as long as he likes."

"It's not proper, and you know it. A man, not related to any of us, in the house. And..." Her voice trailed off, as if she'd been considering being even more cutting and thought better of it. Something about how Golshan was barely a man, he suspected. She looked at Seth. "Don't you deserve better?"

Dilly didn't hesitate for an instant. "I have no complaints about my Seth or our Golshan." That word, it made Seth look at her, eyes wide, but she sailed right on. "And even if I did, which I don't, this is not the time or place. It's the first Christmas we've had Seth back, and the first Golshan's spent with us, and whatever else you might think, it can wait."

Lia opened her mouth to say something else, but before she could, Seth's Mum cut in, all righteous fury.

"Iliithia Honoria Wain Sutcliffe. I am ashamed of you." Lia's full name, all the resounding syllables of it, including her married name. Seth didn't think he'd ever heard Mum do that. Her husband Cephus winced, and Lia subsided into silence, if rather ungracefully.

After a minute, Seth's dad coughed, and asked Thesan a question about one of the student pranks that fall, something Archie had mentioned hearing about from friends still at school. That got the topic well and truly changed, and from there they went on to other things. Not long after the meal wrapped up, Lia packed up the children and left, with Cephus trailing behind her, nodding apologetically.

Everyone else melted into the kitchen to divide the leftovers, wash all the dishes, wash everything else. They were amiably chattering away, including Golshan in the teasing and setting him up to dry the dishes, while others put things away. It let Dilly have a nice sit down. Seth spent his time circling between the great room, making sure she and Mum had plenty of tea, and the kitchen, to help out.

Finally, though, everyone else peeled slowly away. Golshan wheeled himself into the doorway once they were all gone. "Going to have a bath."

It felt like a closed door, but Seth nodded. "Sure." He wanted it not to end on that note for the evening, but he wasn't sure how.

Dilly nudged him. "Come help me get comfy. I know you don't want bed yet, but come chat." She, on the other hand, was clearly ready to be in bed with a good book. Not least because she'd got three new ones for Christmas. "Actually, make me cocoa, and come up?"

Seth nodded, and as Golshan disappeared down the hall, he went to go make a mug of cocoa and tidy up a bit. Ten minutes later, he was knocking on the door upstairs, to their little suite of rooms. A bathing room, a water closet, a little nook. That would do for a crib when the baby was tiny. And Dilly, in bed, in a new nightgown, the lights already set for reading.

He lifted the mug. "Cocoa, love."

"How is he? How are you?" It was the first thing out of her mouth, but she reached out a hand to take the mug as Seth settled on the side of the bed.

"He was in the bath when I got the cocoa." Seth ran his hand through his hair. "I, I don't know. Do I check on him? Do I leave him alone? Do I wait and see if he wants to talk?"

When he looked back, Dilly had a very patient expression on her face. "I will drink my cocoa, and we will talk, and Golshan will have a reasonable amount of time for a bath. And then you will go down there and see how he is."

It was not as if Seth was going to argue. "You don't mind?"

"I," she proclaimed, "Have a book."

Seth snorted. "I am superfluous, then."

"Never. Don't you dare think that." Her voice got fierce. "But we had a grand time last night in bed, and today I have a book. Also my back hurts, or it did, until I found just the right position. So you can tuck me in and go see Golshan." She hesitated for a second. "And if you stay down there overnight, that's fine too."

That made Seth pull back, frowning, trying to figure out where to start with that. "We're not."

"You're near enough everything else." Dilly still sounded deeply amused, but also very sincere. "Don't leave him alone."

Seth hesitated, then closed his eyes. This would be a lot easier if he didn't have to look at anyone. Even Dilly. "Does... does everyone think we are?"

"Near enough every adult in the room knew Golshan's been in and out of people's beds for a good while. And mostly men. Entirely men?" Dilly was not clear on that point.

"Mostly men, but not all."

That made Dilly tilt her head as if she were rearranging all her baking supplies in some new, improved order. She nodded once. "Anyway. They know you're twined around each other. You have been for so long. Honestly, I think Lia's more than a bit jealous. Cephus is a good sort, but they're..." She shrugged. "They're fond. Good partners. But maybe better parents than partners, I don't know. Lia got awfully rigid about things, during the War."

Seth frowned. "Has she been awful to you? Too?" He hadn't really thought about that, he'd been so worried about Golshan. And Dilly had never said anything about it, though Seth had realised there was a bit less back and forth than there might have been, before.

Dilly wriggled her hand. "Rigid." She repeated the word again, having apparently decided it was the best description. "It was hard for her, having Cephus gone. And having two babes in the house, without him to help." He'd been well behind the lines in Belgium, in some administrative role at headquarters, doing analysis and logistics planning. He'd been good at it, from what Seth had heard.

"You didn't say." He didn't want to accuse, and he hoped it didn't sound like that.

Dilly reached to pat his cheek. "It was hard for me too, but different." Then she shook her head. "I wish she hadn't spoiled it today. The morning was so grand."

Seth nodded, then, carefully, he summoned his courage. "You said - our Golshan. Yours and mine."

"Ours." Dilly glanced at him, then away. "I meant it, love. When I said to bring him home. I hadn't..." Her voice caught. "Now he's here. I don't know what to call it, but." She gestured. "The solstice, his customs, I liked those a lot. The food and the poetry and the warmth. This morning, laughing and all together. When we've had a night with the charmlights and someone reading aloud, and being comfortable. It's not awkward. New. But not awkward. Wandering into the kitchen, seeing him there, him being willing to help out. And seeing him with the kids. I want to see him with our daughter."

"So you're not just..." Seth hesitated. "Not just agreeable." He tried out the words.

"I said this summer, I'd want to make him a home, for all the reasons you love him." Seth almost said something, but she set her hand on his. "But now, I want ... I want that for me, too. I don't know what it means, but. Here we are. And we want a thing we can give him, if he's still willing." She chewed on her lip. "He does know what Lia's like."

"He does." She'd been like that for ages, to varying degrees. Seth loved Lia, but he didn't always like her much. He always liked Thesan, and Cel, and Allie when she was up for being around people. "What, what should I tell him?" He felt lost with this. There wasn't enough time to carve something, the way he was working on a sculpture for Dilly.

"You go downstairs. you make it clear he's not alone with this. You're there with him. That I want him here, and I won't let Lia or anyone else drive him away. You, Seth, love, are excellent at being there. Steady. Reliable. Do that. Please." Dilly swallowed, as if this were very potent all of a sudden. Her voice got softer, intense. "You make there be space. Not - not crowded space, or tense space with expectations. Real space. Room to stretch, room to breathe. Space to be with us. Give him that. Please."

Seth leaned forward, brushing a bit of hair from her face, behind her ears. "Not like your house, mmm? Where you grew up?" She'd come from a merchant family with expectations, and everyone had been more than a bit startled when she'd ended up at Schola rather than Dunwich. She didn't miss it, but there were times, like the holidays, when it smarted more than others.

"Not at all. And that's..." She gestured, settling her other hand on her stomach, after a moment. "That's what we want. All of us. Our space, and our people."

Seth smiled and then tugged her hand to his lips to kiss it. "Make you an excellent breakfast in the morning, then. Bring it up to you in bed?"

"That, I like very much. I must say, you worrying

you're not being fair to me seems to keep working out in my favour. Foot rub, the other day. You brushing my hair out. Breakfast in bed."

Seth laughed. "Watch it, love, or I'll start working through a list." Then he let out a long breath. "Been long enough, you think?"

"Mmmhmm. Go see how he's doing. Take care of him. Whatever that is."

CHAPTER 7
THAT NIGHT

Golshan lay on the bed, legs under the blanket and hands laced behind his head. His thoughts were racing, tumbling over each other. The one that kept circling back, shouting in his head, was how quickly he could beg the Gospatricks for a place to go, until he figured something else out. How quickly he could pack his things up. His few things scattered around a room that still smelled of fresh paint and new linens. That wouldn't take long.

He'd broken things here before. A favourite bowl, a vase, a picture frame. A dozen other things, and he counted them up again. Now he'd broken Christmas. He'd always thought it was a bright and shining thing, the way Seth talked about it. And this was Seth's first one back, since the War had torn them away. The first Christmas expecting a baby. The first back with Dilly.

He'd broken it, as completely as a bowl that had shattered to tiny pieces, too small to ever be mended, dropped on the stone floor of the kitchen. And it wasn't anything he'd done, it was just him, taking up space in the world.

There was no getting the glow of this morning back. Even the memory of them explaining the traditions of the stockings, the small delights, he could barely touch that now in his mind.

There was a knock on the door. He ignored it, and after a moment, turned over on his side, facing away from the door. Some small part inside his head crowed at that. He'd had to sleep with his back to the wall as soon as he'd learned how to turn himself over in bed. A hint of safety tucked in there.

His thoughts went back to the way Seth and Dilly were. They were so attuned to each other, like they were passing lines in a song back and forth. They didn't finish each other's sentences, not like he and Seth sometimes did, but they flowed with each other. It was like they'd never been apart.

He knew Seth had missed her every day. He knew it had torn Seth to pieces not to have her nearby. And he'd gathered it was just as bad for Dilly. Well, worse, because Seth had been in danger, and Dilly wasn't. Golshan loved the notes Dilly had sent along when the mail came through. She'd include notes for him, cheerful bad sketches of the local wildlife. But he'd wanted, fleetingly, for someone to send him letters, just for him, long ones. He'd had plenty of friends, but no one but Seth who'd have done that for him.

There was a knock at the door again. He sighed and could not bring himself to answer it.

"It's Seth. Can I come in?"

He didn't want Seth to come in. If he did, all Golshan's resolve to do the right thing would melt away. All his good intentions to leave them, both of them, to a happy life together.

Another knock, then the one word, "Please."

He was not that strong. "Come in." He knew he didn't say it loudly, but the door opened immediately. He heard Seth step in, quiet steps, and the sound of the door closing, but he couldn't bear to turn around. Also, it was a fair bit of work. After a pause, he heard the steps circle around the bed until Seth stood in front of him.

Seth had changed into his pyjamas, a deep green dressing gown belted around his waist. That was a present from Seth's mum, who had given Golshan a similar one in deep gold, along with a vibrantly orange jumper, currently folded on top of his trunk.

Seth took one look at him and shook his head. "Hey."

Golshan shrugged, wordlessly. Some shard of him wanted to ask Seth to sit down, wanted his head in Seth's lap, where everything made sense. And the rest of him knew that had to be a bad idea, that Seth wouldn't do that, wouldn't ever again.

"Can I sit?" Seth asking permission. That felt odd. They'd known each other so long and so well that they didn't need to. The way Seth and Dilly didn't need to, it was all glance and a shift of a hand or a shoulder. The twitch of a finger. He'd spent an afternoon last week idly cataloguing the ways they did that in his head, while Seth puttered around tidying things up to have everyone over.

Golshan waved a hand, his shoulder twitching, mirroring the way Dilly would have, that gesture of wanting the thing that was going to happen. Despite himself.

Seth hesitated, resting a hand on Golshan's shoulder just for a moment. Golshan wondered if he'd meant to do more. He'd leaned forward, as if to say something. But then he squeezed, and stepped back, to kick his slippers off at the end of the bed where they'd be out of the way.

A moment later, he was settled on the bed, on his side,

and facing Golshan. He'd slipped his feet under the covers, and if Golshan moved his feet just an inch, he'd touch Seth's. He didn't. Golshan didn't let himself, he couldn't let himself. That wasn't something they'd ever done. Leaning, yes. Seth carving, while Golshan curled up with his head on one of Seth's thighs, yes. But never like this.

"Can we talk, Golshan, love?"

"You should be with Dilly." It came out before he could take it back. It was what was in his head, the loudest thing at the moment. And it was a true thing. He knew that, too.

Seth shook his head. "Dilly has a book." It sounded like a joke, but that just made Golshan feel more on the outside. Seth watched his reaction, whatever it looked like on his face, then added. "She sent me down to you."

The look on his face must be even more baffling now. "Sent you down?" Golshan wasn't sure what he thought about that.

"We're worried about you. Both of us."

Golshan supposed there might be some reason for that. But he didn't know how to tell Seth, how to tell them both, not to get dragged down, worrying about him. How he didn't want that for them. "Oh." He had to say something. That was the least he could get away with.

"Tell me what you're thinking. Please." It wasn't a command. Seth wasn't the sort of person who gave commands. But it was a request like one of the great standing stones, something that would not be moved by the centuries.

Golshan closed his eyes. He couldn't look at Seth and talk about this. Besides, he knew right where Seth was, inches from him. Close enough that Golshan could feel the warmth of his breath, that he could easily reach out a foot or a hand and touch. He didn't. That wasn't safe.

"Please." Seth repeated it again.

Golshan screwed his eyes closed. "I should leave."

Seth didn't say anything, instead there was a hand on his shoulder, then a moment later, Seth was pulling himself closer, letting that hand come down to his back. Gently, but right there, a touch he could not ignore. The tips of Seth's fingers were half an inch from the worst of the scarring and damage, and Golshan had no idea if Seth knew that.

"Let me talk, please." Seth's voice had an urgency now, like he was barely holding himself in. Seth never rushed things, never had words bubbling over. He thought things through. Golshan didn't know what it meant now, that he could barely keep himself from speaking. "Please."

There was no fighting Seth about this. Seth would say his piece. Golshan didn't want to make a fuss. He wanted, somewhere, deep inside, to slink away into the dark. He wanted to hide for a long time by himself. Maybe sometime a long time from now, he could be the sort of person who appeared out of the blue, here and there. Darting in with a present and disappearing again. Only he was never going to be darting again.

Golshan let his eyes close. "Yes?"

"You're ours, Golshan, love." Seth's voice was suddenly soft but fierce, the way Dilly had been earlier. When she'd said 'our'. When Golshan didn't say anything, Seth went on. "I'm here to make that clear." His hand spread out a little more on Golshan's back, like he wanted to hold more.

Seth hesitated, then. What he said next made Golshan's eyes shoot open. "May I kiss you?"

Kissing wasn't a thing Golshan had done much. Most of his lovers didn't prefer it. The few who had, it had been a quick kiss, a reminder of other things mouths might do. He didn't think Seth knew how to kiss like that.

He shivered, but then he nodded, just once, and closed

his eyes again, waiting for this dream, whatever it was, to pop like a soap bubble and disappear.

It didn't. Seth rearranged himself slightly until the space between them was almost nothing. He didn't expect Golshan to move, to do anything. That was good, because Golshan was sure he couldn't. Even if his legs still worked, everything about this was overwhelming.

The kiss itself was not all brilliance. Their heads were at an odd angle, lying on the pillows as they were. Seth's arm was a little too stretched down his back to make it easy to reposition their heads. What it was, though, was warm. It was real. It was so real it shoved everything else out of his head. All the doubts, all the words, all the fears.

Seth was here. Right here, against him, kissing him, completely present. There was nothing else in the world but Seth and the fact Seth was kissing him. Ever since they were fifteen, Golshan had refused to think about what it might be like. Wanting something he would never get, pining over it, had seemed utterly wrong. Seth did not want kisses, and so Golshan would not even imagine them. It had seemed like a particular blasphemy, a use of force that no one could fight, even in the depths of Golshan's head.

Only now, here they were, on their sides, facing each other, so close he could feel everything. When Golshan pulled back for a moment to breathe, he found he couldn't inhale, that he was caught in the grip of something he couldn't name.

Seth didn't kiss him again, not yet. Instead, he inched himself closer, until his hips were pressed against Golshan's. Pressure was what he felt best, below his waist, and now he felt the pressure of Seth's body, his cock, against his stomach. Of strong legs against his weakened ones. The way Seth edged the toes of one of his feet between Golshan's feet. As if there was still not enough contact, like Seth wanted to wrap him up, entirely.

"Don't go. Stay. With us." Seth finally shifted his hand to come and cup Golshan's cheek, his hand warm. Golshan could almost hear how hard the pulse must be beating. He could certainly feel how Seth was trembling with this. "Please."

"You - you don't, you'll lose...." Golshan felt entirely wrong-footed. All the arguments he'd been rehearsing in his head earlier fell out of his mind.

"Lia was awful. We don't want that sort of awful around. She can be awful somewhere else, not in our home. Your home. All our home. Dilly's. Mine. Yours." Seth had gone fierce again, fierce and earnest, and that hand shifted to Golshan's hair, which had finally grown out to a respectable few inches.

"You'll, tomorrow. Daylight." That sounded even less coherent than the rest of it.

Seth, though, seemed to understand. "We're not going to change our minds tomorrow. I'm sure. Dilly's sure." He let his thumb brush along Golshan's hair, like now he'd started touching, he wanted to get the sense of everything Golshan was, through his hands.

Golshan grunted, frustrated now that this wasn't going the way it needed to.

"Let me talk for a minute. And then you can. And I'll listen." It wasn't as if Golshan could get his words out in a sensible order, so he nodded.

"We were going to ask you to be godfather, did you know? You - I can't imagine who else we'd ask."

It was not where Golshan had expected Seth to start, not at all. Then Seth went on. "Thesan as godmum, of course. She's born to be a delightful auntie. Only. We're going to need to find someone else for godfather. Because we want you to be here. Be ours. Be a parent with us."

"Lia..." The name came out bitter on his tongue.

"Seeing you with her kids, that made it clear. To both of us, me and Dilly. Seeing how you were. Right there with them. Keeping an eye out, letting them cling and climb, and answering their questions, telling stories." Seth swallowed, and then he forged on.

It was only because Golshan knew him so well that he knew Seth was on the edge of something momentous. He managed to get his eyes open, and finally, to shift his hand to settle, tentatively, on Seth's ribs.

Seth let out a long breath, and then went on, his voice softer now. "I don't want you to go. Dilly doesn't. I don't know who I am without you. I don't want to. And she...." His voice went softer. "She said, watching you today with the stockings. What that was like. She wants that. Laughing and being together, and it all being good. Much more than good."

Golshan closed his eyes, and then he was shivering again, shuddering with it, like he hadn't since he was out of his mind in the clearing hospital. He'd thought it was shock, then, and the cold of the trenches, but this felt the same. It shook him, and he didn't remember how to breathe.

A moment later, he was wrapped up in strong arms. It wasn't just the one around his waist. Seth somehow got his other under the pillows, to tug Golshan's head to rest against his chest, his leg a bit more between Golshan's. Golshan couldn't help with that, but it didn't seem to matter.

They lay like that for what seemed like hours, but was probably only a minute or two. Seth was just there, impossibly there. When Golshan finally stopped shaking, he just lay there, breathing in the way Seth smelled. Wood shavings, hints of cedar from the wardrobe and dresser, a hint of turpentine and wood stain, and something that was wholly Seth. His brain wanted to name the spice, the scent of something baking in a room nearby, and it wasn't that. Only it was.

Seth didn't say anything at all, even when Golshan pulled his head back a little more. He did give Golshan a bit more space.

"Let me, let me, my back?" Golshan could feel something in his hip cramping. It wasn't something he'd practised, how to lie in bed with someone. Maybe, just maybe, he had reason to.

Seth immediately released him enough to let Golshan rearrange himself, the little movements of getting an arm behind his body, readjusting, tugging his feet into the right place. Then he was lying back on the pillows, staring up at the ceiling for a good five or six breaths until he turned his head to look at Seth again.

"It's not real. It can't be real."

"Why not?" Seth had settled on his side, and as if he'd been waiting for Golshan to speak, he settled his arm along Golshan's chest, elbow down by his navel.

"You're. You'll lose." Seth's family were a part of him, as much as arms or legs. "You can't, for me."

"Why not?" Seth's voice was firmer now, pushing Golshan to explain himself. Not that he had a good explanation. He swallowed, thinking about what he'd been told, training with his knife and his magic, trying to figure out how to make Seth understand. Then Seth went on, his voice soft but clear. "The War changed me. Of course it did. I don't have patience for the petty things now."

That made some sense, but Golshan hadn't put that together. Maybe he hadn't seen it, and that had his mind spinning off on all the other things he might not have seen, might not have understood.

Seth let him, for a little, before he tapped his shoulder. "Focus on me, love."

Golshan tried, oh, he tried. He closed his eyes to make things easier, and murmured. "Listening." Though now his mind was caught on that endearment, and not just what it was, but how Seth said it.

"I've seen enough broken. Destroyed. Seen enough people argue. Regret. I'm having none of that. I'm wanting the strong joins, the places we fit together, that nothing will shake. Not all the world will fit with that, and if they don't, well, it's a big world out there. May they find the good for them."

Golshan wanted to ask, to argue, again.

Seth went on, like this was rolling downhill now. "Dilly says Lia got more rigid during the War. And I've got..." He shrugged, Golshan could feel it. "Not softer. War makes no one soft. Flexible. Like willow."

"Weaving." Golshan sucked in a breath. "Mourning."

"Remembering." Seth made it a blessing. "Growing."

CHAPTER 8
THAT NIGHT

Seth was watching Golshan - his Golshan, maybe - so closely now. It helped that Golshan's eyes were closed. Otherwise, he'd be watching Seth's every reaction, adding them all in one sharp snap of understanding.

"Growing." Golshan echoed it back at him.

Seth inhaled, wondering about all sorts of things that had been growing in him. "Thinking about what I want. Now I have choices again."

That got Golshan to open one eye to peer at him, then both. "How much time have I taken?" Now, it didn't have that plaintive note. It was a demand, a desire, and that made Seth crow inside his head.

"Since I found you? Oh, I've put in plenty of time with the woodwork."

"Not as much as you would have if I'd..." Golshan waved a hand at his legs.

"It turns out," Seth said, "You can't actually work wood every hour of the day, when you haven't used some of those muscles for years." He kept his tone light, but he remembered the cramps in his shoulders and back. He definitely remembered all the times he'd had to stop. "I'm doing fine now, but I had to work up to it. And I'm a proper journeyman now, I can set my own hours."

"Still. Took plenty of them."

Seth shifted over to kiss Golshan again. It was smoother this time, and his hands were free, so he could get a hand into Golshan's hair. Something in that made Golshan melt back against the pillows, like he'd suddenly stopped fighting, like he was giving himself over to it entirely. Seth went on, as long as he could, pouring all the things he felt into it. It was like he normally did with his carving, letting all the emotions pour out in shapes and the touch of his fingers.

When he finally pulled back, they were both breathless. Golshan was blinking at him, trying to focus. "What changed?"

Seth knew Golshan didn't just mean the kiss. Or he did, but it was about all the things the kiss meant. He hadn't put this into words, not even to Dilly, really, though they'd talked a bit about it the past two weeks.

Most of all, he knew it mattered. He had one chance to get this right. "When you kissed me, I had no idea what to do. You know me. Quick with my hands. Slower with words."

Golshan snorted, but he shifted, making more space for Seth to settle in against him, one arm opening out. Seth took the hint, rearranging, so he was on his side, stretched out, one arm settling on Golshan's chest, head on his shoulder. Golshan was a bit shorter, which should have made this odd, but it wasn't.

Once Seth was properly settled, he cleared his throat and gave it his best. "I didn't know what to think. I didn't even think I liked people like that. Until Dilly showed up. And made her interests clear."

"Tell me about that." Golshan had heard it at the time, certainly, but there was something engaged, now, a mix of thoughtfulness, and a new analysis.

"She finished school, and I was apprenticing." Pleasantly, with Master Adams, living in. "Wednesday afternoon, my half day, Mistress Adams told me there was someone at the door for me. I was all over sawdust. And there she is, basket over her arm, asking if I want to come out for a picnic. And I went and washed up, and she had..." He shook his head. "I found out later she'd asked Mum about it. What I'd like, when I was free, if any of the family were planning to visit that day."

"Were they?" Golshan sounded intrigued now.

"Not after she asked. Mum wrote to cancel, she made up some excuse. And there we were. It took me a while to do more than kiss her cheek. Three months, going out every Wednesday." As he said it, he could feel himself rising to some amount of attention. He was caught between the pressure of Golshan's body and the memories of what his first fumbling attempts had been like with Dilly. He was sure Golshan could feel it. If not directly, certainly in the way Seth was holding his body. "And we didn't have much privacy."

"When did you?" Seth lifted his head, and Golshan went on. "As far as I could tell, you went from seeing her, often, to falling in love. And she's good for you, Seth. She makes you laugh, and she makes you smile, and the smiling's even better. The way you are when you look at her."

Seth waited, a heartbeat or two, hoping, wondering, if Golshan would go on. "You, you look at me a little like that." Golshan hesitated. "Now."

"Somewhere, I fell in love with you. I don't know

when, with you. After apprenticeship, before I found you again. Before you were hurt, I think, but who knows, it was all buried under mud, and we never had any privacy at all, not even for a conversation."

That had all come out in a rush, but Golshan made sense of it. "After I came back from..." He almost said a name, a place, then stopped himself at the last moment. "The one in March."

"Something like that. You were - it was one of the worse ones for you. I just wanted to make it better. I remember that. I wrote to Dilly about it. She's still got the letters, if you want to read it. Talking around it, because of the censors."

There was a long silence, before Golshan let out a burble of laughter, his arm suddenly tugging Seth tighter against him, as he roared with it. When he finally caught his breath, Golshan said, "You sent a love letter about me to your wife?"

"Yes?" Seth's voice was faint now. "I tell her things. I tell you things. I mostly tell Thesan things. And Mum."

"You did not tell your mum you were in love with me." Golshan tried that out. "She'd have said something."

Seth contemplated this. "Mum. This morning. She said you looked happy. And I looked happy. And she approved of anything that made for that kind of happy. Dilly said, later, she'd asked Dilly what she felt. And Dilly's happy. Differently happy than this morning? But happy."

"And what sort of different do we mean?"

This was the other sticking point. Because it was about how Seth had seen himself all his life. It was about knowing a fair bit of Golshan's history with a string of lovers. It was about not knowing a lot of things, including most of what Golshan thought about things now.

"Find I enjoy kissing you." That was the easy part.

They had done that, and Seth might not have kissed many people. Two, both of them under this roof. But he was quite clear about whether they were enjoying it. "I'd..." He swallowed, then stammered it out. "You can feel, maybe. Me enjoying it."

Golshan sucked in a breath, like that had changed something for him. "Are you someone who loves men, then? Or just me, among men?"

"You." That was the easy part. "Don't think I could ever, with someone I didn't know. Very, very well."

Golshan nodded, and then he turned his head, focusing on Seth. "I can feel you. But I won't do anything you don't ask for."

Seth could barely breathe. "And if I ask?"

There was a little twitch of Golshan's shoulder. "My hands work. My mouth. I don't know about the rest, but...." It had an edge to it, but he didn't seem bitter. Not the way he had every right to be.

"I asked the Gospatricks. Well, Nurse Gospatrick. About - about what you could expect."

Golshan's eyes widened. "You didn't."

"I did. To be fair, she'd already asked me what I knew about that sort of thing for you before you were hurt."

"Wait, when?" Golshan pushed himself up on one elbow, and Seth lifted enough to kiss his nose.

"When I was arranging for you to go there. I talked to them, brought your file. Then that Friday, they asked me to come for the day, and see the place, and said they wanted to talk to me. It's the most thorough interview I think I've ever had. You could put the two of them in charge of getting information, and people would cave in minutes."

"I gather that's what Roland's mother does. Well, one of the things. And his father's Major-General Gospatrick."

Seth whistled. "How do you know that? He's the one was trying to keep us from getting thrown away."

"For all the good it did us. But he tried. Because of Roland, from what he didn't say." Golshan waved a hand. "His parents came by a couple of times. What did they ask you?" Trust Golshan to focus back on what mattered here.

"They asked about what your life had been like. Before the War, before you got hurt. How much of it I knew. I gather - um. I gather I knew quite a bit more than most people they ask? And I told them. Not who, the people I knew about. But that you'd preferred men, not exclusively. That you'd had an active sex life, that I wasn't sure what..." He shrugged. "What it'd be like now. I wanted to be honest."

Golshan blinked, and then there was that rolling laughter again. This time it went on and on for a good minute, before it finally settled down into amused chuckles. "I spent my whole time there ducking talking about it. They kept trying."

Seth shook his head. "You could have asked. I suppose I could have told you. But it's not exactly where you start a conversation."

Golshan nodded. "Did they - did you have any other conversations I should know about?"

Seth could feel himself blushing. "I asked, when we were making arrangements to bring you home, what I should know about that. They looked me up and down, and said that you had a right to privacy. But they'd be glad to send someone round to explain your options if and when you wanted to."

The chuckling started up again, until Golshan murmured "They were very clear things might come up, once I was settled." He shook his head. "Pun likely intended." Then he sobered. "I don't know how things work for me now. What works. If anything. But I do know I've always wanted to give my partner pleasure. That's not changed."

Seth hesitated, then said, "Dilly and I've had to adapt. As she's ..." He gestured. "Her shape's changing, what she wants. It's not the same at all as things with you. But it's - she likes what we do a lot. Just she wants different things. Or wants the same things differently. Why don't we ever learn how to talk sensibly about this?" His voice came out plaintively again.

Golshan got his hand up to touch his cheek. "Do you want to try something?"

"Please." Seth had always been better at doing than talking.

"I could touch you. I could use my mouth. Mmm. Maybe not that. I need to figure out the best angles for that. And my hip's..." He shrugged. "Moving around all day was a fair bit of work."

"I could take up learning massage? A touch of physiotherapy?" Seth offered. He'd thought about it already, but he hadn't been able to figure out how to offer that kind of intimacy. Now, of course, it made him smile.

"In your abundant free time." Golshan shook his head. "Can you - would you help me get a pillow behind me? One I can lean into?" That he'd asked, that made Seth think this might actually be real.

"There's a big long one under there somewhere. That, and a sticking charm?" Seth gestured.

"Me on my side. The pillow behind me. You facing me. Then we can both use our hands."

Seth was very glad Golshan had something like a plan here. Seth then swallowed, and added, "Dilly said I could stay the night with you. If you wanted. If that makes a difference to anything."

A hand darted out to grab Seth's wrist, as if Golshan were suddenly drowning. "What?"

"Dilly said I could stay the night with you. If - if we wanted." Seth knew it had to be we, it had to be both of them. It wasn't a thing where one of them made the decision.

"She's sure." Golshan breathed it out, and suddenly it was like a prayer. "You're sure."

Seth nodded, watching Golshan's face carefully now. "We are. Begin as we mean to go on."

That made Golshan snort. Then, his voice suddenly full of his old urgency, he said, "Pillow. Please."

Seth extracted himself from bed, sparing a glance as Golshan worked himself into the position he wanted. It involved a series of obviously practised but rather complex movements to get himself comfortably on his side without his ankles in a knot. He lifted up enough that Seth could get one of the longer pillows from the head of the bed. Seth figured out how to arrange it so Golshan could lean back against it.

Two minutes later, they were properly settled in bed again, facing each other, and Seth didn't know where to look. Golshan had somehow got his pyjama top open without Seth noticing, revealing a fascinatingly furry chest, and Seth had shrugged out of his dressing gown. He blushed, now. "You'll have to, I don't know."

"We touch. We enjoy. Nothing complicated tonight." Then Golshan snorted. "Besides all the everything."

It made Seth smile, too. "We have more time." He had to keep pointing this out to himself. Tonight didn't have to be perfect. It just had to happen, so that other things could. That first cut of the chisel or the knife into perfect smooth wood. If you never began, you never found out what might take shape.

Golshan laughed at that. "World enough and time." Then he slipped his fingers into Seth's "You know how to touch. I'll tell you if something doesn't feel good. All right?"

Seth nodded, and then focused on Golshan's face, watching, as his fingers began to explore. He'd seen Golshan naked before. It was inevitable when they'd cycled from the trenches into the barracks behind the lines. But it certainly wasn't the sort of thing where one could look. Or take any pleasure. That would have ended very badly, all round, and Seth had known it.

He let his fingers move, from shoulder, the places he'd touched before, where his hand had cupped and rested, or he'd patted Golshan on the back for something well done. Then he explored, shifting down, feeling where skin gave way to hair, to the parts of his chest seen much less. There were nicks and scars, most superficial, but one or two that had been deeper.

Golshan shrugged. "Not a safe line of work, duelling."

Seth nodded, and then paused, his hand coming up to cup Golshan's cheek, as he leaned in to kiss again. He took his time now. Golshan didn't kiss anything like Dilly, which just made this feel even more wonderful, that these two people, different in so many ways, were both so welcoming. So warm. So responsive. Golshan arched a little, not directing, not compelling anything, just arching into the kiss, letting Seth learn what pleasures he most enjoyed.

Finally, Seth pulled back, getting his eyes to focus again. "Will you touch me?"

"Thought you'd never ask." There was humour, there, and teasing. But there was also a rough and raw desire that surprised Seth. Surprised them both, because Golshan's eyebrows went up. "Mm. Anything I should know?"

Seth shook his head. "I - I know some things about

what I like. Not enough to tell you what to do." He then grinned, and this felt natural now. "Besides, I shouldn't lecture a master of the craft."

That broke the tension in the room, what little was left, and Golshan snorted. "Right. You let yourself enjoy, we'll worry about me after. Bit fiddly to try and figure both out at once, especially considering."

What followed made Seth's eyes roll back, made his breath come out in pants, and then made him swell and burst. Golshan had a single-minded intensity to his pleasures that was everything and nothing like Seth had expected. He dove into them, even when it was his hand alone that was touching, playing Seth's body like an instrument. Seth made noises he'd never heard himself make before. It wasn't just the gasps and moans, there were those too, but there was the wordless begging. Golshan teased him up to an edge, then backed away, over and over again, always dancing right to the knifepoint, then backing away.

When finally that strong hand - strong as Seth's own - stroked steadily up and up, Seth began to let himself go. When Golshan hissed, "Show me," it was over. Seth felt his hips buck into that gloriously demanding hand, into strength and sureness and certainty. Then there was hot dampness on the sheets between them, on Golshan's hand, and Seth was out of breath, limp with release.

Finally, he got his eyes open again, to find Golshan propped up on one elbow, watching him. "Kiss me, please." It was a request and a desire, and Seth wanted nothing more than to make that wish come true. He sucked in a breath, then moved to kiss, to get an arm around Golshan's back.

They danced back and forth, tongue against tongue, until they were both breathless. When Seth pulled back again, Golshan swallowed, his eyes closing to focus. "Will you touch me? I don't know that…" He stopped, swallowing. "I don't know that anything will happen. I don't want to chase that, not tonight. I don't want to spoil…" He couldn't continue the sentence.

Seth murmured. "Tell me when you've had what you want." Having another man's cock in his hands, that was new. But he knew what to do with something solid, with weight, with fullness. He knew how to let his fingers guide him, the lines and veins, the places that brought forth a gasp. Golshan had not been entirely hard, when he began, but that didn't bother Seth.

They had set so many things aside already, all the assumptions about how things should go. And he thought, in some small corner of his mind, that this might go better when he didn't have experience in how it was with men. He just gave himself over to touching, to taking in Golshan's every reaction. It built and built, until something clenched. No liquid, but every other sign Seth knew made it clear there had been great pleasure there. He carefully backed off, leaving his hand resting on Golshan's thigh.

When Golshan opened his eyes again, he looked entirely blissful, as if he'd fallen into a place where there were no words and none were needed. Seth moved just enough to kiss his cheek, and then settled in to curl up, not caring about the damp spot in the bed. He let Golshan lean, until he was on his back, with Golshan along his side, using him as a pillow.

CHAPTER 9
THE NEXT MORNING

Golshan woke quickly, coming awake startled and trying to remember where he was and what was going on.

Immediately, there was a murmur, right by his ear. "Morning, love."

Golshan let his head fall back. He remembered moving onto his back sometime in the night. Seth was stretched out on his side, a warm solid presence next to him, just waiting.

It didn't feel real. It felt so real everything else in his life was like a shadow. Something of that must have shown in his expression, because Seth reached out to touch his cheek. "Right here, Golshan, love."

"Sure?" Golshan's voice cracked once, and he shivered, closing his eyes again.

"Certain." Seth's thumb brushed against his skin. "Here's my thought. Dilly wanted breakfast in bed. How about I shove along to the loo, and get out of your way? You come out when you're ready. Keep me company while I make up a proper tray for her, and something for us?"

"You've been thinking about this." Golshan considered, then stretched. "It's a fine plan. What do we have for breakfast?"

"Sausages, the ones you like. Eggs. Toast. Mum brought over more jam yesterday, or there's marmalade. Could do some potatoes and onions, if you want to dice for me?"

Golshan felt himself smiling more and more. "Small pleasures." The marmalade and the dicing, both. "I'll be fifteen minutes, maybe. If you had tea ready?"

"Tea it is." Seth rolled out of bed, turning to kiss Golshan once on the lips. Then he was picking up his dressing gown, and sliding into the slippers, padding away out of the room. It was not leaving, nearly so much as deferring this particular pleasure for later, and Golshan had no idea how Seth had managed to make it so clear.

Seth was out of the downstairs loo well before Golshan was settled in his chair and sufficiently sorted for that part of the necessary routine. He cast the charms without thinking about it now, the ones that dealt with the physical realities of his injuries. But then he sat in front of the mirror, looking at himself for a good few minutes.

He'd honestly never expected anyone to want to be with him. Not now. Seth had just rolled right past it, like it wasn't any kind of concern. He'd paid attention to what Golshan liked. He hadn't fussed at all, even when there'd been a bit of awkwardness. And now, this morning, he'd cleared out, so Golshan didn't have to navigate what he needed to do, and someone trying to help.

On the other hand, this was Seth, and Seth had always paid attention to what mattered. He'd always found that line between doing the things Golshan couldn't manage on his own, and the things he could. Turning in assignments, for example. Not one of Golshan's strengths, ever. Or, to be fair, doing many of them. Other people would have nagged, would have got impatient. Seth just figured out where Golshan's limits were, how far his attention would stretch, and worked inside that.

It made him shiver, thinking about what Seth might do with other kinds of being inside, of what they could explore. With anyone else, Golshan would have worried, and now he just couldn't. It would be fine. Better than fine. Whatever they sorted out, together in bed, it would be grand.

Maybe this would work. Maybe, just maybe, there was something that would catch and hold his attention, and it would make everything else possible. It had been like that when Golshan first met Seth, their first week at school. Seth had been in the middle of a knot of boys in their year, kicking a ball around, but he'd seen Golshan standing by himself.

They'd found a tree to climb, a stone wall to walk along, even spotted whales in among the waves. They'd circled back to the cottages with the rest of the first years to find several teachers wondering what they'd been up to. Golshan had known those teachers had something in mind, and he'd worried he'd done something wrong. He was always doing things wrong at home. Seth had just smiled, sunny and completely confident, and talked about what they'd seen, and mentioned that one of the trees wasn't too happy.

The rest of that week had been the same, with Seth tugging at his hand to join in with the other boys and some of the girls. And then at other times, going off to find time where it was just them, where there weren't so many things going on. He somehow knew when it was too much noise and too many different things, and when all those things were just what Golshan wanted.

By the end of the week, it would have killed him to be separated from Seth. He'd meant that hyperbolically for so many years. Then the War came, and he'd known how real it was. He was a shadow of himself, without Seth, and he knew it.

Which, of course, made it all the more ridiculous that he was dallying in the loo. A sensible man would be going along to the kitchen and seeing how far Seth had got with breakfast. By the time he turned the corner into the kitchen, he could hear laughter and voices, and he stopped in the doorway.

Dilly turned to him, from where she was standing, leaning over the table, reaching for one of the cloves from a pomander from the festive decorations. "Golshan! Happy Boxing Day! I gather you had a fine time being convinced last night?"

She was so cheerful about it that Golshan wasn't sure what to do. He glanced at Seth, who came up behind Dilly, one hand on her shoulder, then he shooed her with a hand. "Sit."

"You were supposed to have breakfast in bed?" Golshan offered it tentatively.

Dilly grinned. "Tell that to our little seedling here. Someone woke me up kicking at six this morning. I have, however, waited on having breakfast until someone else cooked it."

"By which she means she had a bit of the leftover goose, and I don't know what else." Seth nudged her. "Sit. Golshan, will you cut things up?"

That, at least, was something Golshan was sure he could do. "Please." He rolled himself to the spot at the end of the kitchen table that they'd set up for him. Dilly settled onto the bench on the long side next to him. A moment later, Seth had a cutting board set out in front of him, with a bowl of four potatoes and an onion. And his favourite knife for the purpose, the one they'd found fit his hand best.

Before he could pick it up, Dilly shifted to touch his hand. She hadn't touched him, mostly. Not least because usually Seth was, and she was on his other side. But it struck him, now, that maybe she'd been restraining herself. It didn't make sense to him.

Then he looked over at her face, and she was watching him. She had a way about her, not like Seth's quiet, an orchard sort of quiet, but more like a meadow, where there might be all sorts of things going on. Most of all, there were things growing and living. Someone, an artist, a poet, might have gone into raptures about her as an earth goddess, with warm brown hair like the woods Seth loved best, and dancing eyes. But it was her smile he'd always liked most. It was a smile that included him, but also had her own secrets.

He swallowed. "What," He stopped, tried again. "What do you think? What do you want out of this?" Then he found the right words. "How do we make you happy too?"

"Oh, love. I already am happy. I mean, look at Seth, look at how he is. Glowing with it. And he said he had a proper good sleep. Nothing woke him."

Seth didn't turn around, but a moment after Golshan looked at him, blinking, Seth murmured. "A nightmare or two a night. Most nights. Quite clear you'll keep me safe."

Golshan filed that away to ask more about later. Not right now, in the glowing morning light, when they had so much else to talk about. After a moment, Dilly went on. "Come to find out, I want a bit of what you two have. If I can."

"I'm afraid you'll have to be a bit more clear, luv."

Golshan didn't want to overstep, he had no idea where any of the lines were anymore.

She didn't move her hand, and he liked that, he found. Instead, she squeezed. "I told Seth this last night. Yesterday morning, when it was just us, it was grand. Laughing and being together. What it's like in the evenings, curling up, and the lights dim. Reading and making things and - no masks, no worries. Just comfort."

Golshan glanced at Seth again, who was just going along with the cooking, but solidly unworried. There was no tension in his back, none of the little signs that Golshan paid such close attention to. He turned back to Dilly, who was just waiting for him.

"You've not had that?" He'd heard bits about her family, here and there, of course. But it wasn't something she talked much about.

"Well, not nearly enough, recently, of you both around, and relaxed. Though may the gods give us many years of peace." Golshan echoed that prayer, fervently, though silently. He didn't want to interrupt her. This was important, it mattered. After a moment, she went on. "My family wants to be proper. Seth's mum's grand. And his dad. I want to do things differently than I grew up with. Warmth." She looked at him, now meeting his eyes. "And you, Golshan, you're warm. All the way through."

He gestured at her, carefully. "And the little one?"

Seth said, without turning around. "I made it clear. We want him to be a parent with us. Proper equal parts."

"Someone's got to teach children to climb trees." Dilly said it absolutely evenly.

Golshan just gaped now, then swallowed. "If you'd forgotten."

"It is December, love, and I'm still working on plans." Seth turned and brought some of what he was working on over to the table. Toast, with pots of raspberry jam and marmalade.

"Plans?" Golshan's voice cracked again, but he reached for one of the pieces of toast and the jar of marmalade. Dilly gestured at him to go first.

"The sort of thing that would horrify the people at the place I found you if they ever heard about it. How do you feel about some climbing ropes and platforms in the orchard? Got to figure out how to get your chair all the way under the trees. Maybe an outside chair, easier on rough ground. Phillip had some ideas about better wheels for that last time I talked to him." It was exceedingly cheerful.

"Ropes. Platforms." Golshan blinked several times and then started laughing. "What did Nurse Gospatrick say?"

"She agrees that your arms still work very well. And once you're used to it, I can't imagine you'll fall out of a tree any more than you used to. Mind, she wants someone to come round and have a look, and consult. But." Seth shrugged. "Choices. Options."

"You seem to have thought of everything." Golshan had to admire the strategy. It was, admittedly, an overwhelming sort of strategy. He appreciated that, even if it was rather much aimed at him. "They would hate it, wouldn't they?" He shook his head. "They weren't awful, there."

"They were far too limited. And that's no good. Not for you. Sausage or bacon?"

"Bacon, please." That was Dilly.

Golshan considered. "Sausage, if it's not too much."

Apparently, that gave Seth a chance at something, and he bent to kiss Golshan's hair. "You're never too much." It left Golshan blinking after him, as Seth moved to get the frying pan off its hook and start up the stove. There was amiable quiet for a bit. That was something else Golshan liked here. No one had a problem with just being together, quietly. Seth had always been like that, but Dilly didn't see the need to chatter just to fill the space.

The food was fantastic. The food with the Wains always had been. A lot of it wasn't what he'd grown up with, but it was solid and filling. It had real flavour, and most of all, it was made by people who cared about doing the thing right. And they didn't even mind about his customs with food, it seemed. Solstice had a glow to it, all alive and glowing. And they'd spent some time tossing ideas back and forth about Nowruz.

When the meal was done and the dishes were washed up and dried, Seth turned around, leaning his hands on the counter behind him. "Do you have any plans for the day?"

"Should I?" Golshan was still getting used to the holiday customs, but no one had said anything specific about Boxing Day.

"Boxing Day is for sprawling around enjoying one's presents and the leftovers. And whatever else." Seth then grinned. "So, um. Dilly wants to go curl up in bed. You want to come join us? Your bed's not big enough for all of us, that was bad planning."

"Don't you go making me a new bed!" Then he frowned. "Yours is upstairs."

"I have arms. And practice with charms to make you lighter. I do it all the time with wood."

It was, admittedly, a very handy sort of skill. Golshan leaned back in his chair, considering. Seth didn't rush him, neither did Dilly, though she settled her hand on top of his again, not apparently noticing how he kept tapping his index finger as he thought.

"I don't like not being able to get around on my own."

"Entirely fair." Seth nodded. "I'm still thinking about if we could build in a rudimentary elevator. Manual, with a crank or something of the kind. I think we could certainly do a small chair for you to use upstairs."

Golshan snorted. "If the ropes in the orchard work, you could just install some over the stairwell. Though keeping the little one out of that might be a trick."

It made Seth crack into a broad grin. "We'll all be learning some unusual skills." Then he tilted his head, just waiting.

Golshan swallowed. "Today, I'd like very much to be upstairs with you." Admitting that he wanted that, it was more terrifying than the War had been, but here he was.

"Just we also need to figure out other ways of doing that. I promise, you'll get my best ideas."

Dilly cleared her throat and said, "I do like the idea of curling up with you. Talking. I don't know what else, now, ever. That's something we'll have to figure out. But the being together." She then grinned, suddenly, like the sun coming out after a rain shower. "Besides, we can both team up to tease Seth. Teasing Seth is the best fun. Did you know he's ticklish?"

That made Golshan look at Seth in an entirely new light. "I had some idea of that, but I admit, not much chance to try it out." He then held up a hand. "You can always say no."

"I am not entirely certain I can say no to something both of you want. I'm fairly sure I don't much want to." He then pushed away from the counter, and said, "How about we go sort that out. You want the loo or anything from your room before we settle in?"

Fifteen minutes later, they were settled in a comfortable pile on Seth and Dilly's bed. Seth had been gloriously strong - he had muscles under his shirts, Golshan had known that for a decade or more.

Trusting Seth not to drop him, not to bump into something, not to be careless was simultaneously the hardest thing he'd done in a long time, and the easiest. So many other people hadn't had a care with him, but Seth was Seth. Those people didn't love him, those people didn't know him, those people didn't hold his heart the same way.

It hadn't been perfect, of course. They'd had to fumble around to figure out a comfortable way for them all to end up. He had ended up in the middle of the bed, propped up on pillows, with Seth on his right side, Dilly on his left. The curve of her belly pressed into him, in a steadiness that he found remarkably reassuring.

After a few shifts, they had settled into a position where Dilly had Seth's hand under hers, resting on Golshan's chest. There was something very soothing about it. Dilly didn't make it quiet in his head the way Seth did, but she also didn't get in the way of what Seth did. She just arched around it.

And arched deliberately a moment later. "Oh." She then changed the angle slightly. "Our seedling's kicking. Do you want to feel?" It took Golshan a moment to realise she meant him. Golshan managed to get his arm free, and then let Dilly put it in what was presumably the right place. Nothing happened for a good ten seconds, then there was an active push under his hand.

"That must be odd." He was caught, for a moment, thinking of how he felt less than he had, and at least at the moment, Dilly was having sensations in entirely unusual places. There was probably some cosmic magical law of parity of sensation or something that applied, but he'd honestly never been good at sympathetic magic theory.

"You have no idea." She then covered his hand with

hers. "I'll keep asking if you want to touch, then." Golshan thought for a moment she might have been intending something else, but he just nodded.

A moment later, she was shifting to get comfortable, letting him claim his hand back. Then she nudged Seth to explain how his parents had set this space up, and whether they wanted to move anything before their lives got terribly busy with a baby.

CHAPTER 10
SATURDAY, JANUARY 3RD, 1920

Seth had quickly come to love Saturday mornings. By mutual agreement, none of them made any particular plans for the first half of the day. Last night, they'd lounged in bed with Dilly until she was ready to sleep. Then Seth and Golshan had come downstairs. It had been a leisurely sort of hedonism, both times, rather than anything more active. There was nothing at all wrong with that, and several things that were very right indeed.

Now, though, an hour after lunch, they were curled up in the great room, looking out the window at fog. Seth had been thinking about going up the road to the pub, with Golshan or Dilly if they wanted, but he had no desire to go out in the mist. He'd been carving, instead, finding that his hands kept turning to small figures of the Schola House animals. Lying down, at ease, mostly. A fox with its nose on its tail, a pair of salmon, curving through carved water, and a mare with her head down grazing all stood in a little row along the shelf now.

When he glanced up, Golshan had turned his chair to

stare out the window. Seth tilted his head. "Penny for your thoughts?"

Golshan pivoted back, with a slight squeak of the wheels, and Seth made a mental note to oil them again. They were still figuring out the maintenance it needed, and the bearings Phillip had used took more oil than they'd thought, maybe. That wasn't hard to fix, it just needed attention. "Come tomorrow, you'll be back in the workshop."

Seth nodded. "I've some orders to be working on, and some designs to test." He was still working on a rocking chair for Dilly, and if that worked out right, he suspected they'd be a popular item for sale. Then he tilted his head. "And you're beginning to feel at loose ends."

"How do you always know what I'm thinking?" Golshan nudged the right wheel, turning sharply to come close to Seth, knee to knee.

"Practice." Seth grinned at him, and then set the carving aside for a moment, folding the cloth in his lap.

"You have things you need to be doing, though. You can't just cater to me."

"Well, for one thing, you deserved to have time to sort out how things work here. And there were the holidays. But now we've got a clear run from wassailing the trees, middle of the month, to your spring festivities. Well, and likely a baby in there somewhere." A week on either side of the equinox, most likely. "You're welcome to do whatever you like with your days. You're always welcome to keep me company. We like your cooking, though it's a bit tricky yet until I get a counter set lower with another sink."

"You're going to a lot of trouble." Golshan sounded dubious.

"The sink's no trouble. Good for small children, which we intend to have around for a while. Or sitting down at, doing dishes, which I am fairly sure Dilly would like right about now."

"I'm not going to talk you out of it." Golshan didn't make it a question, just a statement.

"You aren't." Seth tilted his head. "I did have an idea, but it needs fleshing out."

Golshan shook his head, then pivoted the chair again, lining it up so he could lever himself onto the sofa, beside Seth, thigh to thigh. "Tell me. Or I'll tickle you. You aren't holding anything sharp right now."

Seth laughed. "Anything but that! I knew you'd use it against me." Then he shifted his arm, letting Golshan tuck in next to him. "I keep thinking about all the other people, like you. Well, not precisely like you, you are singular."

Golshan nodded. "But stuck in care homes. No one to come fetch them out, like Orfeo and Eurydice."

"Is that what you think it's like?" That had been the performance piece, their fourth year, when anyone at all likely had been drafted into helping. Neither of them had the right kind of singing voice, but Seth had heard a lot of the rehearsals while working on sets, and Golshan had helped paint them.

Golshan shrugged. "It felt like it. Like if you'd turned around and done the wrong thing, when you left that first time, I'd never have seen you again. If I'd done the wrong thing."

Seth tugged Golshan's hand into his. "There isn't a wrong thing you could do that would keep me from you."

Golshan shivered, and Seth suddenly paid very close attention. "You know what I did. When I was away from the trenches."

"I do. And I also know that was war, and this is not. Well. We still war with ourselves, don't we?"

Golshan's focus snapped into place, almost audible.

"We." It sounded like he was feeling out the shape of the word, like Seth got with a new carving. "More. Please." There was something urgent in his voice now.

"I was in the middle of it too. Maybe it would be different if I'd been behind the lines, like Cephus. Or back here, like other people." He shrugged. "I've been thinking a lot. About people making assumptions."

Golshan's hand shifted, tightening in Seth's. "Penny for them?" It was an echo of earlier, and Seth smiled, settling back into the sofa now.

"Thinking about the play is a good way to go at it. There's a script in people's heads. Noble young men, going off to fight. The ones who come home, you throw them a parade, you send them on their way, return the greatcoat to the nearest train station."

"Wait, you had to turn in the greatcoat?" Golshan was delightfully distracted now.

"The thing was full of lice." It had taken Seth a solid month to stop itching horribly. And that had been with all the charms that a devoted mother and wife used to farm living could apply to the problem. "Yes. They sent us off with the uniform if we wanted, a new suit of clothes or a fee to cover some. Pay, and the promise of a bit more. All sorts of forms. And a requirement to turn the greatcoat in."

"What was it like when you came home?"

"Dilly knew. I'd been able to write letters. There was a portal close enough to the demob camp I'd been able to drop a note, as soon as I knew the date. I had to take the train back. To London, for me. She met me down at the portal down the road. She'd been waiting an hour, I think. Just perched on the wood bench, watching everyone who came through. When it was me, she near knocked me off my feet."

"And the others?"

"Came for supper, and shooed us off to bed. Again." Seth grinned, amused at the memory. Then he said, more quietly. "Plenty of people. They came home, and people don't understand why loud noises make them miserable. Or some flash of colour makes them jump. Why there are things they won't eat, or won't say or won't talk about."

"Plenty of things people won't talk about." Golshan shifted to lean his head on Seth's shoulder. "And people assume there's a way to recover. A narrow path to walk, lined with their approval."

"And if you step off it, no matter how good the reason, there are nasturtiums for you."

"I still think that's denigrating a perfectly nice flower." Golshan squeezed his hand. "Could we grow some?"

"Nasturtiums? We could. You can eat them. They make for a brightly coloured salad. Not unlike you."

"I am not a salad." Golshan managed to keep a straight face for about a second, then he collapsed into laughter on Seth's shoulder.

Seth hugged him tighter. "You are brightly coloured. Makes me feel much better, to see that."

"The convalescent blues were awful. Even more than the uniform in the first place." That made Golshan pause, as if he were lining up dominoes in a row, to get them to make patterns and lines.

Seth let him think for a little, running his thumb over Golshan's hand. It was going to be terribly hard to be out in public, and not touch, but he didn't quite care. He couldn't bring himself to care right now, anyway.

"How do we talk about the nasturtiums? And how there are a whole lot of us who are just ignoring them? Metaphorically , I mean. And that they don't have to stay on that path if they don't want to?"

Seth snorted at that. "Treating them like flowers, not like moral guidelines, you mean."

"That." Golshan grinned at him and went back to leaning.

"I'm thinking that's something you could do. If you wanted." Seth offered it. "Find other people, help them figure out what makes sense for them. Not the script. Maybe help them find the people who care about them. The ones not on the next-of-kin lists. Or maybe they mostly care about their family, but they need a space that understands."

Golshan considered it. "I would have to go places. And there must be stairs."

"So, maybe we make a day a week when I can go with you. Or Dilly, maybe. She can make people feel guilty for having offices up a lot of stairs and get them to come out and talk to you." Seth grinned at the image.

There was a long pause. "How - how does money, I mean. I won't take from you."

"Ah." Seth squeezed. "I make things in the workshop. My apprentice master has a shop in Trellech, we take it turn and turn about to be there. Once a fortnight for me. Mostly small things for the shop, bowls and spoons and some of my carvings, but we've got a couple of chairs on display, information about the beds. It's not as much as I want, but the more I specialise, the better it will get."

"You do like a bit of furniture. That's not the money, though."

"We're doing all right. Nothing fancy, but good country food. Plenty of it. We might need to take on a cow, if Lia's going to keep being difficult, but that's all right. Thesan's made it clear she'll keep our seedling in books, and Mum's going to do it in clothes. I like making things with Phillip, things that help people with injuries, but it's harder to get money from that."

"Wealthy folks have bad backs too." Golshan pointed out. Then he considered. "I have a pension." Golshan was still sorting this out, and Seth let him talk it through. "My share of food, at least. Bed and board."

"Dilly does most of our bookkeeping. And Dad. We'll sit down the next week or so, and sort out a fair number, all right? You know we'd have you, no matter what."

"No reason Dilly shouldn't have the good tea, or whatever else she fancies, within reason. Nice fabric to make curtains out of. Frocks? Does she make frocks?"

Seth laughed. "She did like making your curtains. And we do still have to finish the nursery."

"You really think I can do this? Help other people?" Trust Golshan to circle back.

"Golshan, love. You like talking to people, you always have. Figuring out what makes them interesting. Even in the trenches, you'd always be chatting someone up. And at least there it wasn't for something in private."

Golshan snorted. "Cigarettes, mostly. I'm not sure I can talk to people about nasturtiums the same way."

"Every person's different. Not the same thing, is it? Not so transactional. But that's a lot of what you did at the theatre. I heard your stories. Remember, you can't fool me. And," Seth paused. "I think the Gospatricks thought you'd be good at it. They mentioned, a couple of times, you'd helped talk someone around, just asking questions. You're good at showing people options."

Golshan made a small grumbling sound. "Where do I even start?"

"We could go see the Gospatricks. And you could ask your questions about sex, and we could talk to people there, and I'm sure they know others. And the healers know some. And..." Then Seth broke into giggles.

Golshan gave him a moment, then elbowed him. "And?"

"And you could always go back to that care home and see what they made of you now?"

Golshan went still, and then he too was collapsing in laughter, against Seth's side. There was nothing better in the world.

They had a future. They had ideas. And they had each other, all three of them.

COUNTRY MANNERS

CHAPTER 1
DECEMBER 23RD, 1921 AT THE LEFTON
FAMILY ESTATE

"It's not too late to claim you urgently have to be back in Trellech and on duty." Giles turned, aiming at where he knew Kate was, speaking quietly. "I should have known they'd put you at the far end of the house."

"Is this the sort of house that has secret passages? There must be some way for the servants to move about without running into people. I expect that's part of what Watson is finding out. He's never been in a great house like this before, he's having so much fun." Kate didn't seem upset, at least. Her voice sounded more amused than anything else.

Watson was his valet, new to service that fall. He'd gone bustling off to see to things below stairs, and Giles took a moment to think about what he might make of the place. Kate had found him, a former stage dresser who'd also done some props work. She'd had the sensible thought that someone from the theatre would understand. That he'd know the importance of having things in the same places all the time, of not moving the furniture without warning. All the little things that made Giles largely independent. Giles was quite capable of managing his own blindness, but Kate kept having excellent ideas, and should be encouraged to have more. By everyone, but Giles was determined to do his part there.

Giles snorted. "I spent summers here. There are, but I don't know if there's anything terribly close to where they put you. Tell me about it?"

Kate laughed, and leaned in to kiss his cheek, one hand on his shoulder, so he knew where she was coming from. She was silhouetted by the window behind her, enough he could see the fuzzy shadow of where she was. "First, where do you want these tokens?" She shifted something in her other hand, the tin of small rune-carved stones. "Your bath is across the hall, right?"

"Yes, but I can manage that without one. I don't trust someone not to move it." He considered. "Where's the chair?"

"Let me get out of the way. Three steps straight in front of you." She took a step to the side, and he took three measured steps forward, and could feel the chair brushing against his knee. He turned, settling down into it, quite sure they'd not changed it since he was a schoolboy. He'd had this room then too, all manly deep reds and browns. They were supposed to make him grow up brave and virtuous.

"A token on the dresser. Watson is here, so I will trust to his judgement about ties and cravats and all that. There's one in the hairbrush already." That had been his good idea. He could use the resonance in the charmwork to navigate to any of the charmed stones, based on pitch. As Kate had discovered, it was also terribly handy for remembering where you put your hairbrush. Or if mounted on a bookmark, your book. "This chair, my side of the bed, and did they put a desk in here?"

"They did, but it's rather a poor excuse for one. All beaten up. You want your typewriter here? And the braille slate?" He could hear her rummaging about. "The chair seems sound, though. I'll put the stone by the inkstand."

Giles nodded. "And a stack of paper out, would you?" She'd have remembered that, of course, but they'd discovered over the past months together that checking on each other, talking through what they were doing, made things run smoothly. Besides, he enjoyed hearing her voice, especially when she was relaxed and at ease. He adored the intimacy of it, the way the lilt from Wales snuck in when she wasn't being formal and on guard. No one else heard her voice like that but him.

Once he heard the various small movements stop, he gestured in her direction. "Do you have - you must have a lot of questions. And honestly, you can make your escape when you need to. I really need to be here all week, but there's the portal. You have a journal."

"Lady Alysoun herself had a look at my clothes. I am fully fitted out for a week of holiday meals and festivities. She has even coached me in the intricacies of the sort of Victorian parlour games favoured by aged aunties with opinions." Kate laughed. "Mind, I'm not sure aged aunties without opinions exist. Entirely mythical, surely."

Giles knew when he would not make her change her mind. Kate was good-tempered to a fault, but he'd learned quickly how politely stubborn she could be when pressed to it. It was like moving a mountain, once she decided she was going to be the immovable object. She obviously saw something in his face, because she patted his shoulder again and then bent down to kiss him on the lips. He waved a hand. "Laying out the parameters of the equation."

"As always. Would it make you feel better to go through this one more time? Now that we're here?" She was sounding amused and patient, at least. Like this was a challenge, and she was going to face it. And they had been rather busy, both of them, this past week, so a review was probably helpful on all counts.

"It is the obligatory family gathering. Hosted at the family estate, the greatest of the properties, of course. It's a vast house, something like forty bedrooms. You didn't tell me which one they had you in. That's going to make it hard for you to sneak back to me."

"It is very yellow. Exceedingly yellow. With flowers all over." Kate shrugged. "However, I am not expecting to spend overmuch time there when I'm awake. And at least it's not pink. Pink always makes me feel balky." From how Kate had described her hair - deep auburn - Giles did not imagine it would flatter her.

"And I hope not all the time you're asleep, either." Giles had got very used to waking up with her beside him. Or if not beside him, to the warm indentation and knowledge she'd been there until she went on duty.

"You're sure it's all right for me to sneak up here?" Kate sounded like she was weighing things out again.

"Sneaking into someone's bedroom is a very traditional thing in a house party. There are all sorts of codes about whether you welcome someone doing it." Giles tried to remember what they were. "Leaving things on the doorknob or whatever. And you usually wake early enough to sneak back. Or, you know, go out for a tromp around the grounds."

"Well, it would be good to avoid doing things that

implied I was open to an assignation. The only sex I wish to be having in this house is with you."

Giles shook his head. "It's not terribly likely, since it's just family here. We'll have to see what Watson comes back with, in terms of intelligence. You must be rather far down at the end of that wing, if I remember the colour scheme right. It's been years since I poked around. Not the done thing and all. How do you feel about scaling a trellis or a convenient ladder?"

"It depends on how dressed I am required to be. Being out of uniform is going to be rather a muchness." Kate spent most of her hours in some form of the Guard's uniform, usually in split skirts, blouse, and jacket. She had been acquiring the proper sort of frocks for social events and suppers out, but they were still rather a new puzzle for her.

"Is Istan settled, do you think?" That was the maid who had come with them, since Kate would need someone to do her hair up properly. Normally the young woman - a niece of his housekeeper's - had a broader range of tasks.

"She was hanging things up in the wardrobe when I came up here. She's very good at not fussing, and also at telling me when I need to sit down and let her see to something. All right. What else should I expect? Aged aunts with opinions. Cousins? Your parents, at least I've met them." He heard a slight creak of wood, and the scrape of a chair. He expected she'd pulled the desk chair over to talk.

"It's Father's side of the family. Mother and Father. You did say you were brushing up on the operas Mother likes, which I think is really decent of you, and likely to be insufficiently appreciated."

Kate snorted. "Not my usual thing, but some of them aren't bad? And the performance last month was quite entertaining. Things that come out when it's staged." His mother favoured particularly obscure 18th century operas from the magical community. The performance had been of one about a princess in disguise, from some European kingdom, who had gone through a series of noble but baffling adventures. The music was quite good, though, for once. "And your father is very proper."

"Father has barely admitted I exist since I came back from Flanders. Though, to be fair, he was not a doting papa when I was younger. There's quite a gap in age between me and Caesarius, and Father has never understood mathematics." Giles shrugged, and leaned back. He wished it had been different, but it wasn't.

"Never understood maths, or never understood why you understand them?" Kate considered. "Both. Clearly both. All right. And neither of them approve of me, but they have a hard time overtly disapproving. Except that perhaps this trip is meant to discourage us from marrying."

"There is that." He'd thought about the implications. "The other guests do suggest someone is up to something. My brother and his wife and their children. We'll come back to them. Aunt Lucretia and Uncle Norbert, and their children. Ambrose is apprenticing now, in Materia, based in Trellech. Elisabeta is in her last year at Schola. I don't know what they're like now, it's been years since I saw them." He felt the faint brush of her fingers on his wrist at the dual implication, but he refused to shy away from perfectly good words.

"So not people you were close to, before. Or since." Kate disapproved.

"They sent apologetic cards. After, when I was at St Dunstan's. The sort I didn't mind someone reading aloud." Giles shrugged. He refused to let it hurt him. He had found people who didn't mind, and more to the point, he'd found Kate. She seemed to treat his blindness as just one thing that needed to be negotiated in and amongst all the other things that went with their partnership.

Kate grunted, audibly disapproving of this. "Who else? You said not the other uncle and aunt, but their daughter?"

"Isoline. She's married, I don't know her husband at all. Oswald, I think. They have two children, but both under ten." Giles counted off. "Mother and Father, who will probably say you can call them Delphina and Tiberius, but grudgingly. My brother, yes, we're coming back to him."

Kate picked up, her memory well-trained to sort people out. "Aunt Lucretia and Uncle Norbert, with their children Alponse, who is apprenticing, and Elisabeta who is at Schola." She emphasised the similar sounds from the names and their current pursuit to get them locked in her memory. "What does Uncle Norbert do?"

"Uncle Norbert does something tedious and necessary at the Ministry. Aunt Lucretia does all the ladies' luncheons that Lady Alysoun hates, and would love to get invited to her parties." This time he gave her the cues. Norbert was necessary, Lucretia and ladies. Lord Richard Edgarton was Kate's superior officer in the Guard. But these days, they had regular invites to the Edgartons' social events. Lady Alysoun had been delightfully generous with her time in getting Kate sorted out for her new social obligations at the events Giles went to.

"And then there's Isoline, your cousin once removed, and Oswald, and younger children. What does Oswald do? Does Isoline do anything of note?" Kate was filing things away, still. Again. It made him smile, how stubbornly she was sorting this out, on a trip he wished he hadn't had to ask her to make.

"Isoline has a line in fancy flower arrangements, the

ones that come with enchantments for faster healing or well being or abundance or whatever. She kept sending them, when I came home, and they did no good. I think she was rather offended, and she's still touchy about it."

Kate grunted. "The sort who can't deal with actual injury or illness, just the sort that turns up in a novel and is quickly cured? I've met the type."

"Oswald is second in a firm that does charms for barns and agricultural buildings. Better storage, that sort of thing. I think Isoline thinks it's a bit beneath him, but it's necessary work, and I gather he's quite good at it." Giles considered. "All right. My brother."

Kate shifted, and he felt her hand take his, her fingers calloused but still surprisingly delicate. "Your brother. Caesarius. And his wife Julia - very Roman, all round. And their children, Xenia and Primus. Who is a second child. They had them comparatively late, just before the War."

"But first son. Very Roman, yes." Giles shrugged. "Caesarius is twelve years older. He was already at Schola most of the year by the time I remember anything. I'd see him, out on the grounds, when I was little, and he was home for the hols, but he never had much time for me." He shrugged. "When I got older, he'd come and scold me about all the things I should learn."

"Again, I suspect maths was not on the list." Kate's thumb brushed over the curve of his hand.

"He was always amid the social whirl. Teachers loved him. Charming and bright, and sharp."

Kate spotted it immediately. "But not kind. Not to you. Not to other people?" He didn't know whether to curse her or bless her.

"Not kind, no. Since Flanders, he's left me alone." Giles swallowed. "I expect he'll make you feel awful, sometime. I should have warned you."

Kate tsked, then leaned forward to kiss his lips once. "Remember who I apprenticed with, you. All those posh young men who think they know everything, and have always known everything, and should have everything. I will take you and your maths every day. And he's not going to say anything I haven't heard dozens of times before. This time, I'll have you to tell me it's not true."

He caught at her hand, reaching searchingly for the other. She let him, made it easy for him, and he tugged both her hands together, pressing them between his larger ones. "Always. You know that. You must know that." He could hear the urgency in his own voice, the way something about her cracked all of his reserve open.

"That's why I'm here. Staying. I'm not leaving you alone with them, either. They'll chip away at you." She hesitated. "I looked up their War records. Caesarius and Norbert and Oswald." Kate's voice was quiet. "Why were you the only one in the trenches? Near the front?"

"Younger son, remember? I'm the spare." He didn't regret it, not exactly. He knew he'd saved lives in the middle of the worst day of his life. Somehow. Through raw bloody luck, no skill of his, except that enough of his men had trusted him. But he couldn't quite keep the bitterness out of his voice. Then he blinked. "You looked them up before this?"

"The thing about the Great Families, love, is that there's this book, with all your names and relationships written down. Figuring out where people served is easy, from that. Now, if you wanted to find out about my brothers, you'd have to actually do some work." Kate sounded very amused, and Giles smiled at that. It was good she was. It meant this might not be entirely awful.

"And yet you made me tell you about them. At least twice." Giles shook his head.

"For one, I am still honing my interview techniques. I mean, I expect to be for the rest of my career. And second, how you talk about them tells me things that aren't in any book." She tugged his hand so she could squeeze it. "We haven't talked about your grandmother."

"She's still very upset about Vale." Phillip Vale, who had robbed Giles, fled the country, and been returned in disgrace, to be disowned.

"Even though he's a distant cousin?" Kate asked.

"Grandmama still feels like things were done improperly. Who did them improperly is a troublesome question, mind."

"Not her, though. Am I right? I am right." Kate snorted.

"Not her. She is... she is very Victorian. Mind your ps and qs, call her Mistress Lefton, do your best with the formal manners, shower her with respect, obvious respect. Like, um, who was it you were complaining about, the case two months ago?" A grand old dowager.

"Oh, yes. I can do that again. There's a skill I'm going to keep needing. Perhaps even more than interviewing people to get all the information I want." She hesitated. "So, what are our obligations here? More precisely?"

"Formal suppers. Luncheon together, but if the weather is not horrible, it is acceptable to take a packed lunch out and ramble. I know you need to get your obligatory exercise in." He considered. "They don't really know what to do with you being in the Guard. You're an officer now, and it's not as if you don't have good connections because of it. The Edgartons. Lady Donovan. Various of the others. I'm fairly sure they don't approve, but I can't tell how much of it is because they don't approve of people like me considering marrying."

Kate sighed. "Which is not a thing you can talk people

round about. Perhaps showing them will do something. All right. No one's going to drag me out fox hunting or something? I didn't bring clothes for that."

Also, it involved a number of customs Kate was not fluent in. "Not in this household, not anymore. Grandmama does not care for hounds. But there might be some shooting of pheasants. The next estate over is set up for it, and they invite us over."

Kate snorted. "All right. We will manage, love. And if it gets too horrible, I will invent an excuse that means I have to go to the Guard Hall for the day. But I'd rather not leave you alone with it."

Giles shook his head. "We both rather wish to protect and defend each other, don't we?"

Kate stood, then bent to kiss his cheek. "Well, I'm certainly not swearing to obey. Defend, though, that might do very well. Scandalise a few people, but there we are, some people just need to be scandalised."

Giles laughed. Before he could continue, there was Watson's knock on the door, and he called out, "Come in?"

"Here we are, sir. Mistress Kate." He delighted in referring to her that way, as if she were a lead actress, at least in private. "I have a great deal of news from below stairs. Oh, and let me fix your hair, dear."

Kate laughed - Giles loved the sound of it. "Of course. Both things, please."

CHAPTER 2
BEFORE SUPPER

They were the next to last to make it downstairs to the formal parlour, in the end. Kate had left Giles so she could change into something suitable for the evening. This was a deep green velvet dress with a bodice that fit more like her uniform than it looked. The outfit had met with Lady Alysoun's particular approval. The weight of it felt comfortingly familiar, rather than the finer silk the other women wore.

They also wore rather a lot more jewellery. Kate had traded her Guard pendant for a single opal pendant that Giles had given her shortly after he had proposed that summer. She had earrings in, but that was nothing compared to the glittering jewels that the others wore. Kate didn't think it was just her upbringing and background that made her think it was rather ridiculous to wear that much jewellery to what was purportedly a family gathering.

The room itself was rather Victorian, the sort of style where even the legs of the furniture were hidden by swaths of fabric. It was stuffy, as if the fire had been burning a bit hot for the space. The colours were pleasant enough, varying shades of green, lighter than her dress. She didn't bother to describe that to Giles. He'd been clear earlier she needn't bother with the decorative details unless they mattered.

She leaned toward Giles. "What must be Casaerius - he looks like you - and Julia. She's wearing a dozen gems and something in deep gold silk. Your mother, then your father, then your grandmother at the centre. She's peering over her glasses at us. To the right is Isoline, I think. Blonde, the right age, wearing rather low-cut red, and Oswald, who is wearing a suit, not robes. I don't think your Aunt Lucretia and her family are down here yet."

It was a particular challenge to describe people in a room she hadn't met yet. She and Giles had sorted out how to manage the order, always working left to right so he could keep track. Giles nodded, and she guided him forward, her hand tucked through his arm. It was not the proper way to guide someone, but it looked much better in the sort of social settings where people disapproved of blindness.

She stopped a proper distance away, smiling. Giles waited, trusting that she'd have positioned him precisely, and smiled with a slight bow. "Grandmama. May I present my fiancee, Captain Kate Davies? Kate, my grandmama, Mistress Aurelia Lefton." Kate did her best to smile, made easier by the fact he'd so firmly included the rank she'd worked so hard to earn.

There was stirring, to their left, then a long and awkward silence, before the older woman said, "Giles, it has been far too long." She did not hesitate so much as create a tremendous distance. "Mistress Davies."

Kate was not sure how far to push. Whether she

should. Giles shifted his arm slightly to reassure. "Do, please, call me Kate. I hear my title quite enough at work."

That got more tsking, but Giles had turned toward her, smiling beneath the shaded glasses. He added almost off-handedly, "My room is just as it was, of course. Thank you for having us both." She nodded without saying anything else.

They'd talked about the order. His grandmother, his parents, his brother, and then his aunt and cousin. "Master Lefton, Mistress Lefton." She nodded politely. Giles said, amiably. "Mother, Father."

Delphina spoke, with a "You had an easy journey, I hope?" It was stilted, and Kate was sure she'd almost said it was good to see Giles again. Not that they made much of an effort to spend time with him at other points. They largely preferred London or their country house to Trellech. And besides, Giles had often been at the manor house they'd been investigating or at his rooms in Oxford during the week.

"Very quick, thank you." Giles still sounded entirely pleasant, and Kate did not know how he could navigate it that smoothly. Next, she turned him, subtly as she could. "Caesarius." He dropped her arm to hold out his hand.

There was the long moment, the one she knew he hated, of waiting to see if it would be taken. His brother was not that awful, at least, because after two or three seconds, he reached to shake. "It's been ages." Then, to Kate, he added, "My wife, Julia. Our children are up having supper in the nursery, with Isoline's and Oswald's. So nice for them to have cousins to play with."

Kate smiled. "A pleasure to meet you both." She could use all the polite phrases like a shield or a ward, and she would. Finally, that brought them to Isoline and Oswald. They were perched on a rather delicate looking Victorian sofa, all carved wood and too many pillows taking up space. Once Giles was beside her, he nodded pleasantly. "Isoline, Oswald, my fiancee Kate. It's been forever, hasn't it? Last time we talked, you were still apprenticing, I think?" That was to Oswald, who nodded.

Before he could say anything else or Kate could pass that on, there was a commotion behind them, with people coming in behind them. Kate just had time to whisper the order in Giles's ear before the chaos hit. "So sorry we're late, there was an awful wait for the Bedford Square portal, I can't even tell you."

That must be Lucretia, a rather younger sister to Tiberius. She was not aging gracefully, wearing more makeup than suited her. Her hair and frock were in a style that Kate thought might be outdated by a decade or so. Certainly before the War. Some part of her mind suddenly wanted to figure out if that was a deliberate choice. Lucretia might prefer the corsets and pigeon-fronted gowns with more structure and support, or it could have to do with a lack of money. It was quite possibly both. Kate smiled. Smiling was entirely appropriate in the circumstance.

She stepped sideways with Giles, then settled them onto another small sofa, in the outer edge of the arc of furniture, while the four made their greetings to Mistress Lefton. Giles had only barely got his bearings again when they swept to Tiberius, then around to them. "Giles, goodness. You look surprisingly well." Lucretia's voice was a hair shrill, the kind of tone that made Kate realise the woman was more nervous than she seemed.

Kate thought they really were going to have to set up a bet about what people would say, or how they would say it. She should have suggested it earlier. It was one of their favourite ways to manage tedious meetings. She had not had a chance to add any details to him, but Giles just beamed. "A pleasure, again. It's been years since I've been here, it's good to be back. This is my fiancee, Captain Kate Davies. How are you doing, Aunt Lucretia, Uncle Norbert?"

There was a quiet voice behind Lucretia. "Uncle Giles. Captain Davies." He coughed. "I'm Ambrose. And this is Elisabeta." Ambrose was in that rather gangly stage of young adulthood, looking rather like the photographs Kate had seen of Giles at that age. Elisabeta looked, honestly, a bit sulky.

Kate did not blame her. She suspected she'd looked the same at several family gatherings over the years. But she nodded, along with a "Please call me Kate."

Once they had moved on to the others, Kate spoke quietly. "Your aunt is wearing an older dress, something before the War, and rather a lot of cosmetics. Ambrose, I can see he looks like you at that age, a bit gangly. Elisabeta looks like she'd rather be somewhere else."

"Do please speak up, Mis - Kate." Kate got the sense that her short nickname was apparently also beneath them, but it was better than the wrong title.

"I was just letting Giles know about the layout of the room, Mistress Lefton." She would not beg pardon or make apologies for that.

"Is that really necessary?" That was Julia, her voice rather nasal. "He's been here for yonks."

Giles spoke up, as Kate had been sure he would. "The room, yes. But Kate's a great help, telling me where people are. It seems a small thing, but it makes it much easier to follow the conversation."

There was a murmur from several points in the room, but Kate wasn't able to pin down who, precisely. Giles shifted his hand to cover hers, companionably, and then asked his mother what she'd been enjoying lately. That at least carried them through until it was time for supper. His mother had not been enjoying much, as far as Kate could tell. The conversation was made up of a long string of mildly phrased objections.

It was the sort of thing Kate did not know how to interpret, still. She might never, honestly. Among her people, if you liked something, you said so. If you didn't, you said so, and you probably did your best to avoid doing that again. From the comments Delphina and the others made, among their sort, you did many things and then spent the rest of your time complaining about unimportant details. It seemed a very odd hobby.

The dinner was rather less comfortable for her. They were being informal, as she understood it, which meant she was seated next to Giles, rather than at the opposite end of the table. She had begun to get used to having multiple courses brought out. That was no longer strange. And she had practised with the cutlery and tasting the wine, and all the other skills people seemed to expect her to have.

When Giles was served, his grandmother glanced up. "Oh, someone should see to that." It was sharp, cutting. Kate glanced at his plate, and there was nothing there Giles would find difficult to manage. Chicken, in a cream sauce, with vegetables.

Giles opened his mouth, but one of the servants reached over to take it away. Kate spoke before she meant to. "That's not a problem, Mistress Lefton."

"Are you contradicting me?" Now that sharpness was aimed directly at Kate. Blast.

Giles cleared his throat. "Kate and I share meals, as our schedules allow. I promise, I am quite able to eat without someone cutting the chicken up into bite-sized pieces for me. Or making mush out of the, what is that?"

"Potatoes, turnips, and Brussels sprouts."

"Ah, I thought I caught the sprouts." Giles turned toward where his grandmother was sitting. "No damage to the tablecloth, I'm sure."

He was so insistently patient about it. The rest of the table had near enough gone still and silent. Finally, Mistress Lefton sniffed. "If you insist." She said it as if it were the greatest demand she'd ever heard.

Kate waited for the conversation to begin again, then leaned slightly toward Giles. "Chicken at three, potatoes at seven, turnips at nine, sprouts at eleven. Sauce over most of it."

That made Giles snort once, quietly, and nod. He said nothing directly back to her, but began a conversation with Isoline, on his left, about her children. While eating rather more tidily than most of the other men at the table.

It was, really, an unfortunate tactical decision. The conversation went on for a couple of minutes, with Isoline and Oswald comparing tutoring schools and preparation for exams with Caesarius and Julia. Kate was nearly done with her chicken when she heard, "Such a pity you won't have the opportunity, Giles."

That was a complicated topic. She and Giles had talked about it, of course, before he proposed. They were sensible people, with professional obligations. And hers were, frankly, more complicated than his.

Pregnancy would mean being assigned to office duty in Trellech for the duration. It would mean adjusting a number of things about her work and ongoing training. She was still finding her feet as a Captain, and it was hard won. She didn't want to give people excuses to avoid giving her interesting assignments.

On the other hand, she'd grown up as one of five - three brothers and a sister. She was not entirely sure what she thought about being responsible for a tiny baby, but she did well enough with children once they could talk. And Giles had been clear that a good nanny was in the cards, if she wished to have children. If they wished to.

Beside her, Giles's voice was smooth. Dangerously smooth, but she didn't think his family would notice that part. "I beg pardon?"

"Well, surely, you won't be..." Julia's voice trailed off, delicately.

"You seem to have rather a few misperceptions about things." Again, so very mild. "It's my eyes that suffered from the gas. Not, mmm. More relevant parts."

That brought a round of exclamations from around the table, from nearly everyone else. Kate held still, trying not to show how much she wanted to dig in and bare her teeth and defend her ground.

In the end, it was Mistress Lefton's voice that cut through. "That was not the point, Giles, and you know it. And such crudity."

Giles did not apologise, but he nodded in his grandmother's direction.

Julia did not let it drop. "It's not proper. And, well. It can't be good for a child. Growing up in a household like that. And what you do, Kate. Working." Again, she made the short nickname into near enough an insult.

Giles let his hand shift against her leg, under the table, the little silent pattern of three taps that encouraged her to speak her mind. Kate shrugged. She'd practised that shrug in the mirror every day for three months, to get the right amount of implication into the movement.

"A third of the Guard are women, and about a quarter of the Captains at the moment. We have protocols for those who wish to have children. As we do, though not perhaps immediately after marriage. I am still quite new to my current rank, and there is a great deal to learn."

"Giles, really." That was his mother.

"Yes, Mother?" He was doing a better job tracking the voices than he'd been afraid he would. Though she supposed it helped that the women's voices were fairly distinct in tone, and the men's in pitch. Giles found groups of more than five or six harder to manage, as a rule.

"We had assumed that, well. It is easy to understand why Kate might be willing to overlook your infirmities. There are certainly benefits for her." Making it blatant that they all thought she was after whatever money she could get. She had to admit that his townhome was a rather nicer set of digs than her rooms in the Guard barracks. But the creature comforts were not why she loved Giles. Merely a pleasant benefit. "And I suppose for you, as well, having someone about the place who isn't a servant. I do wish you'd take on another secretary."

"Because the last one worked out so well?" Giles was beginning to lose his patience, Kate could tell that readily. The question was whether the rest of his family would notice in time. Phillip Vale, his last secretary, had been forced on him by the family.

Vale had been awful to Kate, but then he had abandoned Giles and stolen rather a lot of money. He had been sent back from abroad to stand trial, sentenced to gaol for some time, and disowned by his parents. That he'd also had rather an unpleasant opium habit hadn't helped anything, either.

Giles continued. "Watson has been a great help with the practicalities, and Kate's the one who found him. For the rest, Kate lends a hand, or I have a regular appointment with a bookkeeper. Really quite simple, and I have plenty of time for my research and teaching."

"Oh, that, you're not still on about that?" That was Caesarius. "Goodness, that must be a bore. And I don't know how you do it, when you..." He flicked his fingers at Giles's glasses.

Giles did not need Kate to explain that one. "There's a rather fascinating lineage of blind mathematicians, actually. I've a new paper coming out next month, and I'm looking forward to the coming Hilary Term, of course. My students have been settling into the year's work nicely."

It was as if none of them believed he had an active life. Up to Oxford by portal on Monday morning, usually staying there through Thursday afternoon, then coming back to Trellech. Unless there were some good reason for him to do otherwise. He had done that from time to time when Kate was free, or when there was an interesting weekend lecture.

Of course, he continued to consult for the Guard, and that meant being in both places regularly. Giles did find navigating the crowds both at the Trellech portal and the Oxford one a trifle tedious, but that was the only reason to limit the number of trips.

After another awkward silence, Lucretia picked an entirely different topic, some bit of gossip about a family everyone else at the table knew. Something about an alchemist, who'd done something particularly clever. Kate didn't place the name. It at least gave her a break where all she had to do was listen, nod occasionally, and focus on not making further difficulties at the table.

As the meal wound down, there was a general move back to the parlour for music and card games. Giles did not play the latter - at least not without a brailled deck. But Kate was drawn into a game of tarrochi with Isoline, Lucretia, and Oswald. She was not a skilled player. But she'd played more than enough hands while in the Guard barracks or on watch duty at the Guard Hall on a quiet night to not come out the loser. That was Isoline, who seemed rather distracted by something.

They at least kept the conversation firmly on family gossip, about each of the neighbouring estates and the magical families of the area. Kate could listen to that all night. She never knew when something like that might come in handy, whether directly related to a case she was handling or not.

Politeness kept her there until after Giles had got Watson to walk him upstairs. She would have to see either about sneaking up to him later, or finding time when they could talk alone tomorrow morning.

CHAPTER 3
MORNING OF DECEMBER 24TH

The next morning, Giles got himself up promptly and dressed for a country walk. Watson, being a former theatre man, did not care for mornings. Giles tried to do without him until a more reasonable hour. Kate, on the other hand, loved mornings. And even more so on days where she would not be getting in her usual exercise with the Guard.

Watson had laid out his clothes last night when they'd come up after supper. That done, Giles began the careful migration through the house to find Kate's room. He had gone slowly. He knew the house, but he also knew there were any number of places his grandmother might have added a decorative table, or chair, or something else.

It really was a blasted annoyance. He would have understood separate rooms. He had not rubbed his family's noses in the fact that Kate lived with him, in the Trellech townhome, rather than in her rooms at the Guard barracks. At least most of the time. However, putting her at the absolute furthest end of the house was annoying.

Thankfully, Istan had come across him as he was

coming across the top of the staircase on the first floor. She let him take her arm, just above the elbow, and guided him deftly down the hall. Stopping, she said, "Moment, sir." and disappeared inside. Giles waited. He was sure there would be no one else about at this hour other than the servants. The other guests were in his wing, the children up in the nursery rooms on the third floor, above where he was now.

Inside of a minute, Kate was slipping her hands into his. "I didn't expect you."

"A walk, my bright captain?"

Kate leaned to kiss his cheek. "A pleasure. You don't mind if I get a run in somewhere?"

"There should be a reasonable stretch of lane, unless things have changed rather drastically." Kate hesitated. He could hear her start to say something, then stop. "Go on, love."

"Do you mind if we stop by the kitchen? Istan was checking on something for me."

"It will be a while before breakfast." Then he stopped and tilted his head. "Not breakfast."

"I asked about some cream and honey and honey cakes, last night. The cook apparently wants to give them to me herself?"

Giles smiled, pleased. "Cook wants to get a sense of you, I'm sure. I'll back you up. Do you know how to get there?"

"I believe so. Istan gave very clear directions." Kate swallowed. "All right."

Giles took her arm, and let her lead him along, adding a comment about the house here or there. He hadn't been down into the servant's halls for rather longer than the last time he'd been in the house, but as a child, he'd snuck down there regularly.

Once they were down outside the kitchen, Kate cleared her throat. "Pardon? Cook wanted a word, when she has a moment?" It was polite, considerate, and very clear on her place in the hierarchy of the house. Giles was delighted.

It was a minute or two before anyone came over, but Giles could smell the flour and a hint of something else - lemon, lavender, something of the kind. "Master Giles." She sounded delighted. "And you've not come to see me." She then stopped short. People did that, they used perfectly reasonable verbs and then got embarrassed and it ruined any future conversation.

"I've not been back here more than once or twice since the War, Cook, but I'm glad you still remember me fondly. I stole a great many biscuits in my day, didn't I?"

"I'll be making sure there's a basket of them for you, sir, for your room. I heard they were fussing at you at supper." Then, carefully, she added, "You'll be letting me know if there's something you'd prefer?"

"Ah, Cook, you're very kind. I wouldn't have you change a thing. I just need a hand knowing where things are on my plate. It does no good expecting a bit of your excellent chicken when I get a bite of, I don't know, jelly."

It made her laugh warmly, which was what he was hoping for. When she spoke again, it was to Kate. "And you're his lady, then? They've been gossiping about you something fierce, so I hear."

"And I'm sure they've got their opinions." By which Kate made it clear she knew those were not kind. "My parents run an inn out by Cardiff. I know exactly how much work it is feeding a crowd with all their particular demands. I don't want to add to them, but Istan said you wanted to talk to me directly about the cakes?"

"What, pardon, ma'am, but what were you wanting the

cakes and cream and honey for?" Cook, he was sure, was folding her apron up in one hand.

"A proper offering, if I may. I'm new to the land here, but I want to do things right. And Giles will be with me."

"That's a thing that matters to you, ma'am?" Cook let out a breath.

"It is. And besides, making a proper offering is how Giles and I got started, more or less. It does make me want to keep doing things right." Giles would not have put it like that. But he supposed making the offering at Mannering House had been what let them into the gate. That had sent Kate tumbling rather literally into his arms later that day. And what had meant she was now here beside him, braving his family for love. "Honey cakes and honey and cream are how I've always done it. No commitments, no obligations, just a hello."

"Ah, you do know the proper way of it. We've a basket all made up, and some scones for you. There'll be breakfast ready about half nine, Master Giles, in the breakfast room." It was only about half seven now.

"We'll likely be back for that, but if not, I look forward to luncheon. And you can know that Kate and I are both greatly appreciating your food."

He could hear Cook smiling. "Ah, you're a grand tease, Master Giles. The weather's fine, for a wonder. Enjoy your walk." And with that, she showed Kate how to get out the side door and the path down to the lane.

Once they were a good twenty steps from the house, Kate stopped. "There's a woman who truly wishes you well."

"She's been there a long time. Since I was a boy. And I can tell. It's in someone's voice. She was beaming and smiling, I'm sure."

"Oh, yes. And she's supplied us well. There's a bottle

of cream here, and cakes, and a small jar of honey. And the scones. Quite a few scones. And - oh, some flasks of tea."

"Her scones are bliss." Giles sighed happily. "Mrs Meredith is a fine cook and an excellent housekeeper, but it's hard to do all the things she does as well as someone who specialises in cooking."

Kate leaned in to kiss him. "All right. I am relying on your knowledge of the land for a good place to leave this offering. Where are we going?"

"You know they make jokes about the blind leading people." Giles snorted. "Um. There's a farm about a mile down, and I believe there's a healing well most of the way there. It should still have a sign from the road."

"Someone else's farm?" Kate sounded dubious.

"No, it belongs with the house, the manor farm. Provides food and drink for the main house, and they sell the extra on. There's a man and his wife and - um. Some number of children, likely more than three, live further down past the farm."

Kate snorted at the 'likely more than three'. They walked on in silence for a dozen steps. "I see what you mean about windows, now I've got a decent view."

"When we were at Mannering House." The mysterious country home that had disappeared for centuries. "The manor's much newer, of course. Glass was much more the done thing for the holes in your walls, rather than shutters."

Kate laughed at that. "I couldn't stop looking at them last night, and thinking about it, actually." They turned down the lane, from the drive leading to the house, Giles could feel the ground change to something harder packed and properly graded. It wasn't a busy road as roads went, but there was a fair bit of agricultural traffic along here over time, with carts going back and forth. Not at the moment, of course, since it was winter.

"It is, admittedly, a ridiculously large house. It's almost never full up, we're less than half full now. Grandmama gave over a wing to an officer's rest home during the War, and barely noticed except that they cluttered up the lawn on nice days." He kept his tone light. She'd complained - to his mother, to him, to anyone who didn't flee fast enough - for a good two years about it. She'd done the needed thing, but not at all graciously.

Kate, of course, caught a hint of that. "I realise you have been carefully trying to avoid biasing me about your family, Giles, love. But now I have met them, can you give me some proper intelligence, so I might better come out the other side of the week?"

Giles grunted. "That's fair. Only, where do I even begin?"

"Well, for one, I'm a tad surprised they're not insisting on calling you Aegidius. They seem the sort of people who would. Or where everyone has one of the particularly ridiculous posh nicknames. Migs. Plum. Knobs. Bunny. Tibs. Actually, just about any consonant with ibs on the end?"

Giles laughed. "There is that. No, we've always been a bit more formal than that. There's a sort of posh family which is deliberately informal, in a structured way. And then there are families who are distant. We are decidedly distant."

About this point, Kate's stride shifted. "There's a little wooden sign. The well, though the paint's badly faded."

"Lead on, please." Their pace slowed as she made her way along the narrower path, murmuring here or there if there was a rock or a dip in the ground. The commentary was helpful, but it rather got in the way of conversation.

"Here's the well. There's a few ribbons tied up. Wishes? Do your people do that around here?" Kate stopped. "If you stay here, there's a little stone, set to the side."

"That's the right place. About knee height, improbably rounded?" When he'd been a boy, he'd found it almost erotic, the way the stone curved. It was set back, two or three feet from a massive tree.

"Yes." She slipped her arm out of his grasp and took a few steps. He could hear her humming, mostly under her breath, the faint noises of her taking things out of the basket she'd been carrying. Then her voice came out clear. "By honey, by cake, and by cream, I make an offering to thee. Let there be peace between us." She waited, then he heard Kate add an unexpected. "Thank you."

By the time she came back to his side, he was ready for her. She leaned in to kiss him, and he slipped his arm around her waist, taking his time with it. When she pulled back, he grinned. "Feel better now?"

"Mm-hmm. And I think they approve. Shall we walk up to the farm, and then I can find you somewhere to sit while I get a bit of a run in?"

They walked back down the path and turned again onto the lane. He was pleased just to walk along, listening to the birds and the rustle of animals in the grass. "What's the day like?"

"Clear, it doesn't look like rain. Or snow, either. No white Christmas. You told me, festivities tonight, and carollers from the village. Festivities tomorrow, most of the day. I would worry about presents, but both you and Lady Alysoun have approved them as appropriate from someone in my liminal state of acquaintance."

Kate had in fact acquired a mix of books and silk scarves from an artist Alysoun knew well, who could use the coin. She had stubbornly paid with her own money, noting that it meant it would look reasonable from her budget. Giles had a present for her they'd approve of for now - a warm uniform cloak, with a dozen enchantments on it to keep out rain and a good few pockets.

He was looking forward rather more to giving her things in private when they got home. He'd arranged for several books she'd say were far too expensive for a gift. But she'd then pore over them for weeks. Giles loved listening to her read, the little hums and flips of the page and sometimes the scratch of her pen as she took notes.

He was sure she had something for him, and he loved that. It would be something he actually wanted, rather than the obligatory gifts he'd get from his family. Even more awkward ones now, since they couldn't fall back on a handsomely bound diary, a book, or a new pen, or something of the kind.

Kate was quiet for a moment, then said. "There's the farm. Is it all right to go up?"

"Absolutely. It should be fairly quiet. The house is further on, and they likely did the morning feed already."

They turned up the lane to the farm, and Giles let the smells wash over him. He'd always liked a nice, honest farm. There was something wholesome and sturdy about it. A farm had cycles and seasons and there reasons for how they did things. It was soothing. That was the right word.

"It doesn't seem like anyone's about." Kate began talking, quietly. He could feel she was glancing around. "Some sheep and goats out here. I can see cows in the field on the other side of the lane. And I can hear some chickens. I think they're behind the barn."

"There should be a draught horse or two, but they might be in the barn." Giles tried to remember the layout. He'd been down here often enough as a young man, but it had been some years. Farm buildings didn't generally pick up and move, though.

"Barn." Kate agreed. "I'm getting to like horses." She had not grown up riding - she was far more comfortable on a ship, actually. But she had been working on the skill diligently and was getting to be quite good. Giles had had a chat with one of the Guardsmen responsible for the stables a few months ago.

"Horses it is." They came up to the paved yard, then crossed it, until Kate commented, "The barn." It wasn't a step up, but he could feel the ground change under his feet, the kind of thing that could throw him if he didn't have any warning. "Oh, my. You're lovely, aren't you? Big dapple-grey, oh, you're grand."

They both heard the noise at the same time, a little scurrying in the hayloft above the horses. It was the time he hated his blindness the most. He couldn't respond like he had before. He didn't have enough information.

She tapped his hand, the brief signal they'd sorted out, telling him to stay put, she would go investigate. He agreed, just as silently, squeezing her hand once for good measure.

And this was, he thought, the hardest time. He had known, from the first time he realised he was falling in love, that there would be hundreds of these moments. She would launch herself, like a falcon taking flight. And he wouldn't know what she was doing until she came back to him.

He knew her well enough he could hear her moving almost silently across the barn. There was a ladder up the back, he remembered, and the loft ran around the edges of the barn, with space to drop hay down to the horses below. There was a shift, and then a skittering sliding thump, in what he thought was a far stall. He didn't hear a horse over there, but it was hard to tell. It could just have been standing still.

On the other hand, horses generally noticed something coming down into their hay rack. Kate, however, strode over there. He could hear the soles of her boots striking the floor. She wasn't bothering to hide now. There was the sound of the stall door opening, then a "Well, what do we have here." It was her deliberate voice. The one she used when she wanted to establish that she knew what she was doing, but she wasn't sure yet if the situation called for command or charm.

There were muddled noises, and Kate asking if someone was all right. He was about to call out, enough to remind her he was here, when she called to him. "Giles, I'm bringing someone out with me. I need your help to figure out what's best to do. You know the people around here."

"Of course. Should I come over?"

"We'll come to you." He could hear her coaxing someone else along with her, as if whoever it was had her hand, or she had a hand on him. Then she brought him across. "Giles, there's a bench here, and I'm going to move this bale of hay for us to sit on. We have here a young boy, he's about five or six? I'm fairly sure he was hiding up in the hayloft for a bit, but I don't think he's able to say anything."

Giles nodded. He wasn't entirely sure what to do with this. Thankfully, Kate went on. "First, we need something to call you. It's awfully rude to be saying 'boy', isn't it? Can we call you Edward? Michael? Balthazar?" The last one apparently got a reaction, and Kate said cheerfully, "Well, it's a seasonal name, isn't it? But not that. John? Jack? James? Jeremiah? Walter?" Then she paused. "Walter, all right. First thing, are you hungry? Do you need something to drink?"

Giles suspected there was nodding, because Kate reached to take the basket he'd been carrying. "We have some scones here and some tea. Can you drink that from the flask? Here we go." It was not particularly maternal, but it was cheerfully competent. Once the flask was open, she continued. "This is Giles. He's blind, so he can't see you. And because you're not able to talk, at least right now, I'm going to have to tell him about you, and what I notice, all right?"

Giles was rather glad for the forthright explanation, though he could see this was going to be a bit tedious for Kate, translating things both ways. "Pleased to meet you, Walter."

Fortunately, that seemed all right, because Kate said, "So, Walter here looks to be five or six. Brown hair, some freckles. He's wearing good solid clothing, but he looks a bit dirty around the edges. Were you sleeping here last night? He's nodding. Can I go up and look at where you were sleeping? I think we should find you somewhere you can warm up and get clean."

After a moment, Kate said, "Giles, can I leave you together for a minute? I want to go check the loft."

Giles nodded. "You can." He'd certainly hear if the boy moved. He could hear the slight creak of the ropes around the hay bale as he shifted.

"Walter, you keep snacking, and I'll be back in just a jiff." Kate sounded brisk and in control, the way Giles loved best.

CHAPTER 4
THE HOME FARM

Kate had not expected even a minor mystery to fall into her lap. Chances were, the boy had got separated from his family somehow, found the nearest place out of the wind, and was scared. On the other hand, it would give Kate every reason to busy herself doing something useful today. Far more useful than play card games or do whatever other amusements this sort of family got up to. Besides rather cutting gossip, clearly that was a staple. She could give them the gift of gossiping about her in peace.

She glanced over her shoulder before making for the ladder to the loft. Giles was talking quietly, and the boy - Walter - was looking at him with some bafflement. That was fine. Anything that kept him calm and relaxed was a help right now. She climbed up the ladder, glad she'd worn trousers. She didn't fancy risking a run in her stockings against some of the raw bits of wood on this ladder.

At first, she didn't think the loft held anything of note. Everything seemed in order. But something nagged at her. She had planned to do a proper search, as much as she could, anyway, but something drew her over to the corner, to the right of the main door. Someone in a hurry feeding the horses this morning, in the dim winter light, could certainly have missed the way the hay was piled.

There was a little nest there, of a few horse blankets. The hay was stacked high enough in front of it you'd have needed to be quite close to see someone hidden behind it. It would have been warm enough for the night, more or less. She saw nothing terribly personal. This was a night's hideaway, not somewhere the boy had been for days. Or, as far as she could tell, with anyone else.

She was looking around again when she heard Giles call out from below. "Kate? He seems to want to go somewhere."

Kate turned and hurried back down the ladder. They could come back for a more thorough search later. When she got back down on the ground, Walter had Giles's hand, and was tugging toward the door. Giles was still seated, but there was no sense putting him to more difficulty.

"Here, Walter. What do you want?" She kept her voice calm. He looked at her, and then gestured, pointing.

"Is there somewhere you need to go?" He nodded, bobbing his head up and down. "Is it near here?" More nodding, though that seemed a little less certain. "Can you take us?" This time, he looked a little less certain, but then he nodded again.

"All right. Give us a minute, all right? So Giles can come with."

Giles cleared his throat. "I could…"

"I need your knowledge of the area, for one thing." Kate was clear about this. "And as if I'd leave you out of the thing. Here we go, there's my elbow. Walter, you stay close, don't get too far ahead, right? There, he's nodding, about five feet in front."

The boy hesitated when they got back out to the road, looking one way and then the other. Then he turned left, going further away from the house. Giles added, "There isn't too much this way bar the farmer's house, not for a bit. Or I didn't think there was."

Kate considered. "Go on, Walter? We can go this way for a bit."

They got down by the farmer's house, and then Walter started looking around, looking lost. "Walter, hey, love. Did you get turned around? There, he's nodding." She glanced up at Giles, who nodded back. "Walter, how about we go find you somewhere you can get some more food and warm up while we figure out where you came from. Giles? What would you think best?"

"Bring him home. Nanny would be glad of one more. We've plenty of rooms. And... " He gestured. "Plenty of food. We won't be taking from anyone."

"Your parents? Your grandmother. This is not precisely the impression I had intended to make."

"The impression you should make, dear Kate, is that you are an exceptionally competent woman who can take on near any challenge that presents itself. Including them."

Kate snorted. "If you say so. All right, Walter. The food is very good where we're going. And then I can figure out how we find your people."

By the time they go back to the manor, Walter was sagging. They got to the back door, the kitchen door, when Giles said, "Let me."

Kate stepped back and away, pointing things out to Walter in the courtyard, keeping him occupied. There was a moment of conversation, and he turned. "Someone's fetching Nanny."

Kate tugged Walter to sit on a bench, out of the way and settled into a game of "I Spy". Harmless, took nothing more than a little creativity, and it was easy to adjust to children of any age. And with Walter picking the items, he didn't have to do more than nod or shake his head. Within five minutes, an older woman - certainly old enough to have been Giles' nanny, if she'd been young at the time - came out, wearing a sensible dress. "Master Giles, whatever are you doing round this door?"

"We've been having adventures, Nanny." Giles could be exceedingly charming when he wanted to be, and all that charm and joy was coming out now, lighting up his face. "My fiancee, Kate. You'll have to chat with her later. She has all sorts of good ideas about toasting bread in fireplaces. But we found a young boy on our walk this morning, curled up in a stable until he fell out of the loft. He's not able to tell us anything right now, but we thought best to get him somewhere warm and snug while we figure out the next steps."

"Oh. Oh!" Nanny came out. "Well, isn't that a thing? A little boy in a stable. You should have a bath, I'm thinking, and I'm sure we can find some clean clothes that will fit you." She glanced over at Giles. "Sir, if, um, you'll make it all right with the family?"

"That's my next stop. Kate, love? Do we contact the Guard first, or beard my grandmother first?"

Kate considered. "Let me go grab my journal and write. Maybe there's a Guard near here who can be a help. Nanny - um. Is that the proper thing to call you?"

"For someone Master Giles brings home, it is. Elise Fendle, ma'am. I do hope you'll come have a chat sometime while you're here, when the little ones are in bed, or during their rest in the afternoon. Around half one is a good time."

"If I can get away, I'd love that." Kate smiled. "I'm sure you have a fine cuppa."

Nanny beamed. "Just so, ma'am. Master Giles, you can come as well."

Giles laughed, delighted. "Just so. We will leave Walter - that's a name he agreed we could use - with you. And someone will come let you know what's going on as soon as we have an idea ourselves."

Once Nanny had taken Walter off - the boy seemed willing enough to go - Kate said, "My room, so I can write? And we can plan?"

"A fine plan. Your arm, then, dear Kate? If we go through this way, we'll avoid the family until we're ready."

Five minutes later, they were back in Kate's room, and she had written a fairly long note in the journal. Someone in the Guard would be monitoring, and could let her know promptly how to get hold of the nearest of the local Guards. Though there were none terribly near, Kate suspected. The house was rather remote. A good minute after she'd stopped writing, she said, "Why would a boy be alone? Overnight?"

She loved Giles because he knew the difference between when she was thinking out loud, and when she wanted his ideas. Here, she definitely wanted his knowledge of the area. "He got separated from his family, somehow, whoever was taking care of him."

"Someone must have been up there to feed the horses this morning. Why didn't he show himself to them?" Kate settled beside him on the bed, thigh to thigh, and took his hand.

"Fear?" Giles offered it as an option, but without being very committed to it.

"Do you know much about who's around here? Are there travellers?"

Giles frowned at that. "I wouldn't have thought at this time of year. Usually autumn. There's a clearing, further along the road, back in a copse of trees, that they camp in sometimes. I used to watch them training the horses, or, you know, the tinkering. They'd mend pots and pans, that sort of thing."

The chime on her journal went off. "Moment, Giles, love. Let me see what they said." As she read, she grimaced. "The Guard in the nearest village is away for the holiday and there's no one else handy. Can I have a look round and make a full report, they ask. Well. All right."

Giles reached out a hand, and a moment later, she took it, as she always did, squeezing once. "We have solved more challenging problems. The boy is getting food and a warm bath, and he'll be well taken care of. We should see what Grandmama knows. Or more likely, any of the staff, about where we should start asking. And then we can go back to the farm, see if anyone's seen anything, you can do a proper search, and see what we know there."

"There are times when I very much appreciate your logical mind." Kate leaned to kiss his cheek. "And there are times I'm sure the world isn't that simple."

Mistress Lefton was only just up and about, and apparently rather startled that Kate and Giles had already been out. She was not at all pleased to discover an unknown child who did not speak had been dumped on her staff. Giles settled into the chair in the breakfast room, and let her question him.

"You expect my household to feed this boy? For an unknown period of time? He might have a disease. Pests. And it will make more work for the staff."

"Nanny was delighted to see to him. You know she's been bored. And she's perfectly competent with all manner of cleaning methods and charms. The cousins are all well and good, but they're all old enough not to need much care. More some supervision and someone to let them know when it's time for a meal."

Mistress Lefton sniffed unhappily. Giles went on, smoothly. "It turns out there's no Guard able to take over." He glanced at Kate.

"I've been told that the nearest Guardsman is away, and the next one out is ill - ill enough he had to go to Trellech for care. They can get someone out in a day or two, if we don't figure out where Walter's family are by then, but of course it's over the holidays."

Some of the Guard wanted Christmas proper off. Others had been on extended duty for the various events around the Solstice. The Council Keep needed additional security. There were events at the Temple of Healing.

Giles said smoothly. "And of course, you being gracious about it, Grandmama, looks well. Kate's already mentioned that you were kind enough to make sure the poor boy could wash up and get a warm meal."

"Well." It was grudging, but Mistress Lefton finally nodded. "I suppose you need to go and do something, then?" She spoke, for a wonder, directly to Kate.

"Yes, ma'am. I'd like to go look at the barn again, and talk to whoever did the feeding last night and this morning, and then see if we spot anything else."

"We?" That was an arch tone.

"I'll go with her, grandmama. We've done this before."

That earned another sniff. "Be back by tea time, properly washed up and dressed. I won't have you spoiling our holiday with your, your whatever."

Kate bit the inside of her lip and squeezed Giles's hand. After a moment, she managed a polite "Of course not, ma'am." Giles made their farewells, and she guided him out of the room, then out of the house, pausing only to grab their coats and stop by the kitchen door again for some portable refreshments.

It wasn't until they were back down the path that Giles spoke again. "They're going to be awful tonight. You can flee."

Kate snorted. "They were going to be awful, regardless. This gives them something specific to be awful about. And if they choose to be awful about helping a young child, or my doing my duty, that's on them."

Giles relaxed. "You could make an excuse to leave."

"I won't leave you alone with them." Kate turned, pausing for a moment, reaching to touch his cheek with her fingers. "Not now I've seen how they are. Neither of us wants to deal with that alone. Neither of us should need to. United front."

"United." Giles nodded. "What's your plan, then?"

"The barn first, and some investigation charms. I don't suppose you're up for counting for me?"

"Always." He settled his hand more comfortably around her arm. "And then the staff."

"Will they know you? Or are we relying on the family name and my badge?" She'd grabbed it from her room, and her coat was her uniform coat.

"A bit of both, I suspect. Do you want me up in the loft with you?"

Kate hesitated, thinking. "It's a steep ladder." She'd leave it up to him. "And a bit splintery. But once you're up there, there's plenty of space if you don't wander too much."

"Let me give it a try and see how it goes. What do you have on you?"

"My satchel." The one she always kept packed. "Lantern. I'm assuming the charm light, we won't want the oil and matches in a barn."

Giles shuddered. "No. Thank you. Though I'm glad you have them." She'd been careful to cover all her options, ever since she'd been caught without charm light in Mannering House.

Kate continued on, smoothly. "Pocket knife, the good one you got me. A tin with scones and sandwiches from Cook. Two bottles of lemonade and a large flask of tea. My working stones, a notebook and pencil, a coil of strong rope. The usual precautionary tools." Those she kept now in a smart leather kit Giles had got her for her birthday, that kept a proper first aid kit snug and safe. "My journal, in case we do need to summon help. And my usual kit." Several handkerchiefs in varying fabrics, some tweezers, a small set of lockpicks, twine, needle and thread, a flint, and a variety of other handy tools.

"Then we seem reasonably well prepared. Right then, you tell me what you need."

There was still no one in sight when they made it back up to the barn, and nothing seemed to have been moved. She considered. "We can probably assume that anything out of the ordinary here would be noticed, right? Also, I'm not sure what's normal."

"Ask about it when we do that." Giles agreed. "Where's this ladder?"

Kate led him over to it. "Ten rungs, then you're at the top, and clear to go two steps forward from the ladder without running into any trouble. You go first." It was easier for her to give him guidance that way, or lend a hand. He nodded, then tested the stability of the ladder before rummaging for gloves from his pocket to protect his hands.

She'd noticed he preferred to go without them most of the time. It let him get more information from what he touched, but there were definitely times the protection was worth the loss of sensation. He made his way up deftly enough, as she counted out the steps for him, warning him when he was on the last rung. She heard him move forward. They'd practised, over the past year and a half. Now he could take predictable step sizes, and she could use that to help him navigate when she couldn't be there leading.

His family, she was sure, would be outraged. As far as she could tell, they thought he should sit tucked up in a room and only go out under close supervision. She climbed up behind him and found him facing back toward the ladder.

"It smells like a barn." He was amused.

"In other words, all the people who go on about you having better senses because you can't go see can go hang?" she said. "Do you want to sit or do you want to lurk?"

"Oh, sit. Is there a hay bale?" She found him one and got him settled. She'd be a while, most likely. A proper search couldn't be rushed. Once she got him sorted, she set up the charm lantern, and said, "Can you do a steady count?"

She preferred to do this sort of investigation with a structure, casting a charm repeatedly every twenty-five seconds as she slowly moved through the space. His count would help her do it more evenly.

He nodded as she aligned herself with the far right line of the loft. On her mark she cast the first charm and he began counting down from twenty-five. They'd got through to where that nest of blankets was when she thought she saw something glinting. "Hold, please, Giles?"

Giles fell silent, and Kate went over to look at the mussed hay. She thought her eyes must have fooled her for a moment, but then she saw the thing glint again. It wasn't reflecting the charm light, it was something else, but it didn't react to her investigation charm. It didn't react like ordinary magic, anyway.

She was just about to ask Giles about it when she heard steps below, and then a bellowing. "You young bastards come out of here."

Immediately, instinctively, she swooped down, tugging a silk handkerchief out of her toolkit and picked up the object just as a ginger balding head appeared up the ladder. He seemed just as startled to see them as they were to see him.

CHAPTER 5
THE BARN

"What's all this now?" Giles could hear the voice, almost place it, but it had been a long time. He didn't even know where Kate was. This was the kind of thing he found most nerve wracking. Before the War, he'd been quick to adapt to a new situation. Now he had to guess, he couldn't rely on body language. He couldn't move closer or away easily. And at times like this, he had no idea if he was in the midst of an immediate threat.

Thankfully, he knew Kate was there. She had training and experience, and she knew what he needed to know.

"Hello, are you the farmer here?" Kate's voice was clear, and there was a note of something else there. It sounded like her at her best, when whoever she was talking to was more inclined to listen.

"Beg pardon, ma'am." Then he obviously caught the uniform coat. "Are you Guard, ma'am?"

"I am. Are you the farmer?" Giles chortled inside, at how she didn't give anything away.

"We was hearing noises and all." Then he cleared his throat. "Um. Is there a problem, ma'am? Guard?"

"Captain Kate Davies." Kate's voice was crisp now, with all the resonance that meant she wasn't at all nervous. "This is Giles Lefton, my fiancee. We're visiting his family up at the great house for Christmas. He became blind during the War."

Explaining it always made things awkward. Not explaining it, however, made things more awkward.

"Sir. I remember you, sir, when you were here before the War. And they talked about you some."

Giles said, amiably. "A pleasure to be back, largely. We have run into a spot of something interesting, though." His job here was to smooth things along as a representative of the family, no matter how little they might like that.

Kate picked up again smoothly. "We were out for a walk earlier this morning, and we discovered a young boy who'd been hiding in the loft. Over there, where the blankets are. It doesn't look like he disturbed anything, and he'd have been well enough hidden if you fed before the sun was well up."

"You know barns, ma'am? Um. Captain?"

"My parents own an inn, so I did my fair share of time mucking out the stalls and feeding when I was little." Kate was cheerful about it, and Giles hadn't quite realised that it might be something she missed, even if she didn't ride herself. He'd always found that sort of work satisfying, a concrete bit of making order out of chaos, at least for a few hours. It seemed to put the other man at ease.

"Oh." Then he went on. "I'm Wilcox, Ned Wilcox, Captain. We have the farmhouse up the road. One of the lads fed this morning, didn't say anything was out of order. Will you want to speak to him?"

"Please. And anyone else who might know about a

small boy. He wasn't able to speak - perhaps something scared him badly. The boy's with Nanny, at the main house, having a wash and a warm meal. He tumbled out of the hayloft into that empty stall here."

"Ah, that's King. He's out in the paddock early. Good thing, too." There was a hesitation, then a cough. "Thinking you'd best come along with me, if you don't mind? I don't know a boy like that, but my Mum might, she knows everyone in the area."

"That sounds a fine idea. We're sorry to put you out on the holiday, but we'd like to get Walter - that's what we're calling him - back to his people. Why don't you go down the ladder, and Giles and I will follow."

Going down was, as always, a little more tricky than going up. Kate could go first, to tell him when he was down on the last rung. Or she could go second and give him guidance. They did the second this time. It wasn't a long ladder, and sturdy enough. And besides he could feel with his toe when he got to ground level. They managed getting him in through the hole in the floor easily enough, and a minute or two later, he had his hand on her arm. "Lead on."

The walk to the farmhouse didn't take very long, but the wind had picked up a bit, making it chillier than it had been. Then they were being shown into a house of some kind. Giles remembered it, vaguely, from earlier years. Correctly, it turned out, when Kate whispered. "Stone cottage, two stories, shingles on the roof, looks sturdy and well-kept."

The introductions were baffling to him - there were a lot of people, including some younger children moving around. He didn't bother trying to keep people straight. He trusted Kate would sort out a smaller group and then make sure he got their names. It was one of the things he found most frustrating. It was hard to walk into a room with people he didn't know. Dealing with family, like they had last night, was vastly simpler. He knew who was supposed to be there, and he often knew their voices well enough. Once he knew where they were, it was easy.

Or at least it was easy for him. One of his companions at the Refuge had accused him of having a steel-trap mind and bending mathematics for his purposes. It was something rather like a logic problem. Or a geometry problem. Neither were his particular focus, but he'd certainly done plenty of them during his education, and laying things out tidily still came naturally to him.

Five minutes later, someone had taken the children upstairs for a bit, and Kate had explained their purpose in visiting. She turned down any offering except tea, saying they'd have a large meal when they got back, and besides, she didn't want to do them out of any treats. She then accepted a little in the way of gingerbread so as not to be rude.

"So I'm wondering if you know anyone who might be missing him, poor thing." Kate finished up the explanation companionably. Giles had not had much of a chance to hear her at work, not with new people, in the past few months. She had a manner that built confidence, but put people at ease. If she'd been at the front during the War, she'd have made a fine officer. Better than he had, he suspected. She had a rigorous practicality he'd learned too late.

The suggestions came and went in a flurry. Someone would bring up a possible child, then someone else would say that one was too old or too young or too blonde or too obviously freckled.

There was chatter from the others, before one of the older women spoke up. "I'm wondering if it might be that cottage, further out? Where the travellers camp, from time to time."

"You think the boy's one of them?"

That got her a flurry of denials. "There's a woman out there, lives by herself, usually, Mistress Knowle. Her daughter married a traveller, she lets them camp in her field. Not this time of year. No, they come through in May, before the solstice fair. But maybe she'd have a child stay with her, for some reason or another?"

"How far out?"

There was some discussion of that, and then Ned Wilcox coughed. "You know how to drive a pony cart, Captain? If you spent a while in an inn?"

Giles could hear her smile. "I can. If the pony's willing enough."

"We could harness up the cart, give you directions. Spare a lad to go with you?"

Kate hesitated, Giles could hear her weighing the options. "Is it a complicated route?"

"Oh, no. Three miles, maybe four, the lane's marked clearly."

"That's a long way for a boy that age to come on his own." Kate hesitated. "Giles, when do we need to be back for the day, if we're not to insult your grandmother horribly?"

A little bit of insult might actually be a help. His family could use a reminder that Kate - and Giles himself - had duties and responsibilities. He was still sworn to the Guard as a consultant - had duties and responsibilities. "We should be back by four, to wash and change."

"And it's well after one now. It will take us some time to check a couple of the cottages nearest. If we don't find anything, we can go out tomorrow afternoon and go further. How's that? Would that put you out too much, on your Christmas?"

There was discussion back and forth about the best timing, and it was decided that mid-morning would do, if they couldn't figure out where the boy came from before that. Kate nodded. "If I hear back that they're able to get another Guard out here, I'll let you know. Is there a riding horse they could borrow if needed?"

Wilcox was glad to offer a choice of mounts - three, up from one, the year before, and the two draught horses. Giles could ride still, but going through countryside Kate didn't know well was a risk, and he'd rather not. It seemed unfair to the horse, for one thing.

All the arrangements made, Wilcox walked them back out to the lane. He promised that he'd check around in the barn again and see if he found any other clues or suggestions of where the boy had come from.

Once they were down the lane again, following a map he'd sketched out, Kate asked, carefully. "Did he seem very eager to get us out of his barn? Unusually eager?"

Giles contemplated that. "What was his face like when he came up?"

"I don't think he knew about the boy. But he was startled to see us, grown adults. We weren't trying to keep quiet, particularly, either." She stopped. "I don't know enough about how farms work. It looked fairly ordinary to me. Hay and straw."

"It's winter. They won't be fed much grain. That's probably downstairs, protected against the rats." Giles considered. "You didn't see any barrels or crates or anything?"

"You're thinking smugglers. Granted, I was thinking about smugglers too. Though I don't know what would come through here."

"Quite." The land around the estate was steadily worked farmland, enough to sustain folks comfortably, but not the sort of place that usually led to riches or a smuggler's hoard. "And he did bring us into the house. So either he assumed we didn't spot anything out of the ordinary, or thought we wouldn't bring it up with all his kin."

"His mother was sharp as anything. She's the one who mentioned that far cottage." Kate let out a puff of breath. "I wish we could get up there tonight, but I don't see how it's doable. That's far enough that even if I went on my own, I couldn't get there and back again before dark, and that's not a safe thing."

"Not in an area you don't know well, no. I'd worry."

She patted his hand on her arm with his free one. "And you're normally so good about not worrying too much. Even when I come home with terrifying tales."

"I know exactly how fearless you are, Kate, my love. And I also know just how careful and well-trained you are, and how committed you are to keeping in practice. I won't hold you back from that. But I am glad you're not wanting to go ride off into the twilight."

"Besides," Kate said. "It would leave you alone with your family. And I'm fairly sure that's not kind."

Giles snorted. "I'm glad you're not going to." He paused. "And you can't even claim duties somewhere else right now."

"Not unless there's a true emergency and they call everyone in. And it won't get Walter back to his family, and that matters."

They walked along for another twenty steps before Giles asked, "What do you think happened with him?"

"I honestly don't know. There are the fairly benign things, that he got lost, found the nearest safe space. But if that's the case, why didn't he go to the farmhouse itself? It's not far, he must have seen the chimney smoke."

"What was the weather like last night? Or this morning? But no, you thought he was there overnight."

"There was a little nest of blankets, I think so. Horse blankets are convenient for that. And if he'd been around in the morning, around feeding time, sneaking in, someone would have noticed him, right?"

"Probably. Though if they're shorthanded due to the holiday." Giles shook his head. "What are the other possibilities?"

"That he was abandoned here, for some reason. It happens, you know it does."

Giles grimaced. "A family who couldn't feed him, or something happened, leaving him where he'd be found. He didn't look injured or anything?"

Kate grunted. "No blood, no bruises, no signs of having done more than the usual amount of rolling around in dirt your average boy gets up to. I suspect his clothes had been handed down a couple of times, but they were competently patched."

"I appreciate your eye for mending. As should your superior officers." Giles grinned. "That's the sort of thing I had to have carefully explained to me in my day."

"I'm fairly sure if we started talking about the mathematical implications of thread counts, you'd make better sense of it." She snorted, and walked along in silence for a bit before she asked, "Is there folklore around here I ought to know about? Fatae tales or anything of the kind?"

"Nothing terribly close. By which I mean the usual collection of healing wells, random stones in fields some people think mean things, a ghost story or six in most large houses. And there's probably a black dog lurking around somewhere grimly."

Kate laughed at that. "So nothing out of the usual, then."

"Nothing terribly active or threatening, so far as I know. Mind, I'm sure I don't know all the local stories."

"Well. I suppose we check the cottages we can get to now, go back, have a hot bath, and brace ourselves for the evening."

"Duty calls in unexpected directions." Giles kept his voice light, but he was still worried about the strain on Kate.

"I acquired clothing for this sort of thing. I don't think any frock that required four fittings can be described as 'unexpected'."

Giles shook his head, then he flinched, and he didn't catch it quickly enough.

Kate shifted slightly. "What?" Her voice was persistent. That was the way he put it in his head.

"Last night, you didn't catch the comment?" He could never tell what she heard and ignored, or what she had somehow missed, without asking.

"Your brother? I didn't catch what he said. I'm sure it wasn't flattering to one or both of us, and I'm sure you changed the subject. Can't change his mind, it's sensible not to waste your energy."

That made Giles stop short, feeling the tug on Kate's arm, though she stopped immediately as well. "Has he said anything to you? Or Julia? Or any of them?"

"Just the ordinary run-of-the-mill disapproval. Just like as at supper. What did he say to you?" She put more emphasis on it this time.

"That he saw no reason you should be nicely dressed. It wasn't like I could appreciate it." Giles repeated it, flatly. "Which is miles from sense."

Kate hesitated. He knew she had a different relationship with her brothers. For one thing, she had relationships with her brothers. And even with her sister, where things were a bit more tricky. She didn't see them often - all three of the brothers earned their livelihood on the sea one way or another. But they wrote, and he'd met all of them, even her parents and sister. They were loud and chaotic and a bit prone to dropping into a line of music if given an excuse. The food had been excellent, and whatever their other issues with him, the blindness had been awkward for an hour or two, no longer.

"Go on. Say what you're thinking." He had a sense now of how she likely looked. Whenever they hit one of these points, where she thought she was about to be terribly rude, dangerously rude, she got very quiet and still.

"It's - why do they care so much about it? That you're happy? That you're independent from them? That you're not tucked up into a dark room at some care home, out of the way. Or I suppose your family has plenty of attics."

Giles shook his head. "Some people, that's just what happened. They wither away, there's nothing of them left. Or they're at their family's mercy for all the small things. News, or someone to read to them, or new clothes, or whatever they want for their hobbies or interests." He'd heard a few heartbreaking stories from others he knew. The people none of them could save, because they'd been walled in by family who said they were helping, and were doing anything but.

"You might not see the frock, but I know full well you can touch it. The velvet, I know you like the velvet."

"And the silk. I like the sound of you in silk. I can hear right where you are, how you're walking. How you're filling the room."

Kate snorted. "You're ridiculous, Giles, love." She didn't mind, though, that he was.

"And there's absolutely no reason you should not have a wardrobe of fine dresses. Well, besides the fact you wear a uniform nine times out of ten, and you seem to want books about the place rather than multiple wardrobes."

"As you do too, so you don't get to complain." She leaned over to kiss his cheek. "Come on. We'll investigate, go back, wash up, and do our duty."

CHAPTER 6

CHRISTMAS EVE AT SUPPER

Kate felt entirely restricted. In her movement, in her dress, in what she could say. Now that they were well into the Christmas eve supper, she could feel her mind stultifying.

"It is custom here to attend midnight mass in the village church. Will you be joining us, Kate?" That was Mistress Lefton. Kate felt Giles touch her arm. They'd talked through this on the way back this afternoon. And before that.

"Mistress Lefton, I'm afraid I don't know all your customs, but I would be glad to join you." She had known, agreeing to this visit, that she'd miss the plygain service. Not that she'd been able to go for several years, because of her duty assignments, but still.

"Are you Church of England or something else?" That was Julia, her nose rather firmly in the air.

"Chapel, mostly. Is your midnight mass the usual sorts of carols and such, then?"

"What else would there be?" That was Mistress Lefton, sounding baffled.

"There's a tradition among many in Wales, of a service at three in the morning, running, oh, a good two or three hours. The plygain service. There are songs, not the carols common other places, sung in harmony. They tell a story, a sermon, the life of Christ. Groups of three or four men, usually, but some women as well. It's..." Kate let her shoulder shrug, feeling the fabric of the low neckline shift. Well, lower, it wasn't the full collared shirt of her uniform, everything was lower than that. "It's a community event, coming together to make song in the deepest part of the night."

"Hmph. All very secretive." Mistress Lefton sniffed again.

A plygain service was anything but, you could see the lights for miles. At their home chapel, there were torches. At Gran's, up in the mountains, everyone brought their own candle, and there would be a hundred lights ablaze. Kate shrugged minutely. "I am glad to come to your service, of course, and it will be a joy to see how you celebrate."

There was really no way to answer that without being overtly difficult, and so the table subsided into little sharp fragments of conversation. After a few minutes, someone down at the far end of the table asked, almost idly, "You won't be out again tomorrow?"

Giles tapped her foot with his, and said, equally amiably. "We've arranged to borrow the farm's pony cart. We had no luck today, and Kate's sure - as am I - that someone must be frantic to find the boy.'

"It's not proper. interfering with the customs. And you haven't thought at all, Giles, about the implications for the Wilcoxes."

"Oh, we checked with them first, before making the arrangements. We'll be here for breakfast, in the morning, and seeing the little ones with their stockings, and then go out, and be back in time for Christmas supper." The family had it mid-afternoon, which made things easier. Kate suspected it involved a very large goose, and they took time to cook, no matter how much magic might help with parts of it.

Mistress Lefton narrowed her eyes. Kate was finding there were many expressions here they didn't have a quick tactile shorthand to convey. They would need to solve that sometime, really. It wasn't as if they could ignore all of his family forever. Even if it was likely very tempting for both of them.

It made Kate wistful for her own family. She'd felt distant from them all through her apprenticeship. Before that, really, when she'd ended up at Schola unexpectedly. When she'd been a schoolgirl, they'd told her it was about the strength of her magic. It wasn't. Or at least, it wasn't just that.

Captain Edgarton, who had the benefit of having seen all her files back to her earliest tests, had laid it out for her when she'd been promoted. Someone had seen in her a potential. It wasn't fate. No one in the Ministry wanted to admit to trusting to the threads of fate to make decisions. But there was some sign, something intangible, that had suggested she was worth keeping an eye on.

And for the posh families, the ones with power, the Majors and Captains of the Guard, that meant sending her to Schola, and then encouraging her into apprentice-ship. They didn't know how to do it any other way than the old worn pathways they'd followed for centuries.

Kate had left that meeting with Captain Edgarton feeling put out and wronged. People had been making decisions for her for years, without so much as bothering to hint what was going on. He'd done it too, and for a few days, she had wondered if it had broken any trust she had in him. She'd felt herself unmoored, a ship battered by a storm in the harbour, unable to move somewhere safer, tossed and shaken.

Giles had noticed, nearly immediately. She had gone to his house, found her favourite chair in the library. He'd come in an hour later, and before she'd said two words, he had come over to her, as deft as could be. Ten minutes later, he'd got it all out of her, somehow. An hour later, they'd been curled up on the sofa, talking through each piece.

What her choices were. He'd come back to that over and over again. She had been gifted with certain opportunities, without knowing about them. Now, she could choose what she did.

Giles had found it delightful that she had instinctively come home to him. That she had not lost her temper or stormed off. It gave them, he pointed out, many more options. There were all sorts of strategies she could pursue. Each of them could come to her fingers and her lips as smoothly as he counted up sums and made the numbers dance.

She had gone back to work, to Captain Edgarton, resolute. If they thought she might have some use, she would demonstrate it to them. And in the end, she trusted him enough to ask what she should do. That had been far more useful and reassuring. That she had shown early promise, but then they hadn't been sure what to do with her. The War had thrown a wrench in whatever plans they might have had. She had proved her flexibility, her gift for steady understanding, but she hadn't been able to serve overseas.

She let the conversation flow around her until the end of the meal. As everyone began to migrate toward the drawing room, she found her shoulders a bit colder than she wanted. Or perhaps she was just taking any chance for a brief freedom. "Pardon me for just a moment, I want to stop in my room and find a shawl."

Giles turned his cheek to her, and she kissed him. "I'll just be a minute. Do you want to come along with me?"

He suddenly smiled. "Oh, yes." They made their way up to her room, ignoring the various disapproving noises.

"Honestly, you'd think we were sneaking off for other things. Which, for the record, I miss, but somehow have no desire to do under your grandmother's roof." Kate said. "I just - there's something about the neckline of this frock that always makes me feel entirely unarmoured."

"It is a delightful chest, as I have reason to know. But I entirely understand why you might not want it on display. For one thing, it always struck me as rather draughty."

Kate laughed. "Let me find a shawl, and a brooch." She went over to her wardrobe, rummaging to find a delicately knit shawl. The thread was quite fine. Her aunt had spun and knit it herself, but it had charms twisted into the stitches for warmth. It was as cosy as the thickest shawl or sweater Kate had ever worn.

She hesitated at her dressing table. Kate had brought her small selection of jewellery with her, of course, a few brooches and decorative pins for her hair and such. She was wearing her one good necklace, her Guard medallion safely tucked in her jewellery box for the night. Giles spoke while she was still deciding.

"The parlour games will be rather dire, I'm afraid. I suspect they're all going to be referencing things you've not yet had a chance to learn."

She picked up the brooch that seemed to draw her hand, distracted now. "Not yet had a chance to learn? Is that what you think?"

"You soak up knowledge, Kate, you know you do. Like the ground soaks up rain."

"Very poetic tonight. All right. How do we do this thing? I don't mind the midnight mass, not at all. Not my usual, but I haven't had that for a few years."

Giles held out his hand to her, and she quickly finished pinning the brooch in place before she slipped her fingers into his. "Next year, we can go to yours."

"Next year," Kate said, "Will be our first year as a married couple, and we can establish our own customs."

"We could, indeed. But they could include going to the plygain, if you wanted. There are portals and such."

She stood on her toes to kiss his cheek, then his lips, more tenderly. "There are. That's a problem for later."

"Now is for going downstairs and facing their general disgruntlement at our contentment." Giles agreed. "I will make this up to you, Kate."

Kate brought his hand to her lips. "This is temporary. By the end of the week, we'll be back snug in your house, and regular routine. Well, as regular as we get."

He laughed. "Which is how we like it, yes. Always a bit of a change."

Kate shook her head. "You're going to get going on permutations of the universe again, I know you. We'll be here all night if you do, and they'll be thinking all the wrong things. Come on."

When they got downstairs again, everyone was settled in, and Ambrose looked up. "We're just finishing a game of Consequences." He then looked abashed. "Pardon, we'll need to swap over to something else, won't we?" Since it involved writing a sentence, folding the paper, and passing it along, it was not a game Giles could play by himself anymore. Not unless he played with people who read braille.

Giles shrugged. "We could pair up, if people liked. Or play something else. Don't let me spoil the fun." His voice was even and relaxed. Kate knew perfectly well he hadn't found such things entirely amusing when he could see. He'd much rather have a mathematical game, a chess puzzle to sort out, or something of the kind.

Mistress Lefton said, a bit sharply. "Penultimate line, everyone. And the consequence, then your answer. Fold it and pass it along."

Kate amiably passed a piece of paper across from Ambrose to his mother, and then they did the last line, "And the world said." Everyone scribbled, more or less dutifully.

Then, of course, everyone had to read them. The first couple didn't particularly catch Kate's ear. They had been perfectly adequate, but not unusually amusing. Then, fourth or fifth, something stood out. She couldn't tell what.

"Joyful Edmund met honest Susan at the start of the path to talk. He wore a bright purple frock coat. She wore a deep black cloak. He bowed and carried on. She hid what was most precious. And the consequence was that a child was reborn. And the world said Noel."

It seemed a trick of her ears, at first, and she hesitated. "Pardon. Could you read that again?" She kept her voice mild, expecting there would be a complaint. Instead, rather her to her surprise, Delphina read it again, leaning over her husband's arm. Kate listened fiercely now. She'd thought she must have misheard something. That 'reborn', for one. But no, each word was as she'd heard it the first time.

"Thank you." She did her best to make her voice as warm as possible.

"Do you need anything else?" This time, she felt Giles's hand close on her arm for a moment. He'd heard something, too. She wasn't sure whether to read the tone as honestly helpful, or as the edged, cutting response to Kate overstepping some invisible line.

"Oh, no, thank you." Again, she made her voice easy, using all the tricks she'd been taught to put someone at ease. "It makes an unusually compelling story, doesn't it? Not all of them do. Please, do go on."

Delphina read the rest of them, and those were again more mediocre. Kate, though, couldn't stop thinking about the images of that one version. It was as if she could see the start of the path, a man in a bright purple coat, a woman in a black cloak. She let them talk on until she heard Ambrose clear his voice. "We should play something Cousin Giles can play."

There was a silence, a waiting sort of silence. Giles said, comfortably. "I don't mind. But while you're thinking of something else, how about, hmm. The parson's cat is an elegant cat."

"The parson's cat is an elevated cat." That was from Lucretia, clearly familiar with cats.

"The parson's cat is an emerald cat." Sentences continued around the circle of chairs. The family were, it turned out, rather good at this. There was a round of words beginning with e going round the room a dozen times before Tiberius finally faltered, and then picked up with "The parson's cat is a fastidious cat."

Somehow, the rhythm, the quickness of it, helped settle everyone down. When they took a pause - they'd hit Q, a letter that was a challenge even for people with extensive vocabularies, Mistress Lefton waved a hand. "Enough for now, enough for now. More tea." It was an order, not an offer, and Lucretia got up to pour.

Kate hesitated for a moment, but she could feel the small tug of something complex just below her breastbone.

"Mistress Lefton, I'm always curious about family traditions. Not just the family magics, though of course those are also fascinating. The various ways they come out. Giles and I had to do quite a lot of research, for the Mannering House investigation, of course. But I'd love to hear more about the family history, the traditions."

"Oh. Oh!" That was a rather pleased sound, more than Kate had expected. Mistress Lefton accepted the cup of tea her daughter offered, and then settled back in her chair. "Well, of course, you have realised we are quite an old family in these parts and in Albion. Back to the Romans."

Kate nodded. "I work closely with Captain Edgarton. He and his wife have a similar family background. They've been kind enough to invite me to their home." She didn't mean to name drop, not exactly. She always found it rather awkward. In this case, however, it had a greater impact than she expected.

Delphinia spoke up, "I've had so little time to talk to Lady Edgarton, but she's always seemed so kind. She makes it to very few of the larger social events. It's always quite a victory to get her to accept one's invitations. And you know her well?"

Kate kept from snorting. Lady Alysoun made it to relatively few events because of particular health issues. And because she refused to spend her energy on things she found entirely tedious, with no larger benefit. She and Captain Edgarton threw their own parties. Well, Lord Edgarton, in that context. The man juggled a half-dozen roles with apparent ease. At any rate, Kate was now cheerfully invited, and Giles as well. Interesting people with creative ideas about conversation, as a rule. And a few other gatherings, to meet their necessary social obligations.

Kate wasn't invited to those. The Edgartons saw no point in boring their friends.

"I've had the pleasure." Kate said. "Though it's Giles who is responsible for more of the social invitations."

Giles picked up smoothly, "I've known the Edgartons since before the War, some of the Guard consulting I did right after university."

Something in the topic, perhaps, opened things up. They followed along with a good ten minutes, amiable minutes, about various social events. Kate and Giles had been to several of the Temple of Healing garden parties that past summer, and that had produced some interesting conversational gossip. And they were invited to a ball in early January, assuming that Kate did not have an urgent case to handle.

Much to her surprise, Mistress Lefton softened enough to inquire about her work.

"I'd hate to bore anyone." Kate said, promptly. But instead of the polite demurrals she expected, everyone actually sounded interested. She squeezed Giles's hand and then chose her words carefully. "I'm sure you know I met Giles while assisting in the investigation of Mannering House. It had gone missing for several hundred years."

"Gone missing?" That was Elisabeta. "How does a house go missing?"

"It turns out that - we think during the Midsummer Faire in 1485 or so - the owner did a ritual to call the Fatae back. This would have been not long after the Pact. It didn't work. Or rather, it did something very odd. He died, and the house was, near as we can tell, not fully in this world, and not fully anywhere else. It was like that for a long time, until the last gasp of the ritual materials gave out."

There were gasps all round, and then Lucretia asked, "How on earth do you investigate something like that?"

"Very carefully." Kate grinned. It had been quite a process. "We got locked in the house, initially, and had to find our way out." That led her off into a handful of stories about the various portions of the investigation. Giles chimed in, and within five minutes, everyone was laughing, in a cheerful mood that lasted through their return from church.

She was left with a faint sense of something odd that she could not pin down. But if the world were going to be odd, better cheerful than otherwise, really.

CHAPTER 7
GILES'S ROOM

As the party made their way back from the church, Giles murmured in Kate's ear. "Walk me up?"

Kate patted his hand, and when the various couples and families separated in the foyer, she simply walked him upstairs without comment. That part surprised Giles.

The whole tone of the evening, after supper, was puzzling him. Something had changed, as if all the even numbers had turned odd, while he wasn't paying attention. He'd expected his family to keep picking at her, at them, all evening. There might be a brief lull in hostilities for the actual service itself, but he'd expected it to pick up again afterwards.

It hadn't. And he knew his family, enjoyed a number of them well enough individually, even if as a group they could be a muchness. Something was odd. He couldn't decide whether to figure out what, or let it be.

Kate got the door, nudging it open, then saying, "Should I let you be?"

"Come in, please." Giles turned back to her as soon as he was alongside the bed. "Stay a bit?"

"Won't they notice? And I do need sleep." She sounded wistful, though, and it wasn't as though she left.

Giles snorted. "I am turning into an awful influence. I know you've a potion in your trunk for wakefulness, if you need it. And I know you hate them, and sensibly so." They were not at all good for the system. Borrowing energy from yourself had an unpleasant downhill slide in the aftermath.

"I do have one. I don't want to take it, it feels particularly awful in the winter. And honestly, I don't think it puts me in the best mood to be driving an unfamiliar horse and pony cart. Be kind to our four-footed friends and all that." Kate hadn't moved, though.

"Come sit for a bit, at least. Where I can kiss you. There has been a lack of kissing. Even with all the mistletoe that's about the place, I'm sure."

"Your relatives aren't much for kissing, I've noticed. Where did you pick up the taste for it?"

"With you, Kate love. With you." He waved a hand. He'd had a number of delightful evenings and following mornings with various women before the War, but it had been a matter of mutual pleasure, not mutual affection. There was, as he had found out, quite a difference.

They had tended to be professional women, their magic coiled around them. Kate was just as professional, just as committed to her work, but her magic felt more like a guard dog. A well-trained one, the sort who curled up at your feet until called upon. Fur and a bit of a snore and the warm weight.

Giles undressed quickly, holding out his hand twice to make sure the cufflinks got back to their proper place. Each time he felt Kate's fingers brush his, then the little heavy clink of them going into their proper box. The magnetic closure would keep the lid in place. He could do it himself, but he found the cufflinks the most fiddly of his required clothing by a long shot.

"You must have kissed other people. You were quite good at it."

"A few. None like you." Giles waited for her to brush his arm with her fingers, before he worked on undoing his jacket, then his shirt. He wanted nothing more than to curl up in bed with her, the way they would at home, all warm and nestling into the feathers of the bed and blankets. Giles turned, then his fingers brushed across her shoulder as she moved, and he felt something different under his fingers.

It wasn't anything so obvious as a spark of magic, the kind that nipped at his skin, but it had a gravity to it. "Kate, love?" He kept his voice quiet.

She noticed his change in focus. She so reliably did. "Yes?" A little hint of uncertainty.

"What brooch are you wearing?"

There was a sudden silence, the kind where she didn't even breathe. She was still long enough for Giles to feel his heart beat a half-dozen times. When she spoke again, her voice had a different sound to it, a hollowness. "I - I don't know. Or I do know. It's complicated."

"Come sit down." He knew that sound, when a dozen past decisions had come shattering through your mind. When you realised that the next thing you did might be your salvation or your death. He'd heard her make it a handful of times, in the investigation of Mannering House. Twice, since, when she was retelling some series of events in her work. Hearing the moment when she realised some-thing had been far more dangerous than she'd allowed herself to know at the time.

It took them a minute to arrange themselves. Giles

settled with his back braced on pillows up against the head-board, with Kate kicking off her shoes and settling in beside him. He figured out where her hand was, and slipped his fingers into hers, leaving her right hand free. "Tell me about it. What is it like? Don't touch it yet, mm?"

Kate let out a breath. "I - I shouldn't be wearing it, right?"

"Tell me about it." He was sure she was tangling up inside her head, and he wouldn't let her do that alone if he could help it. "Start at the top, work around like a clock, if there isn't something better."

She snorted. "Do you have a silk handkerchief? It would be easier."

Giles considered. On one hand, if it were pinned on her clothing, they both knew where it was. If she took it off, that was less likely. On the other hand, it meant she was wearing it. If it was what he was beginning to suspect, wearing it was a particular kind of magical act. The kind of thing that properly needed a whole new verb voice to make clear.

"Can you take the shawl off over your head without touching the brooch? And then set it in your lap so I can't touch the brooch by accident?"

"I think so." Kate shifted away from him, carefully. He could feel the shift of the air as the fabric moved, and the faint inescapable whiff of lanolin from the wool of the shawl. "It's circular and made of silver, with small stones. Seven of them, though there are eight points on the wheel. The gap is where the brooch pin loops around."

"A penannular style, then? Can you give me a sense of the stones?"

"Penannular, yes. The tongue is like my guard brooch, with the formal uniform, just this is a full circle with the open gap at the end." She considered. "I can't tell entirely with it in my lap, but they do look rather like the Fatae stones. Or at least a set of them."

"For all that inaccuracy." Certain sources had the tendency to assume that each of the Fatae lines had a single stone associated with it. The reality was much more like the stones used for various pendants of rank and training. Half a dozen stones of a suitable colour might be used, depending on what was available at the time and the individual quality and personal preference. "Cabochon?"

"That's the smooth round carving, instead of faceting, right?" Kate, to be fair, had not had overmuch familiarity with gemstones before Mannering House.

"Exactly."

"I think they match up. I'd want to look in better light, and with a magnifying glass."

"Set in silver, you said. Flat, hammered, shaped, something else?"

Kate hesitated. "Round. I can't tell without handling it more. Like a thick wire that had been flattened for the stones, and shaped. It's rather smooth, though. I'd think it was moulded, only that's wrong."

"Lost-wax casting." Giles murmured it to himself, but the silence from Kate meant he'd spoken a little louder. When he realised, he spoke up. "You make a shape from wax or soft clay, and then form a mould around it. You remove the original and then use that to cast the metal. Quite effective, especially if you want to make multiple pieces that are similar. Here, you'd set the gems later."

"You know what it is." Kate's voice had an edge to it, the little burr of her childhood accent.

"I think so. It would take testing. If I'm right, you'll need to visit the Guard Hall promptly."

There was a slight crack in her voice. "Is it dangerous? To you? To me?"

Trust her to think of him first. He did the same with her. "Not exactly. You're not touching it now?"

She must have shaken her head, and then caught the movement. "No. It's in my lap. Should I move it?"

"If you can avoid touching it, put it somewhere else on the bed, where we won't touch it accidentally. Actually, no. The desk, that would be good."

She made a series of movements - putting the shawl far enough away on the bed she could move, then getting out. He heard the small noise of her feet on the carpet, the shift of the desk chair, and then she came back, settling in beside him. "Tell me what it is, please."

"I can't tell without testing. But have you ever heard of a Pleasing Token?"

He felt her reaction, before he heard anything. She went still against his arm again. Then she was shaking her head, making her shoulder twitch where she was leaning against his shoulder. "It can't be."

"It fits the description. And the effect." He spread out his hands. "You can't deny that my family were entirely pleasant to you, after you put it on."

"They're incredibly rare. I've never even seen one. I mean, I know there are some."

"Two in the Guard currently. One held by one of the Council. I've heard of three more in the hands of Lords. No, two Lords, one Lady. There are rumours of a few others. No one's ever heard of more than eight or nine at once."

"It's a myth. And it's against the Pact, surely." She pulled her feet up closer on the bed, as if being too near it, on the desk, was too much. "But having eight or nine makes no sense. Either there should be none, or, I don't know. Dozens?"

Giles laughed and shifted to get his arm better around

her waist. "To make it worse, they sometimes disappear. Fairly often when the holder dies, it will just vanish."

"Now, Giles, you are pulling my leg. You must be."

"You can go do the research when we get back to Trellech." He leaned back a bit. "Though there are some other things you need to do. Before the research." He could feel her shoulder hitch again. "You must have questions."

"I'd like answers." Her voice had gone tight, and he squeezed with his arm, gently. He'd handled that badly. Kate was tremendous, competent, gifted, but she could get prickly when she felt uncertain. Or something made her feel stupid.

"Let me explain what I know. Bear with me, all right? I'm dredging up things from a protocol briefing I read a decade ago."

"This leaves the question of why you were reading such a thing." Her voice went softer. At least a touch.

Giles snorted. "You remember, I told you about that cryptography analysis that led to a number of foreign visitors and all those interviews? The local party was someone who had a Pleasing Token. We had to figure out how to work around it so as not to alter either the truth magics, or insult the foreign dignitaries. And we were already having an awful time with translations."

"Which languages?"

"French and German were easy, but there was someone who insisted on Schweizerdeutsch, and someone else who wanted Luxembourgish. Which was not the simple thing to manage."

That made her snort with amusement. "No. A linguist, or something of the kind?"

"One of the Scali men for the Schweizerdeutsch. And they managed to track down an art historian who had also done a fair bit of translation work while living in Luxembourg for the other. The dignitaries were rather put out, actually, which just made us sure something was up. Solved without the Token, thankfully, or we might have had an international incident on our hands." He considered. "More than the one we had."

Kate had settled again. "Fair enough." She let out a long breath. "Tell me about these things, please."

"Of course." He'd been about to. "They're considered to be a gift to the worthy. There are concerns about abuse, of course, but the people who are given them are the last people who'd abuse them. That is, they think, why there's often a couple in the Guard. Your sworn oaths limit an abuse of power. There's a double layer of protection there. The people who have them tend to be the people least likely to make a demand, except to save a life or right a necessary wrong."

"I don't see myself like that." She stopped, then, with an impatient, frustrated sound, and Giles waited, just holding her. After a long silence, where he could feel her hand clench and release against his leg, she spoke again. "Not like some noble knight."

"No, that's the man you work for." Richard, honestly, was the model of a modern knight. Giles had wondered, more than once, what he'd have been like without Lady Alysoun's influence, if he'd have ended up honourable but remote from the world.

Again, it made Kate snort with amusement. "Fair. Why me, though? I'm nothing special."

"Where did you find it? Sometime today, surely?"

"When Wilcox surprised us in the barn. I'd just seen it. Something made me pick it up. It was on the floor, just lying there. I caught a glint of the metal."

"So it's possible it was up there when Walter was. Or that he knows it. But - I suspect not. The lore has it that they show up when only the person they wish will see. And I certainly wasn't going to spot anything, shining or not, on the floor of a dim hayloft." He had a little remaining vision in his left eye on a good day with clear lighting, not too bright. And frankly, it had not been a very good day for that, even without the hayloft.

Kate caught some note of that and shifted to take his hand. "You had been counting, and I - I picked it up. In a silk handkerchief from my kit, I wasn't foolish."

"If the token wanted you to have it, it might have nudged a little. What did you do then?"

"It was in my bag, when we came back, and I put it on the dresser before supper, off to one side, after Istan was done with my hair. I - I must have picked it up when I came to get the shawl." She made another frustrated noise. "And now, what will your family think of me?"

"Were you thinking anything in particular? You know what it's like to feed your magic to something. Did it feel like that? Anything else you noticed?"

Kate shrugged her shoulder slightly. "I could feel the weight of it." He could hear her working through it. "A pleasant sort of weight, like a warm blanket, a proper wool duvet. Comforting. But it didn't feel like feeding a stove or a keep-cold box, or anything like that. You're right that I've done that often enough."

There, now she was thinking smoothly again, she'd sort everything out herself. "They've been around a long time, just so rare it's difficult to study. They don't work for other people."

"They don't?" Kate shifted, leaning a bit more against him.

"I know people have tried. I don't recall the details. You could hand it to me, and it wouldn't do a thing." Giles considered the next part, how to put it the way he wanted.

"You'll need to report it promptly. There's a process for filing them."

"So I shouldn't wear it. I should pack it away safely until we get back to Trellech?"

"I didn't say that." Giles snorted. "Ask whoever's on duty, who's ranking. They'll advise. There are some concerns about giving insult, the idea you might be refusing the gift. Go write them tonight, see if you have an answer in the morning."

Kate wriggled against him. "I'm not sure I like the sound of that. Feeling like I need to. What does it do, anyway?"

"It makes people more interested in doing what pleases you. So long as what pleases you is in their interest. It wouldn't stop someone bound to attack you from doing so. It's not that strong? There's an awful story about an attack in the Civil War. Don't rely on it." Despite himself, he could hear his voice crack.

Kate took his hands in hers, twisting. "I won't. I promise you. Giles, it's an honour I'm not sure how to carry, but I will do right by it, as much as I can. But I won't..." She took the sort of breath that always made him imagine she was squaring her shoulders to face a challenge head on. "I won't trust it to save me. That's denying my skills."

"There you go, that's sensible. And if you do wear it, and it makes my family less awful, well. That's a kindness in the world, isn't it? And it's not hurting anyone."

There was another snort. "Your ethics are a tad flexible, Giles, love."

"In this case, I feel I have more than given them every possible chance. Them being catty and unpleasant isn't doing any good for anyone, including them."

Kate tapped his hand. "Let me think about it. That is a

temptation, mind, and I'm not sure what I think about temptations. In the meantime, I must go write to see what I am supposed to do about this complicated and legendary magical item that's come into my possession. I have no idea what they're going to think about letting me go off for the holidays ever again at this rate."

"We could hire ourselves out to find lost magical relics every seasonal celebration? It would certainly be interesting. And we've done rather well, so far, with the oddly magical."

"Or the magically odd." She got off the bed, coming around to his side after gathering her things from the desk. Carefully, he presumed. She leaned to kiss him. "Sweet dreams, Giles, love. I'll be up a bit yet."

"May it go smoothly."

CHAPTER 8
CHRISTMAS MORNING, IN A PONY CART

"You know where we're going?" Giles was settled beside her in the cart. She had expected a pony cart, with a bench and open sides. Instead, she had found a governess cart, meant to be driven from inside the wicker-work basket of the cart itself. Kate had been dubious about it. As anyone sensible would be about a cart where you had to sit diagonally at the back to one side, the reins in your hands.

However, it meant that Giles could sit comfortably facing her. They could tuck two baskets with various supplies and Kate's satchel of working tools in the front of the cart, tidily out of the way. The weather was surprisingly promising, clear and bright by mid-morning. They were still in a long period of drought, so she hadn't exactly been expecting rain, but it did mean they were less likely to bog down on the road.

"I have a map. I have reviewed the map five times. Also, it really is basically following the road until we get to a couple of landmarks, then turn right. We might need to leave the pony at that point, but it won't be a long walk."

Milo was barely a pony, a Welsh cob, she thought, a deep and rather showy bay. More even-tempered than the dapple-grey mare she'd first met in the barn. Milo meant they could take the much more manageable governess cart, rather than a larger cart with one of the draught horses. Privately, Kate also thought they'd earned their holiday. They'd apparently been in heavy demand on loan to bring extra wood to the larger houses along the main road. And to help cart food and guests for the festivities as well, for the better part of the week.

"Walk on, Milo." Kate clucked, and the cob stepped out neatly. She kept him to a walk until they were on the main road, with a much smoother surface. Once they were going straight, she raised the pitch of her voice again. "Trot up, trot up." The pony picked up steadily, and soon they were moving well along. Kate had checked with Wilcox, and he thought they could make distance easily inside an hour.

It turned out to be forty-five minutes to the first major landmark, even with giving Milo regular breaks to walk. They passed no one else on the road. Giles rode along largely in silence, though Kate thought he might be enjoying the breeze. She'd not asked how much time he spent in the surrounding countryside as a boy, but she was beginning to suspect he'd roamed freely.

"It feels good to be outside for a bit. And it's not too cold. You said you know where we're going? Did you come out this way a lot? There's no other noticeable lanes or roads turning off, though."

Giles snorted as she pulled Milo back to a walk to give him a bit of a rest. "Nanny didn't do outdoors, other than the garden. But I'd go off for a ride with one of the grooms when I was here. He didn't much care how far we went. It was a break for him, both from other work, and a chance to be on a horse instead of at their feet. So we'd both go have a grand time. Grandfather was alive, and he was Master of the Hunt at the time. When I was fifteen, I got to ride out with them."

Kate considered what to say, and as he so often did, he heard what she wasn't committing to. "Foxes are pests for farmers, remember. And it was rare we actually caught one. Clever foxes in these parts, I think."

"Did you wear, what are they called, pinks?"

Giles laughed. "Oh, no. Too young and inexperienced for that. Grandfather ruled with an iron fist. And I didn't keep it up when I was at University, of course, and he died right around when I finished. If I'd ended up living in the country, I'd have earned my pinks, I suppose. There's a lot of work that goes into the whole thing, and a lot of standing around having conversations with people. I preferred my maths. And then the cryptography, of course."

"Of course." Kate laughed. "Right. We're maybe fifteen minutes out. We have a plan. Any changes?"

"Not until we get the lay of the land, which we can't do until we get there."

"Right. Trot up, Milo, trot up."

Finally, she saw the points she'd been told to look for. There was a particular sign on the road, a pile of stones that had apparently been there five years, and then a lane turning right, to the north. She steered Milo up onto the narrower road, letting him slow and pick his way along. They made it all the way up to a small cottage before she pulled him up and found a tree to fasten him to, then came to collect Giles.

"There's a cottage, I don't see - no, there's a little curl of smoke, but not much of a fire. There doesn't seem to be anyone around, no footprints, no signs of trouble."

"Do you want to go on yourself, without me?"

Kate hesitated. It would be simpler, certainly. And if there was someone inside who meant harm, much easier for her to handle it without being concerned about telling Giles the critical information. "You stay here, to the side. I'll call you in, the usual method, if it's safe."

"Also." Giles sounded amused. "It allows you to be friendly and competent. That often goes over well."

Kate shook her head. "You have some bias. Right, here I go." She walked up to the cottage door and knocked solidly. "Mistress Knowle?"

She heard a faint noise inside. "Mistress Knowle?"

The noise repeated, but did not become more coherent. Kate didn't think whoever it was sounded upset or angry, so she called out "I'm a Captain in the Guard. I will come in on a count of ten." It was a risk, giving that much warning, but the noises she could hear did not sound threatening. Worrisome, rather.

She opened the door, the hinges squeaking, and found a cottage. It was a simple workman's cottage, one up, one down, that she'd seen dozens of times before. The main room here was kitchen, working space, and the centre of the house. There was a nook for a bed and a steep staircase up one side to a sleeping area and perhaps storage under the roof.

What she found was an elderly woman, curled up in a mess of blankets, by the remains of a smouldering fire in the hearth. There was no wood left in the bin to the side, nor coal, and the temperature in the cottage was already on the cooler side. "Mistress Knowles." Kate came around and went down on one knee. "May I be of help?"

The woman blinked at her. There were more than a few hints of ongoing pain there - her pupils were black, barely rimmed by a pale blue. "A Guard." Her voice cracked, and Kate saw there was a bucket of water, now empty.

"Are you hurt, Mistress?" She kept her voice even.

Mistress Knowle - or at least Kate had to assume that's who it was - nodded. She gestured again towards something beyond the hearth.

"Water?" Kate asked, and got another nod, more urgently.

"I'll be right back." She went and found a large ceramic crock, checked that it was clean, and went to look for whether there was a pump or a well. Kate found a pump outside to the back, and filled the crock, then found a mug as well, bringing them both back inside. She filled the mug and bent to hand it down. "Drink it a little at a time if you've been without. Let me tell my partner what's going on, and then I'll see about getting things sorted."

The woman nodded, and Kate decided disappearing for a minute was safe enough. She came back out, walking over to Giles rather than calling across the yard. "I believe I've found Mistress Knowles, but it looks like she was injured. The fire's near burned out, she ran out of water. I'm letting her have a mug of clean water in peace before I ask her a lot of questions. Are you all right waiting out here with Milo for a little? Twenty minutes, maybe, until I know enough to figure out who we're getting out here?"

"Guide me back to the cart so I can sit, and I'll be fine. You said you'd packed a blanket. If it's more than twenty minutes, come fetch me?"

"I'll come fetch you sooner if she's comfortable." Kate blew out a breath. "Right." She was sorting out all the many things that would need to be done, now that she had some idea which path they were going down.

Giles reached out a hand toward her, and she took it. "Step at a time. Get me back to the cart, and I'll be fine."

She nodded, tucked his hand under her arm, and made sure he was settled in the cart. He pulled his braille slate and stylus out from the basket, and settled in. "I'll write a letter while I wait. I've been meaning to write to Boffin."

Kate rolled her eyes. "You and your nicknames. Right. Back in a few, yell if you get too cold."

When she came back into the cottage she knocked once. This time she got a louder response. She found Mistress Knowle more upright, leaning against a table leg, the mug loose in her hands. She seemed to have gathered up some sense of dignity, but Kate settled right down on the floor. "May I ask you some questions now, so we can get some help?"

"My grandson." Then she added, "Call me Ada, please."

"A boy, five or six years old, dark hair? Freckles? Sturdily dressed, he had a dark green shirt and a brown jacket?"

"My grandson. Walter."

Kate laughed, almost despite herself, settling down to find Ada looking at her, baffled. "We've found him." Kate said, promptly. "He's safe and sound and being taken care of. Can I ask what happened to you, first, so we can see about getting some help?"

Ada let out a sigh of relief, setting the mug beside her. "I was so worried, he's young."

"He was very brave. He really is safe. What happened?" She hated to press, and it was unlikely there was some urgent medical need at this late point, but you could never be entirely sure.

"I fell. Heard my ankle go." Kate could fill in the sound, all too easily. She'd been around for a number of training injuries and otherwise. "And then I couldn't get up, even with the chair. Got him to pull some bedding for me, leave me some water, told him where to go. But then he was gone, and didn't come back, and the fire...." Her voice trailed off.

"When's the last you ate?"

"Yesterday. There should be..." She grimaced.

"May I look for some food? And was it the ankle, just that? You didn't hit your head, or bump your ribs? Any trouble breathing?"

Ada shifted a little, peering at Kate. "You know what questions to ask."

"I do. They train us, so when we come across someone hurt, we can make sure we get the most useful bits to the Healers right away. I'm going to see about some food for you, how's that. Just a bit to keep you going, and then I'll write to the Healers."

Ada grimaced. "I'm not anyone. They won't approve."

"You're one of Albion. It might be Christmas, but we'll be getting someone out here. On horseback, so they can make good time from the portal. That's what they're there for. And then we'll see about getting you and Walter in the same place. He was scared, he's been quiet, not talking. But I suggested a whole set of names to him, and he picked Walter out of the list."

Ada nodded, and Kate got up to rummage for some rolls and cheese or something of the kind. She found a soft farm cheese, and rolls, and a bit of butter. The fat would be a goodness, but the milk had gone sour in the last day. She found a plate and brought them back down to the floor. She was about to settle down again, when Ada said, "You have a partner?"

This was delicate. "My fiancé, Giles. He's a consultant with the Guard."

"Why didn't he come in with you?" Well, that was blunt, but it at least made it easier to explain.

"He was blinded in the War. A new place, where someone might not want you around, that's more of a risk for him. He's out with the pony cart. I'd think about getting you out to that. But I'm thinking we don't want to be jogging your ankle on the ruts on the road without a Healer's approval, do we? So."

"Go fetch the man. There's some wood out back, if you, though." She swallowed.

"I can do a warming charm. Give me a minute. Safer than building up the fire if we might take you away with us for a bit. Do you have a cow or chickens or anything else that needs feeding?"

"Chickens, penned, out back, they should be fine if the water's not froze over."

Kate nodded. "Let me go see about that, and bring Giles along, then we can make you warmer, and get a Healer out." She waited a moment, but when there was no further response, she went out the back, found the chickens reasonably happy and secure, and came around to the pony cart. "You're welcome to come inside. We'll be a bit, I want to get a Healer out. Actually, let me go back down to the road, leave a sign to mark the lane. Can I have your handkerchief?"

The one he was wearing at the moment in his pocket was a bright red, it would stand out well. He handed it over and she pulled out her pocket knife, cutting it into three strips and knotting them together to make one long piece. "Back in a minute."

She trotted down the lane, finding a branch to tie the red fabric round, and cutting a symbol into the bark of the tree for good measure, a healing blessing.

Once she was back, Giles had put away his stylus and was tucking the page he'd been working on back into his bag. "What happened?"

"Slipped, broke her ankle. I don't think there's anything worse. She's making sense, breathing normally, her eyes are fine. There's some pain, but nothing that suggests a head injury. But they're so remote here. She sent Walter - and that is his name, so good work us - off for help, I think. Her grandson."

"And my role here is to back you up and make charming conversation about the local area until we get a Healer, then. All right. There's space for me out of the way?"

"There's a proper table and chairs, I was going to say." They sorted that out, fairly promptly, and a minute or three later, Kate was settling Giles in a chair, facing Ada. "Ada, this is my fiance Giles Lefton. His grandmother's in the manor house, about four miles down the road? Walter ended up at their home farm."

Ada swallowed, and Kate could read all the signs of someone who was sure there was going to be trouble. Giles said, his voice pleasant. "I knew your cottage was up here. I remember the travellers visiting in the summers when I was younger."

"My youngest." Ada sounded bemused. "Walter's her child. She's expecting again, and I said I'd keep him for the winter, so they had less work with him underfoot and another babe on the way. And to be honest, he's been grand to have around. But sir, I didn't mean to make a fuss, or - your family, sir."

Giles waved a hand. "I am quite clear that coming between Kate and her duty will end badly for anyone who tries, not that I want to. And you're not precisely a tenant, if I remember the bounds correctly, but you're near enough. A season of charity, certainly." He leaned forward conspiratorially. "Besides, you're saving us both from some rather tedious parlour games."

"Or gossip. Now we're here, they can gossip about us. Better all round." Kate could tell her cue. "Now, if I can ask some questions, we'll see about writing for a Healer and see what they say."

It turned out, as Kate worked her way through the various questions, that Ada was not suffering from other injuries. She was feeling better now she'd had some food, though Kate rather wanted to get something warm into her. Ten minutes later, she looked up from her journal, after getting a reasonably prompt response to her inquiry.

"They're sending someone off to the portal shortly, and it should be," She rummaged for her pocket watch. "About half-past twelve, maybe nearer one. We are under a strong request to be back for Christmas dinner, but making sure you're sorted comes first."

Giles said calmly, "If they say you can come in the cart, we can bring you back along for food and to see Walter."

"You said he hadn't talked?" Now that the most urgent needs were tended, Ada was fretting over that.

"He'd hidden up in the barn on the home farm, up in the loft with the hay. Nice and snug in some blankets over the night, but I suspect something might have scared him. He didn't say anything to me, but we turned him over to Giles' old nanny. There are some other children there, and I know he had a bath and a good, solid meal last night, and more today. Not the easiest of Christmases, but we'll get you back safe together as soon as we can."

That left Kate time - more than enough time - to work on tidying the place up, in case Ada needed to be gone for a few days. She asked what to do about this thing or that thing, to leave it in good shape, but mostly she relied on what she'd learned in her parents' inn. Giles, bless him, chatted away amiably about the county, tidbits of gossip he'd picked up from half a dozen conversations. He was utterly unselfconscious about his own situation, though Kate suspected Ada had more than a few questions.

By the time she heard the horse outside, and a call from a Healer, she'd put the entire cottage back to rights, discarded the sour milk, fed the chickens a bit of grain, gathered their eggs, and generally made the place easier to manage. The Healer was a young man she'd worked with before a time or two, with an excellent manner with his patients. It certainly eased her own nerves about what they'd find when they got back to the manor - and the particular challenge of the Pleasing Token currently tucked into the jewellery box on her dressing table.

CHAPTER 9
THE SITTING ROOM

"Grandmama." Giles waited a bare moment for the squawk of distaste to subside. "You can agree to this graciously and come out looking well to everyone involved. Or you can be difficult, and we can call in the appropriate legal remedies."

"You wouldn't." Her voice was sharp and icy. "You were raised better than that. I cannot believe that..."

His father broke in, cautiously. "I gather Giles is right. Aid must be rendered appropriately. It's one of the obligations."

"Not you as well. Do keep quiet, Tiberius, that is no help."

Giles leaned back, letting his fingers brush against Kate's arm. She was rigid next to him. The Healer had thankfully turned up promptly enough, and set Ada's ankle thoroughly with a charm to keep it immobile for several days until the area Healer could come out. Unfortunately, that meant they had got back to the house with bare minutes to wash up and change, and been plunged right back into familial disapproval.

Kate had chosen not to wear the Pleasing Token. He didn't need to be able to see her to be sure.

"It is only for a few days, until the ankle is on the mend, and they can get one of her children back to lend a hand. Cook says it is no trouble at all to add another seat in the servant's hall for her. Or to make up the bed down there so she doesn't have to manage any stairs. And Walter's delighted to know she's safe, poor lad. He must have been terrified and not sure how to say anything useful."

"You brought all of this down on us. All this fuss and bother."

He felt Kate's shift before she spoke. A little tap of one finger, the quiet sign that he knew meant she was preparing herself. He wasn't even sure she was aware she did it.

"I would have thought charity might come even easier at Christmas, surely? A family, in need of a warm place to lay their heads, a boy found in a stable." There was an edge to Kate's voice that Giles simultaneously delighted in and worried about.

The room was utterly silent for a good five breaths. Giles wanted desperately to know what his grandmother looked like. At the end of that count, Kate continued, her voice utterly even. "My family does well enough for itself these days. But when I was young, there were several winters where it was not a sure thing we'd have a festive meal for the day. In my work, I've certainly seen plenty of people who had to do without or who went to tremendous lengths to keep their families as safe as they could. And anyone with brains between their ears who's lived through the War must have dozens of stories of regrets."

"You are not mistress here." Grandmama's voice was cutting sharp.

"And you are not acting as one." Kate's reply was just

as clear, steady as she was in her best moments. "No one is asking you to do the work, to make the beds, to cook more food, to bring in more water. All that is asked of you is permission to share what you already have in abundance. Excess, even. For a few days, until everything can be settled out and Ada Knowles seen back to her own home with kindness."

"How dare you, as a guest here." Grandmama was working herself up now, her voice getting more shrill. Giles was not sure how to intervene.

Kate held her ground, bracing her shoulders, squaring herself in her seat. "I have made oaths about the safety of the men and women and children of Albion. So has Giles, some the same, some different. Clearly, that sets us apart in ways you find uncomfortable and distressing. But all those things you value, your home, your traditions, your feast, your rituals. Those were won by people looking out for others. I am asking you to live up to that."

"Giles, are you allowing her to do this?" Grandmama was insistent now.

"Kate is not intending to pledge to obey me when we marry, so allow doesn't really come into it, does it?" Giles kept his own voice clear. "Besides, I agree with her. It is a simple thing to permit. If you aren't willing, we'll pile Ada and Walter off to Trellech." He shrugged. "If we do that, though, I won't be back. Not this holiday, not ever. You've made it clear what you think of me, when you think of me. And what you think of Kate."

There was another of those shocked silences. Kate was about to say something in his ear. He could feel the warmth of her breath. Before she could, though, he heard Aunt Lucretia. "But they might have, I don't know, pests. An infestation."

"There are all sorts of ordinary precautions for that.

Nanny checked Walter for any illness or any such things when he arrived, and the Healer did the same for Ada. Part of my job is to know about these things, and make sure they're done as needed." Kate's voice was still clear.

There was another long silence, then Lucretia spoke, her voice smaller. "Do you intend to keep working?"

Kate took a breath and let it out. Giles could hear and feel it. When she spoke again, her tone was entirely different. "I'm sorry. This is not what you expected for your holiday. You didn't know what to expect with me. You're not familiar with how Giles handles things. And then we had an unexpected challenge or three. But the truth is that these two people need help. A warm place to sleep, with good food, and the company of the others below stairs, those will do them a world of good. If we hadn't been here, I don't know how long it would have been before Ada got help. Perhaps too long, she said on the way here, no one would likely have checked on her for days. Not until the 27th, at least. She was nearly out of water, the fire was embers, it's colder out tonight."

Kate let that rest there. No one spoke.

Giles picked up after a moment. "I have a life that isn't what I expected, but that has many grand things in it. Kate first and foremost. I am very happy with my teaching, with the consulting work I do for the Guard and the Ministry, some of which is in high demand. There are three other people who can do what I do, and to be frank, I do it better and faster most of the time."

Someone in the room snorted. His brother, he expected. Giles went on. "I don't expect you to fully understand. I don't expect you to learn braille, or even the basics of how I manage the ordinary things in life. I came back for the holidays because I wondered if there is a space where I am welcome, as part of the family. And where my wife-to-be is as well. If that is not the case, then we will make it easier for everyone and not put you through this challenge again." He shrugged. "If you like, we could go back to Trellech tonight."

"It's a disgrace." That was Julia. He could hear the shrillness in her voice. "You've never given much care for the family before now."

Giles couldn't exactly argue with that. And he did not want to be wantonly difficult at the moment. There was no point in making this worse than it was. After he considered his options, he shrugged. "I've never been given much care. I am grateful for the childhood I had, for an excellent nanny, for my tutors, for tutoring school and Schola. But I am also quite clear that those are things done by my parents because they were expected. It was convenient that I fit into those goals."

"And now?" That was his father, who sounded suddenly tired. "We lost face, that matter over Vale."

"I lost rather more than that." Giles could not keep himself from snapping slightly. "He stole a substantial sum from me. He abandoned me. If Kate had not been able to summon help and then aid me herself, I would have died in that house. I relied on him for certain specific tasks, and he failed at them."

He'd never said it so bluntly before. There was another awkward silence, then Julia spoke before she thought better of it. "That's not what he..." Then she realised what she was saying and went silent.

That explained some things. Several things. Giles made himself wait, take a breath, lean back. All the little tricks of movement that would indicate he was in control. He was, after all. Kate was beside him. He was not reliant on Vale for anything anymore. "What did he tell you, then? I am beginning to think there are at least two different stories."

There was silence again, but this time it was his grandmother who finally spoke. Just the one word, the name. "Julia." It held a warning.

Grudgingly, Julia spoke. "He'd see Caesarius at the club every few weeks. I wasn't there most of those times." She made it clear by her voice she considered Bourne's to be the realm of certain men. "But he'd complain about how he had to do everything for you. Help you dress. Cut up your food, like you would for a baby. Guide you everywhere. That it was a constant drain, he never got any time to himself."

Giles raised an eyebrow. "He never got any time to himself, but yet he was down the club, when Caesarius was there, regularly." Honestly, some people couldn't solve the most obvious logic puzzles when they were staring the problem in the eye.

The silence this time had a different quality. Quivery. To his surprise, the next comment came from his right, where Lucretia and her family were arrayed. He was sure it was Ambrose. "If he was so - obligated as that, he wouldn't have been at the club so much."

"Quite right, Ambrose." He might as well praise broadly. The young man had earned it. "I suppose none of you paid much attention to when I was at St Dunstan's and the Refuge. They taught me how to manage most things myself. I can't see, no, I can't read print. But most men of our class have a valet or a man who sees to their clothes. I manage my food just fine once I know what's on my plate. I'm quite independent at home, or any place I know well enough. Even this one, where I've not stayed for years. Bar being careful of a side table or chair someone's moved without telling me."

Lucretia ventured, "So why did you need Vale's help, then?"

"Many men of our class also have a private secretary, especially if they have varying obligations. Such as my teaching and consulting. I am more use to the University and the Guard if I can focus on my work, not dealing with routine correspondence or bills. Vale was expected to handle print materials, and either read them aloud for me or put them into braille if they were something I needed to reference. There's a thing much like a typewriter. He handled the household needs, bills and orders and banking. He picked up materials from the library. Three hours work, most days, if that, and if I didn't need a hand getting through Portal Square, much of the day and evening free."

"The square?" That was Ambrose again, because he murmured, "Pardon."

"It's a fine question. A fair number of veterans, those with lasting injuries or who spent time at the Front, have a hard time with crowds. Some jump at loud sounds, or unexpected ones. Some, like me, can't navigate a crowd comfortably. Others are more likely to fall if jostled, or can't risk another injury." He shrugs. "My man now, he does fine with that."

"Not Kate." That was Aunt Lucretia. Kate, mind, was being very patient.

Giles snorted. "Kate has her own work and her own commitments. And I would not dream of getting in the way of that."

There was a hesitation, and then his mother, of all people, asked, "We have been making assumptions about your future, then, as well?" She wasn't exactly asking about children, or about what marriage would mean, not in so many words, but Giles knew that was what she was after.

He glanced at Kate beside him, the gesture still instinctive, even though it didn't get him meaningful information.

"Kate, love?" If she wished to field this one, she had every right.

She squeezed his hand, and she must have been thinking about this, for when she spoke it was smooth and easy, considering. "I have worked hard, over a decade in the Guard, to earn my current rank. I am excellent at what I do. That's been acknowledged by a number of the Majors and senior Captains. I intend to keep doing that work, so long as I can. It isn't safe, we both know that. But we know both the ways in which it is not safe and the protections we can take, far better than most. I do not take foolish risks, I do my best to be prepared."

There was no immediate question when she paused, so she went on. "Before Giles proposed, we had of course talked about it. Just as Giles expects to have a man, I gather nannies are a done thing. My former superior officer, Captain Edgarton - Lord Edgarton - is a devoted family man, well known for it. He and I have talked about how to make that work. I would need time away from active duty in the field, but that happens for all sorts of reasons, men as well as women. I'm not quite ready for that, not this coming year. But in two years? Quite possibly. Making no promises, of course."

Giles said, promptly, "A great deal can change in a year or two. Having seen Richard Edgarton with his family when his two were younger, before the War, I suspect I'd quite like being a father. I'd want to do things properly. But there's no reason we couldn't."

His grandmother spoke, cutting through someone else about to say something. "Very clarifying." Her voice had that sharp edge, but when she continued, it was easier. "Let us turn the topic to something more festive. Ada Knowles and her grandson may stay. Giles, Kate, you have had a long day. If you wish to retire after the meal, you may of course do so. We had planned to drive out to the Boxing Day hunt and watch them. Or I believe Ambrose wanted to explore the estate a bit."

"I'd be glad to go with you, Ambrose. And Kate, do you want to learn my old haunts?" Giles could tell an olive branch when it was offered.

"I would, thank you." Kate's tone made it clear the thanks was more general. The conversation turned to a bit of gossip about the neighbours, certainly a festive tradition. Then it went on to a discussion of some of the Trellech holiday concerts that his mother had been to.

They did not escape upstairs immediately after supper. The conversation stayed on pleasant topics for an hour or two, but when they broke out the cards again, Giles said, "It has been a long day. Kate, would you walk up with me?"

"And protect you from side tables, yes." She was teasing, amiably.

He waited until they were back in his room, with the door properly closed and a charm for privacy as an additional protection. Then he promptly stripped out of the formal jacket, then the shirt. Kate made a contented sound. She had rather a taste for seeing him shed clothing, he'd discovered.

"Do you want to change into something more comfortable and come back up?" he asked. "You weren't wearing the token."

"The conversation would have gone very differently at supper if I had been." Kate settled on the bed. It creaked as she leaned back. "This was better."

Giles turned toward her, frowning. He could, he thought, see the point of that. Still, he asked. "Explain it to me?"

"Come sit." He came and sat where he expected there

to be space, and she leaned up against him. "You've had enough of the basic first aid training from the Healers."

"I have." He was now sure he was missing something.

"If we didn't sort this out, it was going to continue being difficult. Probably for a very long time to come. None of us wants that. Even your brother and his wife, who were most inclined to be difficult at the moment."

Giles snorted. "Yes." He shook his head. "I should have known Vale was giving off the wrong impression."

"That's my point. If we didn't lance the infection now, it would just linger. Being poisonous and awful. Now," He could feel her shrug. "I don't know what it's going to be like in six months. But either way, it will be more honest."

Giles nodded slowly. Then he offered, cautiously. "What does that mean about your sister?"

"I was sure you were going to ask when you saw the point. How do you feel about a trip there, overnight, for New Year's?"

"Any particular festivities?" Giles half-remembered something, but he was never entirely sure without checking which customs Kate's family might or might not follow.

"Callenig - children go round reciting poetry and rhymes and getting treats, mostly. It keeps the little ones occupied. They carry around a token, three evergreen twigs, with an apple or orange on top - my family holds that the apple is the more traditional. With cloves or sliced almonds in the top, there are different favoured patterns for the magical effect. And a sprig from the nearest hedge. Being gifted it is good luck. And some families, the boys carry water from the local well, to bless everyone they encounter."

Giles nodded. "That sounds manageable. And your sister?"

Kate sighed, but it was an amiable sigh. "I'll see about sorting things out with her. At least making the attempt."

"It takes both sides. You can only do your part."

Kate shifted to take his hand. "True. Tomorrow with Ambrose?"

"Tomorrow. Don't you go anywhere yet. We've time together, in private. I have some ideas."

CHAPTER 10

DECEMBER 30TH, THEIR HOME IN
TRELLECH.

On the 30th, they got home. Kate went upstairs to change into something far more comfortable. When she came back downstairs, she found Giles in his favourite chair in the library, pipe out, looking deeply contented.

"The pipe, even."

"Grandmama doesn't care for the smell. Neither does Mother."

Kate snorted. "I've always found it sort of comforting? My father has a pipe. And one of my brothers." Kate settled down in the facing chair. "Are you sure you want to go to my family tomorrow?"

"Quite sure. For one thing, it will be a change, won't it?" He grinned in her direction. "For the other, we're only staying a night. Are you sure it's all right with the Guard?"

Kate nodded. "As four different people pointed out, I worked a fair bit of the holiday. Getting another day or two off is entirely reasonable. Especially since I tied things up so tidily with a bow in the aftermath."

"And did you say anything about your suspicions about Wilcox?"

Kate laughed. "Oh, right, you were talking to Ambrose, weren't you, before they left? I had a word with Wilcox. I said, in as many words, that I hadn't seen anything that made me need to make a report, but if he had sense, he'd make sure to stop doing whatever it was."

"And what did he do?" Giles leaned forward.

"Turned pale, stammered something, and went off to see about one of the horses, so sorry. That's all right. I'm fairly it was smuggling or evading a tax or a fee, and if I put the fear of something into him, that should do well enough."

Giles nodded. "And Ada?"

"She is tidily settled back into her cottage. One of her nieces from the next village over came to keep an eye on things - and Walter - for a few weeks until the ankle mends properly. Just the right amount of fuss, honestly. I think most of what was needed was someone who can fetch the water and go for help more promptly if there's a need. She brought a pony with her, so that will help."

Giles smiled and puffed on his pipe. Kate knew that expression, the way his mouth quirked when he was thinking. She leaned back and waited. After a good two minutes, he asked, "My family?"

Kate shrugged, knowing he couldn't see it, and then said, "What about them?" in a tone she felt conveyed the shrug properly.

"They were less awful, the last few days?" He had the measuring note in his voice, weighing out awful and more awful and less awful. Not awful was not an option. They were both clear about that.

"Less awful." Kate agreed with that, then fell silent again to see what Giles would do.

"I would understand," he said. "If you never wanted to spend much time with them."

Kate considered her options here. "Do you want to?"

He grimaced, one of the faces he made when he was caught in his own logic. "Yes and no, and that's the rub of it."

"It always is. If it were easy, either way, it would be a simple arithmetic problem. Instead, we find ourselves inside imaginary numbers, or something." She knew she was getting the mathematical analogy somewhat wrong. That was part of the point.

Giles snorted. Then he gathered his thoughts up, and said, "Tell me what you want, Kate. Please. If you could have any of the range of choices from my family."

Kate considered. "This calls for tea. You want some?"

"You're simply postponing the inevitable. But yes, please. There should be cream. I'm sure Mrs Meredith put some out this morning before we got back."

Kate went over to the sideboard to check and called back, "Cream, lemon, honey."

"Lemon and honey for me." He knew she'd want the cream, of course. And perhaps a little honey. She set up the cups while she waited for the kettle to boil, then all the little fiddly gestures of setting up the pot. He let her be in quiet, the way they were both comfortable, so she could think.

By the time the tea had steeped and she brought the tray back, she had enough of an answer to be going on with. She set the tray down. "Cup here, tray on the table in the centre. And all right."

Giles gestured with his free hand. "Go on."

"I am not interested in going somewhere where they do not respect my work. Or where they can only fit me into a very limited box. Especially," Her voice turned wry, "When that box is based on my apparent failings of profession, family, child-bearing, or anything like that."

"Quite. You are many things, Kate, but you have never been inclined to the humiliation sort of masochism. Sensibly. You can stand your ground. You did with them, you did with Vale, I've heard you do it other times. But it is not your chosen hobby."

"A necessary obligation, rather. I do think that that - is confrontation the word? - on Christmas Day seems to have settled some of it. Certainly the next few days were much more pleasant." Kate considered. "Your mother is a woman of specific interests, none of which I share, but she is delightfully acerbic about the follies of the opera world, if you get her going. The same about the tomb rubbings. I am not the daughter-in-law she imagined, but she has Julia for that."

Giles chuckled. "She does, yes. And Father?"

Kate sipped her tea. "He doesn't know what to do with me, what to do with a woman who isn't all about dresses and flower arranging and whatever other decorous hobbies there are. But when we went out into the woods on Boxing Day, he knew all about the land, and I appreciate that. I think I get on better with your parents independently, rather than at the same time."

"To be fair," Giles said, "They do too."

It make Kate cackle, the way he said it so drily. "There's a truth for you. All right. I quite liked your Aunt Lucretia, once I got to know her. And I think Lady Alysoun might find her an interesting contact, actually. A couple of things she said about connections between various of the society ladies."

"You really think so?" Giles turned toward her, reconsidering his aunt in that light.

"She's sharper than she comes across. She's like a sepia

image, isn't she? Rather caught in the past, but it gives her a sense of where she's come from. I think she's never been encouraged in it. I certainly couldn't, properly, but Lady Alysoun might."

Giles snorted. "You can't ever set down your work, can you?"

"You don't either. I know perfectly well you were thinking about your next paper through most of yesterday evening. Listening with one ear."

He spread his hands. "And you were thinking about how to arrange things as you pick up your duties again. We are a good match that way."

"Never bored." Which made Kate decide on the next of his family to discuss. "I actually had several good chats with Oswald. Seeing as how I'm professionally interested in charms on buildings. Even if agricultural storage isn't my usual line. I think he was surprised I was as widely read as I am? But he was fine. Isoline, however..."

"Yes?" Giles leaned forward again, setting his cup down.

"I suspect she's having an affair, and no, I can't pin down precisely why. It was all the subtle body language, the way she angled away from Oswald. Or glanced at the clock. There's really no reason to, in a family evening, if you don't have to catch a portal or a train."

"Unless you're thinking of what someone else is doing in that moment. Quite. Huh. You might well be right."

"Does it bother you?" Kate leaned back, watching him closely now.

"It would bother me rather a lot if you were. Because I would be wondering what I was failing at, with you. Not that I expect that to be too much of a problem. But that she is? If you fall over evidence, I suppose we can talk about what to do then. But it doesn't seem likely."

"No, well-bred society matrons with a fluid sort of daily schedule generally manage to keep things private quite well. She's got loads of excuses for being somewhere, a private home, for an extended period because of the flower arranging."

Giles nodded. "Not our business, fundamentally. At least as it stands. All right. Norbert?"

"I get enough paperwork at work, but he's harmless enough? Mostly? I kept feeling like he was waiting for me to slip and say something indiscreet? Which of course I wouldn't."

"That is rather like him, yes. Anyone else?"

"I thought you were getting on rather well with Ambrose. And I enjoyed talking to Elisabeta, though obviously, she's still at school and it's not like she's free to make her own schedule."

"You did seem to be getting on well, talking about some of the options. Ambrose is rather clever, yes, and I'd like to talk to him more, honestly. Do you mind seeing if he'd like to come round for supper sometime, if we can find an evening that works."

"Certainly. So that leaves your brother and Julia."

Giles sighed. "I wanted to look up to him, you know? All my life."

"We cleared the air a bit, and they were better, after that." She shrugged. "I don't feel like I need to see them often. I don't mind the occasional familial visit, so long as they're civil. But they are..." Kate hesitated.

"Go on, Kate. You're not going to offend me by speaking truth." Giles's voice was clear and certain.

"They've chosen to shape themselves certain ways. Been encouraged to do that. But there's a spark of curiosity in you, and in your mother. And Ambrose, and a different thread of it, in Lucretia and Norbert, I think. It entirely passed Caesarius by, didn't it?"

Giles leaned back, tapping his fingers together while he thought about it. "That's a fair way to put it. He'd likely have been better off if he'd had to work for a living, honestly. Or have some passion."

"And instead, it's being landed gentry. And I know from the Edgartons that that's quite a lot of work, actually, to do properly. But it's not the sort of work that inspires everyone."

"And you think my brother would be happier with some inspiration in his life?"

"Wouldn't most people? I have no idea how you'd convince him to try it, though. I suppose all we can do is to be encouraging to their children, as time and opportunity allows."

Giles caught a note in her voice. "You feel strongly about that, then?"

"Oh, yes. That's one of the purposes of aunts and uncles, Mum always said. So that you've more than just your parents to talk to, to look up to. People who do things a bit differently, or who you just - you don't see them every day. It's easier to talk about things with them. My uncles, you know about them."

The two uncles, both village Guard, who'd inspired her to work hard and go into the same line of work. They'd never tried to talk her out of it, and she loved them for that. They had been brutally honest about what she'd need to succeed, in as far as they knew. And these days, they admitted they didn't know what being based in Trellech needed. Or what being a Captain needed. But they could make sure she was treating the Guards working for her well. That had done wonders this past week.

Giles coughed. "Penny for your thoughts?"

"Thinking about my uncles. And the benefits of reputation. Let me come back to that?" She tucked that thought away, going on. "Your grandmother is a grand example of her time. She's duly terrifying, with high standards, but it's clear she wants good things for her family, even if she's not at all sure how to make that happen."

"You think that's it?"

Kate shrugged again. "It makes people crabby, in that particular way, hadn't you noticed? Like they're, oh, like a swan. Paddling frantically under the surface, doing their best to look gorgeous and entirely composed above water, and with a long snaking neck to peck at people with if needed."

Giles tilted his head. "That's a thing. I touched one, once. Well, a taxidermy one. They're just as much a joy to touch as you'd think."

Kate blinked. "You have?"

"The Refuge took us on an outing to Potter's Museum of Curiosities. You know, one of those odd little Victorian museums? This one had animals in all sorts of odd positions, but also a number of other examples of the art form. A tactile museum, they called it. There was apparently a trend for them in the Victorian era? We were talking about what information you get from touching something, versus seeing it, or hearing it. Very informative, actually."

"And much safer than handling a living one, certainly." Kate agreed. "All right." She swallowed. "About reputation."

"Yes?" He leaned forward again, as if waiting to see if she'd bring up the other topic, the elephant in the room of the Pleasing Token.

"I keep thinking about what my uncles told me, over and over again. That having the right reputation eases things. Someone who does good work, who isn't too rigid about the protocol that doesn't actually matter, who's fair, who understands the ..." She frowned. "They said the scale of what they're asking. If something is easy for the person you're asking, or harder."

"You have a good sense of that, with the Penelopes, I've noticed. You don't always know all the options. But you're quite good at figuring out if it's a complicated thing or a simple one, something they do all the time or something new."

"And you want to ask for new things, and complicated ones. I mean, sometimes that's what you need. But also that's a way of showing respect for the work. If you always ask people for the easy things, that doesn't let them shine. And they get bored, and they do less good work. No one wins."

Giles snorted. "Huh. That's a way to put that. And you were thinking about it because?"

"Because when I asked for help, I got it in spades. Despite the holiday. They didn't send out twenty Guards to do a full search, but that would have been disproportionate. But as soon as I had something concrete..."

"You got the Healer out promptly, and more people to help. No, I see what you mean. And..." His voice trailed off.

"And I have an appointment to go talk to Captain Edgarton and Lady Donovan, and one or two other people they recommended tomorrow, about the token." She paused and Giles took a sip of his tea to let her come to it in her own time.

"I honestly don't know what I think about it. What it means, being judged by someone distant, or perhaps not distant enough at all. You know how I felt when it was Captain Edgarton, and everyone else."

Giles nodded. "An uncomfortable sensation of being watched. Inspected."

"I don't think I'll know how I feel about it for a good while. It's not a thing to be hasty about. I know don't want to wear it more until I better understand how it works, as much as anyone does. They said they'd see about an introduction to the Guards who have one. A particularly elite club. Once I've done that, I'll have a better sense of how to go on with it."

"That's fair. And until then?"

"I've been talking to it? That sounds ridiculous, doesn't it? But if it's, they say some magical objects have awareness? And this is certainly a complex one. People talk to plants and pets and all that."

Giles held up his hands. "You needn't convince me. Fair enough. I'm curious what you learn, whatever you feel you can share with me, of course. But I also understand if there's something you can't talk about, or not yet."

"You are?" Kate wasn't sure how to put how she felt about that into words.

"It chose you and not me, didn't it? And I've always known there are things you can't tell me, in the line of your work. The same as there are things I can't tell you about my cryptography projects. We'll manage."

"By talking about everything else, yes." Kate was about to say more when there was a knock on the door.

"Yes?" Giles called out.

The door opened, with Mistress Meredith, the housekeeper, beaming at them. "Beg pardon, Master Giles, but there's a young man come by in hopes you were at home to guests. Your cousin Ambrose, he's grown so tall. He wondered if you might have a few minutes, or if he could arrange a time to talk to you?"

Giles tilted his head, the little inquisitive expression on

his face. Leaving the question to her. "Show him in, please, Mistress Meredith. We still have tea in the pot, but check if he'd like any of your excellent scones or whatever you have on hand?"

She beamed and bustled off. Kate chuckled. "Seems you made an impression as well."

"A fine thing. And a fine way to begin building something for the coming year, isn't it?"

As Ambrose came in, Kate could see him glancing around, taking in the arrangement of the room, and Giles's desk. He came over promptly, and said, "Cousin Giles, Kate. I'm hoping you can help me, something I didn't want to discuss anywhere near the rest of the family."

Kate could not decide whether she liked being asked for help more or being included in that family. It would be a grand year, she could tell already.

CHASING LEGENDS

CHAPTER I

"Thesan, Isembard, don't you have obligations somewhere else?" That was Richart, next to her, lifting his glass in a toast to them. "Not that I mind a feast. Or your delightful company."

That was the point of this week. No one sensible minded a feast, particularly one as delightfully cooked as this one. She'd done a bit of it, even. The kitchen staff had let her have space in the oven for honey cakes, and they'd used her family's recipe for a mead sauce for the roast chicken. She could taste the honey so clearly, with all its promise of reward for hard work.

"You know why, Richart, you've been in enough meetings about it." She enjoyed teasing him, and all the more so the past term. Something in him had begun to relax, now that Ibis had settled in as a teacher. Not quite so twitchy. She looked out across the Great Hall.

"Humour me. Besides, Hypatia wasn't in the meetings." He gestured to the other end of the table, at Ibis's sister, sitting down across from him. "Or Cammie." Pross's daughter was across the table from Hypatia. They'd rearranged the staff table for the week, with six seats on each side, Helena reigning from the centre. It meant they could talk comfortably across the table without perpetually getting up to move as the conversation shifted.

There were fewer people than she'd hoped when she first planned this, just a dozen. Thesan herself, and Isembard. Alexander, here as their guest. Helena, Dipti, Linta, Ibis, and Richart were the others from among the teachers, along with Lane from the library. And then Pross, her daughter, and Ibis's sister.

Though, to be fair, their colleagues also had families, also had people who wanted this time with them. As she did, for that matter, though she and Isembard were splitting their festive season in three directions. Here, her family, and the obligations of a Council family.

All her memories of festive gatherings were twenty people or more jammed into wherever they could sit, children running around. This was a dozen people rattling around a huge and impressive hall. But they had a fine group, and she was especially glad Ibis had invited Pross.

Including Pross meant they had two current students to round things out. Cammie was having a fine first year so far, and showing a good deal of promise. Hypatia was one of the shining stars of Thesan's advanced astronomy classes, as well as in several other subjects.

Honestly, while Thesan missed chatting with Raphaela or Borea, she was glad of a smaller group for the moment. Navigating her family was one thing, threading her way through reviving long-neglected traditions of the school with her sometimes dubious colleagues was another thing entirely. The people here were the ones decidedly amenable to her idea of anchoring the school a bit more in the customs that had got dusty. They'd have a chance for an enormous feast at New Year's, when the entire village was invited and their fellow staff would be back.

"Hypatia asked me about it in October, for the record. As soon as she saw the books in my office." Thesan could never resist a chance to give a bit of a lecture and at least here she knew it would be reasonably welcome. "You know Helena and I have been talking for a year about returning to some of the old customs of Schola. Not the awful ones - there was a decades long fad for cold bracing baths, or early morning callisthenics."

Isembard, beside her, opened his mouth. She nudged him, grinning. "You don't want to get out of a warm bed any more than the students do. If for somewhat different reasons."

That brought a rumble of amused laughter from their colleagues. As soon as their relationship had become public, Isembard had settled into a quiet but delightfully visible appreciation of her virtues, in a decorous way. Visible, audible, and tactile, honestly. For her part, Thesan loved seeing how much she could tease by innuendo in appropriate settings, in the staff room or meals like tonight.

They were en famille, as Alexander was fond of saying, and she would take advantage of it. Deliberately, actually, because that kind of conversation, that kind of laughter, was bringing them together in a way she'd never felt before. Not here, not as an adult, not outside her family circles or closest friends.

"But the feasting, that's a tradition we're delighted to pick up. The harvest feast for Michaelmas. The ancestral one last month, though that took a lot of coordination. And now, twelve days of feasting and enjoying the pleasures of the castle while the students are gone. There's a bit in one of the manuscripts I looked at - this is the one pinned on the staffroom door - about languid reading at all hours, wherever one's desires lead."

Lane, their librarian, snorted. "I can vouch for the fact you've all taken rather a lot of books from the library. Good show. At least until they all need shelving."

Thesan nodded. "So, we are realists. It used to be Solstice to New Year's, but certain of us have obligations for Solstice." She nodded at Alexander, across the table from Isembard, who had looked dashingly handsome at this year's Council dancing. Something had changed a bit for him this year, and it looked good on him, even if she wasn't entirely sure what or why. Perhaps it was beginning to put down roots in Albion again. She and Isembard had done their bit, too.

"That does not explain your personal obligations. We all know your anniversary is tonight. Having been at the wedding last year." Richart wasn't letting it drop.

Isembard cut in, shifting to run his fingers along her arm, teasingly. "Our first wedding anniversary is indeed tonight. But first, we can think of no better place to spend it. And second, it's on the twenty-third to give us every reason to skip parties we don't want to be at later in the week for the rest of our lives. And we're using it as an excuse to skip out on some of Thesan's extended family tomorrow, though we'll see her closer family Christmas Day."

It had been his idea, actually, given the flurry of Council social events that littered the calendar at this time of year. Either they could celebrate the anniversary on the proper day, or they could beg off of a later party and claim they'd not yet managed their anniversary, so sorry. Or both. She suspected some years it would be both.

"That's rather a neat bit of calculation." That was Pross, who was still finding her feet. It wasn't only that Ibis had just finished his first term teaching, or that she and Ibis were still courting without firm long-term plans or commitments, though those were both true.

She was also neither fish nor fowl. Pross was not a teacher, though Thesan suspected she might well end up as one of the Trivium teachers in a year or two. She wasn't from the village proper, not yet, though she was working toward taking over the bookshop there when the current owner retired. Pross was a mother, but her daughter Cammie was growing up.

Thesan had liked Pross so far, the conversations they'd managed, but she hoped they'd become much better friends in time. She could stand to have more friends, and especially someone nearer her own age than most of the current staff.

"That, I'm afraid, is a side effect of marrying into the great and noble house of Fortier." It made both Isembard and Alexander grimace. That, of course, was not the way one put it in proper protocol.

"I'd call you a barbarian, Thesan, but you actually read enough Greek I can't bring myself to." Alexander waved a hand. "They might have consulted me about the social implications. I must say I'd rather be here than any of my other invitations on offer."

"You could always agree to come back and teach." Helena leaned forward. "Not that Borea isn't doing wonderfully. We've done very well with new staff this year, may it long continue." She lifted her glass. Thesan agreed wholeheartedly. Borea was made of good humour and steady teaching. It wasn't Alexander's beloved endless questions, but she had a keen eye for getting her students to think through the issues of safety and practicality in their ritual work.

"No, no. I would much rather flit here and there,

appearing for the occasional lecture or to keep Isembard on his toes. I prefer to be an honoured guest, thank you. Much less marking involved."

Alexander was, she suspected, a tiny bit drunk. Not with alcohol. She'd learned he had a tremendous capacity for that. Rather, he was drunk on not needing to be so much on guard. He was, in fact, staying in the guest room in their still-new rooms on the fourth floor of the tower. She was sure there would be more drinking and more conversation after the feast, likely well into the night. She was very much looking forward to that.

Isembard nodded. "And that's the traditions we want. The company and the good food - is there a spare bit of honey cake? - and the excellent conversation. I still hold out hopes of getting a couple of stories out of you, finally."

"It's good to have a challenge in life." Alexander was deadpan. Before he could say anything else, however, there was a massive knock, pounding on the huge oak doors of the Great Hall. They'd closed them to keep the heat in a bit, but they weren't locked.

Before anyone could say anything, Alexander was up and out of his chair. He barely glanced at Thesan or Isembard, just pushed his chair back and out of his way, so Isembard could scramble under the table rather than going around it. Or over it. That would not have ended well, given his knee. Or the good dishes.

There were three spaced out knocks in total, just enough time for Isembard to take his position next to Alexander. She could see now what they must have been like, together, in the War. They moved independently, always knowing where the other was. They were a pair of hunting hounds, or something more sharp and primal, like wolves. Both of them had taken defensive postures, but without offering any immediate threat.

"May I, Helena?" Alexander didn't turn to look at her.

"Of course. I trust your judgement." Helena's voice was clear. "Everyone, please stay seated, unless Alexander or Isembard suggest otherwise." Her tone, however, made it clear they should be prepared for anything.

That got a fleeting grunt of amusement from Alexander. Then, he raised his voice, pitching it to carry clearly. Isembard must have cast the charm to make it louder, Thesan just caught the last flick of his fingers and a murmur under his breath. "Who would enter?"

The great doors swung open, hitting the massive stone walls of the hall with an echoing thud. A man strode in, tall enough to be framed in the door, at least seven or eight feet in height, and with broad shoulders to match. His skin was the green of a new holly leaf, while his hair was darker, more like older vines.

He might have stepped out of Merlin's own time. There was an extravagance of a fur-lined cloak pinned to his shoulders and trailing out behind him. Her eye was drawn to the intricate embroidery along the collar and hem of his long tunic. Thesan was sure it anchored powerful magic, even if she had no idea what half of it meant.

He wore no armour, but a jewelled belt held a scabbard and sword, and she was sure the boots he wore held a knife or two snugly against his calves. He held a holly bough in one hand, the red berries peeping out, and perhaps what might be mistletoe, as well, twined around the holly.

He swept in, coming up to within ten feet of the dais where they sat, and he bowed, though he never looked down. Alexander and Isembard hadn't moved. "I would speak to the Lady of the school." His voice was just as rich as his clothing, an echoing baritone. The few words were modern, at least, not matching his archaic clothing.

Helena stood. When Thesan glanced over at her, she caught a quiver of one hand, but when Helena spoke, her voice was clear and crisp. "Sir, I am Lady of the school. Some of our own are gathered here to celebrate."

That made the great green man laugh, a hearty sound. "Well said, lady, well said." He glanced around, then, as if taking in dozens of changes large and small in the hall. Thesan, all of a sudden, knew what had to happen. It would terrify Isembard and also Alexander, but she couldn't help that.

Thesan stood, reaching for a clean plate. She gathered up a slice of honey cake, along with some slivers of cheese, some figs, some sausage, and a little of the chicken in mead sauce. Tucking a fork under her thumb, she picked up her own almost-full goblet of mead. She came around the table, knowing Isembard saw her out of the corner of his eye. The green man turned all his attention to her, and no one else moved.

She walked forward, down the side stairs of the dais step by step, and then over to in front of their unexpected guest. She could feel Isembard behind to her right, a foot or two above her, and Alexander, both near vibrating. "We are gathered to feast in community tonight. May we offer you hospitality?"

That brought forth another laugh, this one somehow warm and approving. "You are a wise and generous lady." He spread his hands, the holly waving. "I am properly met. In my turn, I pledge I mean no harm to any here, but come in search of truth and knowledge."

Helena, behind her, hesitated for only a moment. "Then be welcome, good sir knight. We are a place that treasures both. May we bring a chair or table for your comfort?"

"With your permission, I will bring my own." He waited a moment, and Helena must have nodded. The floor shifted, before and behind him, vines and saplings rising from the bare stone and shaping themselves into a broad chair and table.

Thesan wanted to take a step back, several steps. This was strange and new, and moving far too fast for her. And yet, each part was something ancient, something she'd had her whole life to learn. How you made someone welcome. How you showed you weren't a threat. The green knight gestured at the surface, and Thesan set down the goblet and plate.

"You are welcome, sir, to more, of course." She wasn't at all sure what to say now, and she was sure Isembard didn't want her nearly so close to someone so clearly powerful, magical, and utterly unknown.

He turned a smile on her, and half-bowed, as he sat down. "I will be well fed with this, mistress of stars. You were kind to think of it." It was rather like being in the full face of the sun. Like being a plant that turned toward it, for all both of those were rather foreign desires of Thesan's.

And there was also, indefinably, a sense that something had changed with her offer, something to their benefit. The man must have caught something, because he added, laughing, now. "Go reassure your husband all is well, wise lady."

She ducked her head and went back up. Isembard had nominally relaxed, but she could see the tension in his shoulders. He walked toward the end of the dais to meet her as she came up the stairs. "You terrified me." He wasn't upset with her, not exactly, but he was shaken and trying to cover it.

Thesan swallowed, saying what she'd only just found words for. "You didn't feel anything in the wards."

It hit Isembard immediately, and he swallowed, hesitated for only a moment, and then turned to bow towards the green man, who seemed entirely focused on tasting his meal. Then he offered Thesan his hand, to escort her back to her place and take his own seat. The green man did not look up again until Thesan and Isembard were settled, and until Alexander had taken his own chair. Though Alexander kept his turned out to face the hall, where he could move in an instant if needed.

When he looked up, the green man said, "The honey is local, of course?"

"From Schola's hives. It's a family recipe. The mead is from my mother, a family gift."

There was another silence, though this one felt less awkward. The green man took a few more bites, a sip of the mead, then he lifted his cup. "My blessings on your marriage, then, that is toasted with so rich a drink." He leaned back, like a king on his throne, entirely confident in his power. She'd seen Alexander, or a few other of the Council in that pose, now and again, but it seemed a faint shadow of the real thing.

"I am come to see what Schola is now, in these days." When he spoke, it was almost lazy, but it was that same laziness Isembard or Alexander had, of power that was merely resting. "I am welcomed, and so I will not beg a blow of your most bold knight, nor tease, for this is a fortress of learning, not of battle." That acknowledged the various deceptions of ancient stories, at least, though Thesan could not at the moment place which ones.

Helena nodded, and then asked, choosing her words

with care, "What would you know of Schola? We are not all her teachers, nor all teachers - we have here guests, and friends and even two students." Hypatia and Cammie were being quiet, at least, though they were holding hands across the table, with Cammie craning around to watch.

"I offer a quest. A challenge, a chance for learning of all kinds, for those young enough to put down deep tap roots here, those who will hold the castle for decades to come." The green man spread his hands. "If three or perhaps four of your company venture forth, deep below the keep, they will find something not seen for many years and learn much to Schola's benefit. I bid you come, in tomorrow's light, and learn what you may learn."

Thesan frowned for a moment. There was more there than just his words. She knew it, as surely as she knew which way was north when the stars were out. Something else he wasn't saying. She glanced at the others, but Isembard and Alexander weren't moving, weren't letting anything show.

As she looked back at their guest, he disappeared as quickly as he had arrived. All the food vanished with him. He left only the empty goblet and plate resting upon the stone floor, as all the wood and vines that had made his table and chair disappeared.

There was utter silence for a good minute, until Helena said, her voice shaking now. "Alexander, please." Begging him to make sense of it.

Alexander took a breath, and turned his chair back to face the table, but the first thing he said was to Thesan herself. "What made you offer food so quickly?"

"Good manners." It came out of her mouth before she could think of anything else, but it was true for all that. "Mum's stories. It needed doing."

Alexander let out a sigh. "It might have gone very

differently, otherwise. That was well done, for all we've fallen into a mystery. An ancient one. And not one I know of."

There was a buzz around the table. Pross spoke up, surprising them all. "You know the tale of Gawain and the Green Knight. This man looked much the same as the tale, and I swear, I expected him to ask to trade blows."

Thesan nodded. "Only there's no knight pure of heart here, not the way they meant Gawain was." Isembard grunted next to her, but he didn't argue. She knew enough of the depths of his War, to know he had not counted himself as any kind of pure for a decade now. Alexander, either, and the rest of them were not made for swinging a sword. Or an axe.

Isembard shifted to take her hand. "I was scared out of my mind." She was proud of him, all in a rush, for saying it out loud. He'd kept that kind of thing rammed down inside his heart for so long.

She squeezed his hand, and he slid his fingers through hers. Thesan leaned to kiss his cheek, before she said, "What do we do, then? Three or four of our company."

"Young enough for tap roots. That leaves me out on both counts." Alexander sounded both relieved and disappointed.

Helena snorted, relaxing now they were more into the usual sort of wrangle, the practised one about the division of labour. "I am certainly not young. Nor Linta or Richart or Dipti."

Lane coughed, leaning on the table. "He said three or four. I would have said, Thesan, that you and Isembard would make a great deal of sense. You know the school's lore, as well as any of us, myself included." It had been a pet project since Thesan's first year of teaching, wanting to understand where she lived the way she understood the land she'd grown up on. Lane went on. "Isembard has a number of useful skills, I'm sure, besides the ones we all know about."

"I am..." Isembard let out a long breath. "If there is a threat to the school, it is my job to defend it. Protective magics professor, and all. Though Thesan is right. I felt nothing in the wards before the knock, nor did I feel any threat after. Clearly, the man can come and go as quick as a thought, but still."

Helena considered. "I didn't either. That is rather telling, isn't it? All right. Are you willing?"

Thesan nodded. "Willing enough. Nervous. I am not stupid." There was a chuckle down the table, because anyone sensible would be nervous. "But I'm also - how often does some legend out of the earliest lore of the castle show up for supper?"

That made Alexander laugh more freely. "You have a hint of a reference, then?"

"I have to check my notes upstairs. Nothing solid, if it's what I think. Simply some of the argument for the sentience of the castle, the depths of the magic. I do have a guess as to where he meant, though. There's what looks like it should be a sea cave, down on the beach, well above the current tideline." Thesan glanced at Isembard. "That's two, then. Who else?"

Pross coughed, and said, "I am wondering." She gestured. "I am not of Schola. But I wonder about Ibis."

"He did say three or four." Ibis was still finding his way among their company, but Thesan had already come to appreciate his ability to aim at the heart of a question. "Might Pross come with us? In my line of work, I've found that a mind like a steel trap for lore and history is worth its weight in gold. Having two along would only double our fortune." That was a rather glorious joint compliment, to both Thesan and Pross, and elegantly managed.

"It occurs to me that Pross might be a welcome addition for other reasons, standing as a representative of the village, or near enough. Besides her knowledge, which I quite agree, might be very useful. One mind only holds so much." Thesan offered the compliment back. But also, she had that feeling, an itch, about how Schola was the school, but not just the school, and never had been.

Pross laughed at that and nodded. "Fair, fair. Cammie, you'll stay with Richart, please, or in the library, so someone knows where you are." Cammie nodded, and had the good sense not to argue.

"If you are willing, then." Helena glanced around. "The resources of the castle are yours, whatever food or supplies you think you might wish to take with you."

Isembard nodded once. "Ibis, Pross, perhaps you'll join us upstairs after the meal? Alexander, I want you for the planning."

"As if I would be anywhere else." Alexander lifted his glass. "For the moment, a toast to learning more in the day to come."

They all echoed the toast, then did their best to resume the ordinary conversation of the meal as best they could.

CHAPTER 2
THESAN AND ISEMBARD'S ROOMS

Once they got back upstairs to their rooms, Isembard went to pour drinks. It was partly to be hospitable and partly to give him something to do. It would be wrong to snap at his wife, and he also didn't want to, but he needed to settle himself and quickly.

Thesan went to swap out of her festive clothes into something more comfortable and grab the relevant notebook. Isembard glanced around, making sure the seating was in order. Two sofas, a scattering of easy chairs, they had set up their sitting room for convivial gatherings, at least.

Alexander settled into the chair he'd claimed as his own, and Ibis and Pross glanced around. "Where should we sit?"

"Either sofa is fine. We'll take the other. Drinks? We've more of the mead, a very good cider from near Thesan's family, wine, or brandy." He nodded at Alexander at the last, and Alexander nodded back. He hoped the others couldn't hear the strained note in his voice, but he was sure Alexander did.

And he could not, for the life of him, figure out how he felt about Thesan's choices downstairs.

She came back then, in a more comfortable dress, a deep green that suited her blonde hair and pale eyes, like a late summer field. He couldn't help but smile, seeing her, and she came straight over to him. "You don't like me taking risks, I know. Mead for me, love, please."

Of course she was that blunt and that clear about it. It made him smile, despite everything. "Not much." He let out a long breath. "We'll talk it through. You had reason, you always have reason." If he reminded himself often enough, perhaps he'd be more certain of it.

She kissed his cheek, gently. "I try to. I'd have asked if there was time, but there wasn't. Come on." She turned back to the other three, and said, "Anyone have space around the edges for some biscuits, or shall I not bother? Or there's some decorative marzipan."

"Both, please." That was Alexander, watching Thesan now just as carefully. "But come sit, dear lady, before Isembard explodes."

That made her snort, and they promptly settled on the sofa. There was a long and awkward silence before Alexander gestured at Thesan. Isembard couldn't help a spike of frustration. They'd come to each other as adults, able to set how they were going to be with each other where he seemed stuck in all the old awful habits.

Before Thesan could speak, however, Pross cleared her throat. "I beg pardon, and I'm clear I'm missing quite a few things. But can you explain the interrelationships a bit more? I am clear, Isembard, Thesan, that you are happily married, give or take different approaches to the world."

She favoured Ibis with a smile, warmly teasing, and it made Isembard relax a bit. Then Pross went on. "But I am not clear, pardon, on why Alexander is here, and not, say, Helena."

Isembard glanced from Alexander to Thesan. Alexander shrugged. He always preferred to allow other people to explain things, and Isembard sighed. "Alexander was one of my mentors from the time I started school, and my brother before me. During the War, we fought together, until 1917, when we went our own ways." He did not get into the details, how Perry's death had broken things for them, made it impossible to be together and focus on the task at hand.

Thesan nodded. "And then Alexander came back to teach, for two years, and they had to sort out how things were now."

"You keep telling people things, love." Isembard couldn't help being amused. He was so used to everyone keeping their thoughts close, but Thesan's instinct was to share the information, not hoard it. He was coming to believe her way was far better, as a long-term strategy, at least with one's friends and allies, but it was still foreign to him.

"You don't, and Alexander won't. He loves the obscurity." Thesan leaned back. "I respect Alexander's skills and wisdom a great deal. And of course he has a stunningly excellent personal library, access to the Council collection, and I'm sure dozens of resources I don't even know about and so can't envy properly."

It was the note in Thesan's voice that was persuasive. "And he's a terrible influence on you, love." He added, "He has a tremendous book trunk, and he gave her one as a wedding gift. Which I must say is entirely sensible, given that she spends time here, the country home on my side, and at the Astronomy Guild spaces on a regular basis."

Thesan just looked smug. "It is nearly the finest gift I

have been given in my life." She squeezed Isembard's hand. He knew that she treasured the telescope he'd got her as a betrothal gift even more. Barely, some days.

Pross blinked at her. "You're not from that sort of family, though?"

"Goodness, no. Honest English farmers, going all the way back. Fourth Families." She lifted the glass of mead she was holding. "Our customs are all about orchards and honey and the farm making it through another year. I tolerate the ridiculousness of the Great Families and their social obligations. I don't much enjoy them, but I can do the dance, anyway. My apprentice mistress made sure I could. A lot of the higher-up folk in my Guild don't have to work for a living. It's much easier to go look at stars all night, mind, if you don't have to get up first thing in the morning."

Ibis snorted. "That's the most logical explanation for it I've heard yet. You're right, though, about what it takes to support a research career." He glanced around the room. "So. You both fought in the War. Do we think it is a fighting sort of challenge?"

Isembard swallowed. "I admit, I was not sanguine about Thesan stepping out like that." He let his voice trail off, and Thesan immediately put her hand on his knee.

"He did say he didn't intend any harm. Which is a statement to come back to." Then Thesan held up her hand. "First, love, I was sure, I don't know how, but I knew offering hospitality was the needful thing. Second, though I didn't figure it out until later, you'd have sensed a threat before I did." She added more to Pross than Ibis, "As the Protective magics professor, Isembard is responsible for the wards, under the head's guidance. And it's not Helena's best skill set at all, so mostly she leaves it up to him, and whoever he wishes to consult."

Alexander said, promptly. "Me, mostly. But that's a formality, he's always already been considering everything I suggest." He then shrugged one shoulder. "I led a small group on covert missions for the first half of the War, including Isembard. We know each other's skills well, despite the decade since, and a number of changes." He then flicked his fingers. "Why did you take the risk, Thesan, besides that?"

Thesan grinned. "I remember your discussion with Orion and Claudio last spring. The one about choosing when to act, you were talking about one of the challenges you and Perry took on. Those have been Isembard's particular charges, Pross. Claudio's in his last year, Orion's apprenticing now." Ibis had Claudio in class and had his own reasons to be careful around Orion's family.

She went on promptly. "You were talking about the advantages of height. I can do maths in my head, especially anything involving angles. You could have aimed over me quite safely if you'd actually wanted to fight. Given he was near enough a giant. Long enough for me to drop to the ground and get out of the way, at any rate."

Isembard could feel his face go through a dozen shifts, and he finally let out a wry grunt. "This is why I say you're smarter, love."

"In this case, it's foresight. You know I worry about getting in the middle of some Council mess. We've practised it."

Ibis tilted his head. Rather birdlike, Isembard realised, like his namesake. "You duel?"

For her part, Thesan looked at him, and said, "You did something in the War other than fighting, didn't you? It's good exercise, it keeps me on my toes. It makes me feel more confident about being up on the top of the tower at night with a group of sometimes very stubborn and occasionally difficult students." She gestured. "You saw them. Different reflexes, isn't it? You step back and want to get the big picture of what's going on, I've noticed."

Ibis blinked at her, then he nodded. "Intelligence work. I can take care of myself, but it's more about getting out of trouble long enough to bring information back." He gestured with one hand at Alexander. "As I'm sure he figured out."

Alexander settled back with a lazy smile. Clearly, he had, but Isembard was glad of the information. He didn't begrudge that sort of work. Isembard wasn't made for it, but everything he'd seen from Ibis suggested he'd been both good at it and diligent about following every last thread as far as he could. He nodded. "No problems here."

Pross looked from one to the other. "Now you've all taken each other's measure." She sounded amused. "Ibis can take care of himself, though as you said, Thesan, violence didn't seem on offer. You said you'd done some research?"

Thesan nodded, and Isembard shifted to settle an arm across the back of the sofa, behind her. She shifted to lean into it, accepting the implied apology for doubting her sense as gently as she always did that sort of thing. "People think it's very odd. But I always thought it was only sensible to learn as much as I could about where I expect to live the rest of my life. When I started teaching, I picked up a hobby of searching out old lore about the keep, in particular, and Schola in general."

"I'm sure you have very organised notes." Pross said, nodding at the notebook. "Given that's number, what, volume twenty-three? I can't quite read from here."

"Twenty-three." Thesan agreed. "Out of, um." She flushed. "Forty-five and counting."

Isembard snorted. "There is a reason she needed the

book trunk. It's rather ridiculous, though to be fair, a lot of the notes are charm-duplicated, and that just takes up space, I gather."

Thesan nudged him with her elbow. "And four of them have to do with the salle, so don't you complain too much."

"I am not. We should, however, get on with our planning. So do you have references to mysterious green men? Or other legendary figures? And what they might be asking us to do when we find the cave? It's not as if finding the cave or the meadow or the tree or the whatever is the end of the story. Ever." Isembard settled back to give Thesan space to thumb through her notes, resting his hand on her back.

"It's so complicated how the legend may or may not be a real being. Do we trust the tales tell us the truth of the man before us? Or do we assume they exaggerate or leave things out? I can't help thinking of the Gawain legend, though we're already making noticeable departures." Pross frowned, as if trying to catch a stray thought.

"There were probably several dozen versions of that tale floating around at least, and we only know the surviving one." Ibis must have caught something in Isembard's expression. "I only know about it because Pross and I had a delightful debate with Carillon and Lizzie about it at the end of the summer. Or rather, they debated, and I learned quite a few things. Not my area of expertise."

The way he said it, generously, made Isembard feel better about himself, and also like Ibis better as well. The man was competent as a teacher, even in his first months. He handled students surprisingly well for someone who had neither taught before nor raised children of his own. On the other hand, the Materia rooms were across from Isembard's salle, and he'd heard Ibis talk through his research with students enough times this autumn to know the man knew his field well. Focused on what people had done hundreds, even thousands of years ago, but with an eye to what that meant they knew now.

Isembard enjoyed a good book. But he was given more to the practicalities of how to do the thing rather than the distant analysis of how people did it hundreds of years ago. He sometimes felt out of his league around the rest of the professors.

"I remember acting it out." He nodded slightly. "With Perry." He didn't explain that, because he still didn't know how to without risking hurting Alexander more. Perry had been his best friend, and Alexander's chosen heir, the sort of matched hearts and minds that had nothing to do with bloodline. "But that was a different lifetime ago."

Ibis caught something in the comment, and gestured, letting Pross tell the story. "That's Arthurian, of course, though written rather later, the version that survived. A green knight - much like this one, skin and hair green as well, and a large man, near enough a giant."

That much matched up, certainly. Pross went on. "He comes striding in, no armour, but challenges one of the knights to a test, each taking a stroke at the other's neck. Gawain agrees, after some discussion. He strikes the man's head from his neck, only the green man picks it up and says he'll look forward to seeing Gawain for an exchange of blows. There's the usual sort of travel sequence, and Gawain fetches up at a remote estate. There is a trading of gifts and temptations, there are dozens of books analysing the ritual magic elements of the items." She waved a hand at Alexander.

He picked up, readily. "Quite a few, yes, and quite a lot written about the rituals of exchange. The original text predates the Pact, of course, so there is a strong implication in a great deal of the research that the Green Man and his Lady were Fatae. Not the Seven Sisters, clearly, at least on his account, but something of the kind. Only..."

Isembard saw that at once. "Only here he was, without the proper rituals for negotiation." He was suddenly aware that Ibis and Pross were staring at him, and sighed. He had possibly said rather too much.

Alexander, though, just chuckled. "In this case, I think we may discuss the generalities freely." He settled back, more something than Isembard had seen him in a good while. Relaxed, but it wasn't just that. He was actively engaged, wanting to be engaged in this puzzle, not just responding out of duty. He'd seen flashes of it while Alexander was here as a teacher, but it had been flickers, passing in and out in a few hours, in conversations like this. This visit, though, it had lasted and deepened.

"That's yours to decide." Isembard glanced at Thesan, who had found the spot she wanted in her notes, but she waved for them to go ahead.

"I am, as you both know, a Council Member, one of that august body charged by Richard the Third to take on the land magics and obligations thereunto. And also, therefore, responsible for ensuring the Pact is followed by both sides of the agreement. Managing our own is mostly straightforward. Every so often - by which I mean a few times a year to a few times a decade - someone gets the bright idea to try some ritual to open a door to the Fatae. Sometimes the Guard mends it, sometimes the Council does. Sometimes someone stumbles into some ancient magic and needs to be fished out, or we need to sort out what's going on."

"All of that is logical enough." Ibis agreed, carefully. "My father's estate has an ancient portal near it. There's a certain amount of checking it that has to happen every five years or so."

"The other part of it, of course, is that sometimes we do in fact need to talk to our counterparts, or the nearest diplomatic equivalent. That's normally the Seven Sisters, though not always. It is separate from what might be considered ongoing cooperation under well-defined treaty terms. With some of the Fatae who live belowground, about mining, for example, or some of the shipping." He gestured at the ocean, the side of the island with the coves. "The mermaids, who I suspect you know more about than I do, Ibis."

"Seal House does have that reputation among Schola's houses, yes. Not my area of specialty, but I've met them a few times." Ibis agreed. Isembard suddenly suspected it was more than that, but that probably wasn't relevant at the moment.

"If there are new negotiations needed, the Council handles that. Honestly, it's often 'pardon the idiot, here are the steps we have taken. Do you mind lending a hand on your side?' They have it happen too, sometimes, or we'd feel much worse about the whole thing. I use idiot in the original Greek sense, mind. Someone who is a private person, not acting as part of the community, who cares more for their own interests than that of the polis."

Thesan snorted at that. "But the point remains that our honoured guest was here without any of those rituals. Which, if we follow our second year Trivium lessons in logic, allows one of four answers. He is Fatae but the proper rituals were done by someone else, he is not Fatae, or he is breaking those agreements." She tilted her head. "Or, that his agreement to be here is much older than the Pact, and was grandfathered in."

"I admit that that last option seems remarkably plausible." Alexander agreed. "Given the evidence."

"He did walk in like he knew every stone of the place."

Isembard said. "And he knew us. Did you notice? Thesan, love, he called you mistress of stars."

She tilted her head. "And knew you for my husband, and a blessing on our marriage, and ... he asked about the mead, the way he asked about it." Thesan added to Pross and Ibis. "I mentioned my family has honey traditions. We make a special batch - not this one - for drinking at funerals. If we have some left when the year is done, we get very drunk and count our blessings then. But it's a particular sort of tradition, and not a common one anymore, I gather."

"And the wedding mead." Alexander said.

"Mum was very put out. We moved so quickly on getting married, so what we're drinking tonight is what she put up the night before our wedding." Thesan lifted her glass. "And we have more we'll keep, of course, for later anniversaries."

Pross shook her head. "I've seen references, but it is rather particular." She lifted her glass. "I feel honoured to share it, then."

Thesan smiled broadly at her. "So. We're clear the man is not human, or not now, if he ever was. I suppose that's a fifth category, this research hypothesis is rapidly getting out of control."

It made Alexander laugh, at least, and his eyes crinkled in delight. "That leaves the question of what you bring with you." He gestured with his fingers. "Isembard, I would bring a knife, but a working knife, not a fighting knife. He would consider a knife a daily tool, in a way we mostly do not, but you might want one."

Isembard had been thinking much the same thing. "Sensible clothing. Ankle boots or something else sturdy that protects the feet." He knew Thesan had good boots, since she had a tendency to want to climb small mountains at night to get an unobstructed view from the top. "Walking staffs if you have them, a sturdy piece of wood is good for many things."

Thesan nodded. "Offerings. I mean, food and drink, but I think we should bring a flask of the mead, at least. Cream, and honey cake. He liked the honey cake." She had a note of pride there, and well she should. First, it was excellent honey cake, and second, it wasn't every day a magical being out of legend approved of your baking.

"Pen and paper and a pencil." Pross said, promptly. "And chalk and charcoals, in case there are mazes or a place we need to leave an arrow or some such."

"Not the most reliable way to find your way out. Do not trust to thread, either, though it might be a good addition." Alexander sounded both amused and a bit worried. "Do you know much about caves?" He asked it somewhere between Ibis and Thesan.

Thesan said, "There are small caves along the coast edge, but there's one spot that looks for all the world like it should have an opening, and it doesn't. I'm thinking that is the place we start."

"I agree." Ibis was steepling his hands. "I'd recommend one of our archaeology kits - there are flags for finds, paintbrushes, trowels for smaller digging. They don't take much space. A healer's kit. I'm assuming you have a good one, Isembard?"

Isembard did and nodded. "Your sewing kit, Thesan. Again, small useful objects. I have a full set of working stones. Thesan has a small set. You?"

Ibis shook his head. "Not our thing, as a rule. Though I do have a selection of talismans for protection and well-being that my mother insists on showering us with at regular intervals. By mail, or I'd have more bumps on my head."

"And how are you in challenging physical settings? Thesan likes a good ramble, and doesn't mind hills or I believe caves." Isembard was working through the practicalities. "I learned a lot in the War." Thesan shook her head, making it clear she had no objections to hills or caves.

There was a tiny hesitation, the kind of communication forged in some shared adversity, the sort of thing that he and Thesan were only beginning to feel sure of for themselves. Then Pross spoke. "We spent last summer in cramped quarters in a barrow with only one entrance. We're fine underground."

"Well." Isembard swallowed. "We should all get some rest. Alexander, will you come see us off, as far as the road to the beach, at least?"

"I would be honoured." With that, he stood, breaking the little party up. "I will, if you don't mind, make a pass around the keep to make sure all is as it should be. I remember the patrol route well enough. Then I will retire to my room with a book, and let you two sort what you need." Ibis and Pross nodded, and stood as well, to go back down to Ibis's cottage, a short way from the school. That was all that could be usefully done until tomorrow.

CHAPTER 3
THE SHORELINE ON THE MORNING OF
DECEMBER 24TH

Pross shivered in the morning chill, even with a warm cloak on. They were all dressed sensibly, layers with good boots. It was rather like going mountaineering, which she'd done a few times. She had a walking stick in her off hand, and a satchel over her shoulder, just as Ibis and Thesan and Isembard did.

They had left Helena and Alexander at the top of the road, along with Cammie and Hypatia, who had come along to see them off. Alexander had promised them an unusual language lesson, which she suspected involved Demotic script, as well as Arabic. But it would certainly entertain them. And keep them out of the way, which was the more important part.

Her hand was tucked through Ibis's arm. He'd navigated the rocky path down to the beach as if he'd done it hundreds of times before, which he apparently had. It struck her again how different people's experiences of Schola were.

She'd spent her time as a student in the library and the house library and the house study rooms - well, as any proper member of Owl House should. Ibis had apparently been down on the coastline more than a few times. She assumed that Isembard had spent much of his time in the salle, and Thesan up on top of the keep's tower. Much as they spent their time now.

She envied Thesan, having such a clear idea of what she wanted to do, and having a decade of experience at it, even now in her mid-thirties. Pross was ten years older, and was only beginning to figure out what she really wanted. She'd gone from learning bookselling - which she enjoyed - to having Cammie, to the War and holding things together while Octavian was elsewhere.

Then there had been a long and quiet unexpected widowhood until meeting Ibis at the beginning of the year. It had been a whirlwind since then. First the investigation of the lost hoard, and all the risks and threats it had brought with it from people who grabbed at power. It had made it clear Ibis needed a role somewhere other than the Research Society, where he'd been a fellow. When he'd had the interview to be the Materia professor here at Schola, it had seemed like a gift, if a startling and unexpected one.

Now her life was uprooted again, in all the best ways, but it made her envy and yearn for those deep foundations. Now, she was picking her way through a rocky beach, to find a cave that might not be there, to chase a legend. She snorted, mostly to herself, and Ibis peered at her. "What's so funny?"

"I was just thinking about the difference between last year and this year. I mean, look at this? But you and I have done things just as strange."

He patted her arm. "I'm curious. That's what the last year changed for me. I want to know about the mystery."

Thesan led the way along to a point about halfway across the beach, maybe an eighth of a mile. She turned to face the cliffs, and Pross immediately understood what she'd meant last night. There were two shapes, almost like pillars, weathered out of the stone, and a long dark shadow of a gap.

Ibis said, "I've tried to get in there. It looks like there's space, and then it narrows down to nothing." Pross wanted to ask him if he'd tried it using all of his skills, but she couldn't begin to hint at it, not here. She suspected Isembard was sharper than he let on, in terms of piecing things together, and she knew she had to be careful with Ibis's secrets.

"When did you last look?" Isembard was peering at it up and down. "And do we think a charm or two for information would be a bad idea?"

"Which one, love?" Thesan asked, while she circled up to one side of the gap.

Ibis shrugged. "A fortnight ago, give or take? No, more like three weeks. Richart came down after that." He walked up, looking around the entrance. "No. Wait. This is different. The space is actually there."

Isembard cleared his throat. "I was thinking Alcade's Second? But we could just try the obvious, and see what happens when we walk in? Me first, I think? Beyond that - Ibis, then Pross, then Thesan?" Pross wasn't sure what to make of that order, or whether this meant Isembard would be automatically assuming she wasn't competent. On the other hand, she certainly wasn't a competent duellist, and she had to assume he was. For a multitude of reasons. So she nodded.

Thesan said cheerfully, "That's because he trusts me to do what he says if something's urgent, without arguing." Which was a fair reason, Pross supposed. And if Thesan practised duelling with her husband, she presumably had some skill there, which Pross certainly didn't.

One by one, they quieted and went into the gap between the rocks. It was not, despite Ibis's comments, a tight fit at all. It was a good few inches on either side of Pross's body, without even turning sideways.

She heard the men in front of her make a noise, a sound of startlement but not panic. By the time she came through, they'd got a lantern lit, then the second. As soon as she got into the cavern, she understood why. It was quite tall, a good twenty or thirty feet, reaching up what must be halfway up the cliff. If, mind, the cliff and the cavern were in the same bit of reality. It was entirely possible they'd crossed into some liminal realm.

The light, though, that reflected a shimmering, opalescent cavern. It was rather like being underwater, but in a world of silver and pearl rather than blues and greens. There were arches of stone, something like the great cathedral in Shrewsbury, near where her in-laws still lived. But of course, these were shaped differently, moulded and worn out of the stone rather than built up. They weren't stalagmites and stalactites, either, not exactly.

"Fairytale rules apply?" Pross asked it without thinking, the way she'd taught Cammie to be careful of unknown magic. Ibis, at least, had heard her use it before, and smiled at her.

Thesan looked quizzical, while Isembard seemed to be scanning the space for any sign of threat or concern. "How do you define that?"

"It's what I taught Cammie, when she came across some new magic. Don't eat or drink anything without checking with me or another adult. Don't pick up anything without permission. And if you meet someone who you don't know, be very polite and help them if you can, without taking on an obligation."

"Has it come up often? That seems a useful set of

guidelines." Thesan did the same thing, glancing around, but she was obviously also keeping an ear out for what Isembard was doing. Nothing seemed to be moving, though the flickers of the light made that a bit hard to spot.

Ibis was looking around, the way he got when he was puzzling through some new bit of research. Pross knew better than to jog his elbow or interrupt, so she took a step or two to one side.

"We should make a map, at the least." Thesan rummaged in the pocket of her cloak, and came out with a small notebook, folding it over, and pulling what must be a pencil out, before starting to sketch. Pross couldn't see the map itself. The angles were all wrong, but she couldn't help being focused on how smoothly Thesan made the lines and shapes. She supposed astronomy would teach a certain amount of that, of the spatial relationships, even if maps were on a very different scale than the stars.

Once she'd got a few lines sketched in, Thesan looked up. "Locational magic, rather than astronomy proper. I've done enough sketches for sites and some other specifics that I got good at the basic layout drawing out of self-preservation."

"So we all have some unexpected talents, then? That one's useful." Ibis nodded. "I've a good hand with it as well, archaeology. If we need a second."

Isembard, she could see, had moved forward, into the centre of the huge cavern, looking around at the edges. He turned back. "How about we take each side, two by two? Don't touch anything, but keep an eye out for anything unusual. Or anything like a door or archway. Meet in the middle, we'll discuss the next step there."

"The obvious pairs?" Ibis straightened up.

"We're used to working together that way, both sets of

us?" Pross noticed how Isembard had taken charge, even though Ibis was a couple of years older. On the other hand, Isembard clearly had experience in war and conflict, and Ibis had less. Also, Ibis wasn't arguing, and it wasn't her fight to have, at least not here and now. Especially when, really, the suggestions were sensible and she would rather be with Ibis.

They took the right side, in the end, and Thesan and Isembard took the left. Going up their side, they could see a couple of shadows that might or might not be tunnels, but nothing definitive. There didn't seem to be tidepools, per se, but there did seem to be some source of water somewhere. They could hear it burbling in two spots. She suddenly wondered when the tides were. Getting caught in here would be horrific.

Ibis must have caught something of her expression. "We're well up above the tide line, it's a neap tide, and we're not yet anywhere near spring." When she blinked at him, he added, "Highest tides on a full moon or new moon around the spring equinox. This spring, I'll show you, all right?" Then he grinned. "Right now, we're in a waning moon. It's winter, there's no storm nearby, and it would take quite a lot to get above the tide line anyway."

"I am glad someone knows a reassuring amount about that. Not part of my life."

"Well, London and the more foresty part of the New Forest. Tides aren't the dominant natural event, are they? At least if you don't make your living near the water."

"And water and bookstores, generally a bad mix." Pross relaxed a bit. The fact Ibis could tease was tremendously reassuring. "You're taking this as an adventure, then?"

He hesitated before he answered, but he nodded. "The green knight - he had a sword, can we call him a knight?"

"I feel that's fair, unless and until we have a better

label?" Pross hadn't really thought about it in detail, but a sword like that did have implications, historically speaking.

"He was clear that no harm was meant. Which means that I don't think there are, what's the word. I think we could get hurt, but I don't think it's some hidden pitfall. The natural risks of caves, perhaps, or anyone can slip and fall in the safest room in the world. But I don't believe there's an imminent threat we must spot."

"Why not?"

Ibis shrugged, gesturing with his chin across the cavern. "Do you think Thesan would be here if there were a threat? At least not without an argument that went far into the night? They're both reasonably well-rested, they're getting along comfortably, he's listening to her ideas without any kind of defensiveness, and she's making them without feeling like she's overstepping."

"When you put it like that." Pross shook her head. "That's the kind of thing you were doing in the War, then?" They'd talked a bit about his service and hers, but not in a great deal of detail. They had, to be fair, been focused on more interesting things.

"A fair bit of it. The quieter patterns, the ways people, even if they're not talking about something, give hints away that there's a lurking problem." Ibis shrugged.

"And you don't mind him taking the lead?" Pross felt she had to ask. Now they had a moment alone.

"By Wadjet, no." He grinned. "Protective goddess." Which Pross had more or less placed, but she appreciated the clarifications. There were rather a lot of Egyptian powers to keep straight. "I saw him last night, same as you did. He knows what he's doing when it comes to this sort of thing. He has extensive field experience, which none of the rest of us do. And he had a point about how the protection of Schola and her people falls under his duties, in particular."

"Do you think they explained that to him before he took the role?" Pross couldn't help wondering how you asked that. She'd got a sense, from things Isembard and Thesan had mentioned in passing, that neither of them had expected him to be a professor lasting for decades to come. Not originally, anyway. For all it was clear they were making their home here for the foreseeable future.

"I hope so. I suspect not. I have gathered the previous headmaster - Alvis Osborne - was very, um. How did Linta put it. Detached, during the previous decade or three, from anything other than his own particular interests."

Pross blinked. "That's almost blunt, for academic commentary."

Ibis snorted. "Very. I did ask Richart about it after she said that. He's the only one I feel I could ask, at least yet." He gestured with a hand. "Maybe this will change that."

"What did Richart say?" Pross glanced over at a shadow, then decided it was simply a curve of the cave wall.

"Richart made it clear that Alvis had been told he could resign, or the heads of House would make sure he left. They have, in some ways, more direct power than the Head. He had been neglectful. Not directly dangerous to students, but refusing to make space or time for concerns, letting petty squabbles get in the way. Richart didn't go into that, mind."

"He doesn't gossip much, does he? But he's sharing the information you really need to know. That's fair enough."

Ibis grinned suddenly. "He said if I make it through the year and agree to come back, then he'll tell me the gossip. But it's good for me to make my own judgements about people and situations. Unless something unusual comes up."

"Wasn't that his approach in class, too?" Pross considered. Sympathetic magic, Richart's field, relied on both established connections, but also the wielder's own ideas of what fit together.

"He is consistent like that. Wait, look, over here. Does that look like a proper passage to you?" Ibis held up the lantern, peering at it.

"I think that's a shadow? But look, over there, it does seem that's a solid wall, and is that ..." She pointed. Behind a row of stalagmites, she could now see something that looked remarkably like a door. Or at least, like it should be a door. It had that sort of solidity, but it didn't seem to be made out of wood.

Ibis nodded, then gestured across at Isembard and Thesan, who had come up the other side. They were about twenty feet apart now, with various stone outcroppings curving between them. Then they made their way to meet the others in the centre. "Is that the way in, do you think?"

"It seems likely. We didn't see anything that looked promising." Isembard looked it up and down. "That seems like, oh, what's the model you were showing me, love, with the rotating door?"

"I wanted a secret door to our rooms, but several people talked me out of it. The ones that turn around a rod through the centre. A pivot hinge."

"She may have talked me into one from the sitting room to our private office." Isembard admitted. "But that's not a weight-bearing wall, which makes rather a difference. Shall we investigate?"

There was indeed an archway that looked rather door shaped. But where a door might be, there was a flat smooth rock surface. It might fit inside the archway, it might not, it was impossible to tell. Isembard gestured again, and went to peer at the side of it, and Ibis repeated it on their side.

"Any sign of - anything?" Isembard frowned. "I admit that engineering is not precisely one of my better skills."

Thesan shifted. Pross caught the movement, a small gesture of reassurance, that made her sure that whatever experience he had was something unpleasant in the War. Not the trenches, she assumed, from the bits and pieces she'd threaded together.

"A small hole." She could hear the catch in his voice, but she wasn't sure the others would. It had a hollow note, which told her everything about the size of the hole. It would be big enough for something she could hold in her hands.

He came back to her side, and she reached to touch his elbow, as Isembard asked, "Where?"

"On the ground, six inches back from - if that's a door." Ibis frowned, clearly thinking through the implications.

Thesan followed her husband to look at it, then came back to peer at the door. "May I touch it, Isembard?"

"Me first." He came back around. "Now I do want to try a charm. We'll feel ridiculous if one of the standard opening cantrips works first thing."

Ibis was shaken out of his musing enough to say, "I don't think it's that easy."

Indeed, it wasn't. Isembard cast a charm light first. Partly, Pross thought, to make sure it didn't cause some unintended reaction. When two charm lights, one on either side of the door, didn't do anything, he reached to press the edges of the door. He used his height - he must be six foot three, at least - to reach up above. Then he tried a set of charms, in remarkably rapid sequence, after Thesan stepped back to join Pross and Ibis.

Ibis blinked at the range of them, and Thesan added, "That's some professional bohort playing for you. More to the point, tutoring Orion and Claudio, and the school team last year. They did quite well in the league matches, and he has grand hopes this year, even if Orion's left school."

Isembard ran through another chain of charms, and then turned back, shaking his head. "Nothing I can sort out." He grimaced. "So the question is, are we meant to explore through that hole? I am not inclined to stick a hand in. A walking stick, maybe."

Ibis swallowed. Then there was the tiny shiver of his shoulders. "Let me have another look."

CHAPTER 4
THE FIRST CAVERN

Ibis could feel his stomach lurch. He'd had a sense as soon as he'd seen the hole. It might have been crafted as a challenge, specifically for him. And of course, it was the first challenge they were facing.

He wanted, desperately, to have something to measure it against. He wished he knew what the green knight had meant, whether they could trust that nothing would be harmful. Whether the knight was even speaking the same connotative dialect that they were.

The knight had spoken in modern English. Oh, a little aged around the edges, like he'd not trotted it out for a century or two, but not even so far back as Shakespeare, de Vere, or Lanier. That implied he had a modern interpretation of harm, but that couldn't be a sure thing. For one thing, it's not like there was a modern agreement on the term, outside of the narrow negotiations of a duelling salle or bohort field.

Now, Ibis sucked in a breath, and went to peer at the hole in the stone again. Six or so inches high, five wide, it was near enough a half-circle. He was fairly sure he'd fit through there. If he took the risk.

He straightened and came back to the group. Pross was watching him, and she held out a hand. She knew what he was wrestling with, at least. He wasn't alone with it to sort it out. Ibis hesitated. "Pross, a word? In private?"

Isembard gestured. "If you wouldn't mind, stay where we have a good line of sight? Fifteen feet in either direction should be fine. Just in case."

Ibis nodded and drew Pross back in the direction they'd come from. He stood with his back to Isembard and Thesan. He trusted them to watch his back, but he had no idea if either of them could read lips or use some other charm or gift. "You know what I'm thinking." He kept his voice low, a bare whisper.

"What do you need to do it?" Pross, thank all his blessings, was pragmatic. She had learned, this past spring, why he was so private about it. They'd talked about it a number of times since. He didn't think she understood all of it. He wasn't sure anyone could if they weren't able to themselves. But she did well with it, as a rule.

"They'll have opinions." He couldn't keep a slight quaver out of his voice.

Pross glanced over his shoulder, through the darkness of the cavern back to the other two, and the charm light. "You said Thesan gets on well with Richart, and he likes her. Do you think she knows about him?"

Ibis had not been able to bring himself to ask, actually. It would imply things he wasn't ready to sort through yet. Trust wasn't transitive, especially in the places it most mattered. If Richart had trusted her with his secret, then Ibis felt better doing so. But he didn't know if she knew, or whether she'd told her husband, or whether Richart had said anything else that might be relevant. Critical.

"I haven't asked." Even to him, it sounded feeble.

Pross clucked her tongue. "Do you see an alternative?"

There was a long silence, a good half minute. Finally, Ibis shook his head. "No. Not unless they have some trick they haven't mentioned."

"Let us go and ask, and if there isn't any other idea, well. Will you?" Pross reached to take his other hand in hers.

"Needs must. I don't like it. But I don't know what else to do." And he felt they needed to do something. He could feel a tug on his magic, something that had weight and insistence about it.

"Let us go discuss it like civilised and skilled people with words at our disposal. And I'll be right with you, if they're awful."

Ibis closed his eyes, and nodded. He offered a brief prayer under his breath, in the ancient form, for strength and grace and clarity of tongue, finishing with "May Djheuty guide me."

He must have said the last bit near enough out loud, because Pross squeezed his hand as they came back to the others.

"I have a skill, one I keep private."

Thesan's eyes lit up. She was not shy about her knowledge. He suspected most people would miss it; it was subtle, only a term talking with her regularly made it obvious to him. Well, and the exceedingly personal nature of the skill. It made him deeply sensitive to any hint about it. She didn't ask him about it, didn't say anything. She just put her hand on Isembard's arm and waited.

In the end, perhaps it was easier to show them. Ibis took a deep breath and then drew his magic into him. He made the peculiar twist in his head that the shifting required, and felt himself shrink down to a few bare inches above the ground, on tiny and stubby legs. He could feel the senses change, the way a hedgehog's nose worked, smelling the cool stone of the cave, and a thread of something else that was more like moss.

The first thing he heard was Thesan's delighted warm laugh, and a "Oh, that's grand. That's truly grand." Then she must have looked at Pross, because she added, "Not a surprise to you?"

"Not anymore." Pross was more cautious, waiting to see Isembard's reactions.

The other man was quiet for a long time, long enough to make Ibis nervous. "And a hedgehog?"

Something in his tone, the way he sounded honestly, a bit baffled, made Pross relax. She snorted. Ibis could hear the moment she'd decided Isembard wasn't a threat. "Have you ever met anyone more likely to be a hedgehog? Prickly as he can be?" Then she added, "Change back, love, so we can discuss strategy?"

Pross knew he could change several times without a rest if it were called on. And he knew they had brought along plenty of food and drink and a few restorative potions if need be. This shift was more about spreading himself out, growing back into his body, and he concentrated on it ferociously for a dozen seconds. It wasn't fast, either way, not for him. He brushed his hands off on his trousers, almost instinctively, feeling the stone of the cave under his paws still.

Once he had done that, he forced himself to look at Thesan and Isembard. Thesan had her head cocked, considering him. Her hand had slipped into her husband's, perhaps to encourage him to be moderate? Ibis wasn't sure at all how to read Isembard, in particular.

There was a moment's hesitation, then Isembard offered his hand. "I can see why you might not tell people.

Glad to have your skills." It was the sort of thing men did on the bohort field, or in an army mess. Then he glanced at Thesan, and added, wryly. "Also, she had a word in my ear last year about shifting and my unexamined biases. More than a few words."

Ibis let out a long breath, then nodded. "You'll keep it confidential, then?"

"I won't tell anyone you don't tell me I can." Isembard agreed. "Though I'm glad I know. There are a couple of matters related to the Schola wards where, honestly, that might be quite helpful."

Thesan patted his arm. "You are getting ahead of yourself." She then added, after a moment. "I've known about Richart for a few years, and he told Isembard last autumn. There was an unfortunate worry with a snare."

"But you haven't seen him?" Ibis considered that.

"Thesan has. I haven't, not changing, and not up close. Just a hare, silhouetted in the twilight, before it went bounding off. It's quite an impressive bit of magic, isn't it?" Isembard seemed firmly settled in how the thing might be used, which honestly Ibis found reassuring and worrying in equal terms.

Reassuring, because there were no signs Isembard considered him less than human, like some of the Great Families were about shifters. Worrisome because that's how too many people had ended up dead during the War, and before the War, and back through history.

Isembard must have caught something about that. "Richart also explained that one of the requirements for the head of Seal House is being able to tell that someone can shift. And to be able to help them if they're learning it. Which rather implies the ability itself, though not uniformly."

"Which you've been thinking about ever since. Personally, I was suspecting that Richart was pleased to have you apply for the position. It means he might have someone he's willing to turn the House over to in due course. Your ability just makes that more likely, doesn't it?" Then she brushed off her hands. It seemed like that explained something important to her. "That can wait until we are tucked up cosy and warm on the other end of this. What do you need to be able to do this safely? The hole's big enough we could pass through a small lantern, or supplies, likely?"

Pross laughed. "I like your practicality, Thesan. Do we have a smaller lantern we could put a charm light in? The bigger ones would be a tight squeeze. I don't want to risk breaking them. And there's... do we have any idea what happens when Ibis gets inside?"

"That's the question, isn't it? Is this challenge designed to press him to reveal his secret? I think that is a logical enough conclusion. In which case, presumably, he can go inside, undo a latch or something, and we move on. If, on the other hand, there is more to the challenge, then I don't know what we do."

Isembard nodded. "Do you feel like you can handle yourself long enough to change again and come back, if you need to?"

"I don't think I know how to answer that question." Ibis said, honestly. "I was in Intelligence in the War, but I only shifted once or twice. They didn't know." Or at least he hadn't told them, and he kept that dark and terrifying fear tightly knotted in the back of his mind where it couldn't wander. "But it's not the first time I've been in an unknown situation."

Isembard grunted. "Well said." There was a respect there that Ibis hadn't heard from Isembard before. The man had been friendly, genial, an agreeable colleague, but Ibis had not got much of a sense of him beyond that.

They'd been busy, their specialities didn't much overlap, and Ibis was still settling into the school.

Thesan, for her part, had taken a step back. "Pross, have you done any reading about architecture?"

"A little about many things." Pross said. "Why?"

"Look at those two stalactites, how they run all the way up to the ceiling. Do you think there's a chance the door is set in like a portcullis, or something of the kind, with ropes to pull it up?"

Pross joined Thesan, facing the thing that looked like it ought to be a door. "Not a pivot door?"

"If it's a pivot door - at least the ones my brother has made - it will need some sort of bar or latch to hold it closed. On the other side, since it's clearly not on this one. If it's a portcullis, it would be ropes or chains. You could get a good tall door without us seeing the ropes, depending on how they were set up."

"You have a point. Which means Ibis changing again once he's inside, but we'd assume that, really."

"Unless there is a hedgehog-shaped lever to trigger something. And honestly, I'm not sure I'd trust that." Thesan said. "This is an interesting sort of challenge, isn't it? All about the need to trust, and yet, you don't want to take that foolishly far."

"Foolish trust has not generally been a problem in my life." Ibis pointed out, with some dignity.

"Rather not, from everything your sister says." Thesan was teasing gently, rather the way Hypatia teased him when she was in a good mood and not around her other teachers.

He raised an eyebrow. "Clearly, we should talk more about my sister. Now, however." He took a breath. "Any reason I shouldn't go reconnoitre that hole now?"

"Let me get the lantern ready. Thesan, the small one,

do you have it? We should be able to set it inside so you can get a good look before you enter."

"I don't need much light as - as a hedgehog." He hadn't said it out loud, often. "But I suppose it will be useful opening things up."

Thesan nodded, and rummaged in her satchel, pulling out a small lantern that fit tidily on her outstretched palm. She considered. "Let me light it. You both might need your strength for other things. Any reason we need to preserve night vision, do you think?"

Isembard snorted at that, but he didn't argue. "I think we can rely on the lantern. Or let our eyes adjust later, if we need." A moment later, she had it lit with a steady but muted golden glow. He supposed that must be a charm she did regularly, given the classes on the tower. Isembard ducked over to the tiny hole again, getting on hands and knees to push the lantern in, and peer around as best he could.

"Don't see anything right nearby. The lantern's to the right as you enter, away from that door slab." He stood up, a bit creakily, and Ibis remembered he had a bad knee. Not that he seemed inclined to let it stop him from doing things.

"Right." Ibis let out a long breath. "Here goes, then." He called his magic to him. It might be his imagination, but it felt like it came a bit more smoothly this time, like wrapping a cloak around him. Then he was down on the ground, nosing at the dust and chill of the cave floor, before he went trotting along. The light from the lantern was almost too bright now. He was glad she hadn't made it brighter, but it did let him peer around from the hole, to see what else was there.

Of course, his eyes didn't work the way they did when he had two legs. Everything was rather faded. He'd described it to Pross one night this summer as being sepia-toned, looking at older photographs or prints that had faded and smudged. It was more than enough for him to tell there wasn't some lurking figure or immediate danger.

More to the point, he didn't hear or smell anything amiss. He could hear the others, the small sounds of their boots on stone or a breath. Nothing in the passageway, even when he scampered a few feet down the passage and back. There were no new smells, either. That stone, over-whelmingly, the salt bite of the sea air, and again that faint scent of forest loam and moss, an earthy dampness rather than an ocean one.

There was plenty of space. A long passage stretched back under the island. It ran, he thought, roughly back toward the school, but he wasn't at all certain of the angle. The ceiling height was difficult to judge in his current form, but he thought it must be a good nine or ten feet high. And then, yes, as he snuffled at the front of the passage, he could smell a faint shift of moving air. It was the kind of thing that indicated a gap, however infinitesimal, beneath the door.

Satisfied he'd learned all in this form that he could, he gathered himself and transformed again. Once more, it seemed curiously easier than he'd expected. He breathed in again, and let it out, then called out. "Having a look now." Ibis had to remind himself that they worried. His hedgehog thought much less about that sort of thing, about the emotions and connections. It, he, was much more concerned with safety and food and where he could find what he needed.

Now that his eyes were adjusting to the light, he could see there were what looked like two ropes hanging down one side of the passage. He reached out, almost touching one, then took a breath and curled his fingers around it.

When he pulled, it was clearly a pulley. The rope on the other side ran up. Ibis could hear - could nearly feel - the scrape of stone against stone, before the panel in front of him began to lift.

It was not easy going. Even with magic in play, as he suspected there was, stone was heavy. The engineering, though, made him think of his Egyptian ancestors, moving massive blocks to build the pyramids. Steadily, the stone lifted. When he let go of tension on the rope, it held in place. That was promising, that there was some sort of precaution, though he also spotted a hook on the wall that should work. A jamb cleat, he thought that was the name, from one of his trips back to England by ship when he was a child.

He called out again. "Come around to the front."

There was a murmur from outside, too muffled for Ibis to make out, especially as he kept pulling the stone up and up. By the time he had it to about head height, he could see the other three, standing back enough to be well out of the way. Pross was glancing between him and the stone above, and Thesan pointed at something, out of his line of sight.

Ibis pulled the rope at an angle, enough he could work a loop over that jamb cleat, testing it until he was sure it would hold properly. Then he smiled at them, and made a bow. "A passage, though I have not explored it at all."

"Well done." Isembard's praise was warm. And, Ibis was startled to realise, also very welcome. He had taken a risk, even if it was a thoughtful and necessary one, and Isembard knew it and respected it.

Thesan smiled at him. "We were commenting on how it seemed to be quite well designed." She came to peer at the rope, looking up toward where it disappeared to what must be the pulley. "Do we go on, then?"

"It seems we must?" That was Pross, as she rummaged in her satchel for a flask of tea, opening it and handing it over to Ibis without a word. They'd got used to reading each other that way this summer, and it was an intimacy he was particularly grateful for now. "Once we've made sure we're as prepared as can be for what's next."

CHAPTER 5
THE FIRST CAVERN

Thesan glanced around. "Now we have determined the next step, should we take a breather, and sort out what we're doing? Somewhere with a little seating space?"

Isembard glanced around. "Out in the cavern, here?" He gestured at the hallway leading off into the darkness, beyond where they now stood.

"If we sit here, we can lean our backs against something, be aware if anything is coming in either direction, and have somewhere to put the lanterns?" Pross pointed this out amiably. "Having spent rather a long time inside an excavation, don't underestimate having something to lean against."

Isembard snorted. "Oh, I won't. Here, then." He grimaced, and settled down with his back against one wall. Thesan settled in beside him, closer to the entrance, while Pross and Ibis mirrored them. The passage was wide enough both men could stretch out their legs without worrying about hitting the other side.

Pross pulled out her flask of tea, and offered it round. Thesan, however, considered Ibis. "Are you all right?"

He ran his hand over his face, through his hair. "I feel like I'm missing something. That was a challenge, obviously. But it was, I don't know how to measure the challenge."

Isembard opened his mouth, then closed it again, and let Thesan talk. She loved that about him, that he was willing to settle back and observe and think. "Can you lay that out, since I feel like I'm missing something too."

Ibis shrugged, and gestured, summoning a little green point of light that hovered like a lonely star, as he talked. "We have the green knight, which I think we may call him for ease of identification. Allowing as how he didn't give a name, and he carried a sword."

"No sign of a horse, but I agree the sword is indicative." Pross said, amused.

Ibis nodded, then flicked another dot of light into existence, this one a glowing red. "He presents a challenge. We discussed this, at length last night, that he said a chance for learning. A quest. But he promised no harm would come to us, just something not seen for many years."

"We are," Thesan pointed out. "In a cave. It restricts the vision, a cave does."

"We seem to be asked to go deeper into it. You said last night that you thought there was more beneath the keep than can be found from the foundations."

Thesan nodded. She had not, honestly, talked much about it last night because she had not talked much about it with anyone. Some with Isembard, over the last year. It was, as he'd said last night, one of his particular duties to see to the wards and protections that were woven into Schola's walls. Saying it out loud, even in the comforting dark and soft charm light from the lanterns, felt like she was exposing something fragile and vulnerable.

Not unlike Ibis must have felt. "As I said, the records are scant. You'll get a flurry for fifteen years, of every tiny bill or barter with the village. Then there'll be a hundred year span where there's a line or two in a great bound volume that says, roughly, "The well-being of the school has continued as before." She shrugged. "I gather you appreciate that kind of problem, in your own research."

Ibis snorted and relaxed a bit. "I do. It's quite peculiar, isn't it? And of course, they leave out all the actually useful bits, such as a clearly marked plan of the foundations, or later additions."

"Exactly. The earliest detailed plan we have of the seven houses, the expansion of the curtain wall around the keep, is about twenty-five years after they were built. And there are notes on it, saying things were changed, but not what they were changed from. Most tedious."

"It did help me locate three hidden passages, and a window people were fond of sneaking out of." Isembard pointed out. "So it was some use."

Pross tilted her head, a wisp of hair bobbing in the light. "Do they do that often?"

"Usually the young men who like a challenge, and who are not yet convinced of their own mortality." Isembard said, shaking his head.

"By which he means he catches one or another of a certain bunch in the wards every month or so. Though less this year." Thesan said. "Orion was a surprisingly good influence."

Ibis stiffened slightly, and Isembard waved his hand. "You keep worrying about it. I don't care for Orion's uncle any more than you did, and now he's bound by oath for the foreseeable future. I honestly expect he's going to work himself into apoplexy sooner than later. Orion was headed down that road, but I hope I've done a fair bit to change his mind."

Thesan grinned. "More than a bit. Didn't you say he'd written last week? We got distracted, and I know we'll see him on Monday, at the Carringtons. Assuming all goes well here."

"If it doesn't, you won't have to make pleasant conversation with half a dozen people you'd rather avoid." Isembard snorted. "I do apologise for the social obligations."

"I knew what I was getting when I married you." Thesan pointed out, then she shrugged. "Pardon, we are still remarkably like newlyweds, and periodically give into the temptation of sappiness."

Pross blinked at her. "I find it rather charming, honestly? It's not that common with, well, older couples? People who have found each other in maturity?"

That made Isembard laugh. "I feel I am only barely qualified on that count. And a number of the difficult conversations are with various ladies who wish I had chosen them. Or dallied longer, or a number of other wishes best not repeated in public. So the blame all falls to me. Thesan is very gracious, putting up with it."

Thesan was watching Pross closely, more than Ibis, and she saw the little inhale. "Again, I knew what I was marrying. Mostly, we ignore the social obligations during term time. I grit my teeth for the necessary events over the winter holidays and a few things over the summer. Honestly, I mostly hole up with a couple of the people who like books and being interesting, and we do well enough. Alexander knows them all, of course, and he's been delighted to have the excuse of explaining things to me."

"The man does like an explanation." Pross agreed. "And he's quite good at it."

"Alexander likes an explanation on his own terms. He's like a sphinx at other times, he always has been." Isembard shook his head. "I can't decide if I'm glad he's not here, or wishing he were, for the record."

Thesan considered. "Wishing he was here, because he'd be delighted by it? But also, he'd..." She tried to find the words for it. "Seeing you last night, the two of you, how you responded. I'd not seen that directly, before."

She must have had a queer note in her voice. Isembard immediately focused all his attention on her, taking her right hand in his left, and bringing it to his lips. "Did we alarm you?"

"Oh, no. And oh, yes. But you made it clear, both of you, what you were like. How you know each other, in that particular way. I'm glad you don't need to call on it often, but it..." Thesan searched for words. "You are superb, and it was a joy to see your skill. What you are brilliant at."

There was a tiny silence, a gaping one, in the near-dark, before Ibis spoke, his voice low and clear. "I never had that, in my War. Working so closely with people I could trust to match my competence."

Thesan looked at him, peering across the passage. She had got the sense, the past term, that he had been quietly lonely, desperately isolated, before he'd met Pross. Not from things he'd said, even. He was prickly as a hedgehog, as Pross had noted.

It was more what his sister had said, her obvious delight in seeing him relax. Ibis was more than twice Hypatia's age, but Hypatia had an old soul, and what Thesan's mother would have called a worrying heart. She saw things about her brother no one else could or had.

Isembard nodded. "Being alone with it - ah, I don't wish that on anyone." Thesan filed away the thought that she should check with Seth and Golshan about whether one of their groups of veterans might suit Ibis. Or whether Isembard was inclined to invite him along of his own accord. That was a problem for later, at some point after this cave.

It made her clear her throat. "So. This cave."

Her husband laughed, and relaxed again. He was like that, settling into the necessary work with good will, even if it were strange or difficult. It was, with the benefit of some time to sort it out, one of the things she most loved about him. He was unstinting with himself. That could cause problems, and had already, but he had a generosity of heart like a lighthouse. To the right eyes, at least, as she hoped hers were. "This cave." he agreed. "We're heading back toward the school, aren't we?"

Thesan nodded. "I wrote down the headings last night, but that doesn't answer for the distance, not precisely. And I'm not sure any of us wants to muck around with measured strides."

"Even if we could, with the various bits of rock in the way." Isembard agreed. "Do you think it will matter?"

Thesan shrugged. "Philosophically, no? If we are heading back to the foundation of the keep, then we are heading to the foundation of the keep. If we aren't, we aren't. If we have passed through some threshold into another space, not bounded by a nutshell, then no measurements we have will do us any good anyway."

She caught Pross's expression, which was hovering between amused and baffled, and repeated. "Philosophical. The nature of space and time, or at least their magics, are part of my field, I consider myself quite well read in both.

But I admit this is not a problem discussed in the extant literature."

"There's another paper for you to write up this winter. Besides that one on timing and the royal stars you've been working on." Isembard still sounded relaxed, which made her tilt her head to peer at him.

"It doesn't bother you?"

"Being bothered seems a waste of energy. We decided to come here, for good reason. We have some assurances that we will not be harmed, but will be challenged. If the other challenges are like this was, then we'll manage. Or we won't manage, but I trust we'll give it our best." Isembard shrugged. "The War burned worrying out of me, more or less. Though now I say that, I'm glad Alexander isn't here. This is a place where those habits might be the exactly wrong thing. Our instincts last night were not yours, love, and yours was better."

Pross half-lifted her hand in the pause, then put it down, as if she were in class, before snorting at herself. "So what do we do? Is this just a festive scavenger hunt?"

Ibis grunted. "Not entirely festive." He curled his arms around himself for a moment, then stopped, changed his mind visibly, and settled one around Pross's shoulder. It made her smile, and Thesan as well. "I hoped you would be reasonable, but that doesn't mean it felt reasonable."

There was a silence there, before Isembard nodded. "So we might expect more of the same. He did say it would be a chance for learning of all kinds." He flicked his fingers. "The part I'm trying to figure out, reasoning in advance of the visible chart," He nodded at Thesan, who appreciated the metaphor. "Is what the goal is."

"He was specific about wanting younger staff." Pross frowned. "Well, and possibly me. But you're all the youngest of the teaching staff, aren't you? And by a fair bit."

"It depends how you count the library and infirmary staff, but yes." Isembard shook his head. "We've been circling around that in staff meetings for the past year and a half, about ossification."

Pross hesitated. "I noticed there wasn't a lot of explanation about why Alvis Osborne retired then. Rather precipitously, considering? I'd have expected an announcement in October or November, feting him the rest of the year. Then the glorious announcement of a new head, quite possibly from outside the school."

When Isembard's chin went up in startlement, Pross added, "My father's in the Colonial Service, my late husband was a researcher. I understand how these things are done. The timing suggests something significant happened in what, mid-April?"

Thesan let out a breath, glanced at Isembard, and got a tiny nod from him. "You're very good. So you know. We had a series of odd events here that year - Isembard's second. One of the new Trivium teachers was being exceptionally difficult. She's long gone, thankfully. But Alvis was absolutely no help at all."

She shrugged. "We've gone round and round about this since then. I've got on well with Helena since I started. We don't share academic interests, exactly, but they overlap well enough without putting us in competition for the same resources. You'll understand that, I'm sure."

Pross laughed. "Oh, entirely, yes. It's always a bit fraught, working with someone in the exact same area of the field. Either you're deep in each other's pockets, or you're looking over your shoulder to see what they're up to and if it's better than what you're doing."

Thesan nodded. "But it turns out, we're well aligned on..." She shrugs. "They'd made fun of me, a bit, teasing me about my interest in the ancient mysteries of the school. There are all sorts of tales, of course, various legends and lights. A few ghost stories. But no one really took me seriously."

"But you kept at it anyway." Pross gestured, vaguely back toward the keep. "And then here comes someone out of those legends. You were going to come down here whether or not anyone else thought it was a good idea, weren't you?"

"I would have had a very long argument with my husband about it, but I think my wards and protections are still good enough to slow him down enough." Thesan grinned sideways at Isembard. "He doesn't yet know all my secrets."

"That would be the danger of collaborating. Or not danger, the other thing. Challenge, certainly. I want to make sure she can get away from danger, if the situation ever does call for it." Isembard shrugged. "Being related to the Council isn't entirely an easy place to be. Nor my brother and sister-in-law. They've been disturbingly mild recently."

Ibis nodded. "I - I admit, I had expected you told each other everything."

"Good grief, no. For one thing, we haven't nearly had time for everything, we both had lives before we met." Thesan shook her head. "For another, I'm clear there's a whole host of things Isembard will never tell me, and that's fair. The War, but other things, too. And I'm clear there are things he can't tell me, that are oaths and promises, made on the Pact."

Isembard opened his mouth, then closed it, and she touched his arm. Ibis hesitated, then murmured, "We all have those, I suppose. You don't mind?"

Thesan waved her hand and went on. "We're not some pure and innocent couple, meeting in our first year of school after sheltered childhoods." She then leaned to rest her head on Isembard's shoulder. "Though I will grant he has more of a history than I do."

Pross nodded. "That's sensible. And a thing we've been sorting out, ourselves. Though we might have to go out to Egypt to do some of it." She sounded a little resigned, to Thesan's ears. A moment later, Pross added, "We're none too sure what his mother will think of me, but we hope Cammie will be entirely charming. We're thinking to go for a few weeks at the end of the school year, before Hypatia starts her apprenticeship."

"That's just sensible. Enough time to travel." Thesan yanked her attention back to the puzzle at hand. "So. There are all these traditions, many more honoured in the breach than in the observance, and Helena and I basically decided we'd start them up again. Some of them are what you've seen, feasts and shared celebrations. The things that bring a community together. Some are to do with the Houses, the Heads of House have been doing a bit more with the House magics, more deliberately."

Ibis nodded. "I've helped with a few of those in Seal House - well, it's why I've been down to this beach so often recently. Richart approves, but I'm sure you know that. He said it sets up the right sort of resonance, in the house, a sort of purring in the magic."

"That's a new way to put it, but I like that." Thesan said. She tilted her head. "Richart's calmer this year. There used to be this edge, under everything. Wanting to check on his burrow, to borrow the metaphor. Now it's smoother. He's more sure of having help."

Ibis blinked at her several times, then cleared his

throat. "Oh." He considered that information, as if it threw dozens of conversations into a new light. "He's been deliberately letting me make my own judgements. He didn't explain about Alvis, for example, the details. He said he will if I decide to stay."

"Seeing what you do without other people biasing you. That's sensible, and just what I'd expect from him." Thesan liked Richart, and she let it show. "Back to the celebrations. Most of this is quite new, mind. We've only barely got through a yearly cycle, and a lot of the first autumn was a bit garbled. I found a particularly useful book that I finally got to read while we were holed up for our honeymoon."

Isembard tapped his fingers on her arm. "Which was full of glorious privacy, books, and bed. Not necessarily in that order."

"And delightful on all counts. Also stars. I get very cranky without stars."

"We can't have that at all." Isembard agreed. "Anyway, she woke me up at something like five in the morning one day, just bubbling over about something she'd found that put things properly in sequence. What was it you said, like a loom? All the parts working together, making something larger?"

"It's more like some sheep, a sheepdog, carding combs, a spinning wheel, and then a loom. But yes. Pieces feeding into pieces, over and over again. Getting refined, each time." Thesan watched the other two. Ibis had his head tilted, thinking hard, while Pross was listening intently.

Ibis spoke after a moment. "I'd be interested in comparing what you found, the details, with some of the temple magics. The ancient ones. I admit, I wasn't paying proper attention this autumn."

"Your first term teaching, you were swamped, everyone

sensible is. If you're not swamped, you're doing it entirely wrong." Thesan spread her hands. "Anyway. I'm wondering if that's what happened. If we did something right, and some dusty long-ignored magic felt like it was welcome again."

CHAPTER 6
THE SECOND CAVERN

"We should get on." Isembard gestured at the passageway. "Everyone ready?"

Everyone was. Isembard checked to make sure the lanterns were well distributed. Thesan knew her mythology rather well, since so many of the tales tangled up with the stars. She was pulling a roll of thick thread out of her bag, and attaching one piece of it to the rope of the door. Then she spooled it out to rest on the ground. "To find our way back if we need to. I have some chalk, too. As Alexander says, don't rely just on the thread."

Pross nodded approvingly. "Better than breadcrumbs." Isembard had not got to know Pross well so far, but he was rapidly coming to appreciate her sense. She and Thesan got on well, and that was also promising. Once they were all standing and ready, he said, "Right. This way. Steady as we go."

The passage ran near enough straight ahead for a good hundred yards. Possibly further, as it was awful to judge distance in the dark. Suddenly, though, it began to twist, a sinuous curve without any openings. That wound around, completely confusing his sense of direction - though not his compass, thankfully. Their path was leading steadily west, back toward the keep.

All of a sudden, they came out into another cavern, but this one was lit with charm lights. It was not a home, not exactly, but it had a sense of being decorated, or arranged. There was a regularity to the layout that wasn't purely natural. Or probably not purely natural? Isembard couldn't be sure. There was some sort of charm glow that lit the centre of the room, rather like a ballroom would be, but he couldn't see where the light was coming from.

A moment later, he saw a shift of some movement at the far end of the cavern. It began as a mix of darkness and glow that his eyes couldn't focus on. Everyone stopped behind him. He must have put his hand up without thinking about it. The shape shifted again, and then a woman stepped forward.

When she came forward, she held out her hands, palm up, indicating that she was working no charm. Or at least, that seemed the way he was meant to read it, in keeping with the forms of etiquette that Thesan had so thoroughly reminded him about. Isembard was under no illusions here. Anyone who appeared in this space, like that, might be capable of magic he had only heard of in wisps of tales and legend.

As soon as she took another step or two under the light, Isembard knew that this was a lady of great power. He couldn't have explained, entirely, how he knew. There was a curve to the energy, the way it felt when Livia and Garin took their proper parts with the Land magic. Livia never stinted that, for all her other difficulties.

What the lady before him offered was the same flavour, but more like a river in the spring, bursting with water, rather than a measured canal. There was a weight to it, a pressure that he could feel against his skin. And she was utterly confident.

She was shorter than Thesan, likely a foot shorter than Isembard's six feet and three inches. Her robes were of flowing dark fabric, the sort of shade that might have been black or deep blue or dark green, perhaps even purple. The glow from above seemed to change the colours as he watched. He could see the hint of fur lined sleeves and weight to the skirts that he knew must come from fine-woven heavy wool. Most of all, though, she carried herself like a lady out of the tapestries at Arundel, the ones that recalled the roots of the family.

He did, however, know how to be polite. His mother had drilled him, endlessly, in the proper form. And Alexander had taught him half a dozen of the older forms, because they mattered for duelling. He'd never expected to need to use them with someone else.

He bowed low, deciding at the last moment to use the placements Alexander had taught him that went back to the Merovingian kings. When he straightened up, she was laughing, a melodious sound. When she spoke, she spoke in English, a bit accented but clear and modern.

"A nobleman of nearby lands, then?" She spread her own hands and then curtsied. It was not like the movements Isembard knew from the far more modern dances. It was something properly called a reverence. Beneath her robe, she must be bending her knees, but she moved so smoothly it was as though she swam through the air.

When she straightened, she looked at him, direct and confident. Isembard wondered, now, if this is what it had been like in the time of the trouveres and the courts of love. And if this was the kind of sure power Eleanor of Aquitaine had held. They lived in a different time, and his life was filled with women who were many things, but not queens.

She glanced at each of the others, then, taking her time but lingering on Thesan. It was as if she were weighing something or measuring something. Isembard instinctively wanted to step in front of his wife, to shield her with magic, and he also knew that would be a grave insult. He managed not to move, but he was sure this queen had spotted how his muscles tensed and his weight shifted.

When the lady looked back at him, she smiled. "You are a noble knight, sir. But we are not here to call upon your prowess in battle. Not today."

That was ominous. Ominous and baffling, especially that plural. Did she mean herself, a royal we? Did she mean herself and the knight? If she were a queen, was he actually her king? And what did she mean by calling Isembard himself a knight?

Isembard swallowed, gathering himself. This was where Alexander would have been incredibly useful. He would have known how to use his words far more precisely, to build the shape he wanted. All Isembard could manage was, "Great lady, our greetings." She nodded at that, graciously, but didn't say anything at all. "We are here at the bidding of a green knight."

There was an instant where something flickered across her face. Wistfulness, perhaps, some moment of hope or possibility. But then everything smoothed out. "And you have made it to the second cave." That melodious voice had a burble of laughter behind it now, some barely-covered joy.

"Lady." Isembard inclined his head.

She took pity on them. Or at least, he thought she took pity on them for a moment, but then she continued. "Your journey through this cave is simple. I ask for but one thing, a kiss. A kiss that is meant, truly given." Then she focused on Isembard again. "From you, good sir knight."

Isembard felt every muscle in his back tense. He was sure it showed, just as he was utterly unsure what he felt, the tangle of emotions. She was a beautiful woman, if terrifyingly magical. She asked for a kiss. Thesan knew about his past, but he could scarcely turn and look at her, or ask what she felt about this. He wasn't sure if she would consider this insult or betrayal or sensible.

It was not as if they had been in a situation like this, or discussed it. Difficult conversation with parents of students, yes. Various possible threats to the school, certainly. How to get enough time together between her evening classes and his patrol schedule, of course. That one felt like a constant accompaniment to their days. What to do if a queen made of magic wanted a kiss? Absolutely not.

Before he could figure out what to say, he felt a hand slip into his, as he held it out. It was the posture used when escorting a partner onto the dance floor for the Council dances or the other formal occasions. Thesan inclined her head at the queen. Her voice was clear when she spoke. "May we ask questions, lady?"

That brought another laugh, this one loud enough to echo in the cavern. Again, it was pleased, delighted, as if this were the best fun she had had in centuries.

"You may, and you ask so well, that pleases me already."

Thesan nodded, and Isembard could feel her relax just slightly. "First, what may we call you? I am Thesan, this is Isembard, Pross, and Ibis."

The lady smiled more broadly. "Proserpina and Thutmose, as well." Giving the other two their full names. "You are all well named, a god of scribes, a goddess of the dawn, one of the spring and the dead, and a great hero."

Then her voice got softer, sharing a confidence. "Do you all find it a great deal to live up to?"

There was a silence, as all of them inhaled, before Ibis spoke. "Often, lady."

It apparently reminded her. "You may call me Glaslyn, or lady, as you prefer." They all had enough Welsh to make sense of that. 'Glas' was that word used for blue and green and shades between, even shading to silver. And 'lyn' was lake. A variable, changeable lady, and with even more echoes back to the tales of Arthur.

Thesan nodded, taking that in, then she nodded, "Glaslyn." She then asked, "One kiss, truly meant, from my husband."

The lady nodded. "Do you object?" Here, for the first time, was the first note of challenge.

"You know our names. I must assume you know other things about us as well." Thesan was choosing her words carefully. "We had not discussed such a challenge coming up, but I trust my husband's heart. A kiss may be truly meant in many ways, and I am, after all, right here. My fears can tell me no stories about what happened behind my back."

Isembard shifted slightly. They had talked, over the past years, about his past, and he had thought Thesan had no concerns. And truly, it didn't sound like she had meaningful ones. But his past still fought with their present. He would have to remember to bring it up, after all this was over, and see if he could do more to reassure her.

Then, he realised, he could. He had her hand in his, a tug brought her closer, into his arms. He bent to kiss her, the kind of kiss they'd rarely shared in front of others. The sort of kiss that rivalled the one at their marriage oaths, or the opening of the dancing at the ball afterwards.

She trusted him, let him gather her into his arms and

support her, and she followed his lead. He pressed against her, holding, wanting, letting the certainty of what he knew they had wash over him and through him. He hoped, desperately, she felt the same thing.

When he finally pulled back, she was smiling, reaching to touch his cheek before she turned around to face the lady, tucked against one of his shoulders. The lady was laughing now, soundlessly, the delighted expression of a young woman whose greatest delight has been offered to her.

"I will not ask for that, mistress of stars." She sounded confiding now, the way one talked to a friend. "I offer a gift for that kiss, as well. Beyond your passage forward. It has a cost, however."

"A gift?" Isembard asked this question, keeping his arm around Thesan's waist. It gave him something to do with his hand for one thing. "And a cost."

She nodded. "Give me a kiss, and you win your passage. The gift, though... " She considered, her head tilted, a perfection of poise and coiled power. Isembard was no artist at all, but he desperately wanted to preserve that image. He wanted to show it to every woman he taught to duel, and most of the men, as well. "I can give someone the knowledge of how to protect Schola, hold her walls and keep her people safe. There is a cost."

Isembard sucked in a breath, feeling it rush past his teeth. Part of him wanted that, burned with needing it. The rest of him, the more jaded and sensible parts, wondered how great the cost would be.

He managed to even out his voice to ask, "The cost, great lady?"

Glaslyn inclined her head and now she focused solely on him, speaking quietly, the way you did to one you loved and trusted, but had to tell a difficult thing. "The cost is that you will give up one horrible memory of a thing you have done. A memory that burns inside you, that you come back to in the darkest time of the night. It will be gone."

There was complete silence for a long minute, just the charm light above, the faint shifts of colour on the lady's dress as she breathed. Isembard rocked back slightly on his heels. It seemed, in the first moment, like the greatest gift. He'd wanted it, to lose the memory of any one of the awful things he had done, the things he regretted most from the War.

He had a number to choose from, and each of them weighed him down. Stone piled on stone. The thought that might lessen, even slightly, felt like bliss.

Then the rest of him caught up. He might no longer have the memory, but would that leave the guilt, the shame, the horror at what he'd done? Would that be better or worse than the memory itself? She had said it was a cost, but how could you weigh that? How could you begin to make that choice? He felt that giving it up might be cheating himself. Might be cheating those others in the memory, whichever memory it might be.

Thesan brushed her fingers against his, and it drew him back to his body. Isembard coughed, gathering his words. "It is a cost, lady, in exchange for a great gift. Would I, pardon, I do not know how best to ask this. Would I remember the regret and the rest of it, the...." He hesitated, glancing sideways at Ibis and Pross. "The shame and guilt?"

Glaslyn smiled, and this time it was gentle and benefic. Praise for his courage, perhaps. "You would. But you would no longer have that memory to catch you, unaware. It would be changed, without the anchor there."

Isembard swallowed, then he nudged Thesan to look up at him. "Love." He put all the emotion into it he could, no longer caring that anyone else was there. "Will you make sure I don't forget what matters most. What I never want to do again. How I never want to feel again?"

She nodded, solemn, reaching to touch his cheek and then cup it. "Always." She had been thinking too, because what she said was, "Our wedding day, we promised each other a number of things. But most of all, we promised to let each other flourish. This," She gestured, at the cave, back toward the school. "I know what that knowledge means to you."

Isembard felt a rush of relief, that he didn't have to explain, didn't have to find words. He bent to kiss her again, this time on the forehead, and then she pulled away.

"Lady." He made another reverence. "Your blessing and your gifts are most welcome, and I will pay this cost." He kept his voice steady. Alexander would likely curse him, for not hedging the promise. But Isembard knew, deep in his soul, that this was not a thing you could possibly barter for or hedge around with protections. You dove into the water and you swam, it was the only way.

The great queen nodded once regally and held out her hands. Thesan squeezed his arm once, and stepped back, moving to stand next to Pross. Isembard felt awkward for a moment, knowing they were watching, knowing how intimate this was. Then he was within a few feet of her, and he could feel the pulse of her magic, a low hum that enfolded him. He'd felt nothing like it except, from time to time, in the depths of Schola's keep, among the ritual baths.

Then she reached for him, taking each of his hands in one of hers, and she turned her face up to his. And she let him choose. She waited, perfectly balanced, as if she could wait for centuries. He would have to choose this, to enter into it.

He took a breath, and dove, bringing his lips down to

hers, one hand shifting to under her elbow. He didn't dare touch her further, in case that might be some insult, but he had to touch her more than just her fingers. Her lips were soft against his, then they were kissing, his tongue slipping against her skin, and she was opening to him.

More than just physically. He could feel a wave sweep over him, settling around him like a cloak. Not just a cloak, it was as if he had sturdy boots on his feet, made for sure footing. A sword at his hip, a knife in the top of his boot, a wand against his arm, all the tools he might use to protect and defend. A sense of weight, over his shoulders, of armour and mail. And over all of it, a cloak that swept around him, sheltering everyone until it passed.

It would take him years to understand all he learned in that moment. Only he knew, as well as he knew his own name, that if it was needed, he could draw on it instantly.

That wave passed, and then he felt something else. It was as if there was a touch deep in his mind. It was delicate and deft, but it did not cut or burn. Instead, one moment, there were flashes of memories through his mind, all the worst moments, buzzing like hornets. The deaths he'd most regretted.

The one that lingered most was of two teenagers, barely old enough to choose to fight, who reminded him far too much of his students now. Innocents in the wrong place at the worst time. He remembered his wand coming up; he remembered their faces as they knew what would happen.

Then that tumult went still, like a bright light going dark. A star disappearing. Bigger than he'd realised, as if it was agitating so many other memories, in ways he had only dimly understood. He could feel the edges, the space that a moment ago had been sparking and aching. It ached, but that quiet made him shudder, almost making him drop to his knees.

Then she pulled back from the kiss. He felt as if he had not done the thing properly, had not been true to it. Only she had given gifts. When he opened his eyes, she was smiling at him. It was the way Thesan smiled at him, the way his mother had smiled at him when he was little. The kind of smile that loved him in all his parts.

Glaslyn touched his cheek. "Tend us well." There was that odd note in her voice again, a wistfulness. Before he could make sense of that, or say anything further, she stepped back once, twice, and then disappeared into shadow and was gone.

CHAPTER 7

THE SECOND CAVERN

There was silence as the four of them stood in the light at the centre of the cavern. Ibis had no desire to startle Isembard. It was neither sensible nor kind. The man had just touched legend and myth, and no one came out of that unscathed, even if the great lady had been notably gentle in her gifts.

Instead, he slipped his hand into Pross's. Watching Thesan and Isembard made him think of what he and Pross might find. They had known each other for less than a year, and they were still finding their way with each other. She had been married before, and widowed, and he had lovers. But those were different, with other people.

Seeing a pair a bit further along their own path made him wonder what he and Pross might be in another year. And how the marriage charms would settle on them if they chose that. What they looked like to others.

Ibis also could not help but wonder what it would be like to meet Hetheru or Djehuty or some other great lady or lord of the Netjer. The gods and goddesses of his mother's people. The legends here, they were his as well, he supposed, but they were not the ones he knew as deeply.

After minutes in the quiet, Isembard let out a breath, and shifted. Thesan slipped her hand into his, and then he turned to Ibis and Pross. "Pardon."

Ibis inclined his head. "Are you well?" Men did not often ask such things of other men. On the other hand, they were comrades in arms, and that made it a practical question.

Isembard glanced at Thesan, and Ibis knew in that moment, he would answer, for his wife if for no other reason. "It is as if someone handed me armour, sword, sturdy boots, and a cloak. The weight of it, and the tools I need. I'm still getting the feel of it. I suspect I will be for some time." He shrugged. "It is not so often you are given the choice."

"More often the gods choose as they may, and we are their pawns," Ibis agreed.

That made Isembard tilt his head. "I could not decide. Is she made of magic itself? A goddess? A timeless queen?"

Thesan added, when his voice trailed off. "A personification of Schola, or some aspect of the place? Some creation of the founding mages and teachers?" Then she added. "I don't think that last one, for the record."

It broke the lingering tension. Pross said in response. "I want to consult several dozen papers now. Books. Private journals. And I'm sure there are hundreds more I don't know about. And yet..."

Ibis turned to her. "Yes, love?" He was not accustomed to the endearment in front of others, but something about the intimacy of the situation the four found themselves in made it come easily.

She caught it as well, and when she smiled at him it was all joy, glowing in her eyes, before she answered. "I am thinking that this is the sort of mystery, a religious mystery, an initiatory mystery, that we must experience. Not treat as an academic study."

Thesan nodded. "We are all scholars. Yes, even you, love." That was to her husband, of course, who grimaced at it but didn't argue. Ibis suddenly wondered if the man didn't think himself a match for the others at the table in the Great Hall. It was ridiculous. Isembard had certainly held his own at any meal Ibis had heard him at. And his students knew their work and its theoretical underpinnings as thoroughly as anyone could ask.

"But you are right, Pross." Thesan went on. "We make our way through by being sensibly curious. Not foolhardy, but willing to take the risk, to rise to the challenge of experience. And I suppose that means we need to go on. Everyone ready?"

There was a mutual pause. Before anyone else said anything, Isembard cleared his throat. "I - I think I want to know what I have lost. What I need you to hold for me, love." In the charm light his face shifted, looking suddenly stricken. "I didn't think of the cost it would ask of you."

Thesan stood on her toes to kiss his lips, just once, tenderly. "I agreed. I knew what I was agreeing to. And besides, I wasn't there."

"I don't know how to find out what I no longer remember." Isembard closed his eyes, not sure how to navigate this.

Thesan caught up his hand. "Do we do this here and now, or does it wait?" She didn't look at Ibis and Pross, but it was clear to Ibis what she was asking. Did they talk about shame and guilt and the horrors of the War in front of relative strangers. Who might, for all they knew, use the information against them later. Not that he would, not that Pross would. But it was a sensible fear, as sensible as his fear of sharing his shape-shifting was and would always be.

Isembard inhaled. "Experiencing the mystery." He nodded at Ibis and Pross. "If you don't mind?"

Pross spoke for them both. "Whatever you wish, here."

Thesan didn't hesitate. "Do you remember a story you told me of children, in a house outside of the trenches?"

Isembard's eyes widened, and then he nodded. "I remember. The younger one had black hair."

Thesan nodded in reply. "Like that, love." She had clearly been using it as a test to let him find how this worked. She then went through half a dozen other memories. It was clear, from how she asked, that she knew enough about them.

Perhaps Isembard had told her, though that must have taken tremendous courage. Perhaps she had pieced it together from bits of nightmares, or things he said in unguarded moments. She had mentioned that autumn that her work was in part learning what you could not see by watching what you could. He suspected it made it difficult to hide something from her she wanted to know.

They had a rhythm to it, though. Her voice was clear, gentle, above all, kind. The best of her Schola house, of Horse House. She was going through the conversation the way a mare sure of her place in the herd guided things, not with force or strength, but with inexorable stubbornness.

Thesan didn't flinch from the work. The older he got, the more he admired that particular virtue. Mind, it was one Pross shared, and that reminded him to squeeze her hand again and feel her squeeze back.

Then, Ibis heard Thesan say, the pitch of her voice not changing. "Do you remember a story of two young men, the age of our fourth or fifth years. The cusp of becoming full-grown men."

There was a long silence, and Isembard's eyes half-closed again. Then he shook his head. "Not two young men, together. A boy and a girl, who ran." A lucky escape, Ibis thought, from the expression. Then Isembard closed his eyes all the way. "Was that the worst thing, then?"

Thesan took both his hands in hers. "It was the one that hurt you most. And kept hurting you most, now you are here. The one that had the most risk of poisoning your teaching." That made something in Ibis clench. The way she was so ruthless about finding the truth of it. "You don't remember a hilltop, and two boys, seventeen or so?"

Isembard shook his head. "No. What should I remember now? Tell me, tell me again, as often as I need to hear it."

"That even in the midst of the War, you hated what it made you do. That you swore to yourself you'd do something different." Her voice caught. "That you came home and in time, you chose a different path than the one they made you take. Where your skills protect. I will remind you if you veer. Your other memories will remind you. But that, love." She let out her breath, and it was half a sob. "That was the memory that woke you up, over and over, that made you hate yourself."

Isembard pulled her close against his chest, arms around her, burying his face in her hair for a long moment. Ibis got his hand around Pross, and she leaned against him, wordlessly. Finally, Isembard pulled back. "Thank you, love. We, we should get on. Talk about it more later."

They all recognised a man who needed time to think about what he was feeling. Thesan didn't take any insult. She just stepped back. "Always."

Pross took a moment to leave a chalk marking at the entrance they had come in, and another at the pathway that led deeper into the island. For all they'd worried about getting lost, there was more and more evidence that these caves were manmade at one time, the way there was only one clear path. Or at least they had been altered to make them so, by men or by the Fatae.

This time the passageway was wider, broad enough for them to walk comfortably pair and pair. Isembard and Thesan went first. Pross whispered, when they were some distance in, "We're being led, aren't we?"

"I was thinking the place had been deliberately shaped. Not a purely natural cave, certainly. Not a barrow, not a pyramid, but there are elements of both?"

Pross snorted. "Now you have a new monograph in mind, I can tell."

Before he could say anything else, they came out, rather suddenly, in a new cavern. This one was clearly designed, with great archways between stone pillars. Those looked natural, but as if someone had grown them like the portals were grown, great branching trees made of stone and curves.

The first thing that caught the eye were giant tapestries, hanging in each archway, triumphant banners with vibrant colours, all reds and greens and blues and golds and purple. The second thing was the head of the space, where an altar might be in a temple, set on a dais. There was a broad pool of water, and a ridge around the back which glowed with the light from candles and charms. The whole place was bright, glowing enough to make Ibis need to blink and let his eyes adjust.

By the time his eyes adjusted, Thesan had been drawn to the hangings, and Pross had joined her. They were heraldic, the sort of thing that was full of symbols and meaning, but would take time to tease out.

Isembard glanced at him. "I don't suppose either of you packed a camera?"

"Good thought, but no. They're bulky. I have something that will do well, though." He rummaged in his shoulder bag, and brought out the hardbacked sketchbook he always carried. "I'm not an artist, but I can do a solid archaeological sketch. This is near enough that."

Isembard clapped him on the shoulder. "Excellent."

They took their time with that, mutually clearly wanting to soak in the tapestries before approaching that altar, if that was what it was. There were fourteen, in total, and Ibis could get down the details and proportions quickly enough. By the time he finished, the others had settled at the entrance to the chamber, pulling out a little to eat, flasks of tea, for a bit more refreshment.

"May I see?" Pross leaned over his shoulder, and he showed her the sketches, then turned the notebook so Isembard and Thesan could see.

Thesan tapped one. "That's an older form of the Horse heraldry. And I think I've seen this before, but I can't remember where." She tapped the one facing it. "Well, that's true with most of them. Faint memory. I'm not so good with pictures as I am with stars. That's why we take notes."

Ibis snorted. "Exactly." Then he glanced at the head of the room. "You all aren't sure what to do with that either?" he asked.

Pross shook her head. "It feels like a temple, or a church. Salisbury Cathedral, or the Temple of Healing, I don't know. I'm a bit afraid of doing something wrong."

Ibis glanced at Thesan and Isembard. Isembard spread his hands. "I'm familiar with the Council magics, the forms they let anyone outside the Council see, but we are not a religious family."

Thesan nodded. "And my family are about the local

customs, the orchards and the bees and the garden. Do you have more ideas?"

Ibis nodded. "A bit. My mother's family, they keep some of the older customs. The offerings in temples. The sacred pool. And you said you thought some of the water beneath the keep was important. This might be some of the same source." He looked up at the dais, and then around. "If they created this for us, I think we could be very rude, but I think we'd have to try to be. I think they set it up so we would know what to do."

He couldn't explain why he thought that, other than that was what had happened twice so far. Stories did like their threes. At any rate, the others didn't ask. The other three nodded, and they finished the meal in silence, then wrapped up all the materials to bring them along. Finally, slowly, they stood, and went forward together.

The dais had a great still pool of water, ideal for scrying. As soon as they all stood in front of it, the lower rim, the colours shifted. Ibis looked up for a moment to get a better view of the other items. Candles. Four offering bowls. A bowl of water and ladle for ritual cleansing, at either end. And the scent of something ancient and sacred. Moss and wood and deep forest flowers, things he only knew from his father's lands.

When he looked back, the image in the pool had come to rest. The first image had no one in it, nothing but a broad forest, ranging up and down over hills. The land stretched as far as the eye could see, no sign of an island, seen from above as if from some hawk or eagle.

The view swooped down, through a meadow, along a path. He could see stocky dun horses, a fox, saw a boar open its mouth for a silent roar, and then in the depths as the bird flew near a cave, a great bear, shaggy and brown. It made him wonder, sharply, where the coastline was, or a river, for salmon and seal. There must be owls in that wood, and those would be the seven house animals.

Before he could ask or even take it all in, the scene changed again. A village, now on an island. They had, he thought, skipped over thousands and thousands of years. This was Bronze Age, or maybe Iron Age. He didn't know the details well enough, not here in Wales. But there were huts and a central fire, and people coming and going, too far away to make out faces.

The scenes changed, again and again, letting them trace how the village grew. At one point, it went from a clear golden image, a village that scattered and wandered along half of the island, to something that had clusters. One larger home, not large or lavish, but big enough for people to gather, a bit like the longhouses that had gone before. There was one, then as the scenes changed, four, five, ten.

Thesan let out a little gasp. "Seventh century or so. When the masters and mistresses formed the school." She named them, but Ibis barely heard the names. He was so fascinated by seeing history alive, searching out all the little details archaeologists argued over. He could learn the names later that went with this place.

Before he could soak in all of it, the scene changed again, and this time, the Keep was being built. First an older form of wood and palisades, perched at the top of the tallest hill. Then wood gave way to stone, and then the stone curtain wall went up. It was like rushing through a book, no time to savour the good parts. Seeing it unfold was breathtakingly beautiful, full of all of history's sweep and humanity.

The people changed, too. They got taller. Their skin and hair came in more shades and colours, the clothing changed. As it approached the present, the rate of change slowed until the image crystallised. He could see Pross, younger, a babe in her arms, walking with a man who he knew from the photo on her desk. Her late husband, Octavian. He'd never met the man, but his first thought was to slip an arm around her waist.

Pross nestled against him. She spoke almost in a whisper. "We were bringing Cammie to meet our teachers. He'd wanted to show her off, introduce her." The image lingered for a moment, then changed again. Ibis sitting outside, on the beach, talking to Richart.

"We'd been down to the shore for class, and I'd asked him a question. He didn't rush back, he didn't..." Ibis remembered that day, though he wasn't sure if Richart would, even with a reminder. It had been a turning point for Ibis, but not memorable for anyone else, surely. "I'd asked if I should follow my mother's line or my father's. He looked at me and said he thought I should make my own. He didn't try to tell me what to do, he just - told me it was possible."

Pross leaned against him a bit more, silently supporting. He could hear Thesan inhale, then speak. "He remembers. He told me about it, a little. We were talking about how we hope for those moments as teachers, and we often don't know if they take. With you, he was hopeful. More sure now." That had a hint of humour to it. But before she could go on, there was another scene.

This was Isembard and a young man. They were on the bohort field, laughing and roughhousing. It was the purest kind of friendship and trust, the kind Ibis had never really known as a student. Never been brave enough to let himself try, if he were honest with himself. Isembard reached out a hand, not touching the water. "Perry." He was fixed on it for as long as the image stayed. Youth and life and freedom and the love of a trusted friend, all things Ibis thought he had lost in the War.

The last image was of Thesan and for Thesan. They all knew the other man, Professor Baldwin, they'd all had him as a professor. But here, he was different. He wasn't lecturing, dry and rather formal. He and Thesan were in his office, holding cups of tea.

There was another woman, much older, around Professor Baldwin's age, gesturing with one hand, and Professor Baldwin was grinning ear to ear. "Mistress Eridana, my apprentice mistress." Thesan was watching them now, enrapt. "They were - they were talking about how to impress the Guild. How they knew I could learn what I needed, how they were committed to giving me the tools I needed."

Then that last image faded, and the pool went still.

CHAPTER 8
THE THIRD CAVERN

There was silence again. The light from the candles danced on the pool, causing hints of images. Pross waited for one of the others to say something. They had more right, surely. This was, as Thesan had said, where they were making their lives. She was a visitor, at least for the moment. Even if she wanted to be far more than a visitor, to have a bed she shared with Ibis in his cottage, each and every night.

But none of them spoke. Finally, carefully, she cleared her throat. "Seeing it." She shook her head. "Seeing people." Ibis still had Richart in his life, or had Richart back in his life. But the other three of them, this was a glimpse of people they loved and had lost. Or so she assumed, anyway.

Thesan was focused on her husband, and Pross certainly couldn't ask who Perry was. It was obvious, why he mattered. The War, she assumed. It was almost always the War, with people their age. Old enough to have been adults when it began, young enough to have been in the worst of it, one way or another.

Then, something struck her. "The lady said tend us well." Pross nodded at the altar. "Here?"

That shook Ibis out of his own thoughts. "That seems very simple. Here, but not just here?"

Isembard was quiet but Thesan seemed reassured enough by some small shift in his posture to consider the question. "We brought offerings. Here is a place to leave them? Only." She shook her head, unsatisfied. "It feels impersonal. Even the mead and the honey cake."

"It wants a touch of the personal." Ibis had stepped back slightly. His voice came from over Pross's shoulder. She glanced up, and he was considering the space. "This isn't..." He grimaced. "My instincts, in ritual, are for my mother's practices. My father wasn't a ritualist, not formally."

Pross nodded, and then Isembard shook his shoulders, like settling something. "Alexander thinks well of your instincts," he said. "And I know the forms, but I am not...." He swallowed. "I am going to have to learn how to, how to hold that space?" He was feeling his way through the words, they all heard it. "If you have something you think will work, I defer to your knowledge."

Ibis nodded. "I'm - Dhejuty is the god of scribes, and the scribes were in the temples. There is a great deal of lore about making the offering properly, that the formation of words is magic. The same and different than what we all learned here." Being able to draw on that common education, that seemed to reassure Ibis, Pross could hear it. "You make an offering to restore what was lost or broken or damaged."

"This is..." Thesan hesitated. "Whatever lore there was about how we honour them here, in their place, has been lost. Or buried, or secreted away. The old forms."

Ibis nodded, half closing his eyes. "A temple can sleep."

he said. "A statue. A figure." He looked up at the altar ahead of them, and they all looked as well. There were no statues, no figures, no pictures.

Thesan considered. "In my family, you might offer a bit of hair or nail clippings. Something that's yours. Blood, in some family lines." She glanced at Isembard, who nodded. It didn't surprise Pross that the Fortiers went in for that kind of thing. It was good solid magical practice, but it tended to put people off.

Ibis nodded. "Hair is traditional in many places. Pross, love, do you have your scissors handy? I think." He looked up, then gathered himself, making a decision. She had seen that in him, all during the summer, how he had become more and more comfortable stepping into taking the lead, being the one who chose the path. She'd wondered how that would work with Isembard.

Pross had always heard that the Council families, many of the Lords of the Land could be grasping. Unwilling to share any hint of power. And Isembard's family was both, and he'd carried himself like a man who had everything come to his hands readily. Only, here, he seemed willing enough to share power, to trust in other people's skills. She nodded, and rummaged in her bag for a small sewing kit, bringing out the scissors. "How much?"

"A meaningful lock, if no one minds? If you take it from the back of the head, here..." He indicated a spot about an inch or two behind his ear. "It won't show much as it grows out."

Pross snorted. "You've done this before, then. Right." Ibis bent his head down, and she cut one of the long curls. It felt both blasphemous and proper, all at once. So many of their customs in Albion held that hair had power. Magically, materially, it did. It was a link to find them, a way to affect them, an intimacy that was about the household, not about sex.

She pressed the curl into Ibis's hand, and went to Thesan, who undid her own hair from a bun at the base of her neck. She'd never seen Thesan's hair loose before, since she kept it up most of the time. It had a beautiful wave to it, and a colour a bit like her namesake dawn's light. She found a small lock, twisted it, and then cut it loose, waiting until Thesan had the long strands well in her hand, before letting go.

Isembard hesitated. "Would you mind if Thesan did it?"

Pross shook her head. "Not at all." Thesan handed over her hair to her husband and then took the scissors as Pross stepped back. "I should have brought the locket." She murmured, and something about that put Isembard at ease. Some private joke, Pross assumed.

When Thesan handed the scissors back, Pross turned to Ibis. "Will you?" She pulled her own hair out of its braid, and he snipped a tiny set of strands. She pocketed the scissors awkwardly. Holding hair that might fly away at any moment made things remarkably challenging, even if they were in a cave without too much of a draught.

Thesan seemed to have solved that. By the time the scissors were safely away, Thesan had taken out a tin of honey cake, and Isembard was holding a small ceramic flask. The mead, she assumed. Ibis nodded. "Shall we?"

The altar, if that was the best way to describe it, had a sense of serenity to it. There were no statues, no figures, not exactly. But there was a bas relief, subtle enough to only be visible close up, of a great forest, much like the one they had seen in the pool. There were four plates, each with a small bowl barely an inch across. Ibis went to the one nearest him, and laid his hair in a winding curl around the bowl. He took a cake from the tin that Thesan held out, then a splash from the mead.

He stood in silence, much as he did when working on a translation. Then, he said, slowly, as if he were feeling his way through it. "Lady of heaven, I have opened a light in your temple." He almost went on, but he stopped there, as the candles flared brighter for a moment. A definite response. Ibis closed his eyes and stepped back. Pross knew enough to be fairly sure it was Hetheru, Hathor, who he'd referenced, rather than the lord of scribes.

She went next, placing her hair and cake and pouring the mead carefully. "Great lady and noble lord." She swallowed. "Many are the gifts of memory. Thank you." It was awkward, stilted, but the candles flared again.

Isembard cleared his throat, and made his own offerings, pressing his hair down carefully as the last piece. "When I came here, I thought no one would trust me again. I will do you honour, and keep our people safe." There was something of the bear's roar in his voice, the deep-throated breadth that went far beyond a fox's cry.

Thesan touched his arm, once, briefly, and then she took her own place in front of the last plate. She poured the mead first, then put down the cake and her hair. She sang something, almost wordlessly, what sounded like one of the old charms for blessing fields or orchards. It was not a trained voice, but pleasant enough, and the notes echoed in the cavern. The candles flared one last time, and the glow behind them dimmed, a single row of charmlights illuminating the way deeper into the cave.

Isembard was quieter now, resolute. "I want to stay, but clearly..." He gestured. "We're meant to go on."

"We go on." Thesan agreed, and the two of them made their way around to the next passage, as Ibis and Pross followed. This passage curved again, enough that

Pross certainly lost track of the direction they were going. They were slow curves, but it felt as if that were all the more confusing.

Finally, they came into another cavern, lit only by stars above. No moon, and the ceiling seemed incredibly smooth, as if it had been carved in an even dome, the sky above. Thesan let out a little gasp, and then peered up. She dropped her husband's hand and took steps into the centre. He let her go, though he followed a few steps behind her. Pross glanced at Ibis, and Ibis shrugged. They followed, but giving more distance.

By the time they'd come to the centre of the cavern, Thesan was tugging something out from under the neck of her dress, then opening it. It wasn't a locket; it was some sort of device, and after a moment she pulled the chain from over her head. Isembard said something to her quietly, but she shook her head, now utterly distracted and absorbed.

Pross knew better than to interrupt someone at work. She knew the expression of concentration too well. Both how it felt on her own face, and what it had looked like on Octavian's face, once upon a time, and on Ibis now. And Isembard did not seem worried at all.

After a moment, Thesan asked him to go stand somewhere, three feet away in a particular direction. They'd put the lanterns down, the shades casting light on the floor. In the dim light of the stars, Pross could only see a general gesture. It didn't seem to be ritual magic, or magic of any particular kind at all.

Thesan used whatever device she had. It seemed to be, as best Pross remembered her own astronomy lessons, both an astrolabe and a sextant. She suspected several other things as well. Whatever it told Thesan, however, it was puzzling.

Finally, Thesan waved them over. "I do not know my historical star charts nearly as well as I ought, in this case. But I do believe that the sky above us is..." She gestured with her fingers. "Let me back up." She pointed up. "That is the pole star."

Pross peered up. So did Ibis. He cleared his throat. "That is - not as bright as Polaris should be?" Then he frowned. "Wait."

Thesan grinned for a moment, pleased someone else was keeping up with her. "That is not Polaris. That's Polaris, there. But that." She gestured at the first star. "Is the pole star."

Now that she'd said it, Pross could make sense of it. There was the arch of the bear, there was the curve of the dragon. And there was the end of its tail, or halfway down the tail. She rummaged in her memory. "Thuban?"

"Thuban." Thesan seemed very pleased now.

Isembard cleared his throat. "And that means? You know you've only had so much time for rudimentary astronomy lessons, in amongst our other obligations."

It made her laugh. "And our other pleasures, don't forget that. Over time, over thousands of years, the axis of the earth shifts. The line around which we rotate. We've known about it since the Greeks. That means that the pole star shifts, over time. From Thuban to Polaris, and eventually on to others, in a very large, very slow-moving wheel."

Pross nodded. "And what does that mean?"

"It's hard to tell, without charts here."

Isembard nudged her. "You could not have known you needed charts from thousands of years ago. It is, in fact, impossible to plan for everything."

Thesan snorted and spread her hands. "Anyway. I'm guessing, please do not use this as a measure of my usual precision."

In unison, the other three of them said, "As if." and then there was a round of laughter echoing around the cavern, with Thesan joining in. Isembard settled an arm around her shoulders, since she seemed done with the measuring for the moment.

When the room had settled into quiet again, Thesan said, "Roughly three or four thousand years ago. Give or take five centuries." She shook her head. "I'm wondering. There are stories, if you go back far enough in the legends, of a great forest, stretching all over. Here, and I think over toward Denmark, too. People finding things that are ancient trees in the fishing nets, or ancient bones. Animals that don't live here anymore, and haven't for a long, long time."

"The bear." Pross remembered that. "Wolves."

"Giant elk." Thesan agreed. She was chewing on her lip. Pross could see it in the dim light. "What does that mean, though? Is that when this began?"

As if she'd said a perfect incantation, there was a sudden meteor streaking across the centre of the dome above them, and then the stars began to turn above them. They moved quickly, rapid circles, dizzying circles, for what seemed like minutes. It entranced all of them, but after a time, the stars came to a stop.

Thesan gestured. "Polaris, there." Much more where they expected her to be. Thesan sighed. "I want my charts." It came out louder and more plaintive than she probably meant it to, but Pross smiled. It was terribly annoying, she was sure.

Then, as if they'd paused for Thesan to catch up, the stars moved again, but at a more stately measure. There was a bright flash of light, somewhere too fleeting to get more than a sense of, as they moved, and then another. That brought a brief breathing space, long enough for

Thesan to say, "Is that a supernova." Then, with more certainty, "Scorpius. Around 400 anno domine."

Something in the cavern approved. It wasn't that the stars dipped or dimmed or brightened, but somehow there was a pleasure in the space. The spinning began again, with bright flashes moving forward, with irregular gaps, before things slowed down again.

Then a great bright star appeared. Thesan immediately said, "Lupus, the wolf, there. There's a great deal of lore about that one. Um. 1006, there are records from China, and Egypt." She nodded at Ibis. "And Italy and Switzerland and several other places." The brightness grew until it drowned out some of the stars nearest it. Not so bright nor so large as the moon, but startlingly visible. It circled in the sky, as if the light had lingered for some time, as part of a long dance. Then it faded out, and the procession went on again.

Eventually, things slowed down again, as if waiting for something. The change puzzled even Thesan. There was no flash of light, no shift. She peered up, and took more measurements, and then blinked. "Oh! That's the grand conjunction. 1484. The time of the Pact."

Isembard nodded. "A - that is a conjunction you would surely know. More so now than a year or two ago?"

Thesan turned to smile up at him, and nodded. Another of their small personal jokes. Perhaps related to the Council, in which case Pross had no desire to try and understand it.

Again, that sense of well-being, and this time the stars began to move more slowly. Thesan kept straining. Pross could only envy the focus she was giving to the task. There were so many points of light, all moving. How anyone could tell what was going on was beyond her, even if they waited or slowed from time to time.

The next pause, Thesan nodded rather more quickly. "That one was documented by Tycho Brahe. 1572. He saw a new star in Cassiopeia, there. Do you see?" Everyone nodded, though Pross suspected they - all except Thesan - were straining for it.

Then it occurred to Pross what was going on. "There is a - if someone has a map to sell, or a globe, there are tricks for dating it. The names of the countries or the cities. You can compare it against known lists. It's imperfect, because not everyone hears about the change in name at the same time. But it's close. Is that what this is doing? Giving you information to anchor to a date?"

Thesan nodded. "I think so. It seems, it seems pleased? And there are few enough supernovae, that make a good dating system. There are too many comets, too many eclipses by far. There's one more in 1604, but nothing more recent." She frowned. "Does that mean that - whatever's going on is, um? After that."

"That is the question, isn't it? What's going on. What's needed, here. We've needed Ibis's skills, and Isembard's kiss, and the offerings, and..." Thesan looked up, thinking.

CHAPTER 9
THE FOURTH CAVERN

Thesan's thoughts were racing. It wasn't just the astronomy. Parts of that were familiar, like shrugging into a favourite jumper or picking up a well-loved book. She knew what to do with that, even if doing the observations on the fly was complex.

She wished she had a proper book of charts here. Or references. But she could scarcely have hauled them all with her, and even she had to admit she would not have assumed she'd need the more archaic historical ones.

Now, though, she looked up again, trying to put a finger on something. She felt Isembard's hand on her shoulder, gently, but he didn't rush her or interrupt her. They knew how to be quiet while thinking, the both of them. Good thing, too. It was an essential skill in their marriage. She did hand over her satchel for him to hold, and keep her hands free.

There was a thread nagging at her in the back of her mind. The Pact, the making of the Pact, must have shifted things for Schola. Fewer, perhaps, than other places. The portal was rather older than the Pact, the island was already cloaked in obscuring magic. The wards of the keep had been in place for centuries, by then.

But why had the stars slowed, in their passage, in the curved ceiling? What was it drawing their attention to? Fortunately, she did not have to figure this out alone. "This is here for a reason. We had a puzzle made for Ibis, and one for Isembard, and this is clearly for me. Though equally, we could not have come so far alone."

"Collaboration." Isembard agreed. "Partnership. Trust." He nodded at Ibis, Thesan just caught the shift of his chin. "And the green knight said three or four of us for a reason. Why?"

"This, the stars..." She gestured with her left hand. "There must be something we are meant to do here. I don't see another doorway, closed or not. And it's clearly indicating some things."

Pross peered up, then made a slow pivoting circle, as if considering. "Ibis, you were reading that article about alignments of temples, based on the stars, yes? Is that a technique you could apply here, Thesan?"

Thesan and Isembard both grinned, in unison. "Oh, yes." They'd done several bits of alignment work since that bit with Ptolemy's Third Schema, the first serious magical work they'd done together. She'd helped him realign the protections in the salle last summer, which had been three days of painstaking and often very physical labour, but it had been entirely rewarding.

Thesan added, "We've done it before. Only what are we aligning to? That's the real question. Are we trying to find a date that something occurred? Trying to do something with what the stars tell us?"

She glanced up. They were continuing to move forward slowly.

Pross coughed. "When you got this idea for the feasts,

and the old traditions. Was there a reason? Or was there a reason they were dropped? I'm wondering if that's a point in time to focus on."

Thesan leaned back against Isembard's shoulder a little, as she was thinking, feeling his arm come more sturdily around her waist as he braced himself better. "So, our previous headmaster began teaching in 1860, and he was headmaster from 1895. Thirty years, by the point..." By the point he'd abdicated his responsibilities. This was trickier to talk around, it still felt like disloyalty to her.

Isembard picked up, thankfully. "I wondered, when I began, if he'd been ignoring some of the offerings and duties. We did have a chance to ask him, finally. Or rather Alexander asked, and I listened in. Full weight of the Council behind him, in case they had to help mend anything."

Thesan had not been there for that, but she had heard all about it later. Several times over, as they'd dissected the implications. "He had been neglecting certain pieces, or at least being very perfunctory with them. The minimal easy sort of offering for the seasons."

Pross grimaced. "Oh, like that. What about before that?"

"Ah, that's the interesting part. When Alexander finally got Alvis talking, it came out that he was mostly doing what he'd been told by the headmaster before him, and the headmaster before that. Of course, he's not a ritualist by preference, and his predecessors were Materia and Alchemy, respectively."

Ibis tilted his head. "I can see how Materia would make a good headmaster. And a good headmistress, given Helena. But is there a tendency to Alchemy?"

"Recently, yes, by which we mean three hundred years or so. It's the most respected of the magical arts among certain families. That's a longer discussion though, not for here and now. Which takes us back to 1813. And the records from that headmaster partly got destroyed in a roof leak, and they weren't important enough anyone tried to reconstruct them. We went back to, um, the Act of Union in 1707, because they had to change some things. Everything got written out again. But there's that sizeable gap for most of the 18th century and the early 19th."

"So when we added Scotland, formally." Pross considered. Scottish students had been coming to Albion's schools since the Pact, though not in larger numbers until the last century or so.

Isembard nodded. "So, somewhere in there, between 1707 and 1813, something stopped. They sort of scraped away a fair bit of the older ritual work, in the early 1800s. Progressive ideas, some of which were better than others. Modernising. Alexander has a rant, do ask him for it when we get back. He'll be delighted." He considered. "And you found a bit about how there was a lot of shipping picking up then. That might have had an effect, too."

Thesan snorted. Alexander would indeed be delighted. She nodded, then. "The shipping, who knows. They focused a lot more on the obscuring magics, at that point, anyway. Reasonably." She let out a breath. "So. Are we doing something new here, or are we starting something up after a long interruption?" Finally, the threads in her memory caught a bit. "Wait. Can we go back to what we saw at first in the pool? And then I've a question for you, love."

"You think that was important?" Pross tilted her head. "A great forest, stretching out as far as the eye could see. A few meadows and open spaces, rocky ground, but mostly thick with trees."

"A green man and his lady implies - well. Growth.

Ground." Ibis was trying out the words, as if he weren't sure what language they should be in. "And you said there was an ancient forest, that comes up from the seabed."

Thesan nodded. "Back in our rooms, I've got notes on the legends. There's all sorts of tales about this island. They call it Cantre'r Gwaelod. The Lowland Hundred or the Hundred Under the Sea in English. A whole kingdom where the sea was held back by walls, and there were forests and farms and fields, all through Cardigan Bay. The legends say it was destroyed by negligence, or drink - someone forgetting to close the sea wall at night, or a seduction, depending on which stories you listen to. There are tales about the bells being heard, but we at least know where those come from."

That got a snort. The Schola bells could be heard from anywhere on the island, and they rang at sunset every night. Which might, now she thought about it, be connected.

"You had a question, love?" Isembard shifted his hand a little on the top of her hip.

"I did." Thesan swallowed. "When you kissed her, how did it feel? The - the implication of it, the magic of it, I mean. I'm familiar with your kisses."

Isembard was quiet for a long moment. The stars continued their sedate progression. "That's a hard question to answer. Like diving into cool water. But that sense of the life of a forest, too, now I think of it. Quiet, but knowing there are thousands of lives around you, birds and beasts and trees and insects. Is it both, do you think? Something else? And what does that have to do with stars?"

Ibis said, hesitantly. "The merfolk here talk about the water. The island, the shaping of the island? A very long time ago, the oldest of their legends. And then the hiding of it. That's not something they talk about, not with us. Not that I know of."

Pross coughed. "You've gone far beyond my knowledge, I admit. Though now I'm wondering about... " She waved a hand. "I've spent the last decade and more in the New Forest. I'm more familiar with forest customs. But there are seasons for things. Rising and falling, the May Day dances and offerings, the harvest ones. Turning out the mares and stallions. Is it possible that what's needed is something like that?"

"It would make a fair bit of sense. And what we could find. The problem with what we found in the records, I think, is that we got the script of a play, but not what it looks like staged. There's so much left out."

Thesan took a breath. "We can tell what the feasts had, if there were special ingredients or dishes. They wrote down some of the things that were said, but only the notable bits. The chatelaines have kept most detailed records, and those largely survived. But we're guessing, in several cases - even with the help of Alexander and several other people who know the Council rituals, and the land rituals. I don't think we have them right yet. Well, I'd be surprised if we did, honestly."

Ibis snorted. "That is the perpetual problem of archaeologists. Hullo, we've found this figure. Is it a religious object? Is it a child's toy? Is it a highly enchanted magical object with metaphysical teeth? Did someone just have a particular and somewhat unusual sexual preference?"

That made all of them chuckle and relax a bit. "So. If the stars do point to a particular time, I suppose we figure that out. And then we can use that to do something else, perhaps. Find out more about what got broken in the chain of ritual. At least a date would give us more to work with.

Other rituals to compare to. Or maybe we were looking in the wrong time all along?"

"Time of year, too, yes? Though you might need reference materials for that." Isembard offered it carefully. Thesan knew he was still nervous about his knowledge of her field.

She nodded. Before she could say anything, Pross shook her head. "I keep thinking about the ancient tales of Broceliande. The eternal forest. There are a number of ties to Arthurian tales, and to others. A fountain of youth, Merlin's home, all sorts of enchantments."

Ibis nodded. "If we're positing an ancient forest, it might have stretched down to Brittany, yes? Across some of the Channel?"

None of them were the sort of academic who could answer it. Thesan suspected they'd have to go to the portal keepers for that, but at least she had an idea who to talk to there. "A problem for a bit later, but I agree, worth exploring." Then she swallowed. "All right. So, our next step is to figure out when these stars want us to know about."

She squeezed Isembard's hand, then took a step forward, looking up, and she pitched her voice. "Please, would you show us the time that is most important to understanding what you need?"

There was a slight hesitation, everything going terrifyingly still, and then the movement picked up again. It made her think of the Council dances, the formal ones at the solstices, spinning the magic and feeding it for another turn of the year. The stars spun and spun, faster for a bit, then slowing down again. She knew she wouldn't be able to do all the timing here and now. She could guess, a fair bit, from where the planets were, but that only went so far.

And perhaps something else would present itself. Some better idea. Until then, she'd carry on with what she knew well, and hope for inspiration to come from the steady effort.

As the stars above her slowed again, she began looking for all the small cues. She started, as she always started, from the first she'd learned about the stars, with finding north. There was Polaris, and she automatically made the small adjustments to align herself properly.

What constellations were visible, that would tell her a great deal about the season. She could see the Winter Hexagon clearly. That was a tremendous help. The six stars of the asterism shone out bright and clear. Rigel, Aldebaran, Capella, Pollux, Procyon, Sirius.

And there was Betelgeuse, in the centre, which formed the Winter Triangle. It was in the northeast, which suggested right around the solstice, if what she was seeing was earlier in the evening. That it was in the northeast strongly suggested the season, though. By February it would be rising in the south as well as setting there.

Once she had her bearings, she said, "Winter. Winter solstice. Now to figure out the year."

That took longer. It wasn't so much finding the planets, locating them in the sky, as it was making sure she hadn't missed anything. There was Jupiter, by Aldebaran, in Taurus. Mars was near the horizon, in Pisces. The others weren't visible at all, somewhere below the horizon.

Thesan closed her eyes, trying to figure this out. "Love, did you unpack anything from my bag?"

"I have more sense." Isembard sounded amused. "Why?"

"Ephemeris, please?" There was a momentary silence, then he was rummaging in her bag. Then he handed it over the slim and well-worn volume. She cast a reddish charm light, the one that wouldn't affect her night vision as much, or anyone else's. Some bright spark of the

Astronomy Guild had done some experimentation about it a century ago.

She pieced through the book. It was the astronomical placements, of course, not the astrological ones. Precession continued to have a great deal to answer for. However, she flipped back and forth several times, then ran through the entire period with her fingers, one last time. Everyone else was quiet, very patiently so.

"I can't be sure, not without a lot more maths and checking things. And wishing for a conveniently placed comet or something that is not at all visible. I'd even take a moon phase." The moon had been absent from this, however, which was curious but did make it much easier to see the stars. "But I think 1751. Which makes sense for other reasons."

"The calendar." Pross said it first, but Ibis caught on quickly.

"They changed to the Gregorian calendar in September 1752. But the start of the year, moving it to January rather than Lady Day in March, that was January 1752. And it must have played havoc with all the winter celebrations, one way or another. If something were going to get missed, it makes sense it might be then."

Thesan gestured. "Notebook, love?" Isembard took the ephemeris and handed her a notebook. She sketched out several things, doing a few measurements with the sextant on her necklace again to be sure of the angles. The visible Royal Stars, the major points of constellations, the planets she could see.

However, nothing changed. She had hoped, rather a lot, that saying it would shake something loose. It didn't. Nothing shifted, other than the stars drifting slowly forward in their dance. She ran her hand through her hair, tucking a loose strand behind her ear, while Isembard came up beside her again.

"You and Alexander were talking last year. About the dances. The Council dances." It was a passing thought, a stray one, but she had no other lead to follow here, and it seemed worth asking about at least. She didn't want to admit failure. Ibis had put his trust in them, and Isembard had taken on an incredible oath and burden of knowledge. She wanted to do her part, to share in the burden and the challenge.

Isembard set down both bags and came around to look at her, facing her. "I thought you were asleep. Though it is possible that we said the words 'music of the spheres' a little too loudly in your presence."

CHAPTER 10
THE FOURTH CAVERN

Isembard tried to figure out where to go from here. He remembered the conversation well. They'd been at the country house in Essex on New Year's Day last year. He had thought Thesan was napping on a couch in the library, that she'd fallen asleep with a book. To be fair, it had been a whirlwind week of the wedding, a brief honeymoon, and various social obligations and familial ones.

And to be fair, it wasn't exactly a secret. Not that many people got to see the Council dances, the ones that happened at winter and summer solstice. There were others trotted out for specific occasions, but always those two.

On the other hand, the people who did numbered comfortably in the hundreds. Family of the Council Members, those invited to the relevant gatherings over a lifetime. Isembard knew them because he'd been asked, now and again, to partner some spinster or widow of the Council, which meant he had to know the steps.

Besides, Thesan had been the one to get him thinking

about it. Someone had asked her, earlier that week, about the music of the spheres, and it was obviously an old joke, a teasing point. He'd lost her to a good twenty minutes of arcane magical theory, ritual philosophy, the realities of astronomy, and the fact some people got entirely too fanciful. Alexander had kept quiet for three minutes before he'd flung himself into the conversation.

Isembard had followed about one word in six. He'd been diligently applying himself to remembering what astronomy he'd known once upon a time, and learning more. It was right. And it helped him make sense of what was out on Thesan's desk, what to ask about when they got a spare minute.

She was always finding an article he might be interested in, from the journals. She was often dead on, finding exactly the things that helped with a particular question he was chewing on. He couldn't return the favour, not exactly, but he could pay attention to what she talked about.

So he'd asked Alexander for an explanation, and Alexander, unsurprisingly, had laid out a practical example. They both knew the dances. Why not use that as the framework? The movement of people, in patterns, aligning magic and oath to something far larger than that knot of people, or even that generation, that mattered.

And, of course, there was all sorts of lore about the Fatae dances. Alexander had seen them, a few times, in the greater negotiations, but they were different. The dances were either more individual, more like step dancing. Or they were apparently vast patterns of dozens of people, twice what the Council dances involved at a minimum, more like a horde of warriors moving in unison. Isembard never wanted to see that, thank you.

Now, of course, he had to figure out what to say. "Alexander, in his heart of hearts, thinks the dances are a series of realignments. Between the Council keep, and something in the, what he calls the macrocosm. And from there, radiating out to everyone it touches, bit by bit."

Thesan nodded. "And if I ask him, he probably won't tell me much at all. I'll still ask, though."

"He'd be offended if you didn't, now you know there's a thing to ask about." Isembard smiled, fondly. It was grand to see Alexander have someone else to challenge him. To see how easily Thesan had turned her love of learning into a very real and solid show of her affection for him. Isembard couldn't bring himself to respond the same way. They had far too much history, he and Alexander. He wanted all the best for Alexander, but sometimes it wasn't easy to be with him. He could, however, be delighted that Thesan offered it so generously.

"So." Thesan swallowed. "I think there's only one way to go here. We could argue about this for hours, or days. We can't be sure, we don't have the resources to be sure. We don't have Alexander here, just his voice echoing in our heads." That made Isembard snort and grin, because yes, it did. "We're somewhat lacking in music, but we'll make do."

"What do you need, musically?" Ibis gestured. "We've been known to whistle. Fugues, usually, but not exclusively."

Thesan blinked and then glanced at Isembard. "Love? Your choice."

Isembard thought back to the music, and what would be most relevant, and what he'd talked about with Alexander a year ago. "We want something that speaks to Mars and Venus, if I remember Alexander correctly. Martial, active, something about the syncopation, for the former."

"And for Venus something flowing and voluptuous."

Pross picked that up. "I see the theory. Ibis, do you know..." And she whistled something briefly, a snatch of music that had all the moving presence one might want. Ibis nodded, and picked up the phrase, and then after a moment, Pross settled into a descant that looped and twirled around the more martial line. It wasn't a tune he knew, but it had an open sound to it, the harmonies that made space for magic.

Isembard nodded. It would do well. He held out his hand to his wife, nudging their bags over towards Ibis and Pross. He took several steadying breaths as he escorted Thesan out to the edge of the cavern. The dance he had in mind drew from the Renaissance, the patterns and shifts, the small hops. It was very much a partner dance, and one that Thesan should be able to follow.

Much to his relief, once they started, it was easy. As if they were fitting themselves into something that was already happening, they just had to listen for it. It wasn't coercive; it wasn't worrying. It was like threading himself into a duelling exercise, knowing that each movement had a purpose, and was what mattered most in that moment. Thesan's hand was warm in his, and when he glanced at her, she was smiling, broadly. Delighted with the dance, with him, with everything.

A man could be reborn from that smile. He certainly had been.

They pivoted, touching hands here, then arching away in broad curves before coming together again. Then it was right hand to right hand, pivoting around each other, followed by a little hop and skip. They were like children galloping around with a broom between their legs in play. That feeling caught at him, that it wanted a sense of joy, a memory of a more innocent childhood.

He supposed that made some sense. Schola, well, now,

he really was going to have to talk to Alexander about it. Richart, too. This made him realise how liminal a place Schola was, on near every level. The land and the sea and the shore between them. The horizon and the sky, how overwhelmingly clear it could be from the top of the keep.

How the school was the doorway between childhood and adulthood, how the future was shaped by how each and every person went through that space. And how, magically, he was beginning to realise it stood between the time before the Pact, the ancient magics, the Fatae magic, and things now. Things as they had been for five hundred years.

Isembard almost faltered, before he caught himself at the last moment, and swung his focus back into the dance. It was a lot to hold. He didn't know how Thesan was doing it, so evenly, but he did his best to match her. To match the rolling of the movements, four steps forward, three back, circling and circling in arching dances.

It was pleasure, certainly. The way that dancing was a partnership. It was like he and Perry had known as young men, how they were a pair, working together, having fun together, all tangled up in a joyous knot. He hadn't thought he'd ever get that again. Or at least, not more than a glimpse here or there to remind him of what he'd lost. He'd certainly never expected to find it in a wife.

Until two years ago, he'd assumed that eventually he'd marry someone Garin insisted on, do his duty. At best, they'd have their own wings of the house. If he were lucky, it would be someone who would be pleasant when they were in the same space, not grasping. Someone he could at least have a conversation with.

Instead, his marriage had stargazing and snatched moments between classes, and teasing each other over the supper table. It had swapping out patrol rounds if his knee was complaining or she had a lot of marking. Their marriage had teasing, and being thrown in with her brothers and sisters in a glorious rush of chaos. It meant pillow fights - well, one, so far, but he'd promised more - with her nieces and nephews. Baked goods from her mother, and from Seth's wife, cases of excellent cider.

It was also work, and that's the thing he'd worried over, until Thesan's father, Volans, had sat him down a week or two before the somewhat hurried wedding. He'd been worried the man was going to have some objection. That Volans or Arca had found out more about Isembard's past lovers than was entirely comfortable. Or about Isembard's actions in the War. Either would have been a fair objection, for a father who loved his daughter that way.

But no, it had been a quiet conversation over cocoa with a splash of brandy. All about what Volans learned about marriage over the decades, and by watching his children and his own nieces and nephews grow up and get married. What he thought mattered, and what he'd learned to let go of. Talking as if Isembard was a grown man, able to make his own decisions. Assuming he had his own way of doing things, but perhaps these ideas would be a help.

It made Isembard appreciate accounting rather more than he previously had. Volans had laid it out deftly and gently, the options and the costs, but it wasn't sterile maths, it was something that lived and breathed and had weight and volume.

He made the connections between going to bed angry and the loans you took from the following day. Suggesting that in a steady, boring couple that was bad enough, but in a pair who had other obligations and responsibilities, it would be worse. Who knew what a day would bring, and why not start out on the best foot.

It was, in short, someone caring about him doing well, in a way he'd never had. Alexander had guided him in many ways, but never about relationships. His own father had made the expected sort of gesture at it, but it was more about ignoring things that went badly than shining a light on a better choice. His parents had been a model of how to have a civil, distant relationship. Having someone care, take the time to make sure he could learn what he needed to be a good husband, that had shaken him to his core.

And it certainly set a model for the kind of man he wanted to be now. And perhaps, in not too terribly long, the kind of father. Which was the sort of idea he'd certainly never have had two years ago in more than the most abstract way.

What Volans had come back to, though, again and again, was that marriage was work. It could and should be joyful work, but you had to do your part. A bit more than what you thought was fair, even. Meeting in the middle, letting there be ebb and flow, paying attention to the other's shifts.

Not just the big and obvious ones, the twirls and kicks of the dance of a marriage, but the smaller ones. A bit of tension in the shoulder, a stiffening of the hip, a moment of discomfort. The way those could drag, over time, pulling you away from each other, without even noticing.

Isembard had had a sense that Volans had his own regrets there, but it wasn't the kind of thing he could ask about. When he'd asked Thesan, she said it was a health issue, during the War.

They went once round, and then as they began the second circle, Isembard startled to see a shadow moving against the wall. It was faint in the dim light. Then he saw another, as they spun round, against the far wall.

A moment later, turning again, he saw those shadows resolve into two figures. Glaslyn, and her knight. He was shorter now, taller than she was, but no giant. They paced toward each other, barely keeping to the beat of the music, as if they wanted instead to run and fling themselves into each other's arms.

The next time he got a glimpse, they were dancing, echoing Isembard and Thesan, halfway around the circle. A perfect cycle, a mirror image, their steps as sure and perfect as anyone might ever wish.

Isembard shifted, encouraging Thesan to spin in a circle, under his hand, to circle him, to move ever forward. He could feel the pull of the magic now. It was drawing him forward, inexorably, into something far deeper than a simple dance.

He'd come up early to meet her, that fall, one of the first classes she had with the first years. She'd been talking about the principle of inertia. That the weight of the motion built up, and kept things flowing. He'd always had a more abstract sense of it, but now it was like wearing that cloak, feeling it move with him, almost carry him along.

They made one more circle, another full pass, giving in to the dance and the music and the patterns. As they came to the end of that circuit, Ibis and Pross began slowing the tune, one last repetition of the last lines. Isembard escorted Thesan back to the centre, realising as they were already moving that the other couple were coming to join them. It was as if they had formed out of mist, stepping forward into physical form. They said nothing, and Isembard could not begin to think about speaking himself.

Pross and Ibis had taken a step to one side, forming a near-triangle.

Instead, there was a deep reverence to Thesan and Isembard, and then one to Pross and Ibis. When the lady and her knight straightened up, there was a moment's stillness, and then they faded from sight, dissolving again into mist. They left behind them a scent of the deep forest. Wood, pine, the tannic bite of oak, a burst of some berry. Then that too disappeared, leaving the damp cool scent of the stone.

Thesan closed her eyes, turning to lean against his chest, as she rested her head and caught her breath. Isembard's arms went around her, because he wanted to hold on too. They had done something they didn't understand, except for knowing that it mattered. They stood like that for what could be minutes, what could have been an hour, before Thesan finally pulled back.

She looked up, of course she looked up. Then she smiled, the kind of glowing certainty he'd seen at their wedding, and a few other times. "They're in their proper place." She gestured. "See, there's the Winter Hexagon, but all the planets are in their right places for today. Or at least." She swallowed. "I assume still today."

Isembard grimaced. "We are all trusting that we're not coming out a century later." He glanced over at Thesan, who gestured wordlessly at the sky above them. Which was both a good point and no help at all. "Right. Anyone need refreshments, or shall we - what do we do next?" He'd got so turned around he couldn't remember which way they'd come in, though he was bone-certain that Thesan knew.

That brought a streak of a meteor across the sky, arching to a corner of the cavern. Thesan tugged his hand. "That way." She sounded settled now, reassured, but then she stood on tiptoe, brushing his cheek with her lips. No words, they didn't need them. Sharing the magic, knowing they had, that was grand for now.

Once they got to the opening in the stone - it had not been there before, Isembard would have sworn it - he went first, holding up the lantern. The stone shifted, perhaps twenty feet in, from being hewn out of the rock to being paved, a more orderly sort of passage. It had a domed roof, paving stones under their feet, and a slow incline.

Another ten feet on, Isembard felt a shiver down his spine, and he stopped. The other stopped behind him. Thesan knew to stay back when he held up his hand, and she didn't chatter or ask. He loved that about her, how she paid attention to the small changes. In that, she was like Perry in all the best ways and it made him so glad.

He took a step forward, then three steps back, feeling Thesan back up as he did so. Then forward again before he turned. "We're crossing the outer edge of the curtain wall around the keep." He could feel how the wards fell, like a weighted curtain, spilling over him. More, now. Or rather, he'd always felt them, but he got more information now, it seemed.

Before it had been like going out the door, and knowing if it was raining or not. Now, he knew more about the quality of the weather. Was it a gentle rain, or harsh sun, or a bit breezy. He felt the magic, and decided that if it were weather, it was a mist at dawn, that moment where anything could happen, and be good.

He might be too fanciful. He might be drunk on ancient magic, and not making any sense. But all he could do was go forward.

CHAPTER II

UNDERGROUND

Ibis followed the passage up a slow incline. It felt like the inside of a pyramid or tomb in Egypt, the specific ways those led you along a path. Not the part about death and burial, it didn't have that flavour to the magic. The other thread of their magic, though, that was about rebirth, or at least some people theorised that. Ibis hadn't been sure how you could tell. But the deliberate shaping, the alignment of enchantment to purpose, that felt very much the same here.

There was also tremendous craftsmanship on display, but subtly. He was no engineer or architect, but he'd done enough walkthroughs with men who were to appreciate how the floor was paved smooth, how tidily the ceiling was vaulted. All the things that implied about the strength and design of the building above them.

They made their way slowly up and up, walking for a good few minutes from where Isembard had noticed the wards. The castle was sizable, but Ibis thought that put them somewhere near a corner of the keep itself. A moment later, a door came into view, in the light from

Isembard's lantern. He held it up and nodded. "Thesan, do you know where we are?"

She rummaged for her necklace again and undid something, to hold out a compass. "The cellars of the keep. Possibly below the baths, if there is such a place? There are hints of a deeper cellar vault, but I've never found detailed plans." She gestured behind them. "I'm not entirely sure where the incline started. We're still below ground, though, we've not gone up nearly far enough."

Ibis nodded. "I agree with that. The incline's quite shallow, considering, and we must have been a good sixty feet below the foundations of the keep, if not more."

Isembard nodded. "We open the door?"

Everyone else nodded agreement, and Isembard reached for the latch. It swung open soundlessly, well-oiled. It was a heavy wood door, of oak, but after that first push, it seemed to move smoothly. The door opened into a hallway, a broad one, some twenty feet wide, that ran for about twenty feet before there was a double door.

There was nothing to go but to go forward. At the next doors, they stopped. Thesan had been counting under her breath all along. "This is the core of the keep. It must be."

Isembard nodded. "You walk from the upper stairs across, far more than the rest of us do." He took a breath and let it out. "We go on?"

He looked at Ibis first. "We go on." Not that it was entirely his to decide.

Isembard opened the door. Nothing leapt out, nothing was different. At first. Then Thesan blinked and walked in, Isembard rushing to catch up with her. Ibis could hear over her shoulder. "Of course it's not a danger. Use your eyes. And your magic." Thesan sounded delighted, as if she'd had the best surprise ever on Christmas Day.

As Ibis and Pross followed closely behind, he could see

something come into focus. A great fountain. Not exactly a fountain. There were no shooting jets of water. More like the sacred pools at the Temple of Healing, or the reflecting pool that showed up in some of the Egyptian artwork. This was a circle of water, set within a square that, he thought, mimicked the keep. A moment later, Isembard pointed. "That's the salle. And the other extension, there."

Two smaller protrusions, yes. As they turned around, they could see around the edges of the space, an echo of the curtain walls and the seven student houses that stood there, the library. "Wasn't the water lower when we came in?" Pross peered at it, and they could all see the water was getting higher in the central pool. A moment later, it spilled out to flood the entire area of the keep. Or rather the outline of it, into radiating channels to fill the curtain wall spaces. As the water spread, filling indentations and shimmering, it began to glow softly.

Ibis thought it was a warm light, for all it was more blue than any other shade. It had the living quality of turquoise, for all the shadows of the colour.

Thesan tucked her arm through Isembard's. "Blue. I wonder if that's the connection to Bear House? It always seemed a little odd to me they were blue." Blue was not a colour you generally associated with bears. It was true.

Isembard nodded, distracted. Distracted, Ibis suspected, by the combination of potent magical construction and the sheer beauty of the thing. He and various other archaeologists had tossed around ideas about what the great temples had been like, magically as well as architecturally.

He understood, suddenly, that whatever else had influenced this place, that was part of the mix. Somewhere, perhaps only in a dim memory, passed down over centuries. That water and magic meshed so fluidly, and could touch everything, flow into every crack.

They stood in silence again, as they had after the dance, until Thesan said, a bit regretfully. "We should keep going. See what else there is." She hesitated. "I - I wonder if we'll ever see this again."

Ibis coughed. "I can do a sketch?"

"Oh. Oh, please." Again, that moment of sheer delight and joy. Pross grinned at her, and drew her aside to let Ibis work in peace, as they circled the space, looking at all the little details. He half-listened to them talk, noticing that Isembard was focusing on the walls and wards. He seemed especially interested in the salle and materia rooms, the later additions to the keep, that glowed with a slightly paler light.

Ibis sketched quickly, but as accurately as he could. He couldn't measure, but he could eyeball the distances well enough. He'd had plenty of practice. Here was the keep, here were the walls, here were the paths where the water flowed. He was fairly sure that they were the compass directions, but he'd have to check that later.

Finally, he had a sketch, and he looked up. The others had come back to the centre again, and Pross tilted her head. He lifted his notebook. "Take a look, please, anything I missed?"

Isembard peered at it first, then at some of the lines of the channels for water. "One more branch here." He gestured, and Ibis fixed how the channels branched off. Other than that, they complimented him on his tidy work and detail.

Thesan took one more look around the room, and then swallowed. "We have to, I suppose." There was a door on the other side of the room from where they'd come in, and it opened into a similar hallway, with stairs at the end. The stairs brought them to another door. When they went through that, they found themselves in a small room, a storage space, just off the bathing rooms beneath the keep. The door, once closed, fit the wall perfectly, so closely you could not see the join. Isembard pressed his hand against it and whispered a charm, and the door opened lightly at his touch.

"Your new knowledge, love?" Thesan rested a hand on his arm, and he nodded. "Good. I'm glad. I - I didn't like the idea I'd never see that again."

"Me either." Isembard's voice was a rumble now, something with complicated depths. "Though I think not the caves." He shook his head. "Not investigating that today." His voice had a sharper note in it, and Thesan immediately said, "We'll keep going up."

They all knew the bathing rooms well enough. At first glance, nothing seemed that different. Ibis and Pross had been down here the other night, but after a moment, Ibis said, "Wasn't there a crack in the plaster, there?"

Pross nodded. "You said it looked like a vine, yesterday. But it's entirely gone now." She went over and touched it. "No new plaster, it's completely smooth."

None of them was sure what that meant, so they followed the winding hallway out, to the stairs up, and came up to one side of the great hall. Isembard stopped this time. "We chipped this door." He looked slightly abashed. "In my own school days."

Thesan tilted her head. "You and Perry?"

He nodded. "They never mended it. It was an ancient oak door." He ran his fingers down the edge. "It didn't show much, but I felt bad about it, even when they'd repainted. And now, look. The corner is sharp and perfect."

They were pausing, all of them unsure about whether

to go to the great hall or somewhere else. Or at least, that was what Ibis was unsure about. After a moment, he pulled out his pocket watch, but it had stopped. "Do we - what do we do?"

As Ibis finished speaking, the bells began to ring, they could feel the echoes moving. Six o'clock, the call to supper. Glancing at each other, they walked down the broad hallway toward the doors of the great hall. One of the great doors was open, but the others were all there already.

The first thing they saw as they walked in was a shimmer of magic, touching everything. It was the lightest touch, a sparkle to the air, like a dusting of gold or silver. It caught the eye, then disappeared again.

Alexander was prodding at the great hearth fire on the east wall with a long poker, Hypatia and Cammie were talking to Richart. As soon as the four adults entered, though, both young women were up and out of their chairs, running down the centre aisle between the house tables to meet them. Cammie flung herself at Pross, fiercely enough Pross had to take a step back to catch her balance. Hypatia nearly did the same to Ibis.

"We were worried, where have you been, do you know how long you've been gone?" The two of them said nearly the same thing at the same time, while Ibis patted his sister on the shoulder and Pross tried to reassure her daughter.

By the time Ibis had reassured Hypatia and untangled himself from her arms, Alexander had made his way over. He offered Isembard a hand to shake, then kissed Thesan's hand, nodding at Ibis and Pross. "We were beginning to become a tad concerned. I was seeing what the fire could tell us, though Helena swore she would know if something had gone wrong." Helena, Ibis saw, stood up on the dais, and gestured for them to come up.

It was only once they reached the front of the dais that the great oak doors behind them swung shut with an echoing bang. All four turned as one, as did Alexander, who took up a defensive stance that matched Isembard. Thesan held up her hand, just waiting.

She was right, her instincts had been good about this all along. A moment later, there was that same echoing knock on the door. Helena, above and behind them, called out, her voice magnified by a quick charm, "Come and be welcome, all of good will."

The great doors opened, framing the knight and his lady. The light was behind them for a moment, a silhouette that suggested great antlers for an instant. Those melted away, leaving him in great robes of state, and his lady in a richly embroidered dress. Both were of the deepest green, the kind a man could fall into and never leave, touched with gold and bronze, like the sun was gilding every movement.

As they walked forward, in measured steps, they seemed all formality. But then Ibis caught the brief glance the green knight gave her. The awed one, the one that could not believe his luck. He had seen that expression on Isembard's face a few times this year, and he'd felt it, himself.

And Glaslyn, his lady, she seemed a little unsure of her welcome, perhaps, or shy of the new people. Her knight leaned to murmur something to her, and she rewarded him with a broad smile. She inclined her head toward him, inviting intimacy and sharing her delight at some private amusement.

When they came to the open area, the knight bowed. "May we make ourselves at ease, headmistress?"

Helena nodded. "Please be welcome in the hall." She considered for just a moment, and said, "Richart, would you bring down food and drink for our guests?" As she spoke, the green knight gestured, and the vines and branches rose from the stone again. They spread, shaping throne-like seats for both of them, though Ibis noted there was no armrest separating the two, merely a curve of the seat.

"You are most kind." Glaslyn's voice was louder now than it had been down in the cavern. She turned that smile on Helena. "Please, stay, the four of you. For a moment, if you will." She sat, spreading her skirts to pool around her feet, as her knight summoned a table and then took his own ease.

Of course they stayed, waiting as Richart and Alexander brought down and offered food. Alexander made a full show of manners, offering to the lady with a deep bow, a plate of the carved roast, potatoes, carrots, and a deep red wine. Richart followed, bowing to the green knight, who said something to him quietly that made Richart blush and then smile broadly in relief.

There was silence until Richart and Alexander had retreated to the dais. The knight glanced at his lady, checking with her. It had the feel of a long love, the little gestures of eyebrow and chin and a quirk of a smile. The green knight was clearly confirming something, rather than trusting he knew her wishes in that moment.

Suddenly, he clapped his hands three times. A roar of a hunting horn rang out, and Ibis could hear something, fabric, behind him. He couldn't help but turn his head to see great glowing jewel-tone banners unfurl beneath the windows along the keep's outer wall.

There were seven, for the houses, not quite in order. Boar, Fox, Horse. Then Bear, directly behind Helena's place at the centre of the table, followed by Owl, Salmon, and Seal. Ibis blinked several times, sure his eyes were playing tricks, but the others had the same dumbfounded expression on their faces. Slowly, one by one, they turned back to their guests.

The green knight and his lady looked amused. Both had a goblet in hand, now their outer hand. His left hand was curled around her right, fingers twining. "We thank you." Her voice, as she spoke, was clear. Only someone watching closely would see the way her thumb shifted against her lord's hand, a tiny twitch of nerves.

"You bravely used all your skills." That was meant for Ibis, he was sure, and it hit home as the green knight must have intended.

His lady continued, "You held fast to your commitment and honour." That was certainly meant for Isembard.

"You shared your knowledge and hope for all our people freely." That was for Pross, for the knight inclined his head and lifted his goblet slightly in a toast. Pross squeezed Ibis's arm, beaming and blushing in response.

"And your gift of memory for the dance of the stars is without peer." Glaslyn smiled at Thesan.

There was a space to say something. Ibis could only think of formal ritual words, and those were not the right thing at all. Helena, too, seemed speechless.

Thesan took a breath, and when no one else spoke, she did. "Noble knight, gracious lady. You have challenged our magic and our knowledge. You have drawn on our past, and our present, and spoke to our future." She faltered, for a moment, then said, with all the earnestness she could offer, "I hope you may both remain well and happy." That was a sentiment they could all agree with, and Ibis founding himself sharing that, with everyone else in the room, in a hum of "Hear, hear."

The green knight threw back his head and laughed, then whispered in his lady's ear. She beamed at him, at everyone before her, and lifted her hand, to request silence. When there was quiet again, she said, "It has been a long time, more than two centuries, since a loving couple has taught here together. Longer, still, since one such has held Schola's protections in his hands, heart, and magic. A blessing on you both, and on the children to come."

The blessing settled like a blanket, soothing and certain. It touched them all for a moment, before the lady went on. "And a blessing on all here. You, brave and clever, who helped find a way." That was to Ibis and Pross. Ibis had never considered himself terribly brave, but he suspected he was going to have to find a way to that.

"To the lady of the school, who has the virtues of her house, to welcome, protect, and defend all of good will under our roof. Who had the good sense to make a space where others might flourish." That 'our', that was curious. "We thank you all for what you have done, and what you will do in time." Glaslyn glanced at her lord. "And we thank you for reuniting us, after many years apart."

A shiver of sound echoed in the hall. He could not see anyone on the dais behind him, but Ibis could see how Isembard and Thesan reacted. Thesan did not seem entirely shocked, she was leaning forward, her eyes glowing. The lady laughed, and the laugh broke any tension. "You have many questions, and we have time for only a few. Ask, dear one, ask."

Thesan gathered herself, and Isembard shifted his hand to rest against her back, as if bracing her, giving her more certainty. "I am glad, my lady and my lord." They nodded back at her, but did not speak. "But we are not the first you hoped would help."

The green knight shook his head, sadly. "Two others, before this. More than a century ago. It did - it did not go well. I did not wish to risk that again. Only." He inhaled, sharply. "Only then, you began the old rites, as well as you could, and with excellent heart. I hoped." He glanced at his lady.

Glaslyn inclined her head. "We were separated, walled away from each other, by magic, by neglect, by those who chose form and stolen power over heart and truth. A dozen things built that wall, and we could make no door."

"Or ladder." That was a private joke, again, clearly, and Ibis loved how Glaslyn lit up at it, at the fact that small pleasure was so easily hers again.

"Or ladder." She agreed, her laughter filling the room again. Then she nodded at Alexander, and at Isembard. "You may speak of what has gone on here to whom you judge fit. We have shared with you nothing that can harm us, and much that might heal, in time. And besides." There was a wicked gleam in her eye. "You all say Schola protects herself. I do indeed."

That slammed into Ibis's head. He had so many questions, about whether she was goddess or one of the Fatae, building or personification, or all those things at once. While he was stumbling through those thoughts, unsure how to ask, Thesan spoke again. "Will we see you again, my lord and lady?"

It was the green knight who spoke. "Perhaps, if the magic favours it. More likely in dreams. Know we are here and tending to the island and her many gifts, as you also do."

Then he stood, and his lady with him, the chairs and table disappearing, as he swept her into another kiss, arms twining around her like vines. It was a kiss without shadow or shame, made of mutual delight and joy and adoration. They did not pull apart, but rather faded away from sight, until no sign of them remained but empty plates and goblets.

CHAPTER 12
THE SCHOLA KEEP

Pross felt shaken, as the green knight and his lady disappeared, and she found herself gripping Ibis's arm. The silence stretched out before Helena clapped her hands. "Come up, all of you, and sit. You must be exhausted. We will save the questions until you have had a chance to eat and drink and put your things down. You are all well? You don't need the infirmary?"

Isembard spoke for them all. "We are all very well, but it has been a long day. I'd like a moment to wash up?"

That eased everything. They split up to the various facilities on the ground floor. By the time Pross and Ibis came back, the feast was on the table and plates and mugs of mulled wine were waiting for them. By mutual agreement - or perhaps because no one dared risk Helena's disapproval - they kept the conversation on other topics until they had all eaten and drunk their fill.

Pross glanced around as the plates were cleared, then she coughed. "I suppose we should - how do we do this?"

"We have comfortable space upstairs, if some people don't mind pillows on the floor." Isembard offered.

"I have books." Alexander spoke up promptly. "Lane and I spent our worried waiting time in the library. As you do."

Everyone laughed, because that was certainly what Alexander would do, and it was Lane's natural location. Thesan nodded. "Spares me going and hunting up a couple of titles, I expect."

"Likely." Lane snorted. She pushed a stack of books over for Thesan to peer at and Thesan nodded.

"Everyone is certainly welcome...." Isembard glanced at the table.

Dipti shook her head. "Helena, you go up and talk through things. I'll patrol tonight, shall I? No need for us to all crowd in, and I expect some of the conversation will be far over my head."

"Mine as well. And I think I would rather have the summary once you have sorted out things. Dipti, how about we split the patrol, and have tea in my rooms after?" That was Linta, who Pross did not know terribly well. But she could see how Dipti's maths and Linta's plants were not as immediately relevant. Even if plants did seem a bit central to the whole experience.

But someone could always go fetch them if they turned out to need that expertise right away. Pross had learned long since that the world had two types of people, those who truly enjoyed an intellectual wrangle without an obvious solution, and those who did not.

Fifteen minutes later, they were up in Isembard and Thesan's rooms again. Helena had a comfortable chair, as did Alexander. Pross and Ibis had the larger sofa, with Cammie tucked in next to Pross, and Hypatia on the floor, her long legs tucked under her. Lane had claimed a spare chair from one of the offices, and Richart had the last of the comfortable chairs. Isembard finished bringing round drinks while Thesan had changed clothes and grabbed a new bound journal from her office.

"So many questions," she said, as she settled down, letting Isembard tuck in beside her on the smaller sofa. "Everyone have everything they need right now?" She tugged a small table over to use as a writing desk.

Helena nodded. "Explain. Begin wherever makes sense." She hesitated. "I don't expect you to tell us all of it. Some things are likely not ours to know. Some things you may wish to discuss with each other before you talk to anyone else. You may need to sleep on some, or do more research, or..." She shrugged. "I don't know what you need. But I tell you to do what you need, not try to please me. Even Alexander will probably restrain himself." That was cheerfully teasing, and Alexander snorted.

Pross glanced at the others. "Perhaps if I tell it, and Thesan writes down notes and questions as they come up, and the others fill in?" She felt she had a good sense of what Ibis wouldn't want told. And she honestly didn't know enough of exactly what happened with either Isembard or Thesan to get at secrets without their help.

It was a good choice in the end. Pross began with finding the first cavern, glossing over how they figured out how to open the door. She said only that Ibis had seen a similar construction in the past, and knew how to navigate it. She was sure Richart knew Ibis had shifted, but no one else seemed to find the summary odd.

The second cavern, Isembard picked up after she'd described the scene. Speaking largely to Helena, he said, "I need time to let it settle, but I can feel Schola's wards, like a cloak. A weight, but also a protection." He nodded at Alexander. "I'll have several hundred things to ask you once I can sort through some of it better."

Alexander nodded. "It -" He hesitated. "It is not how

the Council does things. But I am not made just for Council work. Perhaps walking the bounds, tomorrow, in the daylight would be a good start?" Isembard nodded, and they moved on to explaining the third cavern.

Ibis said to Thesan, "You did not seem as surprised as the rest of us that they had been separated."

She shook her head. "It makes more sense in hindsight, seeing them as they were in the great hall. But at first, we saw only one of them, then the other. I caught a glimpse of them coming together in the dance. It wasn't just two people, loving and fond. The dances are about space, distance, as well as connection, the older ones. I don't know. I could see the space."

"You learn what's there by what isn't there. You keep saying it." Isembard was affectionate and amused, and he settled his arm more securely around her shoulders. "I saw the same thing, in the dance, the way they moved toward each other. We needed your eyes there. And your memory." Then he tapped the notebook. "And your ephemeris. We should pick up one for every place you spend time."

"That is not entirely necessary, love, but if you wish to buy me books, I won't complain." Thesan said.

Alexander snorted. "This is how we know it's you." he agreed. "What next?" He leaned forward like a child eager for just one more story before bedtime.

Pross waved a hand, and talked about coming up into the space under the keep, the hallway, the map of the space. Helena frowned. "When did they add the salle and Materia workrooms? Well before the time we're concerned about, but they were on the map. There haven't been many changes to the footprint, honestly, in four hundred years. Some changes to what a space is used for, the interiors. But not the foundations and stonework."

"You had a theory, back when we were first falling in

love." Thesan flashed a smile. From the bits Pross had heard about that year, it was a kinder summary than any other. "About how the wards made a container for learning. Again, I need to think about it, and sleep on it, and experiment carefully. But the way it feels, that is a good way to put it."

"What does it feel like then?" Thesan asked.

"The bowl your mother uses to knead bread." It was a great copper bowl, charmed so that dough didn't stick, but it also gave you something with heft to knead against. "A kitchen, maybe. I don't know."

Thesan said, amiably. "Kitchens, still new to you. Ask Dilly to let you help tomorrow, see what that does."

Isembard blinked at her, suddenly owlish. "Tomorrow?"

"Tomorrow is still Christmas Day. We could beg off, but I'd rather not." She added to the others, "Our family day." Then she focused on her husband again. "You need to walk the bounds. I need to go be in the orchards here, I think. But we don't need to be in Cumbria until one, and we don't need to stay late into the evening."

Helena shook her head. "We're doing our feast here tomorrow, at four. Alexander, did you decide whether we're setting a place for you?"

"If it is not a bother, I will go with Thesan, and her family's generous invitation." Alexander said. "But we will let you know when we are on our way back, for further conversation?"

Helena nodded. "Entirely fair." Isembard looked, Pross thought, a little outnumbered, but in very good humour about it.

Thesan leaned toward Pross. "He's very popular with my nieces and nephews. It's my brother and his family who are hosting. And you had something to ask Golshan, love.

He might have an idea, too. Or know someone with relevant knowledge. I've long since given up trying to figure out what tidbits he picked up like a magpie."

Isembard spread his hands. "I am not arguing. Do you see me arguing? Though, now you say that, I do want to see how Alexander and Golshan get on."

"Hey." Alexander's head came up from where he was peering at a book Lane had handed him. "I heard that, you know."

"You were meant to." Isembard was clearly teasing. Pross was still trying to figure out the relationship between them, but now she was more sure that Isembard still was as well. And it wasn't a mystery that particularly concerned her. She had enough of those to be going on with.

Alexander leaned back. "That brings us to... what happened. What happened to separate them. What happened to bring them back together."

"And," Pross pointed out. "We are not exactly clear on who the Green Knight is. Was. Will be. I'm not even sure what verb tense is appropriate."

"English does not give one nearly enough scope." Alexander agreed, with the grand confidence of someone who was fluent in far more languages than Pross was. "We all saw his introduction. And from what you said, you did not see him again until that dance, and did not speak to him until you were back in the Great Hall."

Pross shook her head. "No. Bar the nuances of the dance. You have as much to go on as we do, there."

"And the lady used the name Glaslyn. Glas, that's the Welsh for that shade that might be blue or green. And lake. And you said there was the water, below."

Thesan nodded. "Water that began flowing again. Because we'd arrived? As we arrived? I don't know. But not with her, necessarily. Though, love, you said it was like diving into water, after."

Something seemed to catch at his memory, but Isembard took a long drink. "She said 'tend us well', after. We couldn't figure it out at the time."

"But if she is Schola, embodied or personified." Ibis said. "Or it could be her and her knight. Or both at the same time. That's the thing about ambiguous language."

Alexander snorted again. He considered. "Ibis, you must be familiar with the pyramid texts. The ritual of the opening of the mouth?"

Ibis was. He had spent three hours last week explaining to Pross the ways people made very wrong-headed translations of them. Not that Pross minded at all, as half of that conversation they'd been stretched out in a very comfortable bed in the lazy aftermath of an excellent time. Ibis nodded. "Pross knows the theory at least." He glanced at the others, and Isembard spread his hands, hoping for an explanation.

Alexander waved a hand at Ibis, deferring to him. "There is a procedure, described in the Pyramid Texts, and depicted in some cases, for a particular ritual. The moment that turns a statue or a carving into a dwelling place for the soul. Where it may be properly fed and tended to." He peered at Alexander. "And you think that's what we did here, in a different ritual form?"

"I do." Alexander leaned back, tapping his fingers on the arm of his chair. "Or at least you created an opening. You could get several dozen journal articles out this, you realise. Each of you. Even you, Isembard."

Isembard said, very mildly. "It's bad form to describe the details of your protections. Thanks, no."

"One of these days, I will get you to publish. Thesan?" Alexander looked at her hopefully.

"If you want to tilt at windmills, you go right ahead. I've got other things to do. I don't know how much I want to talk about it outside of Schola herself." Thesan glanced around. "I feel like the long-term staff has a right to know, the people making their lives here. I don't know how I feel about the Fellows, they're only here for two years."

"Do you oppose telling them?" Helena seemed to be feeling her way with it.

"Oh, I sincerely mean I don't know yet. I definitely need to sleep on it. There are people who have every right to know - Pross, for one, and I know Cammie and Hypatia won't spread it around their Houses. But I also agree with Isembard that sharing too much about your protections - or your vulnerabilities - is a risk. We don't know why they were parted, after all. I - I don't think I could bear doing that to them again. Having a hand in it."

Alexander had nodded along, following the line of thought without any overt sign of agreement or disagreement. "What exactly did you all promise? I assume you made a bargain. Tell me you made a sensible bargain, a thoughtful one."

"We didn't, actually." Isembard's voice cut through a rumble of other questions, smooth and full of the aristocratic drawl he usually muted somewhat. "I did think about what you'd say. Your voice is stuck in my head, still." He shrugged. "What they wanted, what they needed. I would have given it freely, with nothing in exchange. You've heard Thesan say it. This is the place we're making our lives. Why wouldn't we want to help? Besides." Another of those little shrugs. "They gave just as much."

"They took a memory." Alexander pointed out. He hadn't asked which one, Pross had noticed, and Isembard hadn't explained. Perhaps Alexander thought he knew, or perhaps he was expecting to get it out of Isembard in the coming days.

"I gave them a memory. One that caused me nightmares. Who knows, perhaps I'll wake Thesan less often now." He leaned in to kiss her cheek, and then rolled himself upright in one smooth movement. He took several steps to pace over by the slit of the window that looked out over the top of the curtain wall and across Cardigan Bay. Thesan didn't attempt to stop him, just let her fingers trail along his arm as he moved. She did watch him, though, soaking in every detail.

"Thesan." Alexander turned his attention to her, and she glanced at him.

"You know better." There was a hint of stone and steel there, and Pross was pleased that Alexander held up his hands in defeat and didn't press.

Thesan then glanced at Pross. "What do you think, then? You are not a professor here, and to the best of my knowledge, you don't intend to be. Though I thought earlier, I suspect Helena will want you to teach a section or two of Trivium, if you settle on the island full time."

Pross blinked several times, then smiled. "Once Cammie's done with it, I would be glad to discuss."

"I should let you handle all my hiring, you and Richart." Helena said, entirely good-natured. "It seems to work out well."

Richart himself had been quiet through most of this, asking a clarifying question here and there. "I think for the moment, your outside perspective is perhaps particularly welcome. Is this something you think more people need to know about? Some of it may well be noticed. Now, or in the coming year. I have no idea if this means the fields will flourish, or the local waters teem with fish, for example."

Pross nodded. "There are - well, we're in orbits and

systems, aren't we, Thesan? One point changing echoes out to all the others." Thesan smiled broadly at that, and Pross was glad to see the other woman relax a bit. Though she was still watching her husband. "I think, at the very least, taking time to work through the implications. The professors and senior staff, for example, who can note any changes in the school. I'm curious what the baths are like now, myself. I volunteer to investigate them thoroughly tomorrow."

That got a laugh from everyone, and Cammie rolling her eyes. That meant all was well, there.

"Do you want to be more involved, then?" Helena had settled back, leaning on one elbow. "You are most welcome as a guest whenever you wish. Though I'm sure Ibis and your daughter also wish time in private with you when you're here."

Pross felt herself flushing. "I've never been good at groups, exactly. Bookselling involves talking to a lot of people, but mostly one by one. But I, yes. I would be pleased and honoured to get to know all of you better. And to spend more time here."

"We'll begin there." Helena's voice made it clear that was all settled. "I'll let the staff know you have the same run of the place as any teacher. Ibis can show you around. That does come with lending privileges in the library, though you'll have to negotiate with Lane about taking things off the island. Join us for supper now and again at the high table."

"I'm sure we can arrange a carrell. Or to have them stay in Ibis's cottage." Lane said, evenly. "I suspect we're going to have rather a long list of lines of research to pursue, and we'll need every hand." She nodded at Isembard. "Save Isembard for the warding work." He had come back over after pouring himself another cider.

Helena nodded. "Well. That seems as settled as we're going to get tonight, doesn't it? We'll need to talk about it as a full staff after the holidays, at least. I'll talk to Dipti about finding an evening we can do it and take our time. And that will give everyone a chance to notice anything that's different or changed, and perhaps a spot of research. For those of us with less active social calendars."

Isembard snorted. "Family obligations wait for no man or woman. On that note, we do have them. I admit I could use a good soak, and some sleep."

"Quite right." Ibis nudged Pross's arm. "Merry Christmas, if we don't see you in the morning. And we'll leave a note of where we are if we're not in the great hall when you get back."

"The best of Yuletides." Thesan agreed. Everyone got up, moving to clear their glasses onto a tray to go down to the kitchens. They then made their way out, with a cheerful chaos of good wishes for the holiday. As Pross glanced back one last time, to smile at Isembard and Thesan, she could see one faint trail of a meteor shooting across the ceiling above their heads. It seemed to be heading straight for the heart of the keep. She smiled more broadly, and then tucked her hand into Ibis's arm, so they could walk back to his cottage.

Whatever else this was, she had a place here. And so did the others.

AUTHOR'S NOTES

Hello, and welcome to the author's notes for Winter's Charm, my winter novella collection. Thank you for visiting with me and some of my much-loved characters in some new situations and spaces. As always, I owe a lot to my editor, Kiya Nicoll, and to my early readers, who all helped make these stories better.

Let's take these notes in order, novella by novella.

Casting Nasturtiums

I need to start by explaining the title. I grew up with the phrase **'casting nasturtiums'** instead of 'casting aspersions' as a family saying. I come from a family of people who like puns and wordplay, so for a long time I thought it was just us that did that. And then I came across it in a Dorothy L. Sayers book, so not just us! The citations I could find for it go back to humour magazines in 1902, with several other cited sources around the time of the Great War.

As Seth notes, the actual flowers are edible, though a bit spicy or peppery, and they come in gloriously bright shades of gold and orange and red. Very suitable for any tale involving Golshan.

Seth refers to the **demobbing** process briefly several times. This was the way that people were cycled out of the Army and back into civilian life. It took quite a long time: Seth's return in the summer of 1919 (more than six months after Armistice Day) is about in the middle of the process. People were demobbed based on a priority system depending on their civilian work (as well as exceptions for all sorts of reasons.)

The first step was being returned to a camp in England, where the soldiers would be processed through the system, paperwork would be sorted out, and so on. Once they could go home, they had to turn in their uniforms, and would get a suit of clothes or money to buy new ones, and they'd turn the great coat in at the train station near their final stop in exchange for some additional money. All rather convoluted.

As Golshan explains, his **paralysis** is primarily due to swelling and damage near his spinal cord - what we would call an incomplete T6 injury these days. The 'incomplete' means that not all of the nerves were damaged, and he does have some sensation, but this is an location of injury that can lead to a number of long-term health concerns around pneumonia, digestive health, and of course all the personal hygiene needs. Magic makes a number of those easier and more straightforward to manage, but it doesn't solve them entirely.

The death rates for any kind of significant spinal injury at the time were about what Seth describes: eight out of ten people died in the first week or two, either from the initial injuries or infection. A number of the others died due to ongoing health issues, later pneumonia, etc.

Convalescent blues deserve a good rant. These were the uniforms assigned to soldiers in long-term hospital or care settings. As noted, they do not have pockets, they were not designed for independent activity of any kind. Similarly the **Bath chairs,** such as the one Golshan is first seen in, don't allow for independent movement at all. They're tall basket shaped chairs that require someone to push you. By design, that person is rather separate from the person in the chair - it's difficult to even have a conversation.

Golshan comes from a **Persian** family who came to Albion just before he started school, due to political unrest. A number of the magical traditions in that region might reasonably focus on a **knife** as a key magical tool, rather than a wand. Golshan's is a pesh-kabz, made with an ivory handle (from before ivory was restricted), and carved and set with suitable stones. An image search for pesh-kabz will turn up some gorgeous knives that are amazing pieces of art.

There are, of course, a number of other seasonal and ritual customs. The poetry and red fruits on the **winter solstice** in Golshan's custom are about the dawn and glow of life. When Golshan thinks about cotton and blades, those are protection rituals for a new baby, done on the sixth day after birth to keep evil or dark spirits from hurting the mother and baby.

You can learn more about Roland **Gospatrick** and his now wife, Elen, in *Carry On*. The epilogue of that book finds them having established the care home, creating a place for people who need different kinds of help than the Temple of Healing can provide. (And to be honest, the Temple of Healing is rather overwhelmed into the 1920s dealing with urgent cases, surgeries, and all the ongoing needs of the magical community.)

The **wheelchair** Seth eventually arranges is based on some of the more unique extant models from the period, the sort that were put together by talented craftsmen, rather than made for general sale. Magic makes some aspects around comfort and balance a bit easier, of course.

Physiotherapy started being used as a term in the 1890s, though it goes in and out of fashion through the 20th century. It's sometimes more used to refer to work with children who've had polio, but also at times with adults.

~

Country Manners

This novella takes place about 18 months after most of the events of *Wards of the Roses*. For those caring about the timeline, Kate was promoted in the spring of 1921, Giles proposed a year after they met, and they are arranging a wedding in February of 1922.

Giles doesn't refer to it in detail here, but his **blindness** is due to being gassed in Flanders during the Great War. He does reference a few tools. There were several models of braillewriter at the time (though the models of the time had some quirks). He also uses a braille slate, designed for writing on the go, and special paper that takes the impressions needed for braille more clearly. He also uses small charmed tokens to help him orient himself in a room or find his way in an unfamiliar space. These are similar to some modern technology tools, but sympathetic magic does make that sort of thing easier!

As Kate notes, making **offerings** to the Fatae has worked out well for them before, and she uses the same offerings of honey cakes and cream that she used in *Wards of the Roses*.

Kate references a couple of **Welsh holiday traditions**. She is, as she notes, chapel (a nonconformist branch of Christianity, the predominant religion in Wales) rather than Church of England, like Giles and his family. The **plygain** services she describes are hours of singing and candlelight, and the Internet has some lovely examples if you do a search. Welsh music often involves glorious harmonies and resonance. The **callenig** rituals she describes for New Years are pretty much exactly as she says.

The **parlour games** they play are both common games of the time. Consequences is one of the many paper games, where you write down a series of phrases (in this case, using a consistent framework, rather like playing Mad Libs). The Parson's Cat is also sometimes known as The Minister's Cat, but since I grew up playing it as The Parson's Cat, so do they.

The **governess cart** is as odd to drive as it sounds like, where you drive diagonally from the back of the cart. It does however allow a governess (presumably the driver) to keep her eyes on all of the children in the cart at all times, which seems entirely sensible. English Heritage has a good video of what it looks like. (Check out https://www.youtube.com/watch?v=znUZFnTLJXw or search on English Heritage Governess Cart and it should turn up.)

Potter's Museum of Curiosities was a real museum with taxidermy animals (don't do a search on the name unless you're all right seeing that!) There were a sizeable number of these museums in the late Victorian, Edwardian, and early 20th centuries. Schools for the blind also had their own tactile museum collections. (This is in fact how I have touched a swan. Do not try with a living swan.)

The Pleasing Token is something I'm delighted to have had a chance to explore. Kate showed up at the end of *Outcrossing* wearing one. I instantly knew that I'd need to write a book about her (as I have since).

I knew when Kate showed up with a Pleasing Token that they were rare and unusual (though Ferry clearly knows what one looks like.) Figuring out how Kate came by it was, as you can see, a whole new story. I expect to explore a bit more of this kind of magic down the road, since I find it entirely fascinating.

~

Chasing Legends

You can of course find how Pross and Ibis met in *Magician's Hoard*, and the story of Thesan and Isembard's romance is in *Eclipse*. As noted, this is a year and a half after the end of *Eclipse* (which ends in the spring of 1925) and a year after Thesan and Isembard got married (rather quickly) that December. It is also just after Ibis's first term as a teacher.

(He interviews for the position in May of 1926, just after the events of *Magician's Hoard*. If you are on my mailing list, there's an extra called *Tea and Meetings* that includes his interview along with other scenes.)

As Pross and others note, there are a number of similarities to the mediaeval poem ***Gawain and the Green Knight***. Written in a dialect of Middle English that didn't survive, by someone usually referred to as the Pearl Poet (for the other major poetic work it's thought they wrote), it's been translated a number of times. (My favourite still is the one done by J.R.R. Tolkien.)

It tells the story of a mysterious green knight who turns up at Arthur's court and who challenges Arthur's most noble knight (Gawain, it turns out) to cut his head off in an exchange of blows. Gawain is hesitant, but does so, and the knight picks up his head, grins, and tells Gawain to come find him next year for the other half of the exchange. Gawain sets out, and ends up in a mysterious castle, with various attempts at temptation.

The question of who authored Shakespeare's plays is a thorny one. Ibis notes a couple of the other notable playwrights of the era, both of whom have been contenders as the 'real' Shakespeare. **Edward de Vere** was the 17th Earl of Oxford, while **Emilia Lanier** was a poet (considered the first woman to be a professional poet in England), deeply connected to the artistic community around the Tudor court. Both wrote a number of other works.

Schola is set on the island of **Cantre'r Gwaelod**. There are tales about the land in Cardigan Bay disappearing, and some versions put that around 600 CE (at the point when teachers of magic settled on the island and didn't want to be bothered, in my world.)

Of course, the geology and history is even more interesting than that, as are the stories of how it became flooded and lost to time. (The island of Schola is roughly five square miles, though the actual shape is something more of a longer narrow arch.)

Much like Doggerland, the primordial forest that lies under the North Sea (stretching between the east coast of Great Britain and the continent), there was once a great forest running from Brittany, covering Cornwall, and much of what is now ocean up through Cardigan Bay. That's known as the **Forest of Borth**, and at certain times (depending on the tides, storms, and what's been uncovered recently), you can see fossilised trees rise from ocean bed.

One challenge for any book that deals with **calendar** dates before 1752 is the change in calendar systems (and, as noted here, the change in when the beginning of the new year fell.) As this Novella notes, 1751 was right before the shift in the start of the year, and a year before the big shift in calendars. It seems a good time for chronological magics to have gotten skewed and tangled.

(This novella also touches on the fact that Scotland was eventually folded into the obligations of Albion's Pact, but Ireland has not been: this is why Ireland is magically under a different system, has its own schools, and is mostly doing its own thing. One of these days, I hope to dig more into that.)

I worked out the **astronomical details** using my trusty copy of Star Walk (an excellent app both for locating current stars, constellations, comets, and celestial objects, but also for scrolling back historically), and a lot of references to figure out what reasonable timing markers might be. Supernovae to the rescue! There aren't that many of them (few enough that an astronomer like Thesan would be able to place them quite accurately), and they're obvious and easy to identify.

The **music of the spheres** refers to a theory tying the movements of the planets to magical workings, basically that you can create music or ritual that draws on the associations of the planets. Marsilio Ficino, a Renaissance philosopher, wrote a lot about it, among others. Thesan is not sure she approves of the theory here, but that's why academic wrangling over beer exists.

Finally, a chance for Ibis and Alexander (both of whom have Egyptian parents, though rather different sorts of magical training from those parents) getting to wrangle over specific rituals. Thanks to Kiya and another friend for consulting not only on the Egyptology, but also what was known about various pieces in the 1920s. The idea of offerings being about restoration, and burials also being about rebirth are somewhat more modern discussions, but the underlying evidence for those theories is present in the archaeology.

Thank you again!

If you'd like more snippets and stories, my mailing list is the place to be. (And of course, for the latest news on upcoming books.) My website (celialake.com) also has more about all my books, including content notes.

Finally, I appreciate reviews left on your preferred book buying platform or review site a great deal. They're a tremendous help for other readers, helping people find books they'll love.

Whatever season you read this in, I hope it's a wonderful one.

ALSO BY CELIA LAKE

The Mysterious Charm Series

Outcrossing

Goblin Fruit

Magician's Hoard

Wards of the Roses

In The Cards

On The Bias

Seven Sisters

The Mysterious Powers Series

Carry On

The Fossil Door

Eclipse

Fool's Gold

Charms of Albion

Pastiche

Sailor's Jewel

Other stories

Complementary

Learn more about the world of Albion and future books at my

website, celialake.com.

Sign up for my newsletter to be the first to hear about future books and learn about fascinating bits of research. Happy reading!

www.ingramcontent.com/pod-product-compliance
Lightning Source LLC
Chambersburg PA
CBHW030705190726
48286CB00001B/183